Saving Euridice

For Barbara and Grant
with affection
mike

Michael J. Smith

This book is a work of fiction. Names and characters, other than historical persons, are fictitious and any resemblance to actual persons, living or dead, is entirely coincidental.

Cover art by Robert J. Grabowski

Supplemental information at Michael Smith's website,
www.TheWhisperingOwl.com

ISBN: 1717315682
ISBN-13: 978-1717315687

For Ski and Suzanne

Acknowledgments

Many capable people, each in his or her unique way, generously helped me turn my initial concept into this finished novel, *Saving Euridice*. I am pleased to acknowledge their significant contributions. While I gladly share the credit for whatever in the novel pleases readers, I hold my kind supporters liable for none of its failings.

First and foremost, thanks to my family, Julie, Adam, and Ariel Smith, for unwavering love, support and patience. In particular, Julie read a draft of the novel and provided perceptive criticism and invaluable suggestions. I couldn't have done this without her.

Ski Grabowski helped with *Saving Euridice's* development. He created the cover art and gave editorial advice and encouragement.

Thanx! to members of my critique group for their sharp pencils, fine literary sense, and kind support: Larry Fowler, Brett Gadbois, and Barbara Winther.

The following resources were helpful to me: John Elliot Gardner's *Bach, Music in the Castle of Heaven. The German War,* by Nicholas Stargardt. For storytelling, *The Writer's Journey* by Christopher Vogler. Yo-Yo Ma's recordings of Bach's *Six Cello Suites* (CBS Masterworks M2K 378267).

I am grateful to people with specific areas of expertise for crucial help. Louis Smith, cello and Bach's Suites. Dr. Charles Helming, orthopedic medicine. Jim Smith, WWII history and living conditions in Germany after the war. Mike Seidel and Suzanne (Cezanne) Arney, Germany after the war. Robert Potter, Omaha and the Orpheum Theater. Ski Grabowski, German language and wines. Tobias Eigen, German language. Veron Mullis, all things computer Eva Giselle, website development.

Finally, thanks to the readers of my other novels, *An Owl's Whisper* and *Cotton and Silk*, who sent words of encouragement and appreciation. You thoughtfulness is fuel for my subsequent work.

Author's Comment on *Saving Euridice*

I am fascinated by the mythic tale of Orpheus and Euridice and by the question, *What is heroism?* This novel combines the two by asking, **Is Orpheus a hero if Euridice doesn't want to be saved?**

Historical context for *Saving Euridice*

Japan's Pearl Harbor attack in December 1941 forced the United States into WWII. In June 1944, the Allies made their D-Day landings in Normandy. In December 1944, Hitler launched a desperate counterstrike, the decisive Battle of the Bulge. When that failed, the Third Reich was doomed. The war in Europe ended in May 1945 with Germany's surrender.

In the Pacific, the war continued, with the Allies preparing to invade the Japanese mainland. Code-named Operation Olympic, the landings were scheduled for late 1945. They were called off in August 1945 after the atomic bombings of Hiroshima and Nagasaki and the Japanese surrender.

After its surrender, Germany was divided into four sectors, each occupied by an Allied nation: Britain in the northwest, the Soviet Union in the east, France in the southwest, and the US in the south central. In 1949, the German Democratic Republic (DDR, referred to as East Germany) took over administration of the Soviet occupation sector. That same year, the other occupation sectors were united (and commonly called West Germany) as the Federal Republic of Germany (BRD). The division of Germany ended in 1989 with reunification.

J. S. Bach and his *Cello Suites*

Johann Sebastian Bach (1685-1750) composed his *Six Suites for Unaccompanied Cello* around 1720. Popularized by the Spanish cellist Pablo Casals, first in concerts then in landmark recordings made in the late 1930s, today they are among the most revered compositions ever written for a solo instrument.

Prologue   Hilda

Perritt's Swimming Beach, near Omaha, Nebraska
Labor Day, 1941

The woman in the leopard-print swimsuit and tortoise-shell sunglasses strolled from her towel to the water's edge. The midday sun was brilliant. The lake sparkled. She glanced up and down the beach. Raising a hand to shade her eyes, she craned her neck, scanning the crush of holiday bathers frolicking in the glittering shallows. "Hilda," she called, "oh, Hilda!" Her face tensed. She pushed by a mother holding an infant and charged into knee-deep water. Cupping her hands at the sides of her mouth, she screamed, "Hilda!" The alarm in her voice brought gawks from the sunbathers on the beach.

Eighty feet away, sitting high above the water in his lifeguard's perch, Winston Drake peered up the line of wet sand to see what the commotion was. Without breaking his gaze from the leopard-print lady, he took a sip through the straw in his Coca Cola and set the bottle down next to his chair. He looked beyond the agitated woman to Buddy Perritt's guard station. The seat was empty. "Rats," muttered Drake. He took off his sunglasses, scurried down the ladder, and sprinted with his life preserver ring toward the woman. Pushing through the circle of people around her, he asked, "What's wrong, ma'am?"

The woman grabbed Drake's Red Cross tank top. "My daughter, Hilda. She was just here."

Drake scanned the surface of the sand-pit swimming lake. "She's in the water?"

"I don't know. I…"

Drake blew his whistle. "Clear the swimming pool," he hollered. "Everyone out!" He looked into the woman's terrified face. "What color's her suit?"

The woman's eyes were wide, her face frozen.

Drake put a hand on her shoulder. "Ma'am, her suit? What color is your Hilda's suit?"

The woman's eyes fluttered. "Red. Candy apple red."

"Somebody go check Concessions. And the bathroom." Drake spotted Buddy walking toward him, licking a Fudgsicle. "Where you been? Man your stand and look for a kid in red. A girl. Keep people out of the pool." He pulled the ring over his arm and charged into the water.

Drake churned away from shore toward the deeper water near the artificial island in the middle of the lake. *Probably nothing,* he thought. *Bet the kid's up getting a coke. Or using the can.* He pictured Buddy Perritt strolling back from the concession stand with Fudgsicle drips running down his chin. *Can't believe Buddy— sneaking off to get a dang ice cream!*

Seconds later in eight feet of water Drake spotted the red suit. At the bottom. Dead-still. He slipped out of the ring, surface dove, and kicked hard to the figure. He grabbed the back of her suit and pushed off the sand. Like a powerful fish, he surged to the surface. He slipped the girl's limp body into the bobbing ring and began towing her for shore. Half way in, he stopped and checked for signs of life. She was slender and tall, probably about the same age he was. "Hang in there, Hilda," he whispered.

Buddy met him in waist-deep water and finished pulling Hilda in.

Drake remained, gasping, in ankle-deep water, hands on his knees. He watched the terrified mother, her fingertips over her mouth, as her child was carried onto dry sand.

When he'd caught some breath, Drake ran to the crowd on the beach. "Need to do Holger-Nielson, Buddy," he panted, "like we practiced."

Buddy looked at him with panic in his eyes.

Drake pushed him aside. He rolled the girl onto her stomach, knelt above her head, and began a series of back presses/arm lifts. He focused on the still girl's face, matted with her brown hair, trying to block out the mother's wails and sobs.

After two minutes, Drake was spent. Buddy tugged his shoulder. "Lemme take over."

Drake sagged onto his side and closed his eyes. The world began to spin and clammy weakness oozed through his arms and legs. He was vomiting when Harley Perritt, Buddy's father and the owner of Perritt's Swimming Beach, charged up.

"What happened, Son?" Harley asked his boy.

Buddy continued the Holger-Nielson procedure. Sweat dotted his forehead. "Nobody saw her go out," he wheezed. "Found her on the bottom out somewhere toward the island."

"Good job, Bud," Harley said. "I'll spell you." He took over. "Go call an ambulance."

Two minutes later Drake relieved Harley. When Buddy returned, the three traded off until the rescue squad arrived.

The medics continued the effort for a couple of minutes, then the leader looked at Drake. His eyes delivered a hopeless prognosis. "Let's get her to the hospital, boys." His men carried the girl on a stretcher, and he escorted the mother to the ambulance. When they drove off, they didn't even run the siren.

Harley Perritt closed the lake for swimming after the ambulance left. But the crowd stayed, standing in small groups, whispering and pointing.

After thirty minutes, swimming at Perritt's resumed. It was Labor Day after all and only mid-afternoon. Harley reckoned he owed it to his clientele not to spoil their holiday over an unfortunate mishap. Besides he'd purchased extra ice cream and hot dogs for this last day of the season, and he wasn't about to let it all go bad.

When Drake's shift ended at 6:00 p.m., Mr. Perritt called him into his office and shut the door. He handed Drake his paycheck. "Don't come back next year, kid. Human life is sacred to me." He pursed his lips like firing Drake pained him, then he ruined the impression with a shrug.

Drake's hands curled into fists. "But it wasn't my fault." He glared at the boss. "Buddy's stand wasn't ten feet from where the kid must've gone in. And he wasn't on duty."

Harley clenched his jaw. "My boy was busy with…something I asked him to do. He told you he'd be gone for a few minutes. Asked you to keep an eye on things." He pointed his index figure at Drake. "Don't deny it!"

3

"He didn't tell me anything."

Harley shook his head slowly. "Look, *you* screwed up, and that poor little girl paid the price. Who knows, I'll probably get sued because of you. Just thank your lucky stars I don't have you locked up." He shrugged again. "Dereliction of duty. Or something. Now scram."

As Drake walked to his car, the air seemed suddenly thin. It wasn't my fault, he told himself. Still that poor little girl, as Mr. Perritt called her, was dead, and if I'd been more on the ball, she might not be.

On the drive home, Drake spotted a police car parked at a diner. He pulled his cap down and cruised slowly by, like he had something to hide. But a block later he felt foolish. If that Hilda girl did drown, it was an accident, pure and simple. And a tragedy for her family. Sure, it gave him and everyone else who'd witnessed it the willies, but no one was to blame, really.

When he got home, Drake was wrung-out. He went to bed without eating.

The next morning, he woke early. It was the first school day after summer vacation, the start of his senior year of high school.

The school year was set to open with a ceremony in the gymnasium. All the students were assembled, waiting for the program to start, when a policeman came on stage. He whispered something to Principal Moore, standing at the podium. The principal looked annoyed at the interruption and said into the microphone, "Mortimer Perritt and Winston Drake, report immediately to my office. Students, remain in your seats. The ceremony will start momentarily."

Drake shuffled behind Buddy Perritt to the principal's office, feeling like he was going to the gallows. The principal said, "Boys, this is Deputy Crenshaw of the county sheriff's office. He wants to speak to both of you about an unfortunate incident that happened yesterday. Mortimer, you'll speak with the deputy first."

Drake sat outside the principal's office. He could hear the rumble of voices, but couldn't make out what was said. After ten minutes Buddy came out. He had a smirk on his face. As he passed Drake, he flashed his middle finger.

The officer called Drake in. The cop was a colossus in a neat tan uniform with a tiny black bow tie. Balding, he had a bushy moustache that curled around his mouth. He sat in the principal's chair with his patrolman's cap, a notebook and three pencils arrayed on the desktop next to his folded hands. "Before yesterday, were you acquainted with Hilda Crabbe, the deceased?"

Drake knew the girl was probably dead, but hearing Crenshaw confirm it made his heart sink. "No, I..." He felt guilty about that, as if knowing her might have made a difference.

The deputy jotted a comment in his notebook. "She apparently attended Grant High in Council Bluffs." He shook his head slowly. "She would've been a sophomore this year."

Crenshaw asked several other questions that barely registered with Drake, who answered them with distraction. He was thinking about Hilda.

The deputy leaned forward, like he was getting to the crucial part of his interview. "Mortimer Perritt said he alerted you to the fact that he'd be away from his post shortly before the incident. Can you confirm that?"

"That's not right, officer. Buddy never said anything to me."

"Never said anything or you didn't hear him?"

Drake squirmed in his seat. "Well, I guess he might've said something and I missed it."

The deputy glared like he'd caught Drake in a lie. He wrote something in his notebook in block capital letters, punctuating it with a period so emphatic it broke the pencil's point. After a few more questions he dismissed Drake with, "That'll be all, *for now.*"

The assembly had ended by the time he left the office, so Drake went straight to class. When he walked into the room, he felt every student's eyes following him to his desk in the front. And he was sure they remained locked on him for the full hour.

At the end of the school day, Drake was standing at his locker with his best friend Rob Drabik when Buddy and a group of his pals strolled past them. "Hey fellas," Buddy said, "you know that big sign in the locker room at my dad's pool saying you gotta shower before swimming? Well, I heard that Iowa girl who drowned didn't pay no attention to it. Guess she figured, 'Why shower now? With Drake as a lifeguard, I'll just wash up on shore later.'"

The boys broke into raucous laughter.

"Perritt's got a big bazoo," Drabik muttered. "Somebody ought to plug it with a fist."

"Yeah—" Drake slammed his locker shut. "—but he's got a point. If I'd done my job, that girl might..." He swallowed and stalked away, Hilda's mother's sobs echoing in his head.

It took him hours to get to sleep that night, and when he did he had the first of many nightmares. Every night for months, they came. Always with the same story line: He was swimming when he felt tugging on his ankle. He looked back and there was Hilda, clutching his foot. Her face was gray with terror. Her eyes dull, unseeing. And her mouth was frozen in mid-scream—*Save me!*

Part I   Cellist's Beau

Heroic Chance

Omaha Beach, Normandy, June 24, 1944

Private First Class Winston Drake had never been a hero. He thought setting foot in France might change that. Pride swelled in his chest as he jumped from the shuttle boat into the waist-deep surf. He held his brand new M-1 rifle high to keep it dry and savored its heft. Splashing through the shallows then onto wet sand, he felt vibrantly alive. Then ten steps up from the water line, he spied a flash of light reflected by something half-buried among the debris from the recent storm. He flicked away gritty sand and picked up the pair of wire-rimmed spectacles that had been buried there. One lens was shattered, one intact. Drake stared at the glasses, not thick and clunky like his, and pondered what they represented, lost and broken on Omaha Beach. He carefully brushed off the rest of the sand and wrapped the glasses in his handkerchief, then tucked them, like some sacred relic, into the shirt pocket over his heart. He scanned the sunny cliffs rising from the beach to *Pointe du Hoc* with its concrete German pillboxes, burned out and quiet now, and the truth set in: He had missed his chance. All the real heroes had already tread this sand and moved on…or been stopped dead. That was eighteen days earlier, at first light on D-Day.

Drake and ten of his First Army Headquarters staff comrades followed Sgt. Dick Rutledge, scrambling over the five-foot wooden seawall and trudging up the steep switchbacks toward the high ground overlooking Omaha Beach. Half way up, Drake was drenched in sweat. Panting. The midday sun beat down and for the last month he hadn't gone running much—too busy. He stopped to clean sea spray from the thick lenses of his spectacles and recalled the day he'd tried to trade the safety of a desk job for a chance to really do something. That was a couple of months earlier, when he was stationed near Portsmouth in England and it became clear an invasion was imminent. The 101st Airborne trained nearby and he'd watched them prepare for battle like a kid in the stands watches DiMaggio take batting practice. He marched in to see his commanding officer. "Sir, the way I see it, these are special times. I mean, history-wise, we're at a fork in the road, with the awful darkness of fascism on one side and the light of democracy on the other. Which path wins out sets the world's whole future. I wanna do my part to make sure we get it right. So I figure to put in for transfer to an outfit fixing to storm some beach on the French coast."

The CO, a paunchy captain named Parker, stared at him for a moment then broke into laughter. "Drake, go to the latrine and take a gander in the mirror at the pipsqueak looking back." He leaned forward and scowled. "Look, there's men cut out to carry an M-1 and fight for real, then there's folks like you and me—fellas meant to do their fighting with a pencil and a ledger. Hell, the army needs all kinds. You're doing your part just as much as some ranger with black grease on his face, clutching a bayonet in his teeth." The officer huffed and opened a manila folder on his desk. He picked up a sheet with the shot records of an infantry company then looked up at Drake. "Besides, I need you here. Request denied. Get your ass back to work."

A piercing whistle and a shout from Sgt. Rutledge, "Hey Private, get the lead out!" brought Drake back to the moment. He slung his rifle over his shoulder and trudged ahead until he caught up with his comrades, waiting for him on the high ground. The men trooped the half-mile to just outside the village of Vierville, arriving about noon. Sitting in an orchard stippled with shell craters from the 6 June naval bombardment, they ate C-rations and took swigs of red wine from a couple of bottles they bought off a farmer. In mid-afternoon, two trucks picked up the men and took them the twenty miles to General Omar Bradley's First Army headquarters at Isigny, where they would be part of the administrative staff.

Drake and Salvatore Pietromonaco, who went by Pete, pitched the tent they'd be sharing. When the shelter was up, Pietromonaco opened his pack and took out a letter. He pulled a package of Lucky Strikes from his jacket pocket and handed one to Drake. Taking one for himself, Pete lit both smokes. He tore open the envelope. Without unfolding the note, he sniffed it. "Now that's how a dame's supposed to smell." He held the note near Drake's face. "Want a whiff?"

Drake pushed the hand away. "Get out of here. I got my own gal."

"Really?" snickered Pete. "When's the last time you heard from her?"

Drake took a deep drag on his Lucky. "Janie writes me…plenty. She's busy though, going to college and stuff."

"Yeah, sure." Pietromonaco lay on his back, unfolded the letter and read.

Drake turned away and sat staring sullenly into the distance. After a while, he pulled the shoe shine kit from his pack, took off his boots, and went to work polishing them.

"*Love and Kisses*," Pete said, holding the letter to his heart. "That's how my Eloise always signs off."

"Ain't that sweet," Drake muttered. He crushed out his cigarette on his boot sole. "Think I'll shave before evening chow." He took his razor to the hygiene tent next to the motor pool.

Standing at the mirror before lathering up, Drake leaned in to size-up his face. His ears stuck out like a Ford coupe with its front doors open—no news there. But his face was nice, friendly looking. As his girl Janie said, he looked *reliable*. He put his glasses on. Yeah, Captain Parker had a point. About him not looking the part of a combat soldier. His puss wasn't like the ones he saw on the paratroopers of the 101st. Their features were chiseled, hard-looking. His were soft, not flabby but—he pushed on his cheek with his index finger—soft. He stroked the whiskers on his chin. They were pliant. When he'd seen rangers coming in from bivouac, their whiskers looked like they could scrape rust off a ship's hull. Drake took off his shirt and glanced around to make sure no one was watching. He struck a muscleman's pose then winced. More 97 pound weakling than Charles Atlas. Shrugging, he took off his glasses and brushed lather on his chin. As he put razor to skin, his spirit brightened: Bravery's more about heart than anything else, Drake told himself, and his heart might be as stalwart as anyone's.

That evening, Drake and Pietromonaco lay smoking in their tent, listening to the thuds of artillery rounds and aerial bombs. "Took some papers to Colonel Asner's tent right after chow," Drake said. "I saw a big map laid out on a table inside. D'you know the front separating our boys from the German Seventh Army is only a dozen miles east of here?"

"That so?" Pete rubbed the stubble on his chin. "Then General Collins and his GIs better damn well stand their ground. Sure don't want to wake up in the middle of the night with some Herman hollering *Achtung!* outside the tent."

Drake put his hand on the M-1 he'd been issued the night before in England. "That's why they gave us these, Pete. We are soldiers after all."

Pietromonaco chuckled. "Shit, they gave us rifles for the transport over here. We turn 'em in to the armory tomorrow, you know. I'm a soldier all right. A paperwork type. Glad to leave the fighting to the infantry."

When the sun was low in the west, the pounding let up. Pietromonaco pushed the tent flap open. "Guess the war's over," he said, laughing. "So, Drake, how come you go by your last name? That some kind of deal from where you grew up or something?"

Drake shrugged. "Nah. Folks back in Omaha mostly go by their given name, same as everywhere. For a while, being named Winston after my uncle who died in the Great War was OK by me. When I started school, everyone, teachers and kids, took to calling me Winnie. No big deal, I figured—it's a nickname, same as any other. Then those damn Winnie the Pooh books got popular. Remember them? Kids took to teasing me on account of having a stuffed bear's name. Well, we moved one summer, and I told everyone in the new school to call me Drake. A few teachers insisted on Winston, but I was able to put Winnie way back in my rear view window, thank goodness."

As the twilight faded, the shooting in the distance picked up again. Drake climbed out of the tent and watched the flashes of explosions light up the low-riding clouds to the east. Droning aircraft flew overhead. "Ought to come out and see the fireworks, Pete. Big doings up at the front."

"Think I'll take a pass." Pietromonaco yawned. "I'm all cozy in here."

Drake lifted the tent flap and looked in. "Way I see it, we're put on this earth for a reason."

"Ain't how I see it. Life's about living, my friend, not making some score."

Drake shook his head. "Doncha wonder about our boys up there right now? Fighting for our future?" He sighed. "I sure do. I'll tell you one thing—that was some deal, them pushing the Germans off those cliffs we saw today. They're heroes."

Pete chuckled. "Good for them."

Drake sighed. "Seriously, being a hero's something no one can take away from you."

"Fiddle-dee-dee!" Pietromonaco sneered. "In a shooting match, it's a damn good way to get yourself killed. I'll take warm and safe, thanks."

"Well, I wish I'd been with 'em on 6 June," Drake said. "Sure, my nuts would've been in my throat, but doing something that big—" He took a last deep drag on his cigarette and crushed it into the empty Spam can they were using as an ashtray. "— together with the guys in your outfit!" Drake shook his head in awe. "Man, that's true brotherhood."

Pietromonaco scoffed. "Got any brothers?"

"Nope."

"Me, I had six of 'em. Believe me, it's no picnic. Big brothers are always looking for a reason to knock you around. And little brothers? Well, they're pesky as flies, getting into your stuff, wanting to tag along." Pietromonaco waved his hands in circles indicating it never ends. "If you want brothers, best join the Elks."

11

"Brothers at home are one thing," Drake said. "But brothers in combat, I reckon that's something way different. Under fire, fellas *depend* on each other for their lives. There's nowhere else that happens. It's real brotherhood, not just some accident of birth. And you got it for keeps."

"Chin up, Drake. I expect this war's a helluva long way from the finish line. Bet you'll get your chance to join the Brotherhood of Infantry Grunts. The B-I-G-time, they call it. Maybe even win you a medal or two. Then, if you survive, you can sit on your porch swing as a doddering old man and stare at those medals and tell anyone who'll listen how great it was *back then*."

Second Chance

With the war simmered down and the holiday season approaching, Drake sat on his swivel chair, figuring he'd have a quiet Saturday morning. He'd work until mid-afternoon then be free for the day. He leaned back. If the roads aren't too bad, he thought, I might go into the village before chow with some of the guys and have a beer at Café Roi de Grèce. He glanced out the window at the fluffy white flakes tumbling down like crippled moths. An inch of snow already covered the sill outside. Have to see how it goes, he told himself.

At 1030 hours, Weems came around passing out mail. Chirping, "Merry Christmas," he tossed a small yellow envelope on Drake's desk.

Drake snatched up the letter and looked at the return address. *Miss Jane Stabler*, elegantly penned in navy blue ink. The breath in his lungs caught—his first word from Janie since he'd left England. But with a moment's reflection on why she'd been so long writing, he stuffed the envelope unopened into his breast pocket.

Minutes later phones all over the building started ringing. Officers and NCOs ran between offices. There was urgent honking outside. Drake went to the window just as a jeep came fishtailing up the snowy road. It slid to a halt across the street, outside the hotel that served as First Army HQ. Three MPs scrambled out. Two of them posted at the front door, their carbines across their chests. The third, a sergeant, dashed inside.

As Corporal Banting rushed by, Drake grabbed his arm. "What the hell's up, Billy?"

Banting glanced over his shoulder. "Big doings. Don't know exactly what, but I heard the Old Man tell Colonel Roberts the whole goddamn German army's hit the 99th Division near Elsenborn." He jerked free of Drake's grasp and hurried off.

Drake stood there, not knowing what to do. He looked at his desk. The two-week old sick call reports he'd been transcribing didn't seem so important.

At 1515 hours Sergeant Rutledge stormed into the office pool area, wearing a helmet and field jacket. He carried an M-1 rifle and his jaw was set like a fighter's, answering the bell. "Gather 'round, men," he growled. He set the rifle on a desk. "You've all heard the rumors. Looks like they're true. Fritz is hitting us big time south of the La Warche River. Five Corps is fully engaged along its entire front. We're shoring-up some of our units down there."

Drake's heart raced. Reinforcing line units! Maybe Fate would give him a shot after all.

Rutledge picked up the clipboard he'd brought. "The following men are shipping out tonight to be rolled into the Thirtieth Division near Malmedy." He glanced at the paperwork. "Albright, Clark, Hanson, Mickelsberry, Pietromonaco, Schuster, and Warren, you're going." He checked off the names with a pencil as he read from the roster. "You seven, report to the mess hall pronto. After chow, get yourselves to the armory for weapons and equipment. Be ready to truck out by eighteen hundred thirty hours." Rutledge forced a grim smile. "Good luck to you, gentlemen." When no one stirred, he hollered, "What the hell are you waiting for, a kick in the butt from Ike?" The seven dashed out, and Rutledge said, "The rest of you, start packing up. Might be moving the HQ west tomorrow, depending on how things shake out." He scanned the faces of the men before him. "OK, let's go to work, fellas." The sergeant picked up his rifle, turned on his heel, and headed away.

Drake fingered the pocket containing Janie's letter and rushed after Rutledge, catching him at the office door. "Sarge, sounds like the war's teetering on the brink. History's on the brink. We owe it to our children to make sure things break right."

"Didn't know you had kids, Drake."

"I don't. But maybe someday..." He thought of Janie's letter. Perhaps it was a sign. "Look, you gotta let me go too. Bet they

14

could use me for something." Drake waited for the sergeant to meet his gaze. "I can do it, sarge."

Rutledge scowled, then his gaze softened. "Sure about that, Private?"

Drake set his jaw. "Yeah, sarge...positive."

Rutledge stared at Drake for a moment. "Never saw much percentage in volunteering, but I do admire it." He nodded. "I'll do what I can, son."

The sergeant was back twenty minutes later. "CO says you're in, Private. Grab some chow and get yourself outfitted." He put a hand on Drake's shoulder. "Remember, be ready to roll by one eight three zero hours."

Drake was fed and packed at 1745. He left his gear on his bunk and slipped away to a storeroom off the barracks where he'd have some privacy. He sat on a five gallon can of floor wax and took the letter from his pocket. He stared at it for a moment, thinking the fact that she'd written *Jane* rather than *Janie* in the return address was a bad sign. Not as bad as the fact that she hadn't written for eight months. He took a deep breath and ripped the envelope open. One page inside—another bad sign. Drake unfolded it and read.

> *November 11, 1944*
> *Dear Drake,*
> *You've been real good at sending me letters. I feel awful that I haven't written back sooner. I do think often of your safety and pray for it.*
> *I wish there was an easier way than just saying it, but I suppose there isn't. I'm writing to tell you I can't be your sweetheart any more. I met a fella at school. He's joined the Marines. You would like him. He went off to basic training two weeks ago and— what can I say—we got married just before he left.*
> *I'm really sorry, Drake, 'cuz you're a swell guy.*
> *Take care,*
> *Janie*

Drake let the hand holding the letter drop to his side. Tears filled his eyes. Stupid, he thought. He'd been pretty sure for a while what the score was. But seeing it in writing, with the finality of marriage tossed in, well, he wasn't ready for that.

But five minutes later, Drake felt strong. It was as if a small, known future had been replaced by one unknown but electric with possibility. Somehow he liked that.

Drake stopped by the office. His buddies, those who weren't going off to the Thirtieth, were scurrying around, sorting papers into *save* and *destroy* piles. Everyone wished him luck. Drake figured they envied him even if they didn't know it, much less say so. On the way out, he stuffed Janie's letter into a cardboard box labeled *burn*.

Drake was outside in full gear at 1815 hours, the first of the reassigned men to turn out. He leaned on a wooden lamppost and lit a Chesterfield. The snow that had been fluffy earlier was now gritty as cinders. It made plinking sounds on his steel helmet. Drake turned the collar of his field jacket up and faced away from the sharp north wind.

By 1830 all eight re-assignees were assembled in front of the HQ building door. Everyone seemed jumpy. Drake too, but he wasn't scared. He'd wished too long and hard for this to flip his lid now.

Sgt. Rutledge came out with cigarettes and good wishes for the men. The mess sergeant brought a platter of sardine and Velveeta cheese sandwiches and an urn of hot coffee. At 1930, the trucks still hadn't arrived. With the food and coffee gone and the wind stronger than ever, Rutledge herded the GIs inside to wait.

Just before midnight, a trio of two-and-a-half-ton trucks pulled up. Rutledge brought his eight men out. "Who's in charge of this circus?" he barked.

A corporal rolled down his window on the passenger side of the lead truck and waved. "That'd be me, Sergeant." He jumped out. "Sparky Hamlin's the name."

"Hamlin, I got a guy going with you who's pretty good with maps," Rutledge pointed to Drake. "You can count on him. How about he rides up front and navigates?"

Hamlin shrugged. "Sure thing. This old crate's heater ain't worth a tinker's damn, so I'd be glad to move to truck two."

Rutledge called Drake over.

Drake hustled over. "What's up, Sarge?"

Rutledge put a hand on his shoulder. "Hamlin, this is Pvt. Drake." He peered into Drake's eyes. "Got a lot of faith in you, kid. The corporal here's agreed to let you ride shotgun in the front truck and navigate. You up for that?"

"Sure, that'd be swell," Drake said.

Hamlin handed a set of maps to Drake. He circled the Thirtieth Division HQ's position between Stavelot and Malmedy and traced the route the convoy would take.

"Do a first rate job, Drake," Rutledge said, "and good luck in the Thirtieth." He looked up at the icy snow streaming down from the sky and blew into his cupped hands. "Helluva night for a drive." He shook his head and scampered inside the HQ building.

The three-truck convoy was ready to leave when a lieutenant from the Intelligence staff ran up near the cab of the lead truck. He yelled, "Who's the NCOIC?"

Drake rolled down his window. "Cpl. Hamlin's in charge, sir. I'll take you to him."

Standing on the running board of the second truck, the lieutenant said, "There's slews of radio reports of funny business going on out there. Phony radio traffic, felled trees blocking roads, ambushes. Even enemy saboteurs wearing GI uniforms and talking English." He brushed gritty snow from his jacket sleeve. "Besides, this weather's going to fight you all the way. Keep on your toes, hear?" He thumped the roof of the cab and jumped down. "Good luck, fellas."

"Thanks sir," Drake said running to the lead truck. The convoy crept forward.

The driver of Drake's truck was Pvt. Jimmy La Roux. He told Drake he was from New Iberia, Louisiana. He pronounced it

Lousy-anna. Over flaming red hair, he wore a dirty gray ball cap with a cardinal bird on the front. And he whistled. Seemed to be partial to *St. Louis Blues* as he did it again and again, improvising on the tune and slapping the steering wheel in time. On the dashboard he'd mounted a plastic Jesus figure with a battery and a built-in light. The only thing he was scared of was snow. "No sir," he said, "ol' Jimmy's drove big rigs from Texas to Florida, Mobile to Nashville but he ain't never drove on no snow. Ain't a natural pairing, rubber and ice."

"Hate to tell you, La Roux," Drake said, "but it may be snowy until April. Just take it easy and you'll be fine. And lay off the brakes. I've driven in snow all my life and the secret's to keep your speed slow and steady." He looked out the window at the bushes on the side of the road. In the headlights, their white floc looked enchanting. "Isn't it beautiful? The snow on everything. Makes up for having to drive on it."

"I reckon. What ain't beautiful is the job the Army gave us tonight—in the space of a night of hauling that passel draftsmen, clerks, cooks, mechanics, and musicians huddled in back, they gotta magically turn into infantrymen. Should've issued me a wand." He shook his head. "No sir, pulling that off will take more than magic. It'll take a fucking miracle."

Drake nodded. "A miracle? That's about right. Doubt if any of us is combat trained. Though you wonder, can any training really prepare a man for that? Somehow every guy who's strapped on a helmet and picked up a rifle's has to reshape his brain. Shove that urge to save his skin aside. Replace it with a sense of duty." He sighed. "It's unnatural. But somehow fellas have done it since history began."

"Somehow," La Roux said.

As the convoy crept down the slippery road, Drake kept his flashlight trained on the map and monitored their progress.

Ninety minutes after setting off, Drake spotted a dark object in the road ahead. "Looks like a board up there. Better swing right and miss it." Thirty seconds later the horn of the second truck blared. La Roux stopped. Drake grabbed his rifle, jumped out and ran back to see what the problem was.

The driver was standing by the front of the number two truck. "Ran over a board full of nails," he yelled to Drake. "Tire's hissing like a hornet. Hafta change it." One man rolled the spare to the front of the truck. Another brought a jack, and they set to work changing the flat.

While they were working, Drake picked up the board. It was studded with long nails driven through on both sides. He recalled that when he'd seen it, it wasn't covered with snow—like it had just been placed in the road. He took the corporal aside to show him the board when the hollow pop, pop, pop of shots and the sizzling zing of rounds filled the frigid air. The driver of truck #2 went down, yelping in pain. Amid GIs hollering and jumping for cover, two more men were hit before the Americans got off a single shot.

Drake jumped behind the truck fender and scanned the bushes along the road where he figured the shooting was coming from. He spotted a muzzle flash and yelled, "Up there." He marked the spot with the beam of his flashlight. Immediately a round came his way, ripping the air and plinking the fender inches from his ear. "He's there," Drake shouted, "about twenty yards out, near that tree." He aimed his M-1 and tried to fire at the spot but the safety was on. He clicked it off and fired an eight round clip in three sets.

Drake was reloading when La Roux ran forward and flung a grenade to the base of the tree. It went off with a flash, smoke, and a thud. The spot went silent.

"Cease fire," the corporal called. "Looks like we got them, but keep down, fellas." He turned to La Roux. "Nice pitching, Jimmy. Get over there and make sure your firecracker did the trick. You be careful now."

A minute later, La Roux called from the bushes, where the smoke of the grenade still hung, "One guy. Deader than a doornail. Y'all want his weapon?"

"Yeah, bring it here," Hamlin bellowed.

La Roux came back carrying the sniper's rifle on his shoulder. "Pineapple 'bout blew the fool's goddamn head off. Hell if it wasn't a fucking farmer! Or a hunter. Wearing overalls and a plaid jacket."

"Damn Belgians," Hamlin growled, "save their lousy asses and this is how they repay you."

"A farmer?" Drake said. "Hunting in the middle of the night? In weather like this?" He took the shooter's rifle from La Roux. "This here's a military rifle, German Mauser. Remember what the lieutenant told us, Hamlin? Those reports of Kraut saboteurs?" He pointed to the board full of nails. "This was an ambush."

Cpl. Hamlin scanned the road side. "You may be right, Private." He turned to the GIs tending the wounded. "Get those fellas loaded up in back of truck number three. Make 'em comfortable till get to a medic. There's bales of blankets in the back of vehicle two." He turned to the men standing next to the spare tire. "Hey, you clowns! Get that goddamn tire changed. You got three minutes!" He looked at his watch then peered into the darkness up the road. "We're sitting ducks stopped here like this."

When the trucks were rolling, Drake turned to La Roux. "Gotta hand it to you, Jimmy. That was one helluva throw you made. The pineapple." He sighed. "Wish I had the arm to do something like that."

La Roux shrugged. "Twern't nothing. I used to pitch for the New Iberia Cardinals. Threw a one-hitter against the Lake Charles Skippers in '41." He took off his hat. "This here's the cap I wore that afternoon. It's my good luck charm, my talisman. Makes me damn near untouchable."

"Cap or no cap," Drake said, "You ran right at that sniper when the rest of us were ducking for cover. You had your chance to be a hero, and you took it."

"Aw, I'm just a Louisiana Cajun with a good right arm. And an ear for whistling." La Roux launched back into *St. Louis Blues*.

"An ear for *that* song at least."

La Roux went silent. He grinned. "Why'd a fella wanna whistle something else when he can whistle the best? That's what I say." He picked up the tune where he left off.

The convoy had been moving for a half hour when La Roux said, "Drake, lookee up ahead." He pointed to a sign lit up by the headlights. It said *Francorchamps* and had an arrow pointing right. "We turn there, I reckon. You said we go through that town, right?"

"Francorchamps, yeah." Drake squinted at the sign then looked back at his road map. "Damn, according to this it's dead ahead. Plumb on the road. Slow down." He showed La Roux the map and pointed to where they were.

La Roux pushed it away. "The sign says turn here. Francorchamps must be just over there." He pointed to the right.

"Dunno," Drake said. "The dang map doesn't indicate any turns."

"Look, we gotta find the Thirtieth pronto-like. Get those wounded boys in to the doc. You wanna fart around with your fucking map, go ahead. Me—I'm fixing to do what the damn sign says." La Roux turned the truck. An instant later it was careening through darkness, down a steep, snowy embankment into an icy creek that paralleled the road. The truck piled into the stream bed with a groan of crunching metal. Steam poured from the radiator.

Until they'd started down, Drake had been frantically looking at his map, trying to make it jibe with the turn La Roux was making. He didn't have time to brace himself before impact, and his face and shoulder slammed unrestrained into the windshield.

Drake's Big Break

Drake came to in the sloping front seat of the truck cab with his pal Pete shaking him. "Can you hear me, buddy?" Pietromonaco yelled. "You OK?"

Drake's eyes fluttered. He raised his hand to the numbed right side of his face and looked at his fingers, covered in blood. No, he wasn't OK. He slipped back into unconsciousness.

When he came to again, Drake was on the ground, wrapped in a blanket. A buck-toothed soldier he didn't know was leaning over him, cleaning the gash under his right eye with a wad of damp gauze. Drake reached up and felt his aching right shoulder, afraid he'd been shot.

"Hey, Rip Van Winkle awakes!" Bucky said. "How you doing, fella?"

"What the hell happened?" Drake stammered.

"You did a number on that truck's windshield with your kisser, that's what. Lucky you were wearing your helmet." Bucky continued wiping the wound. "You look like shit. How do you feel?"

"Like shit." Drake pushed Bucky's hand away and gingerly touched his swollen face. Moving made his chest burn. "Can you see what's up with my shoulder? The right one."

"Your shoulder?" Bucky shrugged. "Don't see blood so I doubt you been shot."

"Feels like I just tried to tackle Bronko Nagurski without shoulder pads."

Bucky felt under Blake's jacket and shirt. He rubbed his fingers together and looked at them. "Aren't bleeding, but you got one helluva goose egg in there. Better leave it for the medics to check out." He gave Drake a drink from his canteen. "Just rest up. We'll haul you up the hill in a minute."

As the GI turned to leave, Drake grabbed his sleeve. "How about La Roux? He OK?"

Bucky grimaced. "Ball cap of his didn't help much when his noggin went through the glass. He ain't good." He squeezed

Drake's arm. "You take it easy. I'll get some guys to help carry you." He hurried off.

The sun was rising on December 17 when the convoy's two remaining trucks pulled into Thirtieth Division's headquarters area near Stavelot. Men were scurrying around like ants on a stirred-up nest.

Drake and the other wounded were taken to the Division Medical Battalion's Collecting Company. After thirty minutes, a young corpsman introduced himself to Drake as Barnes. He quickly evaluated Drake's injuries, jotting notes on a tag attached to his collar buttonhole. "Looks like you broke your collarbone, Private. How is it, pretty sore?" He went to the next litter without waiting for an answer.

When Barnes left, Drake read his diagnosis: *Clearing Station Tag. 1. Laceration to cheek, disinf. and suture. Eval. for concussion. 2. Clavicle Fracture, Non-surg. Ice, Asp, Sling. 4 days bed rest, 6 wk lim duty then reeval.*

Twenty minutes later the corpsman was back. He cleaned Drake's gash with brown soap and iodine then closed the wound with six quick stitches. "We'll let that air dry," he said, giving Drake two aspirin to take and a cold rubber bottle. "Packed this with snow. Alternate applying it to your contused shoulder and your cheek. That'll keep the swelling down. I've recommended four days bed rest and six weeks light duty. You'll be evacuated ASAP. A doctor will do a final evaluation when you get to a hospital." He scribbled more on Drake's tag. "Got any questions?"

"Yeah, what about a guy I came in with?" Drake tried to prop himself up on his elbow but fell back in pain. "Bumped his head when our truck crashed. La Roux's his name. Jimmy La Roux. Little fella. Bright red hair. Is he OK?"

"Sorry, your pal didn't make it. He was gone when you fellas got in this morning."

"God, no." Drake covered his eyes. "Not Jimmy. He saved us last night. A sniper had the whole convoy pinned down. Took 'im out singlehanded. La Roux was a hero."

23

"Yeah, it's lousy business. Look, Private, I gotta run—on account of this Kraut offensive, we got casualties up the kazoo." The medic turned to leave.

"Hey, buddy," Drake called, grabbing the tag pinned to his collar. "I'm doing pretty good here. Can't you change what you wrote on my tag and get me sent up to whatever line unit needs another rifle? It's my only chance—" He clutched Barnes's hand. "—to chalk up something. Like La Roux did. Cut me a break, will you?"

The corpsman jerked his arm away. "Great, I got a wannabe Sergeant York on my hands!"

"Look, La Roux getting killed was my fault. It was my job to get us here safely. Sarge made me navigator." Tears welled in Drake's eyes. "Should've kept us out of that ditch." He sat up. "I think I'm OK. Honest."

The medic squinted at Drake. "Got rocks in that head? Your clavicle's fractured, jackass! You can't march. You can't shoot. Can't fight. Shape you're in, you'd be dead weight to a combat unit." He shook his head scornfully. "Get yourself healed up, then maybe you can do the army some good. Or erase your screw-up. Whatever it is you think you need to do." Artillery boomed in the distance. "Hear that? You'll get your chance—this war ain't going nowhere soon." He crossed his arms. "Now if you don't mind, I have other patients, sane ones, to look after." He strode away.

Alone on his cot, Drake couldn't shake La Roux from his thoughts. He pictured him, cap pushed back on his head. Big grin on his face. Whistling away like a ghost riding the wind. "Jimmy, sorry I messed up," he whispered. "Should have done my job— should've stopped the convoy till I got things figured out—but I didn't. Now you're gone and I ought to be out there, taking your place, doing something big like you did." He wiped his mouth with the back of his hand. "But no, I'm here, taking up a bed like some cripple or something." He pressed his collarbone for the bolt of pain it brought. "Must be jinxed."

24

Drake was evacuated to a field hospital to convalesce for three days. Then he was sent with his sling and a bottle of aspirin back to light duty at First Army Headquarters Battalion, now in Chaudfontaine. In the second day of the German onslaught, they had been evacuated there from Spa. And they weren't in Chaudfontaine long. On Christmas Eve, the HQ was forced by enemy advances to move again, to Tongeren north of Liège.

In the first weeks of the bulge fighting, Drake couldn't stop thinking of the truck crash that killed La Roux. At night he'd replay it in his head, brooding over what he could have done differently. When he was off duty, he'd listen to US Armed Forces Radio and read *Stars and Stripes* to take his mind off the accident. When he could, he'd pump the guys on the intelligence staff for information on the monumental battle, so near yet so far away. Like everyone, he was hungry for news about Bastogne, where the Screaming Eagles of the 101st Airborne were first surrounded by three panzer divisions, then hanging on by their fingernails, and finally relieved on December 26. But what he did most was long for another chance to prove himself.

By mid-January, the Battle of the Bulge was over and the war went quiet again. Drake's shoulder felt better, and he vowed to make himself physically ready should fate pitch another chance his way. He got up early and ran before breakfast. As his clavicle mended, he did more—first calisthenics, then by his birthday, 12 March, when the staff moved to a location near the German city of Bonn, he was doing push-ups and lifting weights.

"Lola"

The Third Reich was crumbling. Caught in a three-jawed vice of British and Americans to the west, Soviets to the east, and allied bombers above, Germany, its army, cities and civilians, was being pulverized.

With the war moving so quickly to resolution and feeling well recovered, Drake thought constantly about transferring to a line unit. On March 26, just after reading in *Stars and Stripes* that thirteen battalions of American infantry had crossed the Rhine two days earlier, Drake opened his desk drawer and there were the broken spectacles he'd picked up on Omaha Beach. That's it, he told himself. Gotta really start pounding on Rutledge about a transfer. The next morning when he was out running, Drake spotted the sergeant walking Bosco, the HQ Battalion mascot, a chocolate Labrador Retriever picked up as a stray puppy in a bombed-out Belgian village. "Morning Sarge," Drake said, running up from behind. He patted the dog's head. "How's it going, Bosco?" He used a handkerchief to wipe the sweat from his forehead. "Nice weather for a walk, eh? Or a run."

"Yeah, Drake, I noticed you were running. Shoulder's feeling pretty good, huh?"

"Like a million bucks."

"And I suppose that means you'll start bugging me again about a transfer. I swear it's between you and George Patton as to who's itchiest to wade into a fight."

Drake took the leash from Rutledge's hand. "If I don't get transferred soon, doggone it, don't look to me like there'll be a much fighting left to wade into."

Rutledge looked around to make sure no one was near them on the path through the swampy field that served as First Army's parade grounds. "Been meaning to talk to you. I caught wind of something that might butter your bread. Unless you got your heart set on marching into Berlin and planting a 30-06 slug right between Adolph Hitler's eyes."

"Like I told you, sarge," Drake said, "I just want to be able to say I did my part. Whatever that is."

Bosco, apparently bored with standing still, jerked on the lead and whined.

"Gimme that leash," Rutledge barked. "Ain't you never owned a dog? You gotta show 'em who's boss." He glared at the dog and snapped, "Heel," as he stepped forward. Bosco padded meekly at his side. "That's more like it."

"Hmm, maybe that's it," Drake said.

"Maybe what's it?" Rutledge growled.

"Dogs...what you said about showing 'em who's boss. Gives me an idea."

"Yeah?"

"Well, us GIs always say the Army treats us like dogs. But what if the Army's the dog here? Like you said, 'gotta show 'em who's boss.' Maybe, rather than requesting a transfer, I should be demanding one." Drake punched his right fist into the palm of his left hand.

Rutledge's brow furrowed. "Are you stupid or something? Listen, the Army's a dog all right. A big, bad mongrel, all teeth and claws. You go telling the Army what to do, it'll bite your fool head off." He sighed and put a hand on Drake's shoulder. "But there's hope. Lemme tell you what I heard. Just between you and me. *Capisce?*"

"Sure," Drake said, "my lips are sealed."

"Apparently, no one's marching into Berlin. Not us, anyway. Roosevelt's given that to Stalin. We're going to pull up short."

"Pull up short? What's that mean?"

"Pull up short? Well, it means...pull up short. Of Berlin. It's that simple." When Drake opened his mouth to speak, Rutledge thrust his palm out. "Shut up and listen. The real question is why." The sergeant nodded knowingly. "Sounds to me like we're cooling it to save our strength for the Japs. That's what I got from a message that came in Friday for General Hodges. Word is, the invasion of Japan's going to be super-duper big time."

"Big as D-Day?"

Rutledge snapped the leash and stopped. He eyed Drake. "Bigger. Anyway, they'll need GIs. Lots of 'em. I expect they'd look kindly on volunteers. I s'pose they'll have to move whole divisions from Europe too. After the shooting's done here, that is."

"So maybe they'd take First Army, lock, stock and barrel?"

Rutledge frowned. "Hope not. Some of us've had our fill of soldiering."

"Look Sarge, do me a favor and let me know when you hear the first peep about needing volunteers for the Pacific." Drake looked into the distance and sighed. "I guess shitloads of guys have had it up to here—" He pointed to his forehead. "—with the war. Maybe I'll feel that way sometime too, *after* I've done something. *Really* done something."

Rutledge chuckled and slapped Drake on the back. "You're an oddball, kid. Sure, I'll keep my eyes peeled for you."

Drake nodded and ran off. Without looking back he waved. "Thanks, sarge."

It was the next afternoon that Drake first saw Stetti.

He was off at 1400 hours and there was a truck going to Bonn for supplies, so he hitched a ride into town. Drake spent an hour strolling the streets and looking inside the Romanesque cathedral, known as the Basilica of St. Martin. He visited the home of Ludwig van Beethoven on *Bonngaße* and came away humming the familiar opening four-note motif of the Fifth Symphony. He ended up at one of the three outside tables of a tavern overlooking the Rhine. The place, called *Die Marionette*, was located on a quaint lane called *An der Windmühle*. Two GIs at another sidewalk table were the *Marionette's* only other customers. Over a meal of wurst and beer, they argued over Fred Astaire films, of all things, and played Acey Deucey. The card game progressed under the dour gaze of the *Marionette's* proprietor, Herr Frick, a beefy codger with a waxed handlebar mustache and a white apron.

Drake sat, sipping a beer and pretending to read *Stars and Stripes*. What he was really doing was eavesdropping on the movie debate: Was Astaire a sap with some moves or an artist? Drake raised his hand and called, *"Ein anderes Bier,"* to the proprietor. He lit a Chesterfield. When Herr Frick brought the drink, Drake offered him a smoke. Frick glared at him and turned up his nose. Then he marched back to his post, standing with his arms crossed in the doorway.

Drake spotted a sleek young woman a hundred feet away and watched her approach. She wore a black and white check dress. A string of pearls and a tiny black hat over brunette hair pulled into a tight bun gave her style which seemed at odds with her youth— about twenty, Drake figured. Her skin was pale and her lipstick was bright red. The girl was tall, statuesque even, with legs that seemed to go from here to December. She was so slender he wondered when she'd had her last square meal. And she was beautiful. Drake couldn't look away.

When she came close to the *Marionette*, her sparkling, green eyes locked on Drake's. Cat's eyes, he thought. And not kitty cat— more like panther. But aside from those eyes, her expression had a playful look that seemed to say, now I'm going to show you something and in return for letting you in on my little game, I'll expect your fealty. She walked by his table, brushing his elbow with her hand, and stopped at the one where the GI pair sat, halting their card game in mid-play. "Good afternoon, my dear gentlemen," she said in English turned sexy with her husky, German-accented tone, something between a growl and a purr.

Both soldiers sprang up awkwardly. The taller one took off his garrison cap and said, "Hubba hubba, *Fräulein*. Wanna join us?" The other GI offered her his chair and pushed the pile of coins in the pot to the side. He pulled another chair for himself from an empty table.

"I'll sit if you have a ciggy for me," she said. "I seem to have left mine at home."

Both men scrambled to produce packs from their pockets. The girl took a cigarette from each. She put one in her purse and raised one to her lips. The GIs raced to get out their lighters for her.

"How 'bout a bite to eat, beautiful?" the tall one said. "And maybe a drink?"

"I can't stay," the girl said. Then she pouted her lips and glanced at her wristwatch. She looked at the plates of sausage the men had. "Perhaps I have time for a—" She peered for a moment into the tall man's eyes. "—bite."

"Hey Fritz," the short GI called, "Come 'ere!"

The proprietor strode to the table. "No Fritz is here working. I am Herr Frick, if you please."

"Sure thing, Fritz," Shorty said. "The lady here would like something to eat." He turned to the girl. "What'll you have, honey?"

She looked at the men's plates then turned to Herr Frick. *"Wurst, bitte. Mit brot. Und ein Glas Wein. Riesling."* She winked. *"Mit Prädikat."*

Frick nodded brusquely and left.

Transfixed, Drake watched the dance. The girl had the two GIs crawling over each other, trying to win the smallest speck of her attention. Sure she was hot enough to turn an ice cream sundae into soup from ten feet away, but Drake was glad she'd chosen them to sit with. Nothing beats watching a pro operate.

Shorty put his arm on the back of the girl's chair. "So, what's your name, hon?"

The girl licked her lips and gazed into his eyes. "Lola."

The men looked gleefully at each other. "Ain't never met a Lola before," Shorty said. He pointed his thumb to his partner. "This here's Harvey, and my name's Al. Pleased to meetcha, Lola."

The three ate and laughed. They ordered another round of drinks and laughed some more. Abruptly, Lola stood. "I really must be going," she said. "Oh, look!" She pointed to a boat on the river. "Isn't she beautiful! What's the name on her side?"

Harvey and Al turned in their chairs and craned their necks to read the name, written in white script on the boat's bow. While they were looking away, Lola scooped most of the coins from the men's Acey Ducey pot into her purse. Drake watched the whole thing happen.

"*Danke schön*, fellows," Lola said. "*Auf wiedersehen*." She stepped to the sidewalk and strode off in the direction from which she'd come. As she passed Drake, she gave him wink and an *our little secret, eh?* smile.

She was two dozen steps away when Al's voice boomed, "What the...? Hey, that little rat's got our goddamn money." With the clatter of boots on the sidewalk, Harvey and Al took off after her.

Stetti

Stumpy Al was no sprinter, but Harvey could really pick up his gangly get-alongs and put 'em down. The way he was moving, Drake figured he'd catch the girl before she reached the corner. He tossed some cash on the table to pay his bill and joined the chase.

Drake raced by Al, who was sucking air after a few strides. He was ten yards away when Harvey grabbed Lola's arm and pinned her shoulders to the front of a printing shop.

"Goddamn Nazi tramp!" Harvey hollered. "Think you can play me for a chump?" He drew back his hand to slap her.

Drake lunged and caught Harvey's arm before he could wallop the girl. "Hold your horses, buddy," Drake panted. "Look at her. She's starving, for God's sake!"

Harvey eyed Lola's pencil-thin arm and bit his lip. He lowered his hand. "If she had asked, we'd have given her something. Didn't have to go swiping our dough."

Al arrived on the scene, gasping. He leaned forward, hands on his knees.

Drake peered into Lola's pale face. He saw deprivation but no fear. He brushed Harvey's hand from her shoulder and put an arm around her. "Fellas, come on. Can't you see the kid's missed some meals? Look, how about I give you something for what she took and the chow you bought her?" He reached into his pocket and pulled out a money clip. "Maybe a little extra, too." He shoved a wad of Deutsche Marks into Harvey's palm.

Drake raised the girl's chin with his fingers and smiled at her. "Bet you got a family to feed too, eh sweetie?"

Lola nodded.

"How 'bout we let her keep the coins she pinched, guys?" Drake said. "The gal's family is hungry."

Harvey eyed the bills Drake had given him and shrugged. "S'pose so." Patting Al's back, he said, "Let's go finish our game." The pair sauntered back up *An der Windmühle* Lane toward the *Marionette*, where Herr Frick was waiting with arms crossed.

As the GIs walked away, Lola took Drake's hand. "You didn't have to save me, you know," she said in English. "I take care of myself."

Drake gawked for a moment at Lola. She was striking, but without the softness of most young, good-looking girls. Her features looked chiseled from stone. Her eyes were cold—exotic, like those of a wild animal. Dangerous. Drake forced himself to look away. "Who said I was saving *you*?" He turned back to her. "Those boys are comrades-in-arms. I was worried you'd clobber 'em."

"Now *you* are alone with me. Perhaps you must worry for yourself." Lola sounded serious.

Drake shrugged. "Aw, I'm too dumb to worry." He winked. "Let me introduce myself. Name's Winston Drake."

"Winston—" There was an edge to her tone. "—like the English Churchill."

"Yeah, but call me Drake. I prefer it. And you're Lola, right?"

She shrugged. "If you say so."

Drake peered into the girl's eyes—they were emeralds, sparkling in brilliant sunshine. Luminous. Spellbinding.

"Are there no green eyes in America?" Lola asked.

"Guess I was staring, huh? Sorry. Sure, there's green eyes, but I don't recall seeing any like yours." Drake glanced at his watch. "I've got an hour before I need to catch a ride back to my post. Any chance you'd like to walk a bit along the river, *Fräulein*?"

Lola studied Drake's face for a moment, like she'd find his character written there. "I suppose so. But I won't pass those men at the *Marionette*. I'll lead us by another direction to the Rhine. Come." She took him down an alley that ended on the riverside street.

As they strolled the broad waterway, Drake slipped his arm around her waist, and doing so, he realized she was a couple of inches taller than he. If she minded that, she didn't let on. Nice she's level-headed, Drake thought, but he squared his shoulders and tried to stretch himself taller, just in case.

Lola played tour guide, pointing out riverside landmarks, most of them now in ruins.

"Your English," Drake said, "it's swell. Did you learn it in school?"

"Yes, in school in England. When I was thirteen, Father took a sabbatical year in Cambridge. It was two years before the war, when Britain and Germany admired each other. Before the English turned on us. I attended classes, learned the language, met many people. I liked the girls."

"And the boys?"

"Too smug for my taste. Too stiff. Perhaps I met only professors' sons. Anyway, I didn't like them." She studied Drake's face. "You certainly don't look like a Winston."

"Never thought I did either. Is that good or bad?"

"I count it as very good. I could never be friendly with a Winston," Lola said. "It would be impossible. Such an awful name!"

"Because of Churchill?" Drake crossed his arms. "Lots of folks on my side don't think much of the name Adolf, either."

Lola stopped and glared at him. "Nor do I."

"My sarge says it's funny how many Germans are claiming that these days. When we take a town, about every house has a bedsheet flag out its window with *Hitler Weg* painted on it. That means *Down with Hitler*, by the way." He chuckled but stopped when he saw darkness flash across Lola's face.

"I know it very well, what *Hitler Weg* means, thank you." Lola pushed Drake's hand from her waist. "What you say about the dishonesty of many German people is true. The day the Wehrmacht ceded Bonn, the grocer on Beckmesser Straße took off his swastika armband and announced himself a resistance fighter since 1939." She stuck out her chin. "Some of us, including me, opposed Nazi ideals from the start. Well, almost from the start—I was a child when Hitler was appointed chancellor. But even then my heart turned to the East and saw a better way."

"Look, I'm sorry I said anything. I hate politics. Let's talk about anything else. Tell me something about Bonn."

Lola exhaled. The anger left her eyes. "All right. Soon we come to what was the *Beethovenhalle*," she said, "the music concert auditorium named for Bonn's most famous figure. Can you guess this man's name?"

"Would that by any chance be, *da, da, da,* **dum**—" Drake intoned the four-note opening of Beethoven's Fifth Symphony. "—good old Ludwig van?" When Lola smiled, he chanced moving his hand back to her waist.

"So, Mr. Drake, you know something of van Beethoven?"

"Yep," Drake said. "I visited his museum this afternoon. Real interesting."

"Like everyone, you know the opening notes to van Beethoven's Fifth Symphony. And you must know, too, his choral symphony, the Ninth. With its *Ode to Joy*. Of course the music thrills me, but even dearer to my heart are the words of Schiller's stirring poem."

"My aunt back in Omaha has it on phonograph record. It'll spark your spirit, all right."

"One of its lines is my *Herzenwunsch*, my dearest desire: *Alle Menschen werden Brüder.* In English, *All men shall be brothers.*" Lola inhaled deeply, like merely saying those words had perfumed the air. She turned to Drake and raised her index finger. "Mark me—one day there will be no *Führers*, no bosses, no serfs, no masters, no slaves. Only *Kamerades*. Equals. The People won't be denied!"

"Well…" Drake shrugged. "We Americans are working on it. 'Bout got Hitler KOed. And the Jap Emperor is on the ropes. Yep, we're getting there."

Lola peered at Drake like he was a child. Like truth was pushing her to point out his naivety. But she remained silent.

Five minutes later they rounded a curve, and Lola pointed to a ruined building, not much more than a pile of bricks. "The *Beethovenhalle* was there. Broken by Mr. Churchill's bombs." She

35

shook her head. "Perhaps he likes his cigars and champagne better than music."

Drake took off his cap. "A slew of great old treasures been destroyed in the war. But to be honest, maybe it was American bombs that did that."

Fire smoldered again in Lola's eyes. "No, it was the English bombs of Churchill, just as it was for Köln, Hamburg.... So many other German cities. The Englanders call it carpet bombing. It sounds so much softer than the truth—that it is terror bombing." She eyed Drake. "You doubt it? In the night. On cities without soldiers. Only women, old men, children. What else can it be? Sowing terror in German hearts. I hear the reports on Radio Berlin that even my home, Dresden, was bombed. A city called the Jewel Box by the world."

"You're from Dresden?" Drake swallowed hard. "Real sorry to hear that, Lola. Sorry for what happened. For whatever it was that happened." He hoped she didn't know the horrific details of the firebombing of Dresden in February.

"My family is there." She gazed into the distance like she might glimpse them. "Every day I look for a letter, a word from them that they are well, but every day I hear nothing. My heart breaks."

Drake wanted to steer the conversation away from the grim story of the firestorm that had consumed Dresden and probably her family too. "It's strange...Hitler turns your stomach, but you can't stand his nemesis, Churchill, either. How does that figure?"

Lola glared at him. "There *is* the fact that both are mass murderers." She closed her eyes and sighed. "I'm sorry to be so blunt." She smiled and took Drake's hand. "I've thought about this question. Perhaps we Germans hate Churchill for his stubbornness. His refusal to quit in 1940, when *anyone* else would have. So many lives were lost because of that willful old man! And for what?"

Drake's cheeks burned. He jerked his hand from hers. "There is the little matter that Churchill throwing in the towel would have put all of Europe under the Nazi boot." He huffed. "You're saying that's no big deal?"

Saving Euridice

Lola took his arm. "It makes but a temporary difference. A small one. Drake, my dear, is the slavery of fascism so much worse than the slavery of capitalism?" She shrugged. "In the end, history's natural course must prevail with Marxism's triumph over whatever enslaves men. It is those who fight nature—the Hitlers and Churchills—who make history bloody."

Drake rolled his eyes. "Whoa." He shook his head. "You bring up blood and recent history without mentioning Stalin? With the millions of Russians slaughtered in the Thirties in Uncle Joe's purges?"

Lola crossed her arms. "Difficult acts but necessary. The privileged always fight the destruction of class. Blood must be spilled to halt them. A society of equals justifies it."

"Sure, equality's good. But there's other things worth the price of blood too. In the US, we fought a revolution and a civil war for freedom. Every red-blooded American believes freedom's worth fighting for."

Lola smiled. "Since socialism is true freedom, the inevitable future will please your countrymen." She nestled close to him. "But enough sharp talk, Drake darling. Better we enjoy our walking…together. Don't you think?"

They strolled for a while in silence, until Lola said, "Before it was leveled, the *Beethovenhalle* was the residence of the Beethoven Orchestra. My orchestra."

"Holy Moses…you're in an actual orchestra?"

"Yes, as principal cellist." She shrugged. "Can my being a musician astonish you so?"

"It's just that you don't look any older than me."

"I'm twenty-one." Lola brushed the side of her finger down Drake's smooth cheek. "About what you must be. Did you think a cellist must be a doddering antique?"

"I didn't know. Never met one before today."

"In 1939, men, be they florists, farmers, cobblers, or cellists, were taken for the army. I came here from Dresden to fill a man's empty chair. I think I fill it rather well."

37

Drake stopped and took Lola's hand. Her fingers were long and stately. Delicate but vibrant. "I'll bet you do." He looked into her eyes and saluted. "Wow…I'm stepping out with an *artiste!*"

Her eyebrows arched. "Such a lucky boy!"

They walked a little farther and came to a bench overlooking the river. "May we sit?" Lola said.

"You bet."

After a quiet moment watching the Rhine's languid flow, the girl said, "Drake, you are a nice man." She faced him. "You deserve my honesty." She peered into his eyes. "I'm not really a Lola. My name is Stetti."

Stuff in Common

Drake was surprised at his reaction to Stetti's announcement. He wasn't sore about being lied to by someone whose skin he'd saved. Rather, his heart soared. The way he saw it, she could have said *Danke* and *Auf Wiedersehen* and gone off looking for the next GI to hustle. But Stetti respected him enough, maybe even cared about him enough, to come clean.

"In truth," Stetti said, "my given name is Euridice, but no one calls me that. Since school times, to my friends and family, I am Stetti. It comes out of our family name of Bloomstedt."

"Whoa there," Drake said, "you're losing me."

"It is quite simple. For me, Lola is in German a *Deckname*. Hmm, in English I think it is called an alias. Not one's real name. There was a famous Lola in Bavarian history. She was the king's mistress. The gossip was that Lola got whatever she wanted." Stetti smiled. "I like that." She touched Drake's hand. "Now for you, I am Stetti—it's simple."

Drake's brow furrowed. "And the Euridice deal?"

"Euridice is my name in the official records. It came by my father. He was a professor of classical studies at the *Polytechnikum Universität* in Dresden. He called his three children after literary favorites of his. My brother is Siegmund and my older sister Norma. As for me, at birth I had no breath. Until the midwife spanked me. Father said the slap brought me back from the dead—" She rolled her eyes. "—so he called me his little Euridice."

Drake rubbed his chin. "Euridice? Hmm, sounds familiar. That from Shakespeare?"

"No, Euridice's story is a Greek myth. She was the wife of Orpheus. He loved her so that when she died, he could not bear the loss and traveled to the Elysian Fields to bring her back to life. Father called Orpheus's love of Euridice redemptive." She scoffed. "I suppose he believed that love so ideal is possible. As for me, I doubt it. My Bohemian schoolmates found Euridice far too bourgeoisie. They decided Stetti was properly playful, so everyone called me that. And now—" She shrugged. "—I see myself as Stetti."

"So, where was it that guy Orpheus went to save Euridice?"

"To the Elysium. It is part of Hades, the place of the dead."

"Hades?" Drake grinned. "Back home we call it hell. Guess you could say Orpheus went to hell and back for the gal he loved." He shook his head. "Talk about loyalty!"

"For the girl he loved?" Stetti peered into Drake's eyes. "No, he traveled to repair his own loss. He went for himself. I believe it is so for most of what we call heroism."

Drake took out his pack of Chesterfields. "That's a frosty way of looking at the world on such a charming evening." He offered a cigarette to Stetti and took one for himself. He struck a match and lit hers. "I s'pose you'd say I gave you that smoke just for the pleasure of seeing your face in the match's glow. Pure selfishness." He lit his own. "You'd be part right."

"Having witnessed what men are capable of, I can't help but view things coldly." She took a long, deep drag on her Chesterfield. "Though this cigarette tastes so good, I might have to reconsider."

"Good old Chesterfields," Drake said, "they're what Bob Hope smokes."

"You Americans, you know your ciggies." Stetti slipped her arm into Drake's. "Shall we walk some more?"

They strolled the sidewalk along the Rhine. "Just thought of something, Stetti," Drake said, gazing at the river. "We got something in common besides age. Neither of us go by our given name." He smiled. "Stuff in common, that's promising."

Stetti giggled. "Perhaps we both choose to hide some truths about ourselves, eh?" She shrugged. "But then, who doesn't?"

"Yeah, who doesn't?" Drake glanced at his watch. "I've got fifteen minutes before I need to head back to the post. Can I walk you home?"

"It is quite near." Stetti pointed vaguely east. "Where must you go?"

"They're picking us up at the train station."

"That is on the way to my home. Just off *Bismarckstraße*." She took Drake's arm. "Come, I will escort you."

When they were a block away, Stetti said, "The *Hauptbahnhof* is just there. I see an American army truck in front. Does it wait for you?"

"Probably." Drake squinted. "Looks like Moynihan in the cab—he's the driver." He bit his lip, less concerned with keeping Tiny Moynihan waiting than he was with calculating how best to ask if he could see her again.

Stetti pulled Drake to a halt before he could say anything. "If you can arrange time off and should you wish, perhaps we could meet next weekend. What do you say?"

"Darned if I wasn't just about to ask you the same thing!" More stuff in common, he thought. "Sure, that'd be swell. I should be able to swing another pass."

"*Schön*," Stetti said. "We can meet Friday, six p.m. A *Ratskeller* called *Fafner's Höhle*." She took out a scrap of paper and a pencil and printed the name in block letters. "It means in English, The Dragon's Cave. Its street is *Moselweg*." She jotted that on the paper. "It's that way—" She pointed. "—a kilometer from this spot."

Drake glanced at the paper. "A kilometer south of here. Got it." He folded it and tucked it into the breast pocket of his jacket. "So, what's a Ratskeller, anyway? Hope it's not a hangout for certain rodents."

"Rodents? Oh, you mean a home for the rats." Stetti smiled. "No it is not, although I have seen mice scurry over the floor of *Fafner's*. I don't think I know an English word for Ratskeller." She shrugged. "It is a tavern under the ground. In a cellar. *Keller* means cellar." She placed a hand on Drake's sleeve. "So, you wish to meet me, darling?"

"Wild horses couldn't keep me away. Nor rats neither."

"That is good—I won't have to shoo the many wild horses from *Fafner's*." Stetti's eyes twinkled. "The next Friday's evening will be special for me, Drake. Now who knows? Maybe it can please you, too." She saluted playfully. "*Auf wiedersehen.*" She turned on her heel and scampered off into the evening before he could ask what she meant.

Drake watched her for a moment, transfixed. He was thinking, will next Friday please me? If I'm seeing you, damn well right it will! Then he dashed to the idling two-and-a-half-ton truck and pulled up there, panting outside the cab.

Tiny Moynihan scowled as he rolled down the window. He looked at his watch and shook his head. "Eleven minutes late, mister. 'Bout left you."

"Shame on you, Tiny. Giving a fella such a hard time. When his only crime's being young and in love." Drake ran to the rear of the truck, jumped in, and hollered. "Aboard." The truck rolled off in a cloud of exhaust, heading out of the city and back to First Army HQ.

Into the Dragon's Cave

First thing after chow the next morning, Sgt. Rutledge sent for Drake. When he arrived, the Sergeant said, "Have a seat, my boy." Drake made himself comfortable. "I talked to the captain about you. About how you want to transfer to the Pacific Theater."

"To a combat outfit, sarge."

"Right, that's what I told him. He said if stuff continues to go well here, in May they'll start transferring men to the Pacific. Volunteers like you plus a few kazillion others." He leaned forward Drake and lowered his voice. "Word is, the invasion of the Japan's going to make Normandy look like a Boy Scout jamboree. They're talking forty fucking divisions."

"Holy mackerel, forty divisions! There's gotta be a spot for me." Drake pursed his lips. "May, huh? That timing ought to work." Drake looked over his shoulder to make sure they were alone. "See, Sarge, I kinda met this gal. A local. In Bonn."

"What? There's rules against fraternizing with enemy civilians. Just last week I gave you a copy of the special orders banning it. What the hell's the matter with you?"

"It's not what you think. I just need some time to…help her get back on her feet."

Rutledge shook his head and sighed. "S'pose you're not the first GI to skirt the fraternization rules. Get it, *skirt*?" He chuckled. "Just keep it on the q. t. But if the beans do spill, you're on your own. You never told me nothing about a German girl. Right, Private?"

"Deal," said Drake.

"And one more thing." Rutledge squinted at Drake. "You best get it through that thick skull of yours, mister—I don't take kindly to looking like a sap. If I arrange this transfer you requested, you better not try to weasel out of it, dame or no dame. *Capisce?*"

Drake shrugged. "I *capisce*. Just want to give this kid a hand. War's been tough on her and her family. It's no big deal."

"Make sure it ain't."

Drake walked out of the sergeant's office. As soon as he rounded the corner down the hallway, he stopped and took out the brown card Rutledge had mentioned, *Special Orders for American German Relations*. It was signed by General John Lee. He reread the orders—they were pretty damn clear. Don't fraternize with Germans! Rule #6 made that plain: *Never to associate with Germans.* But for some reason, Rule #2 jumped off the card at him. *Never to trust Germans, collectively or individually.* Of course, that couldn't apply to Stetti, he figured. Nobody hated the Nazis more than she did. He inhaled deeply, folded the brown card, and stuffed it back into his shirt pocket.

Drake secured a weekend pass. On Friday, he ducked out early, went by the mess hall and talked a cook out of three cans of Spam, six potatoes and five cans of fruit. He grabbed four packs of cigarettes, dumped the provisions in a cardboard box, and caught a ride into Bonn. He booked a room for two nights at *Hotel Heinrich der Heilige*, a *Gasthof* near the train station that catered to GIs. Then he went to a nearby shop. The shelves were mostly bare, but a few things caught his fancy, and he bought them: two jars of strawberry jam, two tins of cookies, a small burlap bag of turnips—he liked turnips, a paper sack of lima beans, a red wood-handled pocketknife, a bottle of a perfume called *Immer*, and a tube of red lipstick.

Recalling the wine Stetti had ordered the week before at Herr Frick's tavern *Marionette*, Drake went to a *Weinstube* next door and asked, "Got any Riesling wine called *mit pretty cat* or something like that?"

The man behind the bar shrugged and said, "No English." Then he held up a finger. "*Ah, Moment.*" He left and a minute later came back with a woman wearing a grimy apron. He nodded to her and said, "*Gut English hier.*"

Drake spoke very slowly. "I want to buy wine. In a bottle." He pantomimed twisting a cork screw into a cork and yanking it out of a bottle, then taking a swig. He pointed to the imaginary bottle in his hand. "Riesling mit pretty cat. A name like that." He made an exaggerated shrug. "Got any?"

44

For a moment the woman seemed confused, then her face lit up. She held up a finger and said, "Ah, you wish for Riesling wine *mit Prädikat*. Special good, eh?"

"That sounds right," said Drake.

The woman brought out two dusty bottles. She wiped them on her apron and showed him the labels. *Qualitätswein mit Prädikat* was printed on each one. "Is *gut, ja?*" she asked.

Drake nodded enthusiastically. "Is *gut.*" He bought both bottles.

Back at his hotel room, Drake piled all his purchases into the box with the cans of food and cigarettes. At 1730, he paid the cousin of the desk clerk to give him a ride to *Fafner's Höhle*, the Dragon Cave tavern where he was to meet Stetti.

As Drake stumbled down the steps, lugging his box of provisions into the cellar tavern, he thought the name Dragon's Cave seemed fitting. It was dark and dingy. The walls were painted a sullen shade of gray and the bar and tables were made of ancient, black walnut. It took Drake's eyes a minute to adjust to the darkness—where the old men smoking and drinking there all watched him coldly in his GI uniform. He set his box on an empty table and scanned the room. Stetti wasn't there. He glanced at his watch. 1810 hours.

For what seemed like forever, Drake sat alone, almost hidden by his box. Behind the bar was a middle-aged woman. She had a linebacker's body and a pock-marked face. The barmaid kept busy warming glasses of dark beer and bringing them to other patrons. But she treated Drake like a leper. He checked his watch. 1830. How long should I wait, he wondered.

One of the old men eying Drake took a grubby blue cap from his pocket. With his glare daring him to react, he put it on and tugged the small bill to snug it up. The hat had a red star on the crest. It looked familiar to Drake. A moment later he knew why—when Lenin was pictured wearing workingman's clothing on propaganda posters, that was the kind of cap he wore. Drake figured the scowling old codger, puffing defiantly on his smudged meerschaum pipe, must've kept it hidden away since the Nazis came to power in 1933.

At 1845, Stetti came down the steps. She looked stunning in a long black gown with a single strand of pearls around her neck— the same ones she'd worn when they met. Against the dark of the room and her dress, the alabaster of her skin and the pearls was luminous. Without looking at Drake she went to the woman at the bar and gave her a hug and a kiss. She turned to the old timer in the Lenin cap and did the same. Only then did she turn to Drake, who rose awkwardly from his chair. She glided to him, took both of his hands in hers, and turned her face to let him kiss her cheek.

Still holding her hands, Drake stepped back and looked at Stetti. "My gracious, you look…radiant!"

"Is it my concert gown or these?" Stetti stroked the strand of pearls. "My mother gave me them when I left home." She leaned toward Drake so he could admire them. "For me, they bring magical protection and inspiration.

He studied the pearls. "They're swell."

She sat at the table, fingering her necklace. "Next to my cello, these pearls are the most precious thing in the world. Except for the People, of course."

Drake shook his head. "To think, you dressed up like this just for me."

Stetti smiled coyly. "I did, darling. For you and others."

"And others?" Drake put the box on the floor and sat.

Stetti winked, her only reply to the question. "You have no drink?" She leaned back in her chair. Without waiting for a reply, she shot a glance to the woman at the bar, who came right over. "Beer is served here. Will you have one?"

"Sure," said Drake.

"*Zwei halbe Dunkel, bitte, Gretchen,*" Stetti said to the server. She turned back to Drake. "I'm sorry to be coming late. I had to get something. For you." She looked at the box next to her chair. "And what have you there?"

"Aw, just a few things I thought you could use. Food and stuff. No big deal."

Stetti's green eyes sparkled. "May I see?"

"Of course." Drake got up and lifted the box to his chair. He proceeded to set the contents on the table top. "A little of this, a little of that."

She plucked the lipstick tube from the cache and checked its bright red color. "I like this," she said, putting it in her pocketbook. She held the knife up. "For Uncle. He likes shaving wood." When she came to the perfume, Stetti's brow furrowed. "*Immer* is a scent for whores. We say, *Immer auf ihren Rücken*. It means *always on their backs*." She pushed it away. "I won't use this."

Drake shrugged and mumbled, "Didn't know." A moment later she was looking at the wine bottles. He said, "Hope it's not a kind only whores drink."

Stetti laughed. "No, anyone who enjoys good wine will like these." She raised one bottle to better read its label in the dim light. "Riesling!" Her eyes sparkled. "Even the sound of the word has music in it! This one is from Bingen, a little village on the Rhine's elbow. Known for its fine Rieslings." She pointed to the label. "You see *Kabinett*, so it is dry. And here, *Qualitätswein mit Prädikat*. That means good quality wine with special characteristics. So it is a nice one." She picked up the other bottle. "Also *Qualitätswein mit Prädikat*, but this one is different. See here: *Spätlese*. It means the grapes are *late picked*. Fully ripe fruit. Sweetness in perfect balance with acidity and minerals." She raised her right hand to her brow. "Sir, I salute your taste in wines!"

Drake smiled broadly.

The barmaid brought two half-liter glasses of dark beer. Stetti and Drake put the provisions back in the box to make room and the woman set the drinks on the table.

Drake pulled out a roll of Marks. "How much do I pay?" he asked Stetti.

"My," Stetti said, her eyes wide at the size of Drake's bankroll, "you are rich as Croesus." The woman who brought the beer shook her head and pointed to the man in the Lenin cap. "Christoph, my old friend, pays," Stetti said and blew the old-timer a kiss.

47

As the barmaid turned to leave, Stetti grabbed her sleeve. She reached into the box, pulled out the perfume bottle, and pushed it into her hand. *"Für Dich."*

The woman smiled. *"Danke,"* she said and scurried off.

"She's OK with that *Immer* perfume?" Drake asked. "Thought you said it was only for, well, hookers."

"Hookers means prostitutes?" Stetti asked. "Maybe because they catch their customers like fishes? I like the word." She glanced at the barmaid, now flirting with a couple of fellows at a nearby table. "Yes, Gretchen is a sometimes hooker. After she finishes working here in *Fafner's Höhle*. People do what they must." Stetti raised her glass of beer. Drake did the same and they tapped glasses. *"Prost!"* she said and took a sip.

When they'd drunk their beers to half-level, Stetti asked, "You like this beer, dark and warm?"

Drake swirled the brew in his glass and took a swig. "It's hearty."

"I have heard you Americans like lager, chilled, but we believe beer is a food, like bread—the richer and tastier the better." Stetti drank then glanced at her watch. "Soon I must leave." Drake's smile disappeared. "First I have something for you."

"Aw, you didn't need—"

"But it is my wish." Stetti smiled. "Heaven...want to go there?" She peered into his eyes. "Tonight, Drake darling, I would take you."

An Evening with *Herr* Bach

Stetti's offer of a heavenly trip knocked Drake for a loop. Sure, he wanted what he assumed she meant. In the last week, he'd even fantasized about it. He shook his head. "I'll say this, you German girls sure aren't shy about taking the driver's seat."

Stetti looked confused. "But our trip to heaven requires no motoring." She opened her purse and took out a slip of yellow paper. A look of pride flashed in her eyes as she handed it to Drake. "For you, darling."

Drake studied the slip. The elegant handwritten script made it look like a certificate.

Euridice Bloomstedt, Solocello
Suiten für Violoncello, Nr. 1, 3, 4.   J. S. Bach
Freitag, den 6. April, 1945.........20:30 Uhr
Akademie der Musik, Hofgarten Platz, Bonn
DM 3.50

"Looks like an announcement or something." Drake said.

"It is a ticket," Stetti said. "Can you make sense of it?"

"Well…at the top, that's you."

"Yes, and *Solocello* means unaccompanied cello… I perform alone. The next line is what I will play. Do you know Bach's cello suites? Tonight I perform three of the six."

"Sorry, all I know is that Bach is a musician. Or was, a real long time ago, I think."

Stetti smiled. "A musician *and* composer. With this ticket you can come to know better the greatest musical genius of all time, Johann Sebastian Bach. I could talk about him and his art for hours. But better I let his music say everything." She pointed to the date on the ticket. "Tonight."

"6 April, that *is* today! This evening at half past eight." He looked at his watch. "Golly, that's less than an hour from now."

Stetti placed her hand on his forearm. "We have time, the music academy is near to here. And I have taken my cello there already. I need only a few moments for tuning her."

"So I'll get to hear you play? Swell." He read the last line. "Three and a half Deutsch Marks—that is the admission, right?"

"It is my gift to you, saying *danke schön* for saving me at *die Marionette* last week."

The man in the Lenin cap came to the table. Stetti introduced Christoph to Drake. She spoke with him for a minute, then he left. "Christoph goes to open the academy hall. He has arranged this concert as a favor for me." She shrugged. "We all need money." Stetti signaled the barmaid. "I will ask Gretchen to have someone bring your box of luxuries to my home tonight. Wish you to walk with me to the Academy now or to stay here for another drink and come afterward?"

"I'd like to walk with you."

When the barmaid came to the table, she and Stetti chatted. Then Gretchen picked up the box and put it behind the bar.

"So, I must make my goodbyes to some people here, then we leave. That pleases you?"

"You betcha," Drake said. "I'll sit tight here."

After stops at several tables, Stetti returned. "Now we go," she said, and they were off.

The walk to the Academy took ten minutes. Waiting at the door, taking tickets, was Christoph, in an ancient, frayed tuxedo. The cap was gone, replaced by a red star lapel pin. What hadn't changed was the meerschaum pipe clenched in his teeth and the look of disdain he cast Drake's way.

Stetti kissed Christoph's cheek and chatted with him for a moment. She turned to Drake. "We will find you a seat now so I can prepare."

Before they could step inside, Christoph pointed the stem of his pipe at Drake and demanded, "*Karte!*"

"Ah, he wants your ticket."

Drake winced. "Gee, I was sort of hoping to keep it as a souvenir."

"That's sweet," Stetti said. She turned to Christoph. "*Als Andenken, Liebling.*"

50

Christoph scowled and waved them in. As they stepped through the door, Stetti whispered to Drake, "I think he is jealous of our friendship."

The small auditorium, a hundred seats total, was a quarter full of patrons talking quietly. Several of them turned to smile and nod to Stetti. She settled Drake in a chair in the fourth row and said, "Enjoy the music." Then she disappeared through a door to the side of the raised stage.

The seats in the hall began to fill. Drake felt everyone eyeing him, whispering, *What's that American doing here? He doesn't belong.* He twiddled his thumbs, wishing for 20:30 to come.

Right on time, the hall lights went down, leaving the brightly-lit stage all the more resplendent. Christoph strode to center stage and began speaking. Drake understood a few words here and there. *"Guten abend, Meine Damen und Herren."* *"Johann Sebastian Bach."* Raising his hand in welcome and turning to stage left, he ended his remarks with, *"Fräulein Euridice Bloomstedt, unsere liebe Stetti."*

There was an ovation as Stetti stepped from the wings, carrying her cherrywood cello. She seemed to glow. Christoph clapped, beaming like a proud parent. He took her forearm and guided her to her place at center stage. The audience applauded and there were even a few shouts of welcome. Drake could feel it—she had them in the palm of her hand without playing a note. In the bright lights, her black gown murmured simple elegance. Her pearls were a string of stars in the night sky, and her face, radiant as the moon, pulled every eye in the hall to it. Drake could hardly breathe.

Christoph held the chair for her and exited. The hall fell silent. It was as if Stetti, alone, motionless in the bright lights, was the center of the universe. Her countenance went from joyful to solemn. Then, like the sun breaking the horizon at dawn, she threw herself into the opening notes of the *Prelude* to *Suite One*. All expression and movement, Stetti filled the hall with Bach's sublime music. It seemed to Drake that she and the cello were a pair of lovers, alone together. The warm tones they made lazed then darted, swelled then condensed…pulsed with life. When the last note of *The First Suite* faded, Stetti inhaled like someone coming out of a trance, and the audience welcomed her back with boomed applause. Twenty seconds later, with a sharp nod of her head, she began *Suite Three*. Lost in the music, unaware of the passage of time, Drake was surprised, even let down, when its final note brought the first half of the program to an end. The music had been delightful, but he understood that seeing Stetti playing it, loving it so, just a few steps away, was what made the experience heaven for him.

When Stetti left the stage for the intermission and the applause subsided, Drake scanned the faces around him. No longer were the other audience members watching him. No longer did six years of war hang on their brows. Now there was only joy, as if they too had been to heaven.

Stetti returned to the stage after fifteen minutes. There was an instant of silence as she stepped from behind the curtain, then the crowd broke into a rapturous welcome back. Her face glowed at the prospect of sharing more of the music she and her audience loved so well. Drake felt lucky to be part of it.

Stetti was well into the *Sarabande* of *Suite Four* when the lights suddenly went out. Christoph was on the stage in seconds with a lighted candle. He put it on the floor in front of Stetti, then lit four more, making an arc of light in front of her. It made Stetti's presence all the more dramatic. Drake found the second part of the concert more amazing than the first. In addition to the candlelight, the first two suites had prepared him to appreciate the variety, the precision, the complex simplicity of the last one. When Stetti bowed the last note of the *Suite Four Gigue*, in that instant before the room erupted in applause, Drake felt complete contentment—like nothing could have been better than eavesdropping on Stetti's and Bach's collaboration.

When the concert was over, most of the audience stayed in the *Akademie* concert hall. Stetti remained in her chair on the stage, and Christoph scurried around, lighting more candles and bringing out bottles of schnapps and small glasses. Some of the people who stayed smoked or drank and conversed in small groups spread throughout the hall. Drake couldn't understand the conversations, but they seemed amicable—probably just old friends chatting. A stream of concert-goers who seemed to know Stetti personally came up to greet her. Drake watched from the side as they hugged and kissed her, held her hand, and laughed with her, all the while talking, perhaps about the concert and how much they had enjoyed it.

After ten minutes, Drake went out to have a smoke. The evening air was cool and crisp. He sat on the entryway steps enjoying the darkness and the breeze, and the time to let his thoughts drift. When he'd finished his cigarette, he decided to go back inside, thank Stetti for the evening, then stroll leisurely to his hotel. He had just opened the door when Stetti walked through it.

"Drake darling, I feared your departure. I am so glad finding you." She leaned forward and kissed his cheek. "And how did you find Mr. Bach's music? To your liking, was it?"

Drake took her hand. "It was swell. The music and how you threw yourself into it. Your face, the bow flying in your hands, I'd say they reflected the music nice as any mirror."

Stetti smiled. "I believe a performer's physical presence has to complement her music. I am passionate about Bach's precision, the clock-like intricacy and sublime elegance of his music—and my carriage must convey that. Besides the suites are a collection of dances. Dances mean movement, progression."

"You and the music—it did fuse into one." Drake grinned. "Gotta say, you weren't kidding about taking me to heaven."

Stetti shrugged. "I wasn't pleased with *The Fourth Suite*. Perhaps the lights breaking...consterned me." She wrinkled her nose. "Consterned, it's not right, is it? In German the word is *bestürzt*."

"Consterned, no doesn't sound right. Hmm, maybe it's upset you're looking for. You mean the lights threw you off track? Right?"

"Yes, I think so. When I am off the tracks, I play too fast. Regrettable, especially on the *Sarabande*. This is a stately piece, requiring dignity and control, and tonight I hurried through it." She shook her head. "Inexcusable."

Drake stroked her arm tenderly. "I thought it was perfect." He smiled. "You looked so fine up there, especially in the candlelight. So absorbed in the music. So beautiful." He closed his eyes and moved his lips toward hers.

Stetti turned her face to the side so he kissed her cheek. "The *Sarabande* was simply too fast. That is a fact. But what can I do about it now?" She shrugged. "Will you walk with me to home?"

"Be happy to," Drake said.

"I must go inside for my cello."

"I'll wait right here."

Stetti went inside. Five minutes later, she returned, a shawl over her shoulders. Christoph was at her side, with the instrument. He glared at Drake, and gave Stetti a kiss on the cheek. Handing her the cello case, he bade her, *"Auf wiedersehen."*

Stetti squeezed Christoph's hand, and off she went with Drake into the evening.

"I can carry your instrument," he said, reaching for it.

Stetti held the case tight. "I always carry her. I remember Father saying, 'A great cellist must have a great cello!' He had her made for me in Italy and from her first tone, I fell in love. Perhaps it is the cherrywood—it makes her unique. Its fire inspires me."

When they were twenty steps away, Drake looked back. Christoph was still at the doorway, watching them like a father watches his child go off for her first day of school. "Speaking of love, he's crazy about you," Drake said.

She turned back and waved. *"Lebwohl, Liebling!"* she called. She smiled at Drake and took his hand. He is my *Schutzengel*. I don't know if there is a word in English. It means an angel that watches for you."

"You mean watches out for you," Drake said, "Sure, we call 'em guardian angels."

"Christoph is my guardian angel then...since I came to Bonn."

54

"What I can't figure out is how he's kept himself in one piece, being a Red and all. I always thought they were the Nazis' blood enemies."

"Of course the National Socialists hate communism. All fascists must, since they are dialectical opposites. If you worship the state, you cannot abide those who worship the People. Have you a ciggy?"

Drake shook two Chesterfields from the pack. He raised them both to his lips and lit them together. He gave her one.

Stetti took a first, deep drag. "Americans…you are the master race of cigarette-making." She winked at him. "Yes, Christoph knew enough to keep his political sympathies to himself. He told me he had been a workers' organizer in Hanover before Hitler became chancellor. After that, anti-Red slogans plastered every wall. So Christoph Bauer vanished—" Stetti snapped her fingers. "—and, *poof!*, Christoph Kunkel materialized in Bonn. Until the Nazis were chased from the city, he kept his red stars hidden and guarded his words. Now he says, 'The Nazi thugs are mostly gone and at seventy-four I am too old to worry about what people think.' I tease him that at seventy-four he has become too senile to worry. But it is true that Nazi loyalists stand behind many doors." She looked at the houses along the street like the Gestapo might be peering from every window. "I am sure his openness inflames them."

They had gone a few blocks, on a narrow street of small, brick apartment buildings, when under a street lamp they came to a tipped-over garbage can blocking the sidewalk. Drake had eased Stetti into the street to go around the obstacle when she said, "Wait!"

She put her cello case down and picked up some small vegetables that had spilled out of the can—two yellow onions banded together at their shriveled tops and four red-skinned, sprouted potatoes. Stetti found a small cardboard box and put the vegetables in it. "Can you hold this for me?" she asked Drake, handing him the box. She moved a piece of newspaper with her

An Evening with Herr Bach

foot and there was a green apple—someone had taken a bite out of it, leaving browned flesh exposed. Stetti grabbed it gleefully and popped it into her box. "This I will slice and fry with an onion." She looked up at the big house in front of them and scowled. "The rich! They value their money but only for the fleeting thrill they feel when they turn it into things which then they care nothing about. To disrespect food when their brothers are starving..." She shook her head in disgust. "Capitalism is a sickness."

"Sure you want this garbage?" Drake asked. "I could buy you some good stuff."

Stetti ripped the box out of Drake's hand. "This is not garbage! How dare you call it so? These potatoes are small, but they are fine. And onions. Have you ever gone for months on end without onions? I dream of them, onions frying in butter. Of course we had no butter either, but they say dreams are born what is out of reach." She held the onion to her nose and inhaled. "The aroma of onions cooking in butter—there is magic to it. And with an apple...!"

"Listen," Drake said, "how about we go out tomorrow and I'll buy you all the onions and apples you can stuff in a bag? Anything you want."

"Buying more? Is that always the answer for the wealthy? You must see that just because you *can* buy more, it does not wipe out the crime of wasting."

"Sure, I see that. I respect it," Drake said. "My family came through the Depression and we had to be real careful. You're right about not wasting food. But that doesn't mean I can't buy you a couple of onions, some butter, and a bag of spuds if I want, does it?"

Stetti thrust the box with her vegetables into Drake's hand. "I will let you prove your virtue by carrying my onions. And tomorrow perhaps we will make a shopping trip."

"Got yourself a deal." Drake grabbed her hand. "Think about any other stuff you'd like to buy tomorrow. I want to help you out. Honest."

"I said *perhaps* we will go." She turned to Drake, her eyes sparkling. "But if we do, for me, buying a piece of cheese would surpass finding the legendary Rheingold."

"Not just a piece, then. We'll get a big hunk."

Stetti took Drake's arm. "Just thinking of cheese makes me shiver." She pulled close to him. "Or darling, is it you?"

"Lots of gals tell me I give 'em the shivers," Drake announced. "Actually, *you give me the creeps*, is what they usually say." He chuckled and glanced at Stetti, who looked confused. "That's a joke, honey." He winked. "So, how much farther to your place?"

"Just two blocks and around a corner."

"And the people you live with? Are they relatives?"

"No," Stetti said. "The Kellers. Birgitta is a physician. She is forty-six. Her husband, Jan-Hendrik, died in the bombing. Just more than one year. He was a teacher of mathematics. Also living there are Jan-Hendrik's mother Katarina and a daughter, Edita. Both sons were taken for the military, Günther for U-boats and Kurt for the *Wehrmacht* to Russia. Both are missing. Yet Birgitta never falters. I marvel at how she sustains."

"Us Americans—" Drake shook his head. "—we can't know how it'd be, having a war right in our backyard."

Drake scanned the bomb-damaged houses along the street. Many were missing bricks or stucco, and all had windows boarded up. A few were vacant hulks. Trees were splintered, and the cobblestoned street was barely passable, with bomb craters crudely repaired by filling with rubble. The farther they walked, the worse the damage.

"This is plain crazy," Drake said. "Bombing a street like this. Where regular folks live. Guess you can't tell what you're hitting when it's night and you're a few miles up."

"It is barbaric. A British crime of war."

Drake furrowed his brow. "But every country does it. What about the Blitz? Didn't you bomb the hell out of London?"

"Me?" Stetti sputtered, pulling her hand from Drake's. "No, *not* me. It was Hitler. Göring. All the Nazi war-makers. I won't be blackened by their sins. And even if every country bombs civilians, does that excuse it?"

Drake looked around. "Seeing this, it's tough to argue with you."

They turned the corner onto a street, *Chorsängerstraße*, the sign read. Most of its houses were shattered, charred, battered. As they approached one large brick structure with its right side smashed as if by a giant's foot, Drake spied an old woman in a dirty yellow dress. In the cool of the springtime evening, she sat on the stone steps leading up to the house. Eying the stars, she sang to them, keeping time by smacking a wooden stick on the stones. At her side were a bottle and a glass with green liquid. Crazy old gal's been doing some drinking, Drake thought, glancing at his watch. What the heck's she doing out so late?

"Katarina!" called Stetti. She ran to the woman, wrapped her in her shawl, and embraced her. "Come," she called to Drake, "I want to show her the potatoes." When he brought the box, Stetti presented the old woman with each item of food. Then she picked up the bottle and the glass and guided Katarina to the door. "Can you wait a moment?" she asked Drake over her shoulder as she whisked the old woman inside.

Drake sat on the stone steps. He took out a cigarette, lit it, and smoked, gazing up at the skyful of Katarina's stars above.

Death in Bonn

Fifteen minutes after she went inside, Stetti came back out. "I am sorry you must wait. Katarina is sometimes confused, and tonight she chilled herself. I have put her to bed."

Drake stood. "Is she all right? Looks like she'd been hitting the bottle pretty good."

"You mean drinking alcohol?" Stetti laughed. "No. Katarina likes *crème de menthe*. But from the war's start you cannot find it. So I mix water, sugar, green foods color and spearmint oil in her bottle." She shrugged. "You don't mind waiting for me?"

"Naw. I had a smoke. Been enjoying the night air. And the sky."

Stetti walked to the top of the stone steps. Drake met her there. She embraced him. "I am so pleased to play for you this evening. But now I must go in."

"Oh...we'll get together tomorrow, right?"

"I will find you at your hotel in the midday. What is its name?"

"The hotel?" Drake pulled out a slip of paper on which he'd written the hotel name and address. "Let's see here. *Hotel Heinrich der Heilige.*"

"I know it. I will come when I can." She winked. "And we shall visit the market."

Drake took her hand.

She pulled away. "Until tomorrow, darling," she said, touching the tip of his nose. "Sleep well." She turned and headed for the door.

"You, too," he called, watching her disappear inside.

Drake found an avenue leading in the direction of his hotel. Within a few blocks it turned lively, with bars and music and mobs of GIs spilling out onto the sidewalk.

At one place across the street from him, several American soldiers from Drake's outfit, who'd obviously had plenty to drink, hollered at him to join them.

"No can do," Drake yelled back without breaking stride. "Got something soft and curvy waiting for me back at the hotel." He whispered, "A pillow." He knew they would laugh and shake their heads if he said he'd been at a concert of Bach's cello music. They'd never understand how wonderful it had been. Never in a million years.

Drake arrived back at *Hotel Heinrich der Heilige* just as the clock in the railway station tower struck midnight. Fifteen minutes later he drifted off to sleep thinking of Stetti's playful tap on his nose.

Drake woke up early and went for a long walk through the old part of the city. Some blocks were rubble and ash, others showed little or no damage. He had a breakfast of fried eggs and spam with toasted rye bread. Afterward he sat in the *Heinrich's* tiny lobby reading *The Black Gang*, a pulpy Bulldog Drummond paperback probably left by some previous GI tenant.

Stetti didn't show up at noon. And not at one, two, or three either. He thought about seeing if something was wrong at her house, if he could find it. But before he could go out looking, he heard raucous laughter on the creaky, narrow stairwell leading down from the upper floors. A moment later, three GIs from HQ battalion appeared. "Hey, Drake old buddy! How's tricks?" said Rusty Turkel, a beefy corporal wearing Groucho Marx-style nose glasses, "wanna go out tom-cattin' with us this evening?"

"Better shed the Halloween get-up, Rusty," Drake said. "Was out this morning, and the place's crawling with MPs just itching to bust a GI's ass for being out of uniform."

"If I see any white caps, I'll lose the comic glasses but quick." Turkel put his hands on his hips. "So, you up for raising a little hell tonight or not?"

"Can't. Got a date."

"*You* got a date?" Felix Martinez shook his head. "That proves it—German dames got shit for brains."

"Aw, shut up, Martinez," Turklel said. "Course the private's got hisself a date." He walked over and put a hand on Drake's shoulder. "One word of advice, pardner. Be real careful now. To paraphrase Bob Hope: 'If the Army wanted you getting the clap, they'd issue it to you.'"

The three GIs laughed.

Drake brushed Turkel's hand off his shoulder. "Make yourselves scarce, fellas. This girl I'm seeing happens to be real classy, something you clowns wouldn't know a thing about." He pointed to the door. "Go on, beat it!"

Before another word was said, the front door burst open. Stetti rushed in, wild-eyed. Her cheeks were streaked with tears. She ran to Drake and threw her arms around his neck. "Oh Drake, they killed him." She broke down in sobs.

Drake rubbed her back. He glared at Turkel and the boys. "Scram," he hissed.

"What's she blubbering about?" Martinez asked Turkel. "Somebody getting killed?"

"I said get lost," Drake hollered, "now!"

The GIs eyed one another and slipped out the door, muttering.

Drake tried to pull back far enough to see Stetti's face, but she clung to him. "Hey…calm down, honey." He stroked her hair. "Can you tell me what happened?"

Stetti trembled and gasped for breath.

"Come on, hon, you're making yourself sick. How about we sit down?" He guided her to a sofa on the other side of the room, and they sat with her face still buried in his chest.

After a moment, Stetti's sobs slowed. She pulled back and peered at Drake with brimming, empty eyes.

"Take it easy, Stetti. There's no hurry. Just try to relax." Drake spied a water pitcher and glasses on the small table next to the hotel desk. "How about a drink? Some water?"

She nodded tentatively.

Drake pulled himself from her and ran to fetch a glass of water. He brought it back and held the brim to her lips so she could take a sip.

The drink seemed to calm her. She breathed in deeply and squeezed Drake's fingers. "Drake, they killed him." Her mouth quivered. "I said to be careful. The monsters did it. I know. He was such a good man. So good to me."

"Who, Stetti? Who was killed?"

Her lips moved. At first no sound came, then she said softly, "Christoph. They killed Christoph."

Thoughts flashed through Drake's head. The monsters? MPs, or maybe GIs? Some of them were real hotheads. Perhaps there was a fight or something. "I'm so sorry, Stetti. I know what he meant to you. I could see last night how close you were." He bit his lip. "What do you mean, someone killed him? You mean like…murder?"

She nodded. "They hated what he stood for. The People. They hated that he had hidden his passion from them all those years." She stood. "We must go to where it happened. Your police are there, investigating. We must tell them who killed Christoph." She pulled Drake to his feet.

Stetti led Drake the four blocks to the scene of the murder, in an alley next to an appliance repair shop. The body had been taken away, but two MPs were still on the scene, taking photographs and sketching diagrams of the area. Drake said, "We can talk to them. Tell 'em what we know."

They approached the MP sergeant drawing the layout of the alley. "Hey sarge, looking into a murder, aren't you? Well, we—"

The MP thrust his palm at Drake's chest. "Who the hell are you?"

"Name's Winston Drake, Private First Class. This is a German national…Stetti's her name. Her nickname, I mean."

The MP glared at Drake. "Move along, Private. We're busy. Besides we got things here pretty well in hand."

"But this girl's a friend of the victim. Thinks she knows—"

The MP poked Drake's belly with his billy club. "I said move it, ass wipe. You can tell your girlfriend here that the old man was just in the wrong place at the wrong time. This was a robbery, open and shut. Found the old fart's wallet lying by the body, empty. Crooks probably snuck up from behind and *bang*, clubbed him on the noggin. A witness saw a passel of kids, hoodlums, hanging around here about the time of the robbery." The MP shrugged.

"Tell her he died real quick if you want. Might make her feel better." He went back to his sketch.

Drake pulled Stetti a few steps away. He leaned close to her ear and said softly, "They think it was a robbery. They got evidence."

Stetti's eyes went wide. She pushed Drake out of the way and ran up to the MP. "You are wrong. They killed Christoph for his beliefs. Not his money. The Nazis did this."

The MP listened, rapping his club into his palm and scowling. He turned to Drake. "Private, you got about two seconds to get this dame out of my face. Or I'll put a dent in that thick, Kraut skull of hers. Tell her there ain't no goddamn Nazis left in town—we run 'em all off. This was a bunch of punk kids mugging an old man for pin money. Tell her we'll catch the little shits." He took a step toward Drake. "Now you two vamoose, or I swear to God you'll wish you had."

Drake pulled Stetti away. "Come on," he said, then he whispered, "this jerk is never going to listen. How about I ask some questions at HQ? For now, try to be patient—"

"Patience is a vice, as bad as sloth," Stetti sneered. "It is the enemy of progress. Action must be my virtue now." She inhaled deeply then exhaled. "Yes, if justice is to happen, I must make it myself. I begin an idea." She pointed to a burned-out building across the street—nothing remained except for the concrete front steps and the brick chimney. "I will sit there to further consider it. Leave me for a half hour, then return. I may need your help."

Drake gave Stetti a cigarette and took one himself. He rolled the thumb wheel on his Zippo and lit them. He took a drag, nodded to her, and walked up the street.

She watched him go, then went to the steps and sat.

Drake was on his way back thirty minutes later when Stetti ran up to him. "I have it all planned. We Germans have a saying, *Spinnen fressen einander.* It means in English, Spiders eat their own. It is their nature...and so it is for fascists. The best way to harm one of them is to entice his comrade to do it for you."

"You said you think it was Nazis who killed Christoph. How do you *know* that? Maybe that MP's right—this was a pack of punks pulling a stick-up that went bad."

"When Christoph didn't come to home last night, his woman searched for him. She found him in the alley. Yes, she saw his empty wallet, but she also found something more. The monsters stuffed his red star pin into his mouth. It was a message from the Nazis. *Communists Out!*"

Drake rubbed his forehead in frustration. "Well, let's say it was Nazis. How does that help us? You need to know exactly who did it, don't you?"

"I have suspicions," said Stetti. "All through the wartime, before even, Bonn has a few *ordinary* citizens whom we all suspected were secretly Gestapo. So every German city has. Although you Americans have come in, these men remain in our midst." She looked over her shoulder. "A villain named Heilbronn is one of them. One night in *Fafner's Höhle,* Christoph wore his red star cap. I saw a man across the room watching him. Glaring. It was Heilbrunn."

"So you got a name! Let's pass it on to the MPs. Bet they'd pick him up as a suspect."

Stetti clenched her jaw. "I don't want him taken as a suspect. I want something surer. Christoph must be revenged. An eye for an eye. And to be certain that happens, I must rely on his Nazi partners' nature: *Spinnen fressen einander.*"

Drake shook his head. "I don't see how—"

Stetti glared at him and grabbed his shirt. "You don't have to see how. Just do as I say."

He froze, wide-eyed.

Stetti's look softened. She slipped her arm into Drake's. "I need something from you, my sweet. Something little. To help me fool the spiders. I need an official American form, stamped with an official seal. A form that authorizes a payment. What you give to a civilian if you must take his car or his chickens."

"You mean a requisition form? DA-5075 I think it is. I got sent to a shop in Belgium last November with that form and a wad

64

of money to pay for a case of wine we drank with Thanksgiving dinner. Had the shopkeeper sign it and left him with a copy."

"This is what I need," Stetti said. "It must be stamped so it looks official. Leave it blank. I will make it complete."

"Whoa, Stetti, you're worrying me. I can't let you get involved in something that risky. You could get in trouble, or maybe wind up hurt or worse, tangling with these gangsters or Gestapo or whatever they are."

Stetti pushed his arm away and stepped back. "I will act. Either you help me or I strike alone." She eyed him then took his hand. "With your American form, Drake, I'll make the spiders do to Heilbrunn what your Hollywood gangster films call *dirty work*. I can stay at arm's length." She squeezed his fingers. "Your help will keep me safe."

"Sure, that's what I want, but—"

"Then get me the requisition form. Stamped. Get it quickly. You won't regret it."

Drake swallowed hard. "You know I'd do about anything for you." He closed his eyes. "Maybe I can bring it to you Wednesday. Somebody has to deliver paperwork to the garrison stationed in town. I could volunteer to do it."

Stetti threw her arms around him. "I knew I could trust you, Drake darling." She shivered and nestled close to him. "With all that has happened, I can't be alone tonight." She ran her hand along the side of his thigh.

Drake's chest tightened. "I think you're saying you wanna come to my hotel room with me. For the night. Is that right?"

She looked at him like a shy child. "May I?"

"Can't think of anything I'd like more," Drake said. "I wasn't counting on it, mind you, but I'll be happy to…"

Stetti took his wrist and looked at his watch. "I haven't eaten all day. Have you?"

"Yeah, but I'm hungry. Let's grab some eats before we head back to the hotel."

Her emerald eyes smoldering, Stetti said, "My biggest hunger is for you. But I think we should eat." She licked the corner of her mouth. "I wish for your stamina tonight."

Drake had to remind himself to breathe. "OK. Let's grab something quick."

Stetti glanced down the street. "A small shop for ham and sausages is near." She pointed. "We can buy it with bread. Would that do?"

"Sounds swell."

Drake purchased sandwiches and bottled beer, and they ate in front of the shop. Then Stetti took his arm and they walked the five blocks back to the hotel.

Love in Bonn

When they were inside Drake's second-floor hotel room, he locked the door. He scanned the place: Pastel stripes, faded with age, lined the wallpaper. The bed's tarnished brass headpiece and mint-green coverlet. The small chest of drawers supporting a lamp with a grimy, ruffled shade and porcelain beer stein base, brimming with ceramic foam. He winced. "Sorry it's…kinda dingy."

Stetti walked to the window. The twilight coming through the filmy pane was the room's only illumination, and standing there, its glow outlined her body. She spent a moment looking down on the street below then pulled the shade down and turned on the lamp. Resting her arm on the chest of drawers, she cocked her head and gazed at Drake. With the tip of her tongue gliding slowly across her upper lip and her breathing audible, Stetti's seductive aura seemed to turn the room's air electric.

He liked that she had on the same black and white check dress she'd worn the night they met. He watched her pull pins from the raven-dark bun on the back of her head. The breath caught in his lungs as she shook her head to let the thick tresses tumble to her shoulders. He sat on the bed and extended his hand to her. When their fingertips touched, he wanted the moment to last forever.

Stetti stood inches from him. She led his hands to the buttons on the front of her dress. When he'd undone them, she fluttered her shoulders and the dress slipped to the floor. She guided Drake to his feet, tugged his necktie loose, and unbuttoned his shirt. Then she laughed for the first time that day. "Do you know it? We're here together, half dressed, and you've never kissed me."

Drake put his hands on Stetti's waist and drew her close. With her arms thrown round his neck, he kissed her as the world around them began to spin. Kissed her like he'd never kissed Janie back home. Kissed her as she pressed herself close. As she slipped off his shirt. His trousers. The kiss ended only when she bent to pull back the coverlet.

Stetti picked up their clothes and strolled to the wooden chair next to the window. Draping the shirt carefully over the back and placing the folded trousers on the seat, she looked over her shoulder to make sure Drake was watching. Without taking her eyes off him, she hung her black and white checked dress on a large nail in the wall near the door. Then she walked slowly back, stopping just in front of him. "Watch me, darling," she purred, her smoldering eyes locking his on her. She stripped off her underwear and posed before him, naked except for her sizzling string of pearls. After a moment, she glided onto the bed and slowly drew the sheet up to her waist.

Drake tore off his undershirt and shorts. He pulled back the cover, taking a moment to glimpse Stetti's sleek, naked form. The whiteness of her skin, its softness, took his breath away. As he slipped in next to her, the touch of her leg on his sent a jolt of heat through him and the scent of her hair was sweet suffocation. He ran his hand over her breast, her belly, the small of her back. When Stetti eased his body onto her, all Drake's ties to the world beyond their bed slipped loose and he drifted into a sea of tumbling warmth, shadows and sparks, murmured sounds. He wanted never to return.

The sensation of Stetti's body slipping away from him nudged Drake awake. Through barely open eyes, he saw her hover over him, studying him, listening to the rhythm of his breathing. As she turned and walked away, his eyes followed her. He was about to call her name when she stopped at the chair with his clothes. Light from the street slipping around the window shade illuminated the room—faintly but enough for him to see her pick up his trousers and pull the money clip of bills from his pocket. The breath froze in his lungs. When she turned and looked his way, Drake closed his eyes to slits and slowed his breathing. She looked back at the money and peeled off ten bills. She stuffed the clip back into the pocket, refolded the pants and set them on the chair. Then she moved to her dress hanging on the wall and pushed the bills she'd taken into the waist pocket.

Drake's eyes darted behind closed lids. His stomach churned. Part of him wanted to jump up and yell, "What the hell are you doing?" but another, fearful part argued to lie there silent and pretend he'd seen nothing. A moment later Stetti slipped back into bed. She curled her warm body to fit the contours of his back and moved her hand to his chest and her mouth to his neck. Within a minute, her breathing slowed and her body relaxed.

Drake lay there, wide-awake, trying to comprehend what had just happened. He recalled the first time he'd seen Stetti—what Harvey, one of the GIs at the *Marionette,* had said when she stole money from his Acey-Deucy pot: "All she had to do was ask. We'd have given her something." That was exactly how Drake felt now. Hadn't he told her, "You know I'd do about anything for you"?

After thirty minutes trying to understand and getting nowhere, Drake decided sleeping on it was the only thing that might help. He struggled to let his mind go blank. The last thing he remembered was staring at Stetti's dress, hanging on the opposite wall.

When Drake woke in the early morning, Stetti was gone from his side. In the dim light he saw her already dressed, sitting on the chair with her legs crossed, watching him. His pack of Chesterfields rested on her thigh. She was smoking one, and with each drag, the tip glowed red, faintly illuminating her face. After he propped himself up on an elbow, she put the cigarettes back in his pocket and walked to the bed. She bent down and kissed him on the lips. "Sleep well, darling?"

"Pretty good," Drake lied. It had taken him at least an hour to get back to sleep after her nocturnal excursion. Now all he wanted to do was figure out how to live with it. Most likely, he was in for a day of wondering bitterly why Stetti had ripped the most wonderful night in his life away from him.

After she'd kissed him, Stetti went back to the chair, sitting just as before. She finished her cigarette and snubbed it out in the ashtray on the floor by her foot. She cleared her throat. "Oh, last night I took money I need from your money clip." She said it matter-of-factly. "If I can, I will return it someday. If I can't—" She shrugged. "—well I suppose I won't. In any case, what matters is that I need it more than you do. You understand that, don't you?"

Drake turned away. He shook his head at what she'd said. Then he looked into Stetti's eyes. "No, not really." He sat on the edge of the bed, covering his bare legs with the sheet. "Listen, I'm glad to give you whatever you want. Anything you need. Anytime. I'd just rather it was me giving than you taking."

Stetti walked to him and took his hand. "Is there really a difference? If you do truly want me to have what I need? If you are not just trying to control me?"

"Seems a little different to me," Drake said. "Especially after last night. Loving each other. I thought we did, anyway."

"Love? Pssh!" Stetti shook her head. "After five years of war, I am not sure the word has any meaning. In German what we did in this bed is called *geschlechtlicher Verkehr*, a rather cold term for something hot. My sister Norma told me a word she learned from an English boy. I like it better—hanky-panky." Her smile vanished. "Drake., life is giving and taking. Last night we each gave to the other, and we each took. Maybe I felt I owed you something. You've been generous with me. Been a friend. And you've promised to help me do the most important thing in the world—revenge a murder." She squeezed his hand. "Besides, last night I *wanted* you. Losing Christoph stabbed a hole in my heart, and I needed...someone to fill it. Those were reasons enough for me. I thought you needed someone too. That I could be her. I wish that was enough."

Drake cocked his head and stared hard at her. He pulled his hand away. "Sounds more like a transaction than love."

Stetti clenched her fists. "I hope you are not equating what happened last night with prostitution just because it involves an exchange. It is never so if what we give each other is *essential*. Surely even you whose vision is distorted by the prism of capitalism can see that."

70

"Where I grew up, what's mine is mine." Drake pulled on his undershorts and jumped to his feet. "I'm free to give it away if I want," he bellowed, "but no one can steal it from me. Anybody should want that freedom."

"Your freedom!" Stetti sneered. "*Your* freedom is inequity's father. It perpetuates misery." Her chin jutted out. "Socialism brings true freedom. Freedom from greed, from uncertainty, from difference. It's freedom from so-called freedom. And from the self."

Drake shrugged. "First you don't know what love means, then you rattle off crap like that? Jeeze! Those sound like words you memorized out of some Red Party manual."

"No, they are the recipe for social justice. By fostering them, the state keeps man's base instincts in check. For his own good." She reached into the pocket of her dress and took out Drake's cash. She held it up for him to see. "Here is your money." She threw it at him. "Take what you love so much."

Drake picked the bills off the floor. "Never said I loved it." He eyed Stetti, angry at being made out the bad guy. "All I wanted was for you to ask before taking it."

"In this world, those who wait for permission die with their hands empty." Stetti paused. "Do you know what I did for two years to keep Birgitta, her family, and me alive? When I tell you, listen with your heart, not your pride." She took a deep breath. "When Herr Hitler treacherously invaded the Soviet Union, life here in Germany became impossible. Malnutrition stalked *every* family. Disease lurked in our homes, schools...everywhere. Our clothing was broken, with no thread for mending. Birgitta had been a successful surgeon before the war, but since 1943, she must work in a public clinic for almost nothing. With students needed for work projects, Jan-Hendrik's school opened only one day per week. He was paid in municipal credits, redeemable after the war, and he died in his own house one night. An English bomb."

Drake's eyes softened. "I'm sure it was tough for all of you."

"Tough?" Stetti scowled. "Rotten is more like it. And there is more. Something also rotten, but believe me, compared to starving, watching your family starve—" She shrugged. "—not really so much. I went to the local home guard garrison and found a sergeant involved in requisitioning for the district. Erber was his name. For two years I lay with the fat, sweating swine. Every week I did for him whatever vulgar thing he asked."

Drake's shoulders sagged. He walked over and took her hand. "Look, I know the war's been hell for you." He pushed the wad of bills back into her pocket. "I guess what got me was just that last night was golden—I didn't want anything to tarnish it."

Stetti touched the cash in her pocket and smiled at Drake. "May I have a ciggy?"

"Oh, so we're asking now, huh?" Drake winked at her and walked to his jacket lying on top of the chest of drawers. He took the Chesterfields from the pocket and shook one out for her. "Seriously, the only thing I want is for what we share—" He glanced at the bed. "—to be something more than a way for you to get what you need." He shrugged. "More than what it was with that German sergeant." He lit the cigarette and handed it to her.

Stetti took a deep drag. "More than my time with Erber? It needn't be said—I *want* to be with you. From the swine I got only disgust." She spat on the floor then was quiet for a moment. "That isn't fully true. I also got pride." Fierceness flared in her eyes. "For by playing Erber's game, I saved my family."

Drake looked away for a moment then turned back to her. He nodded. "I admire that." His eyes twinkled. "I'm glad you want to be with me. And glad I can help." He put his hands on Stetti's waist. "But there's still something I wonder about, honey. Why *did* you tell me about lifting the dough? My money. You might have gotten away with it."

"To *me,* telling you made perfect sense. Because taking your money was good. I needed it more than you. Can't you see, telling you was respect? I wish you could understand. It was honesty I would never have considered giving to Erber."

Drake looked at the floor. "Glad for your honesty. And being honest too, I gotta admit I can't figure where you're coming from half the time."

"I know that for you, seeing truth is difficult. Capitalism has insinuated itself into your thinking. Growing up in America, you were immersed in it. How could you be otherwise? I will have to be patient."

"Swell of you," Drake muttered. "Look, I'll *try* to understand you. That's not the same as buying into your politics. Or admitting I'm defective upstairs." He tapped the side of his head. "*Capisce?*"

Stetti looked confused.

"*Capisce*," Drake said. "That's what my sarge says. Think it's Italian for understand…like, *Do you understand?*"

"Interesting. An American speaking Italian to a German. Perhaps a misunderstanding is inevitable." She shrugged. "Yes, I will be patient with you—it comes from confidence in the truth of my philosophy. One bright day the entire world will rise to embrace it: From each according to his ability to each according to his need. It is coming, Drake…Schiller's joyful new world where *all men shall be brothers.*"

"Guess we'll see." He kissed her. Tentatively at first, then sparked by Stetti's hot response, with fire.

She took Drake's wrist and looked at his watch. "We have two hours before we must leave the hotel. I want to spend it with more hanky-panky." Pushing Drake onto the bed, she ordered, "Watch, darling, what I have for you," and undressed. Then she pulled off his undershorts and eased her body next to his.

Dreaming of Stetti

Drake was back at his desk the next morning, his brain still spinning from the weekend's rollercoaster of emotions. Everything about Stetti confused him. Was he head-over-heels in love with her? Did that sharing mumbo-jumbo she'd spouted after filching his dough make any sense? What about all that commie talk? It sounded OK, noble even, but…. And the biggest question of all: Was Stetti in love with him or with what he could do for her?

He had already gone to the forms files and taken a DA-5075—*Form, Disbursement to Civilian Providers of Requisitioned Goods or Services*. The form came with two built-in carbon copies in addition to the original on top. When Sgt. Rutledge was out getting coffee, Drake had slipped into his office and stamped it *Official First United States Army Document*.

That afternoon, he'd gone to the HQ motor pool. Inside the converted barn was a makeshift office. Pinned on the door was a caricature of a GI with a huge head sporting gigantic horn-rimmed glasses. The cartoon soldier's hands were on his hips and steam shot from his ears as he looked under the hood of a jeep with smoke billowing from its engine. The drawing was captioned *Master Sergeant Earnest C. Belko, Motor Pool NCOIC*.

Drake knocked on the door and entered. The man looking up at him wore glasses almost as oversized as the ones in the cartoon. "Sgt. Belko?"

"That's my name, don't wear it out."

"Sarge, I hear you keep a sign-up sheet for volunteering to drive the documents parcel to the Bonn detachment on Wednesday evenings."

Belko opened a notebook. "Name and outfit."

"It's Drake, Winston Drake. I'm with Sgt. Rutledge's office pool, First Army headquarters battalion."

Belko scribbled Drake's name and unit in the book. "Nice to meet you, Drake. Can you drive this week?"

"Sure. That's what I was hoping to do."

"You're on. Report here at eighteen twenty hours." Belko closed the book. "So where you from, kid?"

"Grew up in Omaha."

"Omaha...So you're from the good old *Show Me* state, eh?"

"*Show Me* state's Missouri, Sarge. Omaha's in Nebraska."

"Ah," said Belko, "ya learn something every day. See you at Wednesday 1820...Omaha."

Back at his desk, Drake's phone rang at 1040 hours. It was Rutledge. "Need to see you in my office ASAP."

Drake hung up the phone and swallowed hard. Had someone seen him swipe the 5075? Or stamp it *Official*? He sweated all the way to Rutledge's office. Standing in front of the door, he decided that if the sergeant asked, he'd say he wanted to get a bunch of pretzels at that bakery in Bonn for Corporal Goldblatt's promotion party at the Enlisted Men's Club. He took a deep breath, opened the door and stepped in.

"Your paperwork's in," Rutledge said, tossing a stapled five-page document across his desk to Drake.

"Paperwork?" Drake scanned the top page. *REASSIGNMENT ORDERS* was the all-caps heading. He looked up at Rutledge. "Is this for me?"

"Yup." Rutledge scuttled around the desk. He grabbed the orders from Drake, studied them for a moment and thrust them in his face, pointing to *Drake, Winston C.* about half way down. "That's you, in case you're confused. Reassignment? To a combat unit? Invasion of Japan? Ring any bells up there in that dusty old attic you call your head?"

"My orders!" Drake said, tracing his index finger down to a line labeled *Organization*. "Hey, I've been reassigned to Sixth Army. Gonna be, anyway, on May first." He flipped to page two. "Hmm, got me shipping out of France on 2 May. Port of Le Havre. Joining up with the Sixth on the Philippine island of Luzon. Says here, for advanced infantry training." He looked up from the papers. "Guess they're going to skip me right over the basics."

"Figure on some pretty intensive work. What I heard from the captain, who heard it from the horse's mouth, is that the invasion is set for late this year or early next. That gives them six months or so to turn you into a killing machine."

"First of May's just three weeks." Drake spent a moment considering what he still needed to get done. "That'll have to be enough time, I guess," he muttered.

Rutledge's eyebrows shot up. "Enough time for what?"

"Oh, just stuff, sarge."

"Stuff like that German gal?"

"Yeah, kind of. It's complicated. For now, I just wanna make sure she's set-up OK. Get it done before I leave. And who knows? Maybe after the war, a guy could…"

"Yeah, *after*…all that's up to you. But don't forget—until May I own your rear end. Don't you go letting anything, and I do mean *anything*, get in the way of your job here. You do and I'll put the kibosh on your reassignment faster than you can say *John Henry.*"

"No need to sweat that, sarge. I won't let you down." Drake folded the orders in half and left the office. Heading back to his desk, he caught himself whistling *The Caisson Song*. He even softly sang the chorus:

"Then it's Hi! Hi! Hee! in the field artillery,
Shout out your numbers loud and strong,
For where e'er you go, you will always know
That those caissons are rolling along."

Wednesday afternoon Drake was so excited, so energized that he ran five miles, in record time for him—just under an hour. He took a quick shower, grabbed a bite to eat, and reported to the motor pool at 1800 hours. He was on his way into Bonn with the documents fifteen minutes later. He dropped off the satchel at the detachment command post and drove toward Stetti's home. Bad as the streets were, he couldn't get closer than two blocks, even in the jeep, so he walked the final leg.

When he came to the house, *Chorsängerstraße 25*, Katarina was sitting on the front steps singing, just as she had been doing on Friday night. She nestled her *"crème de menthe"* bottle in the crook of her elbow and raised her glass in a toast when she saw him.

"Stetti, *bitte*," Drake said, holding the DA-5075 form in the air.

Katarina set the bottle down and eyed him suspiciously. "*England?*" she said.

"*Nein*, American," Drake said. As Katarina went inside, he was glad to have gotten through a conversation needing just *bitte* and *nein*, about the only German words he knew.

Stetti came running out the door. "You're here. I was sure I could count on you, darling." She took Drake's arm. "Let's walk." When they were a dozen steps down the street, Stetti snapped the document from his hand. "So, this is it? Yes, *Disbursement. Services*. And the mark here?" She pointed to the stamp. "It makes the paper official, doesn't it?" She peered wide-eyed at Drake. "So they will believe me."

"So *who* will believe you?"

"The spiders," Stetti said matter-of-factly. "The ones who will revenge Christoph. Unwittingly." She smiled. "Heilbrunn's friends…his killers."

Drake froze in his tracks. "His killers? You never said anything about killing before." He pictured Stetti dealing with Nazi thugs in a dark alleyway. "Jeeze, this is starting to sound like some crazy vendetta in a gangster movie. I'm scared for you, honey."

Stetti glared at Drake. "*You* are scared? What does that matter? Your part is done." She leaned in close to him. "Why don't you just go on?" she growled, pointing down the street. "Leave. A crying baby is no use to me. "

"No, you got it all wrong," Drake said. "I'm worried about *you*. Dealing with a gang of Nazis. Killers. Those spiders as you call 'em." He took her hand.

Stetti eyed him, then half-smiled. "When you met me, I told you I take care of myself. I am smarter than any Nazi…and more resolute. In the end they will blindly do my bidding. Heilbrunn gets his due and Christoph will be revenged…without a smudge on my hands."

Drake huffed. "At least tell me your plan."

"Not yet. Not until it is completed. Then perhaps. So you will stop worrying."

"Promise? 'Cuz I can live with being in the dark for a while…long as I know when you're in the clear."

"Do I promise? Why not? What is a promise but some words?"

They walked along in silence for a minute. Then Drake took Stetti's hand and said, "Listen, I got some news to tell you, too. I've been reassigned. To the Far East. In May."

Stetti showed no reaction.

"You OK with that?" Drake asked.

Stetti shrugged. "Of course. In wartime, we all do what we must. Armies don't ask soldiers if they mind reassignment. If you cannot object, how can I?"

"I requested it. A while ago. Before we met."

"So it is your wish. I am happy for you."

"Like I said, it *was* what I wanted…before I met you. Guess it still is." He took off his garrison cap. "Only, I was hoping I could help you and your family out for a while longer."

Stetti looked away, scowling. "How many times must I say it? I take care of myself."

"I get that. But a little help doesn't hurt. That's what I hope to do." He squeezed her hand. "Long as I'm here, helping out's a piece of cake. It'll be tougher to do when I'm serving in the Pacific. After the war, who knows, maybe someday I'll come back and take care of you full time."

She slapped him. Not hard but with a flinty look in her eyes.

Drake rubbed his cheek. "What the heck are you so sore about?"

"You insulted me. Calling me incapable of caring for myself. Some fairytale damsel."

"Bullcrap!" Drake thrust his index finger at her. "Hey, you said it yourself: From each according to what he's got to each according to her needs." He sighed. "Look, I have a generous uncle named Sam who pays me more than I need." He reached into his pocket and took out his money clip. "And you got a family to feed. Seems real simple to me."

"Can I argue against my own rule? If you wish to help, I ought gracefully to accept."

"Good," Drake said. "Here, take this." He gave her six paper bills.

Stetti took the money and kissed Drake's cheek. She folded it with the DA-5075 form and put it in the pocket of her dress. "I must go home. Heilbrunn still breathes, and every minute that is so gnaws on my soul. I have my plan, now I need to act."

All the way driving back to the HQ, Drake fretted over what Stetti was getting herself into. She was obsessed with that guy Heilbrunn. Even if she was right that he had murdered Christoph, her plan was risky as hell. He lit a cigarette. "Girl's got bloodlust in her heart," he said aloud, exhaling a stream of smoke. "But Stetti's like no girl, no person, I've ever known. If anyone can pull it off, it's her." He sighed and took another drag.

Drake turned his thoughts to what *he* needed to do, something plenty tricky. Ever since he met her, he'd been sweating the question: You've got an obligation to look after Stetti for as long as she needs help—when you leave Bonn, how'll you pull it off? *From Drake according to his ability, to Stetti according to her need.* Now he had a deadline, three weeks. He needed to set something up that would run itself. Sure, he could provide money. But what good is that when there's nothing to buy in the shops? He wanted her taken care of like she would be back in the States. She needed money *and* connections. That's what he owed her.

Turning into the motor pool at 2025 hours, Drake was frustrated. Emotionally exhausted. He was smart—how the heck could a little matter of logistics baffle him so?

"Hello, Omaha," Sgt. Belko boomed as Drake went to the properties book to sign the jeep back in. "How'd my little darling run for you tonight?"

"The jeep? Oh, OK," Drake said. When he saw Belko's disappointed look, he added, "Fine. Got me there and back good as a Cadillac."

"That's what I like to hear." Belko stood and walked in front of his cluttered desk. "I was thinking about you this evening, Omaha. A bunch of us are going to get together for some poker tomorrow night. You seem like a sharp cookie. Bet you play a mean hand of cards, am I right? Thought you might like to join us."

"Aw, I'm not much for cards. Guess I'll pass. But thanks for the invite."

Belko shrugged his shoulders and frowned. "Your call, my boy. But keep it in mind. We play at the enlisted club. Twenty-one hundred hours. Tomorrow."

"Sure," Drake said as he left.

When his spinning head hit the pillow, Drake wondered if he'd be able to sleep. But exhaustion beat out frustration, and in two minutes he was out like a Joe Lewis opponent.

Instantly it seemed, he was dreaming. He was in a hotel or hospital room with Stetti. She was in bed, looking ghostly pale.

"I'm going to look for some soup or something. Do you a world of good."

Stetti shivered. She seemed too weak to speak.

"You'll be here when I get back, right?"

"Maybe." It was little more than an exhaled breath.

Drake left the room, thinking there had to be somewhere close to get a bite to eat. He looked down the hallway in both directions. No reason to go one way over the other, he figured, so he went left. Each door he passed was closed. Each looked identical. At the end of the hallway he turned left. Or was it right? He turned several times more. Three, four, five times...he couldn't remember. He came to a stairwell and went down several floors. He thought he heard voices as he came to a floor, but when he stepped into the hallway there was no one to be found. Just more identical, closed doors.

Drake panicked. He had no idea where he was. No clue where to get some food. No sense of how to get back to Stetti's room. The farther he went, the more his feeling of dread grew. He sat on the floor, trying to remember how to get back. But no luck.

He heard voices again and scrambled to his feet. If he could find someone, they'd help him. Down the hallway, he spotted two people in white lab coats with clipboards. Doctors, Drake figured. He hurried toward them, but his shoe came untied and it felt like it would slip off, so he stopped to tie it. When he looked up, the doctors were gone. Drake's heart sank.

He went on down the hallway, trying the handles of every door. Locked, locked, locked. Drake closed his eyes. What was he thinking, leaving Stetti?

He smelled smoke. Tobacco smoke. He hurried around a corner. Soon he heard voices. And music—Benny Goodman's *Smoke Gets in Your Eyes*. The smoke was thick enough to tint the air blue. The talking, the music grew louder. He went around another corner and saw a slab of light cutting through the haze at the end of the hall. An open doorway! He dashed toward it.

As he got close to the door he heard a familiar voice. "Your call, my boy." It was Belko. Drake looked into the room and there was the sergeant and four other men sitting around a green-felt-covered table, playing cards.

Belko laid his cards on the table and looked at Drake. "Omaha, you made it after all! Hoick yourself up a chair."

"Can't, sarge. I'm lost." Drake felt like bawling. "I gotta rustle up some chow for this girl because she's sick. Gotta take it back to her. Can you help me."

"Sure, Omaha, sure," Belko said, chomping his cigar. "Right after this hand."

Drake sat on a chair next to the door and chewed his lip. The game went on and on, as did the burning in his stomach. "Almost done, sarge?" he said.

Belko about bit off the end of his cigar. "I said right after this hand, goddamnit!"

At last one of the players whooped and threw down his cards. "Bingo," he hollered and began raking in the pile of money at the center of the table. He stood up and said to Drake, "Now let's you and me go find that little lady of yours."

The winner walked into the hallway with Drake and led him the twenty feet to the next room down. He opened the door and held it for Drake. "After you, sir," he said.

Drake stepped into the room and couldn't believe his eyes. There was Stetti, sitting up in bed, eating a bowl of soup. She looked good as new. "You made it back, Drake darling," she said. "I knew you would. This kind man brought me soup. I have strength again."

Drake broke into sobs of joy. "Thought I'd lost you," he blubbered. He turned to the winner. "Sorry about the water works." Then he rushed to Stetti and embraced her.

The next thing Drake knew he was awake, in his bunk. He sat up and looked around the dark barracks. Everyone was sawing logs except a guy at the end of the room who was sitting on his foot locker, reading a letter by flashlight and puffing on a corncob pipe. The smoke was sweet. Like in his dream, it smelled of success.

Before he got back to sleep, Drake had decided he would make it to Belko's card game the next night. After the way the poker players saved the day in his dream, Drake felt obliged to play. Besides, the run of good luck he'd had lately might serve him well at the card table.

Dutch Can Help

Thursday Drake walked into the Enlisted Men's Club just before 2100 hours. He asked the bartender, "Know where Belko's card game is?"

The barkeep looked confused then said, "Oh, you mean Dutch's game?" He pulled a glass from a bin of murky dishwater and swished it in the rinse. "Got an invite?" He dried it with the dishtowel that had been draped over his shoulder.

"Yeah, from Sgt. Belko."

"It's in the back room. There." He pointed to a black door with a hand-lettered *Private* sign on it. "Knock three times, wait a second, then knock once more."

"Thanks," Drake said as he sauntered away. He knocked on the door as prescribed.

"Come on in," a voice boomed from inside.

Drake entered and nodded to Belko. "Decided to take you up on your offer, sarge, That's OK isn't it?"

Belko took the stogie out of his mouth and put it on an ashtray. "Swell. Always room for one more." He grinned. "Fellas, this is my buddy Omaha." Turning in his chair, he put a hand on the shoulder of the fellow to his right. "This here's Dutch Scholz, our host."

Dutch was a small man, good looking with sandy, slicked-back hair and darting eyes. He wore a green sweater vest and smoked a cigarette through an ivory holder. He nodded at Drake then kept looking, like he was studying him.

Belko introduced the other fellows around the table: Walt Cavendish, a big Texan; Rusty Turkel, a lanky personnel specialist Drake knew from HQ Battalion, the guy he'd seen in the lobby of the hotel in Bonn; and Dickie Henderson, a motor pool mechanic from Ohio.

"Pleased to meet you, gents," Drake said.

"Help yourself to a beer and chow." Belko pointed to a table in the corner. "Courtesy of Dutch here."

Drake walked to the table and surveyed the spread: A pan on a hot plate held gray sausages simmering in water. Rolls for the sausages. Mustard. Pickles. Potato salad. There was a wooden case of German beer in green bottles and an opener. And a stack of small metal plates. Drake made himself a sausage sandwich with lots of brown mustard and opened a beer.

Dutch had pulled up another chair for Drake. He sat and ate, waiting to play until he had finished the sandwich. His first hand in—nickel ante, five card draw, Henderson dealing—Drake won the pot, three bucks or so.

At 2140, Belko announced, "And now, gentlemen, a word from our sponsor. In consideration for the sausages and beer, the game'll be suspended for twenty minutes so Dutch can tell us about a little business he runs on the side."

Dutch went around the table shaking hands with everyone. He gave each man a business card. Across the top was printed *Dutch Can Help*. Below that was *Dutch Scholz, Concierge Services*. At the bottom was *Contact HQ, 9ᵗʰ Inf. Div.* When he'd finished the circuit, Dutch stood behind his chair.

Turkel raised his hand. "Got a question, Dutch. Named after that gangster, are you?"

"You are referring to Dutch Schultz, the late bootlegging kingpin, I presume. Different last names, Scholz and Schultz. No I wasn't named after him. I've always presumed he was named after me." Dutch winked, sparking a ripple of chuckles from the men around the table. "Gentlemen, there's more chow and plenty of beer, so help yourself to seconds. In fact, think I'll have another bottle of suds." He got a bottle, opened it, and took a sip. "Who knows what a concierge is?"

The men sitting around the table stared blankly at each other. Cavendish scrunched his nose like a first grader asked to add one plus two. "Not sure but is that what they call the fella who drives a school bus?"

Dutch rolled his eyes. "No, the proper term for that person is, I believe, *bus driver*." He looked at his watch. "In the interest of time, let me tell you. A concierge is member of a hotel's staff who handles dinner and theater reservations, makes recommendations to guests, and sees to the mail. He makes dreams come true. That's what I do too." He swigged his beer and delicately dabbed his lips with a napkin. "You may be asking yourself, 'Why did this fine fellow get into the business of helping people?' The answer is, it's in my blood." He arched his eyebrows. "Like my father and my grandfather before him—" He raised his index finger for emphasis. "—*I* am a Fuller Brush Man. Have been since I was seventeen." He took another sip of beer.

"Let's talk specifics" Dutch leaned in. "You want cigarettes? Any brand, any amount. See me. A wireless radio? I can get you a Philco or an RCA. You want a gift for the special lady in your life…perfume from France, silk lingerie, nylons, lipstick, a lovely scarf? No problem for me to get it for you. How about a nice Nazi souvenir? A luger, or a swastika flag, or an *SS Todenkopf*? Try getting it anywhere else…*You can't!* Imagine, if you will, your pals back home when you show them a sinister, black luger, bragging you took it off the Nazi general you'd just strangled with your bare hands!" He paused to let the image sink in.

Scholz took a list from his pocket and looked it over. "Ah yes. Want champagne? Cognac? Scotch whisky? Ruskie vodka? I can get you anything. And cheap! We're friends, after all." He opened his briefcase and took out photographs. "I said we were friends, didn't I? Maybe you'd like pictures of naked ladies? Look here—" He displayed the pictures. "How about that? Not a stitch on. What goddesses!"

"Whoa," said Turkel, wide-eyed. He grabbed a photo and gazed at it, mesmerized.

"Lemme see!" Henderson said, taking another from Scholz. "Unbelievable." He shook his head.

"Yes," Dutch said, "they're remarkable. And I have dozens to choose from. Blondes, redheads, brunettes…my goodness, here's a tennis player."

Sweat beaded on Cavendish's forehead as he leered at the ample breasts of a corpulent girl holding a plate of spaghetti. "What if a guy wanted the real thing? Not just pictures."

"Glad you asked," Dutch said with a twinkle in his eye. "I have three young beauties on call for parties or private engagements." He took out an 8-by-10 glossy photograph of a blonde in black corset, stockings and high heels with a riding crop and a shiny SS helmet. "Meet *Kommandant* Hotsy-Totsy. For a very modest fee, she'll shed her leather and lace for you in a bawdy blitzkrieg that no panzer can match." He produced another photo. "If your tastes run to redheads, Nurse Inge's for you." The woman in the picture wore only nylons, a nurse's cap and high-heeled shoes, all brilliant white. "Oh, sweet Inge. Her body's potent as penicillin. And I've saved the best for last." Dutch took out a third photo and gazed at it fondly, like it was his girlfriend's graduation portrait. "Ah, Maya, the jungle girl. When first I laid eyes on steamy Maya, all I could say was, 'Super-duper, Frizzle-frazzle, Whoopty-doo, and Razzle-dazzle!'" The raven-haired beauty in the picture wore a leopard skin bathing suit and held a spear decorated with feathers. "You'll never forget her native dance...those impudent hips pumping in feverish frenzy!" Dutch put his palms on the table and leaned forward. "So gentlemen, how may I serve you?"

Cavendish rubbed his chin. "Our CO's got a birthday coming up and I'm arranging the party. How much we talking about for that little jungle girl to make an appearance? Jiggle around a little to bebop music. Who knows? Maybe her leopard skin falls off? What would that run me? In American...I can never figure out these damn German marks."

Dutch gazed at the ceiling for a moment. "Would Maya be expected to, how shall I put it, pleasure the birthday boy?"

"Yeah, pleasuring the major too." Cavendish laughed. "How much for the whole shootin' match?"

"Seeing it's you asking, Walter, I could probably do ninety. Greenbacks, that is. Imagine it, an evening you'll never forget for just ninety bucks! Plus taxi fare for Maya, of course. You won't be disappointed." Dutch smiled. "And I can provide the libations you'll need. Sounds to me like a champagne and whisky affair. How does that strike you?"

"How much for the booze?" Cavendish asked. "Enough, er plenty, for eighteen guys."

"Well, the number two hundred pops into my head. Yes, two hundred should do it. I'll even throw in some beer. In fact, I can make it two eighty for everything, if you pay in full by dinnertime Saturday. Think of it, Walt…split eighteen ways, that's less than sixteen smackers per man! Can that be right?" Dutch paused, apparently checking his math. "Astonishingly, it is." He put a hand on Cavendish's shoulder. "You'll never find a better deal than that, my friend."

Cavendish was hooked.

Turkel signed on for three hours of first aid from Inge, scheduled for the weekend at *Hotel Heinrich der Heilige*. He got a two dollar discount for paying that night. He also ordered souvenirs, a luger semi-automatic pistol and a small Nazi flag. Belko placed an order for a Philco radio and two bottles of Haig & Haig Scotch. Henderson hadn't won a hand yet, so he couldn't afford to buy anything but a half dozen of Dutch's smutty pictures.

When Dutch was done with the others' transactions, he approached Drake, "And what may I do for you, Mr. Omaha?"

Drake looked at his shoes for a moment. "I'm wondering about something, well, different from girls. I got an unusual need. Maybe we can talk about it after the game."

"Ah yes, something calling for discretion." Scholz winked. "I believe I understand."

Drake's brow furrowed then his eyes got wide. "Hold your horses, Dutch. Think you may have the wrong idea. I'm not looking for something *too* different. Let's just talk later."

Dutch nodded. "Sure, Omaha, sure. Just remember, discretion is my middle name."

As the evening progressed and the number of empty beer bottles grew, the size of the betting pots likewise increased, and Dutch won most of them. When things wrapped up at midnight, the transfer of wealth to Dutch Scholz was virtually complete. To ease the sting of that result, he gave each departing player a new Danish toothbrush and toothpowder from Sweden, along with another of his business cards, "to pass along to a friend."

While Belko and the others took their dental supplies and made for the door, mumbling about lousy luck, Drake hung back. "So Dutch, here's the story. I hope, like your card says, you can help me. See, I had this dream last night…aw, never mind that." He waved his hand. "Look, I'm trying to help this girl—" Drake leaned in. "—a German girl. In Bonn."

"Help her…do what?" Dutch said.

"Help her not starve to death, of course. Her and her family."

Dutch shrugged. "Certainly can't have that."

"Yeah. And to boot, I'm shipping out for the Philippines in a couple weeks. So here's the deal: I'll handle things long as I'm still here. What I need is someone like you to keep that up after I leave. Till she gets back on her feet. I'll send you what I can and you use your connections to turn it into food for Stetti. That's the girl's name."

"Not my usual mission," said Dutch, tugging his ear, "but what is a concierge if not versatile? I promise you, as my card says, *Dutch Can Help*." He took out a small notebook and a stubby pencil. He wet the pencil tip on his tongue. "So this is for Omaha. O, M, A, H, A, right? A. K. A. Private Drake…?"

"My name? Well Drake's actually my last name. First name's Winston, as in Churchill. Omaha's what Belko calls me."

"OK, Omaha, so what foods are we talking about here? In general, because I never know exactly what'll be available."

Drake rubbed his chin. "She likes onions. That I know. And butter—told me butter was about impossible for her to get. And she likes potatoes."

"Maybe some tinned meat, eh? Goes good with spuds." Dutch scribbled notes. "By the way, I can usually get my hands on powdered milk, about all I want."

"Yeah, then powdered milk. Hey, you should hear her talking about cheese. That something you can get?"

"Cheese is a piece of cake, Omaha. Swiss is the easiest."

"With the holes, right?"

"Yes, and the holes I include for free. Another one I see a lot of is that stinky stuff from Belgium…I forget the name. Anyway, cheese I can get. Now, it's not cheap."

"That's OK. She likes it." Drake rubbed his chin. "Another thing. Wine. She's nuts for the German stuff they make in the Rhine valley."

Dutch jotted a couple of words. "Got it."

"But she's kind of finicky. She likes Rieslings. And she prefers—damn what's that German word?—all I can ever remember is pretty cat."

Dutch grinned. "Ah, you mean *mit Prädikat*, Omaha. Means the stuff is top-drawer." He kissed his fingertips. "Now I'll warn you, wine like that'll cost you."

"I know. But if you can find some occasionally, toss in a bottle for her. OK?"

"I'll find it. I have a connection. In fact, just last week I got five bottles for a bull colonel up in Ninth Army."

They spent the next ten minutes hammering out the financial end of the deal, which they took to calling *Operation Stetti*. Drake would send money every two weeks, and Dutch would use the cash to purchase food, then deliver it to Stetti. When they shook on it, Drake felt a rush of relief—his obligation to her would be fulfilled even while he was in the Far East meeting his commitment to Uncle Sam.

Wednesday of the following week, Drake was at his desk making bar charts of the number of First Army personnel reporting to sick call. For each week he drew a blue bar to represent battle casualties, a red bar for illnesses, and a green one for GIs with non-combat injuries.

Sgt. Rutledge rushed in and placed a yellow sheet of paper with handwritten notes on top of the chart Drake was making. "Drop the sick call reports. The colonel's on the warpath about what he called a Nazi crime wave in Bonn. If you can call one killing a crime wave. Sounds like General Hodges jumped on his ass pretty good about getting this kind of nasty business nipped in the bud. Anyway, here's the MP's report on what happened. Get it banged out and on the colonel's desk pronto. *Capisce?*"

"Sure thing, sarge," said Drake. He fed a sheet of onionskin paper into his Smith Corona and began the transcription.

<u>Report, Criminal Incident in Occupied Territories</u>

Report Date:	19 APR 1945
Incident Type:	Murder
Incident D&T:	18 APR 1945, betw 0345 hrs. and 0705 hrs.
Victim:	HEILBRUNN, RUDOLF P.
Status:	Deceased
Perpetrator(s):	UNK
Incident Location:	*Bismarckstraße* near *Alte Kirche Platz*, Bonn, Germany
Witnesses:	Bar patrons, prostitute, hotel manager
Details:	Victim's body found 18 Apr 0705 at incident location by locomotive fireman M. Speckmann on his way to work. Victim was last seen 17 Apr 2245 departing a bar with a known prostitute. Prostitute claims she left victim at 18 Apr 0045 passed out in hotel room from heavy drinking. Hotel manager claims to have seen victim, still very drunk, leaving hotel with two unidentified males 18 Apr approx 0345.
	Cause of death preliminarily identified as strangulation by piano wire. Definitive determination pending. Notice pinned to victim's coat reads as follows: *So Ende Aller Hochverrat Gegen Der*

	Führer. Transl: Thus ends every high treason against the Führer.
	Full investigation details, including names of witnesses and interview transcripts, to follow.
Report by:	Porter, J. O., MSgt., US Army

Drake pulled out his Zippo and lit a cigarette. He took the transcription out of the typewriter and held it up next to the yellow sheet original, checking for accuracy. Something about the report tugged at him, but he couldn't put his finger on it. Maybe the place where the body was found, he thought. He'd probably gone right by there. He finished his smoke and walked the report down the hallway toward the colonel's office.

Half way there it hit him—that name! Wasn't Heilbrunn the Nazi goon Stetti suspected of killing Christoph? The guy she'd pledged to exact revenge on? A shiver ran down Drake's spine. He reread the details section and now the statement that *a known prostitute* was involved jumped out at him. A *known* prostitute? Stetti? He looked at the report. With what she'd told him Saturday, how could it be anyone else? The question leapt like a leopard from ambush and sank its teeth in his throat. He thought of their night together. Both the warmth and the theft. Of how casually she had talked about sleeping with that Nazi supply sergeant. He bristled, recalling how she'd turned up her nose at the *Immer* perfume he gave her, like she didn't splash the stuff on whenever she went out whoring. Congratulations old boy, he told himself, that *Immer* may just be the most fitting gift anyone ever gave. He dashed to the latrine and threw up.

When his head stopped spinning, Drake went back to his desk and retyped the report—he'd gotten vomit on the first copy. He hustled it down to the colonel's office then went to see Rutledge. "Sarge, I'm feeling kinda punk. Lost my breakfast in the latrine a minute ago. OK if I go lie down for a bit? I put the typed incident report in the colonel's *IN* box."

"Checked it for typos? The colonel's nuts about sloppy mistakes, you know."

"Yeah, it's done right." Drake bit his lip. "Say sarge, when the full report with the name of that prostitute…with all the names and statements is drafted, can you let me type it up? On account of I started it. OK?"

"S'pose so, if you're back in action by then."

"Sure I'll be. You know, maybe I'm feeling a little better already. In fact, since it's Wednesday, I was figuring to drive the documents satchel into Bonn this evening. Like to help Sgt. Belko out with that when I can."

Rutledge scowled. "So you're too sick to be at your post but well enough to drive into Bonn, eh? Wonder if that German girl might have something to do with your miracle cure?"

"Don't be sore Sarge. I just think a lie-down for an hour will fix me right up."

"OK, get outta here. Just be at your desk this afternoon—" Rutledge winked. "—unless I get a note from your mother."

Revenge, Sweet and Savage

Right after evening chow, Drake grabbed the documents pouch, signed out a jeep from the motor pool, and took off for town. He made his delivery to the detachment CP and headed for *Chorsängerstraße*. Because of the savaged streets, he parked three blocks from Stetti's house and hiked the rest of the way.

Drake was surprised not to find Katarina out front of the house. He pounded on the front door, a heavy, oak-framed antique with two glass plates etched with matching figures of rearing unicorns. A crack in one of the glass panels was crudely mended with amber glue.

Stetti, wearing a white muslin apron, opened the door. "Oh, I'm so happily seeing you, darling," she said softly, hurrying outside and closing the door behind her. Her eyes aflame, she looked to be sure they were alone then gasped, "I've done it!"

Drake frowned. "That's what I hear."

"You know?"

"Saw a report. Strangled with piano wire....Led to the trap by a *known prostitute*." He glared at her. "You could have told me, you know. I wouldn't have judged you."

"I did tell you. Not my plan's details, but that I would fool the spiders into killing one of their own, the murderer Heilbrunn." Stetti wiped her hands on her apron. "That is exactly what I did, and the world is better for it. Now that the deed is done, you can stop worrying."

"Guess I shouldn't ever worry about you. Like you said, you always take care of yourself. Pretty damn well."

Stetti peered at him. "You are upset? Is it because I have told you so few details of my plan? Come, sit here, darling. I don't want you to be angry on me—I want you to be proud." She sat on the step. "I will tell you everything."

Drake sat and crossed his arms. "That'd be a nice change."

Stetti looked around again. Sure that they were alone, she said, "My plan was simple. A man named Benedikt Steiger is the leader of the Nazi element that remains in Bonn. Heilbrunn was one of his men, his *Schläger* in German. I don't know it exactly in

English, but it is a man who…" She drove her fist into the palm of her other hand.

"An enforcer?" suggested Drake. "Gangsters would say 'his muscle.'"

Stetti punched her palm again. "I like this gangster's talk, *his muscle*. All I had to do was convince Steiger that his muscle, Heilbrunn, was a traitor. He would do the rest. Last July there was a failed plot to assassinate Hitler. Did you hear of this?"

"Sure, it was big news. Us GIs couldn't believe it was made public—doesn't it seem kinda embarrassing that your own people are trying to kill you? Anyway, too bad it failed."

"Too bad? More like catastrophic…for Germans at least. The patriotic plotters risked everything in a plan they called *Valkyrie*. If successful, it might have saved Germany. But the attempt failed, and everyone even remotely linked to the conspirators was hunted down and executed. German state radio made many claims that the Allies helped the assassins."

Drake leaned in. "So if you need to get rid of somebody, you got a ready-made story of treason to pin on them. Convenient. So tell me how you did the actual pinning. Only spare me the details of what you and Heilbrunn did that night, please."

Stetti looked surprised. "I did not even see Heilbrunn that night. I know him by sight and by reputation, but I have never spoken with the pig."

Drake shook his head. She was still lying… "You lost me. But that's OK. Just go on with your story."

"Heilbrunn comes by habit for beer at *Fafner's Höhle* on Mondays in the evening. I arranged for my friend Gretchen to wear her Immer perfume and to give him some free drinks. When he begins wobbling, she whispers in his ear, 'Would you like a…' hmm, in German we say *freier Ritt*, literally a free ride. In English, I think it means…a free fuck."

"Whoa there, Stetti, that's a word ladies shouldn't use."

"But you may?" Stetti set her jaw. "This is a stupid convention made by men." She thrust her hands on her hips and glared, daring him to reply. "I won't accept it." Her eyes smoldered. "Fuck, fuck, fuck. What do you say to that?"

Drake looked at the floor.

"Besides, do words really matter? Millions die since five years and a word can offend?" Stetti narrowed her eyes and shook her head. "In any case, I resume my story. Gretchen offers to lie with Heilbrunn for no charge. I can picture his slobbering grin at the offer. She and the pig go to *Der Korsar*, a sleazy hotel she uses for her *business* dealings—I told you before that Gretchen is a sometimes prostitute, didn't I?"

Drake's eyes went wide, and he jumped to his feet. "Gretchen! Of course. It was Gretchen who...." He pulled Stetti up, held her close, and kissed her hard. "I'm sorry I doubted you."

Stetti's brow furrowed. "Doubted me? My resolve? Or perhaps my ingenuity?"

"Never mind." Drake kissed her ear softly. "Just go ahead with your story."

Stetti pulled back enough to see his face. She shrugged. "So, there we have Gretchen with Heilbrunn in a room at *Der Korsar*. She gives him schnapps laced with a sleeping dram I got from Birgitta. When he sleeps, she puts money in his coat pocket and returns to me at *Fafner's Höhle*. This is where your help, getting the American Army certificate, became crucial." She raised her index finger. "A moment."

Stetti ran into the house and came back a minute later with a book. She held it before Drake's nose: *Volkswirtschaft für Hausfrauen*. "Would you like to see?"

"What is it?"

"The title means, *Economics for Housewives*. The Nazis loved giving books like these to all households, part of their program to make model families." She handed it to Drake. "You might be surprised what you find inside."

Flipping through the pages, he found a folded paper stuck inside and took it out. It had been crumpled up, making creases that remained despite the pressing. "Hey, it's that form I gave you, the DA-5075. And someone filled it out."

"It is filled out and signed, as you see, in English by the American Colonel Charles Smith."

"Who's that?"

Stetti curtsied. "That is me of course. Read it."

Drake held the paper up in the faint twilight.

Disbursement to Civilian Providers of Requisitioned Goods or Services

Classification: _ Unclass.   _ Confid.   X Secret

Document Date: 23 DEC 1944

Name of Civilian: Heilbrunn, Rudolph P., German National

Detail of goods or services provided to United States Army by civilian:

Coordination of US Army support for Operation Valkyrie within Germany

Payment(s)

1.   1200 DM, 17 MAR 1944, Paid Prev.

2.   1200 DM, 08 JUL 1944, Paid Prev.

3.   1200 DM, 23 DEC 1944, This PMT

4.   2400 DM, Was to be paid for successful operation. Void, Operation Unsuccessful.

Note: This document fulfills all US Army obligations to above named civilian.

"I don't get it," Drake said.

"As I said, Gretchen put money in the sleeping swine's pocket before she left the room at *Korsar*. As soon as she returned to *Fafner's Höhle* and gave me the room key, I went to the home of Benedikt Steiger, the boss of local Nazis. I pounded his door, waking the wife. I said it was an emergency and he appeared in his bedroom robe. I told him, 'Sir, I am sorry to bother you in the night's middle, but I worry that something I heard is a matter of state security.' I knew I could catch the fish's attention with the words *state security*." Stetti made a fishhook with her finger and caught it inside her own cheek. "'My friend Gretchen,' I tell him, 'is a waitress who sometimes takes money to give a man pleasure.

This night she has a customer who brags to her that he has special influence with Americans. He shows her a lot of money he got from them. He shows her an American document proving he worked for them. Gretchen does not read English, but when she saw the word *Valkyrie* she knows it was a name for the traitors who tried to kill the Führer last year. She becomes afraid and very angry, so when the man went unconscious with drinking schnapps, she takes the paper to me, since I speak some English. When I read it, I too am furious because it says this man worked for the Americans to kill our dear Führer. I think to bring it to you as people say you are a good Party member.'" Stetti wore a wry smile—like she enjoyed reliving the story. "May I have a ciggy, darling?" she asked.

Drake took one out, lit it, and gave it to her.

She took a deep drag. "Hearing my report, Steiger was first angry, but upon reflection, he smiled and told his wife, 'Perhaps I have a chance to show my loyalty to the Führer.'

Since he reads no English, I translated the document aloud. When I read *Heilbrunn*, Steiger's face turned purple. He snatched the paper from my hand and pointed to the name. 'Death to traitors!' he roared, crumpling the paper in fury and flinging it to the floor.

"His wife said, 'But Rudolph is *your* man! What if they think you were also involved?'

"I said, 'She is right. Your best hope is decisive action. Then no one can question you.'

"Steiger picked up the telephone receiver and turned to his wife. 'While I rouse Horst, cut me a couple meters of killing wire. The snips are in my box.' I watched his wife reach under the sofa and pull out a reel of wire. She went to the kitchen.

"While she was gone I picked up our document and stuffed it into my pocket.

"The wife brought back a cutter and clipped off two meters of piano wire."

Stetti playfully blew a smoke ring and poked her finger through it. "When Horst showed up, I took the men to the Korsar hotel where Heilbrunn still slept. I gave them the key and left, knowing they would do the rest."

"So you weren't there when they…did it?"

"I was not, but I can see it all in my mind: Heilbrunn claiming he'd never worked for the Americans. That he knew nothing about the money in his pockets. Swearing his love for the Führer. His screams. Cursing. Begging, I am sure. Bawling like a lamb at the slaughter." Stetti took a deep drag on the Chesterfield and smiled. "Steiger had seen many plead like this. The begging, the years of friendship…it made for nothing in the end."

Drake winced. "That's dirty business. They say piano wire cuts like…."

"The Gestapo used it to execute most of the *Valkyrie* conspirators. For the gruesomeness of it. I suspected Steiger would do the same with Heilbrunn. To make him an example for other would-be traitors."

"That Heilbrunn was a bad guy, no doubt about it. But I don't know…he was set up for something he didn't do."

She stubbed out her cigarette. "He was a monster who murdered many good people. He killed for pleasure." She moved close to Drake and growled, "And he murdered Christoph." She shrank back as if saying that exhausted her. "The best man I have ever known. My teacher. My saint." She glared at Drake. "If you cannot see how right it was to arrange the animal's death, to make sure it was horrible, then leave me—Go!—and never return."

Drake raised his hands in surrender. "Hey, I said he was a bad guy. Bad as they come. He deserved what he got a dozen times over." He shrugged. "All I said was…"

Stetti's mouth curled into a victor's smile. "There is still one task left to close the circle. What I must do now is arrange for the destruction of the mastermind, Steiger. He has served his purpose in eliminating Heilbrunn, and now he can pay for his own crimes."

"If he's the head Nazi still left in town, how about we report him to Allied command? They could round him up."

"But would they prosecute *all* his crimes? Perhaps not. We hear some Nazi mayors are being left in charge. Because they

98

know how to get things done. And because their crimes were long ago, an inconvenient detail for the occupiers, who care only about the future. But the past deserves respect, too. No, I don't trust the Allies to bring down justice on Steiger's head. Not without my *help.*"

Drake took her hand. "Listen, you got Heilbrunn without burning your fingers. How are you going to pull that off again?"

"For Steiger, all I have to do is show your American army police evidence that he murdered Heilbrunn. They must prosecute a murder that happens on their watch."

"But what evidence can you show the MPs?"

"I'll say Steiger bragged of killing Heilbrunn for betraying the Reich. He'll be the moth in a web. Further investigation will uncover more of his dark past. Then—" Stetti waved goodbye. "*Auf wiedersehen*, Herr Steiger." She closed her eyes. "As for *my* fate, it looks dark, but, as Christoph said, good Marxists do what the moment demands, no matter the consequences."

"You can't do that," Drake said. "Steiger's wife knows what really happened. You were at her damn house. She'll know you set up her poor hubby. And she'll tell every stinking Nazi in Steiger's rat nest what you did. You'll get hurt."

"You think I'm afraid?" Stetti glared. "Spark me a ciggy!"

Drake got out another cigarette and lit it for her.

Stetti took a deep drag, making the end glow orange. She pulled up her sleeve and held the cigarette's tip pointing at the inside of her wrist. "I don't let myself fear pain."

Drake's eyes went wide. "No," he barked, leaping to stay her hand. He took the cigarette away. "OK, OK, I know you're tough, honey. But those Nazi goons won't stop at hurting you. Your life won't be worth a plugged nickel."

"What you say is true. But if I must sacrifice myself to get Steiger, I will do it. I couldn't ask anyone else to do this heroic deed in my place..." She peered into his eyes.

Drake's face lit up. "Hey, wouldn't a GI would be beyond their reach? Heck, yes! Fact is, I could finger the ape without getting burned."

Stetti smiled. "I hadn't thought of that. As an American, you *would* be safe in your barracks, wouldn't you?" She took Drake's hands. "Only Steiger would know your story about overhearing him was false." Her eyes were dancing. "This is how it could work: Suppose I take you to the beer hall he likes. Show him to you. Then you go to your army police and tell them you heard a man bragging he had murdered Heilbrunn. That he said he used piano wire he hides under his sofa. You return with the police to the pub and point to him. They arrest Steiger and find the wire used to murder Heilbrunn. Perhaps you testify at his trial. You are safe, your police gladly solve a crime, and Germany is free of a villain. Only Steiger, dangling from a rope, loses."

Drake winced. "Only one hitch—testifying that, I'd be lying. Under oath."

Stetti put her arms around Drake and nuzzled his neck. "How is it a lie," she whispered in his ear, "to tell the police what you know is the truth—that Steiger killed Heilbrunn? The wire under the sofa confirms your story."

"Yeah, the part about him murdering Heilbrunn's true. But the overhearing part isn't."

"You quibble over a triviality?" Stetti's tone was stiletto sharp. "The truth is, he did murder. Not only his henchman Heilbrunn but countless others too. Can you say the tiny fiction that you overheard his confession matters in the face of that gross truth?"

"When you put it that way...."

"So we agree—this lie is good," she purred, licking his ear and kissing it. "Good because justice is what every hero *must* strive for."

"Maybe." Drake pulled away and bit his lip. "Hey, tell me. If I hadn't grabbed your hand, would you have burned yourself? Just to prove a point?"

Stetti's eyes twinkled. "I don't know. I hadn't considered the question." She pulled him close and exhaled warm breath on his neck. "Because I knew you would stop me." She kissed her fingertip and touched his lips, then she turned and went inside.

Pin the Tale on the Donkey

After talking to Stetti, Drake spent the whole ride back to the post thinking about his dilemma—to protect her he'd have to lie.

He'd pretty much always told the truth. Even when he didn't have to, like the time he broke a window in Old Lady Thurmond's cellar. No one had seen him pitch that rock at a rabbit running by her house. After a day of wrestling with his conscience, he knocked on Mrs. Thurmond's door and confessed. She hadn't even known the dang window was broken and let Drake pull weeds in the garden for an hour to square up for it.

Drake was up the next morning at dawn. In the rose-gray twilight, he went for a run to clear his head. As he trotted out the post gate, he was thinking that Stetti knew him pretty well—she could count on his need to protect her from burning cigarettes or Nazi thugs. Before making a half mile, something else was clear: There was no way to talk Stetti out of her plan. Was there any option other than playing the role she cast for him in her scheme to set Steiger up? Later, in the home stretch, with the barracks less than a mile away, Drake resigned himself to going all in with Stetti. As soon as he did that, he felt energized. He sprinted the last leg of his run, a new record distance for him, nine miles, he figured.

Later that morning, Drake asked Rutledge for another weekend pass. He was nervous about doing it—he'd taken more than his fair share already. But the sergeant said OK without batting an eye. Probably figured, the kid's heading over to Asia in a week, to who knows what…ought to cut him some slack.

Late Friday afternoon, 20 April, Drake got a lift in Tiny Moynihan's deuce-and-a-half truck into Bonn. He got a room for the weekend at his regular place, *Hotel Heinrich,* and walked straight to Stetti's house. He stubbed out his cigarette and, feeling tall as Gary Cooper in his favorite film, *Beau Geste*, he told her, "Count me in," when she answered the door.

Stetti threw her arms around his neck and kissed him. "Darling, there is no time to lose." She took his hand. "We must go now to the beer hall he frequents, *Die Glückliche Mönch.*"

On the way, Drake said, "*Glückliche Mönch*…bet that means The Lucky Monk, huh?"

"*Glückliche* can mean lucky or happy. In this case, I've assumed it to be happy, since the sign in front shows a plump, smiling monk holding an enormous beer stein, brimming with foam. But he could just as well be lucky, I suppose." She stopped. "If you have ciggies, give me one."

"They were out of Chesterfields." Drake took out a pack of Lucky Strikes and showed it to her. "Luckies, just like the monk." He put a pair between his lips and lit them both with his Zippo. "Here you go," he said, moving one of the smokes to her mouth.

Stetti took a hearty drag and exhaled. "Here is our plan, comrade. *Die Glückliche Mönch* is a kilometer or so away. When we arrive, I go in first and discretely see if Steiger is there. I expect he will be. Give me two minutes, then come in. Watch, but say nothing. I will stand behind his chair and light a cigarette to show, this is Steiger. Then I will depart. You wait a moment, then join me. Outside, you describe me the man, so we are sure you know him. Then you run to your army police, telling them our story. Bring them inside and point to Steiger. With your testimony, including telling the hiding place of his piano wire, they should do the rest."

Drake inhaled deeply. "Got it." He bit his lip. "But won't Steiger be speaking German? How am I supposed to understand him?"

"You worry too much. You do speak some German. *Bier, Wein, Haus, glückliche.*" Stetti took his hand. "You know *leben* means love, don't you, darling?"

Drake's eyes sparkled.

Ten minutes later they arrived outside *Die Glückliche Mönch.* "You see him?" Stetti pointed to the monk on the sign over the door. "Isn't he happy, just as I said?" She looked around to be sure they were alone. "Give me a ciggy and your lighter. Wait a minute or two then come in." She took a Lucky Strike and the Zippo and disappeared through the door.

Drake glanced at his watch. Two minutes later, he went in. He stayed along the wall. There were a half dozen other GIs inside, so he didn't feel out of place. He spotted Stetti across the smoky room. She made eye contact and sauntered to a spot behind a table with five civilians. Two women, both wearing feathered hats, smoked cigarettes through holders and talked to each other. Three men played cards in silence. Stetti stood behind one of them, a burly man smoking a briar pipe and wearing a gray, brimmed felt hat. She flicked the Zippo's flint wheel and lit her cigarette. Taking a deep drag, she glanced at Drake, then exhaled and exited.

Drake took a moment to study the man out of the corner of his eye, then he turned and walked out.

Stetti was waiting in the shadow of an awning. "You saw him?" When Drake nodded, she said, "Describe him so I am sure you have the right one."

Drake shrugged. "Beefy guy. Smokes a pipe, a big one. Has a jacket with green trim and a wool hat, like a small-brimmed fedora...dirty gray."

"That is Steiger. Now hurry to your military police station near the *Hauptbahnhof.* You know what to tell them...darling." She pressed the Zippo into Drake's hand and kissed him on the cheek.

Drake hustled the mile and a half to the MP detachment HQ. He went in the door and walked up to the soldier behind the desk. "Evening, Corporal," Drake said, taking off his hat. "My name's Drake and I just overheard a civilian telling some of his buddies about what sounds like a shady deal. Something I think you fellas would want to know about."

"I'm Cullen. How's tricks?" The corporal opened his log book. "Said your name's Drake?"

"Yeah, PFC Winston Drake."

"D. r. a. k. e." The corporal scribbled a line in his book. "What outfit you with, Private?"

"HQ battalion, First Army."

The MP wrote down the information. "So, what's up?"

"Well, I'm having a beer at this tavern called the, er, *Glückliche Mönch.* Case you don't know as much German as me, that's the Happy Monk. Know it? Anyway, some guy at the next table's telling his pals about a killing he did. Strangled some guy. Said he was a traitor. Bragged that he killed him with wire he keeps at home, hidden under the sofa."

The MP jotted down what Drake said. "Got a name for the clown you overheard?"

"Nope," Drake said. "But I can describe him. Heck, I can point him out to you if he's still there at the beer hall."

"Let me go back and get Sergeant Porter to see how he wants to handle this." The corporal returned a minute later with a stocky NCO carrying a mug of steaming coffee. Nodding at Drake, Cullen said, "This here is the witness, sarge." He checked his notes. "PFC Winston Drake of headquarters battalion, First Army."

The MP sergeant stirred his coffee and squinted at Drake. "I'm Master Sergeant Porter," He snorted, then took a sip. "Understand you heard some guy talking about killing someone with wire. How about you repeat the whole story for me, Mac."

Drake went through his tale again.

By the end, Porter's eyes were big. "That info might tie into a case we're looking at real hard, Private. Murder with Nazi Party overtones. The Brass's made a big deal of it." He took another slurp of coffee. "So, the corporal told me you thought the jerk might still be at the barrel house where you overheard him, right?"

"Could be. It was less than an hour ago."

"And you could ID him if we go there with you now?"

"You bet," Drake said.

Porter turned to Cullen. "Tell Michaels and Flynn to meet me out front in the jeep. Pronto."

Drake and the sergeant went outside. A moment later an MP jeep screeched to a halt in front of them. They jumped in the back seat and the vehicle sped off.

"Want me to run the siren, sarge?" Michaels, the driver, said over his shoulder.

"Nothin' doing. Don't want this Kraut to know we're coming, do you?"

Five minutes later they stopped in front of *Die Glückliche Mönch.* "Flynn, go around back," Porter barked. "Make sure nobody don't come squirting out there. I'll whistle when we've made the collar." Flynn hustled off. "Drake, you'll come in with Michaels and me. If he's still in there, point out this guy with the big yap. We'll do the rest."

Drake followed the two MPs in. Steiger sat in the same chair. Drake whispered to Sgt. Porter, "That's him, the big palooka there, playing cards. With the gray fedora and the pipe."

Porter licked his lips. "Wait outside," he told Drake out of the side of his mouth.

Drake exited. He barely had time to light a smoke before the MPs came out, pushing Steiger. The veins in the neck of the handcuffed German bulged as he struggled and hollered. Michaels shut him up with a sharp poke in the gut from his night stick. Porter stuck his thumb and index finger into the corners of his mouth and let out a whistle as piercing as a dentist's drill. A moment later Flynn ran up, and the three MPs muscled Steiger into the back seat of the jeep.

Porter shook Drake's hand. "Thanks for the help, Mac. I'm sure the investigators will want to ask you a few questions. We know where to reach you. For now, I'd keep a low profile here in Bonn. Don't want somebody to recognize you as coming in with us when we pinched this asshole." He shrugged. "Best to play it safe."

"Glad I could help, sarge. I'll keep my head down."

Drake watched the jeep speed off, then he walked back to the hotel.

Saturday morning, Drake hiked to Stetti's home. Katarina sat outside on the steps.

"*Stetti, bitte?*" Drake asked.

The old woman's stood. Her eyes got big. "Stetti?" She giggled and rubbed her hands together as if washing them. "Stetti *weg.*" She hummed a tune and looked into the distance. "*Ja, weit weg.*"

Drake didn't understand. "Is Stetti here?" He nodded toward the house. "Stetti?"

"*Nein, nein.*" Katarina shook her head. "*Stetti ist nicht zu Hause.*" She pointed toward the town center. "*Stetti weg.*" She smiled sweetly. "*Auf wiedersehen,*" she chirped and sat down.

Drake sighed. "Whatever." He took out a pencil and pad and wrote: *The rat's been caught, Stetti. I am staying at Hotel Heinrich through tomorrow (Sunday). Come see me there. D.*

He handed the note to Katarina. "For Stetti."

The old woman clutched the paper to her breast. "*Danke, liebe,*" she said, beaming at Drake like he'd given her a Valentine.

Drake pointed to the note. "For Stetti," he repeated and walked away.

Stetti didn't show up Saturday. Drake spent the day waiting in the hotel lobby, not wanting to miss her if she came. In the evening he walked to *Fafner's Höhle*. Stetti wasn't there and Gretchen said she hadn't seen her. He drank a glass of dark beer and went back to the hotel.

Drake got up early Sunday morning and walked to Stetti's house again. No one home. He wrote another note:

> *Dear Stetti, Still want to see you. You got me real worried. I am at the hotel (Heinrich) til late this afternoon. Sunday. Please come so I'll know you are OK.*
>
> *Drake.*
>
> *PS. Remember, I leave Germany in a week. If I don't see you, I'll try to return after the war. If you ever come to America, you can find me in my home town, Omaha in Nebraska, smack dab in the middle of the US. Love you.*

Drake stuck the note under the knocker on the door. He headed for the MP office.

Corporal Cullen was behind the desk there. He had his feet up and was paging through *National Geographic Magazine.*

Drake cleared his throat. "Hi, Corporal. It's me, Drake. Remember? Friday night?"

Cullen closed the magazine and put his feet down. "Friday? Oh yeah. Drake. Sure, I remember."

"I was just walking by and thought I'd ask about something that's got me worried. Haven't had any reports about a German girl, have you? Maybe in some kind of trouble? Hurt maybe?"

Cullen shook his head. "Town's been quiet as a morgue today."

Drake shivered at the word morgue. "Guess you'd hear if a girl got roughed up or hurt or.... Right?"

Cullen shrugged. "Probably."

Drake nodded. "Hey, Cullen, I'll be over at the *Hotel Heinrich der Heilige*. Know it?"

"Yeah," said the MP. "Why?"

"If you hear anything about a German gal in trouble, would you let me know? Name's Stetti. Actually it's Euridice Bloomstedt, but she goes by Stetti. Tall, dark hair, a real looker. I'll be at the hotel till evening. After that you could reach me at First Army HQ."

Cullen jotted a note. "Will do, buddy."

Drake moped back to the hotel. He hung around there as long as he could, then went to the meeting point for his ride back to the battalion.

Sitting in the rear of the deuce-and-a-half on the drive back, Drake couldn't shake the fear that he'd seen Stetti for the last time. In just over a week he'd be shipping out for the Philippines. What if her luck had run out? That was a pretty ruthless gang of thugs she'd taken on. But she was smart. Smart enough to keep a step ahead of them. Maybe she was just laying low. The truck hit a bump, bouncing the men in back all the way up to the canvas top. The jolt made Drake wonder, had Stetti ditched him? Now that Steiger was behind bars, had he fulfilled his usefulness? Like some cigarette smoked down to the butt and flipped into the gutter without a second thought? He looked out the back of the truck at the outskirts of Bonn slipping away into the hazy twilight dusk.

First thing Monday morning, Sgt. Rutledge led an officer to Drake's desk. "This is Captain Miller of the Criminal Investigation Division. He wants to ask you a few questions about some Fritz his people picked up." Rutledge looked at the captain. "Sir, if you want some privacy, you can use the room next door. It's empty today."

"Thanks, Sergeant. That'll be all." When Rutledge left, the captain turned to Drake. "Morning, Private. I just have a few questions. About the conversation you overheard in that bar in Bonn on the evening of 20 April. Let's go sit down."

In the adjoining room Cpt. Miller eased into a leather chair behind the desk. He opened his large brown leather briefcase and took out a binder of papers. Drake sat on a folding metal chair across from the officer.

For a moment, the captain said nothing. He looked Drake in the eye with a withering gaze. Miller was an athletic-looking man with jet black hair, oiled and combed back. He had a pencil-thin mustache and the shadow of a heavy beard. The man's jaw looked like it could take a sledge hammer's blow. Miller glanced at a paper on his desk. "I have you down as PFC Winston Drake. That correct?"

"Yes sir."

Miller nodded. "Let me thank you for your help IDing the suspect. Name's Benedikt Steiger. We've been watching him for weeks, for his reputed Nazi connections. Preventing espion*age*, sabot*age*—whatever *–age* you got—by scum like Steiger is one of our missions."

Drake cleared his throat. "Oh? Didn't know you people got involved in civilian crimes."

"We do for big stuff. Under the Hague Convention of 1907, as a military occupation force we're obliged to maintain order. Washington's given us a broad legal mandate—most cops and judges were up to their ears in black shit during the Nazi years, so we step in when we have to." Miller crossed his arms and leaned back. "But this case looks special. We think the killing may be war-related. Puts it under our jurisdiction, no question."

Drake nodded. "Interesting. So how can I help, Captain?"

Miller pursed his lips. "I just want to clear up a couple of issues in the statement you provided—" He glanced at the paperwork. "—Friday night." He leaned forward.

Drake's throat tightened.

Miller shuffled his papers. "You stated that you overheard Steiger's conversation in a beer hall. Is that correct?"

"Yes, sir. The place's called the *Glückliche Mönch.*" Drake grinned. "That'd be the Happy Monk in English."

"Happy *or* lucky," Miller said without looking up. "Can mean either." He glanced at Drake. "I minored in German at Purdue." He jotted a note. "Were you there with someone?"

"Um…" Drake took a deep breath. "I guess I was alone."

"You *guess* you were alone?"

"I was alone." Drake thought of not seeing Stetti all weekend after Friday night. "I was hoping to see a girl, but she never made it." He shrugged like it didn't matter but the pained look on his face said otherwise.

Miller opened a silver cigarette case. He studied the row of king-size, filtered Pall Malls, as if one might be better than another. He selected a smoke and lit it with a polished Zippo. Taking a deep draw, he eyed Drake for a moment. "Do you often drink by yourself?"

"Heck no. I was pretty much just killing time, hoping, er, Lola showed."

"Women! What's a guy gonna do?" Miller shook his head.

"Haven't seen any reports in Bonn about any girls in hot water, have you?" Drake asked.

"Nope." Miller glanced at his watch. "OK, so you were having a beer alone in a tavern—" He underlined something in his notes. "—in *Die Glückliche Mönch*, correct?"

"Yes, sir. The happy monk. Or lucky."

Miller peered at Drake. "So you speak German pretty well, eh, Private?"

Drake winced. "No. A few words here and there. Lola's taught me some."

"Hmm, barely? Is that how you'd put it?"

"I suppose," Drake said. "I can order a beer and sausage, ask where the latrine is…that kind of stuff."

Miller scribbled a note. "Yet in a crowded, noisy barroom you were able to hear a man speaking *in German* at another table and make out enough, even translate it, to know he was talking about killing a man?"

Drake swallowed. "Bragging. I'd say it was more bragging than just talking."

Miller shrugged. "OK, bragging. Not sure how it explains that acute hearing of yours."

Drake looked at his hands. "He'd been drinking. I guess he was talking loud. Yeah, real loud. Seemed proud of what he was claiming. That's why I say bragging. Pride can make a fella loud, right?"

"Surprising he'd speak so freely, brag as you put it, about strangling someone with an American GI near enough to hear."

Drake glanced at the ceiling. "He was facing the other way— probably didn't see me. And like I said, he'd been drinking. A lot."

"Right." Miller jotted some notes. "So you could *hear* him. What about the translating?"

"Well…I couldn't get every word. But he said the name Heilbrunn. That caught my ear because I had just typed-up a report on a man by that name who'd been found murdered—strangled with wire—in Bonn. Guess I kind of put two and two together."

"You mentioned *wire* in your statement. Can you tell me the German word for wire?"

Drake shifted in his seat. He shook his head.

"It's *Draht*," Miller said. "I'm wondering how you knew to put in your statement that he killed the victim with *Draht* he kept under his sofa. Can you explain that?"

"Well, ah…" Drake bit his lip. "Guess I read in the report that the guy was killed with piano wire and the big guy, this Steiger, used the word piano, same as in English, so I must've guessed the wire part. And he said *unter sofa*, I think. Sounded to me like under the sofa."

Miller studied Drake. "Pretty damn good. By the way, when Steiger's house was searched, we did find piano wire identical to the stuff used to garrote Heilbrunn. It was right where you indicated, under the sofa." Miller closed the binder of papers. "Look Private, sorry to have to give you the third degree. It's just that your story was too good to be true. Lawyers worry about evidence that seems too perfect."

"You're a lawyer, sir?"

"Yep. Pushy as I was, you might have guessed." Miller relaxed in his chair. "So, Sgt. Rutledge tells me you're shipping out for Asia in a week."

"Yes, sir."

"Since you won't be here to testify, I'm going to need an official statement we can use in Steiger's trial. I'll send someone to get it in the next couple of days. OK?"

"Sure," Drake said, "glad to do whatever to put a piece of Nazi scum behind bars."

"'Preciate that." Miller rose to his feet. "Good luck to you in the Pacific, Drake. Counting on you to take out a few Japanese scum while you're over there."

The men shook hands and Miller left.

The next afternoon, a corporal named Mark Forswear brought Drake a typed statement of testimony, based on Miller's notes. "Should you disagree with anything, Private, you can cross it out and initial. If you want to add a detail, just insert it in the margin. Write it in longhand, then initial. You'll sign at the bottom, then I'll notarize it" Forswear handed the document to Drake and sat in a chair next to the desk.

Drake's stomach churned. Chewing on his thumbnail, he stared vaguely at the statement, two dozen lines of small blurry

111

marks on a sheet of paper. "Sorry to be so long." He scratched his ear. "Say, do I really need to be sure about all this stuff?" He huffed. "As if anybody's ever going to read it, anyway."

Forswear pulled a copy of *Stars and Stripes* from his courier bag. "Oh, they'll read it, all right. The lawyers, that is. Take your time. I got all day." He turned to the sports page. "Can you believe those Dodgers?"

Drake thought about telling Forswear he was no longer sure about what had happened, that his memory was foggy. That he couldn't sign. Then he pictured Stetti—she was counting on him, and he'd promised to do his part. He grimaced, dashed his name on the signature line, and pushed the statement across the desk, away from him. "It's right, Corporal, just the way it is."

Taking Care

Drake decided to make a last try to see Stetti before he shipped out. On Wednesday, 25 April, he stopped by Sgt. Belko's office in the motor pool. "How's it going, sarge?

Belko didn't look up from his paperwork. "Swell," he muttered.

"Say, I'd be glad to make the document run into Bonn this evening."

Belko put his pencil down. "Looking to see that little *Fräulein* of yours, eh?" He sipped his coffee. "Ain't going to happen, Omaha. See, Herbie Scolnick already got volunteered to carry the mail. He was late for muster yesterday morning, and Sgt. Bottles wanted to give him extra duty. You can go next week."

Drake's shoulders sagged. "Not going to be here next week. I been reassigned to a line outfit training in the Philippines. Head out Monday. "

Belko frowned. "Oh shit! Now that you mention it, guess I did hear something about that. How'd you get flimflammed into that bonehead deal?"

"I volunteered. Figured it was my last chance to really… do something."

Belko stared at Drake for a moment. "Gotta hand it to you. Probably have more guts than brains, volunteering for a blood bath like that, but still…"

Drake looked at the floor. "See you, sarge." He sauntered away.

He'd just gotten back to his desk when the phone rang. It was Belko. "Guess what, Omaha! I pow-wowed with Sgt. Bottles. Told him it was your last week here and that you needed to drive the satchel into Bonn. He said Scolnick could pull the duty next week. So you're on for this evening, if you still want to go."

"Count me in," Drake said.

Half an hour later Sgt. Rutledge shuffled up to Drake's desk. "Just got off the phone with Belko in the motor pool. Sounds like you're making the document run tonight. Be sure to have that readiness report on my desk before you head out."

"No prob, sarge. I'll have it done in an hour."

"Reason I called Belko was getting you to the train station Monday morning. I requested a jeep so I could drive you there myself."

"Do you know what time?"

"Yeah, your travel orders have been cut." Rutledge tossed a stapled set of papers onto Drake's desk. "They got you on a train heading to Paris at one zero one zero hours."

Drake scanned the orders. "Holy cow, Paris! A night there." He glanced at Rutledge. "Can't gripe about that." He read some more. "They're putting me up in a hotel called *Le Cle d'Ore*. Sounds ritzy, huh? The next day it's off to Le Havre—that's where I sail from."

"It's what you want, right?"

Drake nodded. "Sure is." He didn't look convinced.

"I suppose you'll want a pass Friday night...go see that gal of yours one last time, eh?"

Drake shrugged. "Don't know. She kind of ditched me last weekend."

"Women!" Rutledge shook his head. "You'll never figure 'em out. An enigma, my old man used to say."

"Enigma?" Drake glanced at the ceiling. "That like a mirage or something?"

"Yeah...well, no." Rutledge scratched his head. "With a mirage, if I'm right, you see something that ain't really there. Like in the desert. An enigma's something or someone you just can't figure out. Like a puzzle. A damn hard puzzle. 'Course even the dames you can figure out sometimes get their jollies jerking you around. Wind a fella up like a clockwork toy and giggle as he spins off the table." He put a hand on Drake's shoulder. "Tell you what, kid, you paint the town red this weekend, with or without your little *Fräulein*. She's not the only fish in the sea, ya know. Just be careful. Don't want to pick up the pox on your last weekend in Germany. I'd say get yourself some rubbers, just in case." He leaned in and whispered, "And I don't mean galoshes."

Drake looked at the floor. "Figure I'll try to talk to her tonight, for a minute at least. Hopefully arrange something for the weekend. If she gives me the cold shoulder, I might just hang around here Saturday and Sunday. You know, get stuff ready for Monday morning."

"Up to you. And hey, I said you could *tentatively* figure on the weekend off. If something blows up, all bets are off. *Capisce?*"

"How the heck am I going to get by in Sixth Army without a sergeant talking Italian to me all the time?"

"You'll probably have some tougher-than-leather, fire-breathing son of a buck whipping your rear end into fighting form." Rutledge shook his index finger. "At least you better hope you do. Mean bastard like that can be the difference between a guy making it off some landing beach and him ending up there, rolling back and forth in the surf with a belly full of lead."

From the moment he picked up the documents pouch and headed for Bonn in the jeep, Drake was second guessing himself. I go all this way, hunt for Stetti, and probably won't find her. Worse, I'll find her and she tells me to drop dead. He gritted his teeth and pushed the accelerator to the floor. "Let's get this over with," he muttered.

After dropping off the documents, he headed for Stetti's place on *Chorsängerstraße*. He parked in his usual spot, a couple of blocks from her home, and walked. As he approached the house, he heard whistling. Katarina was sitting in front of Stetti's. Getting closer, Drake saw she was playing a wooden instrument, a recorder. Not exactly playing. More playing with. Making bird sounds. Having fun.

Drake came up next to her. "*Guten Abend*," he said.

The old woman didn't seem to notice him.

He cleared his throat and was about to ask if he could see Stetti when she bolted out the front door. "Oh Drake darling, it's you!" She threw her arms around his neck and kissed his lips.

Katarina stopped playing and sat watching the show with a look of glee on her face. The old gal clapped her hands and chirped, "*Stetti ihm küsse! Stetti ihm küsse!*" Then she jumped up, put her arms around them both, and joined Stetti in kissing Drake.

Stetti put an arm around Katarina. Murmuring *"Liebe, in Haus, ja?,"* she led her inside.

When Stetti came back, Drake said, "I spent all weekend trying to find you. I was worried. Didn't you get my notes?"

She peered at him. "I don't know what to say. Of course, I saw your messages." She shrugged. "I was busy with my comrades, preparing for the changes to come. What could be more important than steering the future?"

"I just wanted was to make sure you were OK."

Stetti glared. "I don't need you worrying on me."

"OK, OK." Drake took her hand. "It's fine. But there's something else—I want to tell you about some arrangements I've made...to take care of you after I leave."

She pulled her hand away. "Take care of me?" Her sparkling green eyes went dark.

Drake blinked. "Sure...and Katarina. And the doctor and her daughter, too."

"They have names. Birgitta and Edita."

"Birgitta and Edita. Yeah, all of you. I wanna make sure you're all OK. Look, I've arranged for someone to get you onions, cheese, all kinds of food. That Riesling wine you like. A guy named Dutch...he'll take care of everything. I just wanted to tell you about it. I thought—"

"You thought what? The first day we met I told you, *I take care of myself.* Don't you see, *everyone* will need onions and potatoes and bread...cheese and meat...for years and years? Helping me—" She pushed him away. "—it means...nothing. My concern is a future for all workers, free of Nazis and capitalists. A future in commune." She sighed and touched his wrist. "I've said it before—you are a good man, Drake. But you are blind to reality. How could you be otherwise? Since birth, you were fed what to think at the capitalist trough."

Drake crossed his arms. "Look, I know I can't feed everyone in Germany. I just wanted to...to help *you*. You're the one who says, from one according to his ability to another according to her need."

Stetti stared at him then brushed his cheek softly with the back of her fingers. "I shouldn't scold you. The shared future *is* most important, but it isn't all that matters." She took his hand in both of hers. "Please tell me about the arrangements you have made. For me and my family." She kissed him. "Please."

Drake squeezed her hands. "It's no big deal really. Some GI who has tons of connections is going to get you food and stuff. Help keep you on your feet. Maybe if there's enough you can even share with your comrades. Anyway, the guy's name is Dutch Scholz. Seems like a square guy. He's the one named me Omaha. Or was it Belko? I forget."

"Omaha? This is your *Spitzname*? As mine is Stetti?"

"*Spitzname*—there's a two-bit word! It's *Sprechen sie Deutsch* for nickname, right?"

Stetti winked. "It's a pity. Your German improves just as you make ready to leave."

"Never know…I might be back some day." He gave Stetti a cigarette and lit it, then he fired up one for himself. "Omaha's my home town. Named after the Omaha Indian tribe. They lived around there."

"Ja, I see this name on your note. The spelling is O, M, A, H, A, is it not?" Stetti smiled. "As a child, my favorite book had pictures of the Indians of America. Then I read and reread each of the adventure novels of Karl May about the Apache Indian chief Winnetou." She closed her eyes and inhaled like the smoke of his campfire was near. "Indians…such majestic people! Can someone see them now in America?"

Drake shrugged. "Maybe. Nowadays they dress about like everyone else. Except in the westerns."

"I wish I could see Indians. Talk to them. Learn. They had the wisdom to establish socialist societies, you know."

"Different tribes were real different, I think. Doubt they thought of themselves as commies, though folks do call 'em redskins, come to think of it."

"I am happy you taught me Omaha. Such a pretty name. And now I can remember your home city."

"Remember and maybe visit someday, huh?"

"The German version of the *Spitzname* custom applies to surnames. My first cello teacher was Frau Frankfurter. In any case, from today I shall gladly think of you as Drake *and* Omaha. But certainly not Winston!"

"Swell. Having you think about me, that is."

Stetti peered into his eyes. "I did think of you this week. Fondly. You've done so much for me, dear friend. I am even preparing a gift, in the hope that I would see you again."

Drake eyes went wide. "A gift? For me?"

"I want to take you once more to heaven," Stetti said. "Not a heaven, perhaps, as sublime as Johann Sebastian Bach's, but one of my own making."

"I'm ready to go there with you anytime." Drake took her in his arms.

"Can you return on this week's end?" Stetti asked, stroking his neck.

"Since I'm shipping out next week, sarge said he'd give me the weekend off." Drake kissed her. "But why do we have to wait?"

"Learn patience, *Liebe*." She pulled away, murmuring, "I like seeing it in a man."

He cocked his head. "Hey, not two weeks ago you said patience was bad. Like laziness."

Stetti smiled. "It is bad in socialists. But good in capitalists." She pecked his cheek and turned to go inside. Over her shoulder she said, "Patient capitalists are easily overthrown."

An Evening in Heaven, Then…

D rake secured a pass for Friday, 27 April. When he got to Bonn, he booked his usual room at *Hotel Heinrich* and set out for Stetti's home.

As soon as he turned the corner onto *Chorsängerstraße*, Drake saw Stetti and Katarina, their faces lit by a lantern, sitting together on the front steps. He called, "Stetti!" and broke into a run. She hurried to the sidewalk and flew into his arms.

Katarina joined their embrace, then said, "*Katarina muß im Hause gehen, ja?*"

"She says she will go into the house," Stetti said. "I have something to fetch inside, so I will take her. You'll wait for my return?"

Drake held up three fingers. "Scout's honor."

Two minutes later Stetti came out with a chair. "And I need something else." She went back inside and returned with her cello and bow. "You sit there." She pointed to the steps. She arranged the chair facing Drake and sat, ready to play.

"You're going to perform?" Drake said. "Right out here?"

"Of course. What better place to make music than under the stars in nature's air?" Stetti placed the bow on her lap. "I improvised a cello piece for you. Before I begin, let me say its story. At the end of the Sixteenth Century in Spain, songs of one particular chord pattern became quite popular. Known as the *folie d'Espagne*, the tune captured Europe. Like American jazz has now. The *folie* theme became a true musical archetype, and hundreds of composers have based works on it. Famous names—Liszt, Vivaldi, Corelli, even Johann Sebastian Bach—to say a few. I have always loved the melody. So this week I worked for my own improvisation on the *folie* bass…with you in mind."

Drake's eyes were wide. "You wrote a song for *me*?"

Stetti giggled. "I didn't write it down." She tapped her temple with her index fingertip. "Except up here. And your song isn't set—it varies and even grows in richness every time I play it. As if it were alive. Would you hear it now?"

"You bet."

Stetti nodded. "First, the basic tune." She began playing. As she went on, the underlying melodic line remained, but with elaboration and decoration. Its pace alternated between leisurely and rollicking. Between simple and ornate. It *was* alive.

From its first notes, the melody ensnared Drake's heart. The improvisation seemed totally accessible to him. Inviting. Sensual. He watched Stetti's face bathed in lantern light…her look of joy, peace. And to think, she connected this music with him!

When Stetti finished playing, she said, "So, how do you think?"

"I was swallowed up completely." Tilting his head, Drake gazed at her face. "I have no idea how long you played. All I know is that if I'm not allowed to hear another note of music, ever, I can't complain. I *have* been to heaven."

"Of course, it is nothing compared to the works of masters like Bach. But I hoped its personal nature—that I created it for you—gives you pleasure."

Drake came over to Stetti. She was still holding her cello and bow when he kissed her.

Stetti leaned her cello on the chair and put down her bow. "I have something else for you. Something to protect you, darling, in the days ahead. In Asia." She reached into the pocket of her skirt and took out a coin. "We call it *ein Zaubermittel*. A protector. By magic."

Drake beheld the silvery disk and her fingertips holding it. "Never seen a magic charm before. I saw a movie about knights one time—they called it a talisman."

Stetti's face lit up. "Also in German! *Einer Talisman*." She pressed the coin into Drake's hand. "When I was a girl studying in England, I won the school competition for cello. My prize was this silver coin. Since the bombing began, I kept it with me always and I remained safe. I believe its power protected me. Now it can protect you."

Drake held the gleaming silver coin up to the lantern light. It looked freshly minted, though the date of 1940 indicated it was five years old. On one side was stately George VI, England's king.

On the other side was a lion standing astride a crown. The denomination was one schilling. "It's really swell of you, but…" Drake winced. "Jeeze, I can't take your good luck charm. If anything happened to you…"

"I'll have my magical pearls. They'll protect me. Always." Stetti blew out the lantern and approached Drake. She pushed the fingers holding the coin to his pocket. When he'd dropped it in, she moved his hand to her waist. Putting her arms around his neck, she pressed her body to his and kissed him. Long and hard. "I won't let you go tonight." She pulled his hand to her breast. "Drake darling, come in with me."

Stetti carried the cello and bow. Drake followed with the chair. At the door she put her finger to her lips and whispered, "With quiet." They crept into the dark house. Drake left the chair where Stetti indicated, and they climbed a flight of stairs lit by moonlight pouring through a window at the landing. Stetti noiselessly opened a door. "My room," she purred. Inside, she placed her instrument on its stand and then stopped in the darkness, toe-to-toe with Drake. She pulled him closer until they were touching, as one, from knee to chest. "For tonight, darling, I am yours and you are mine" She kissed him hotly.

Drake let his hands slide from her shoulders down to the back of her thighs. He slipped them under her skirt. As he inhaled the scent of her hair, the breath in his lungs seemed sweet and thick as syrup. The world around him turned fluid, spinning. Moving with Stetti to the bed, time itself melted into the shadows.

The first notes of dawn's twilight slipping through the window eased Drake out of his vague, contented sleep. Stetti lay naked next to him. She was watching him, her breath on his cheek—caressing his ear then tracing the line of his jaw with a touch light as a springtime breeze. He could imagine nothing nicer.

"You're awake," she breathed. She kissed his face, her tongue running to his ear. "Love me again, darling," she whispered, touching his penis. Then she pounced, straddling his body and making frantic love to him.

121

When they lay spent in each other's arms, Stetti said, "I need a smoke." She got out of bed and put on a knee-length robe, silk with a Japanese motif of white dogwood flowers on navy blue. She left it untied at the waist and took a cigarette from the pack in Drake's jacket pocket. Pulling the robe closed over her knee, she sat on a wooden chair next to a small end table by the window. She tamped the cigarette on the tabletop and lit it with a wooden match.

Drake sat in bed, watching her smoke. Between drags, she held the Chesterfield over an ashtray in front of a framed picture on the table. He couldn't take his eyes off her—her right hand with its long, graceful fingers as it moved with the cigarette to and from her lips; her string of pearls and underneath the cleavage of her breasts exposed in the vee of the open robe; her left hand resting on the silk fabric clinging to her thigh.

When she'd smoked half the cigarette, Stetti stubbed it out. She got up and let the robe drop to the chair. She stood silently for a moment facing him, fingering her pearls. Then she quickly dressed and walked to the bed. "You must leave before Birgitta wakes," she whispered. She waited by the window with arms crossed and watched him get up and slip into his clothes.

"Don't forget your ciggies," Stetti said, nodding to where she'd left them by the ashtray on the table. She watched him go to pick up the package.

As he reached for the Chesterfields, Drake glimpsed the framed picture. At its center was Stetti wearing a short, summery, white cotton frock. She sat on the knee of a handsome young soldier in a German army uniform. With his blond hair combed rakishly back and his pencil-line mustache, he looked like a dashing cavalry officer from a bygone age. Stetti had her arms around his neck. He'd casually placed a hand on her thigh, a cigarette with a ribbon of smoke trailing up from its tip nested between his fingers. They smiled like newlyweds. It struck Drake as an old-time portrait taken in a bordello.

After a moment, Drake bit his lip and pulled his gaze from the picture. When he glanced at Stetti, she was observing him from across the room, curious as a child watching an insect caught on flypaper.

After a moment, she came over and took his hand. Without a word, she led him down the stairs, to the front door. They stepped outside and stood looking into each other's eyes. Drake wanted to ask about the picture, about a million other things, but before he could, Stetti put her fingertips to his lips. "Listen!" she said, cocking her head. Birds were greeting the morning with delirious song. "Nature's own music." She turned back to him. "I won't forget you."

Drake blinked. "But," he stammered, "what about…the rest of the day?"

"I can't," Stetti whispered.

Drake's heart was pounding, his eyes wide. "And later… after the war?"

Stetti shrugged. "After the war, you'll have your life and I'll have mine."

"But I thought we were…friends. More than that, for cripes' sake."

"Even friendship takes time. More than we've had." She kissed his cheek—a punctuation mark, a period, to whatever they'd been—then stepped inside and closed the door.

Drake stood on the porch, unable to accept that something so important to him, so good, was over.

Finally, he traced the grain of the door's wood with his fingertip, lovingly, achingly. Then he walked away.

Part II   A Rehearsal Called Off

Avanti!

D rake's mind was a fog as he left Stetti's house. An hour later, with most of the city still asleep, he found himself outside his hotel, remembering nothing of the trek there. He went inside, plopped onto a lumpy old sofa in the lobby, and took out his cigarettes. Seeing the Chesterfields shot his mind back to Stetti's room, to the image of that white package sitting on the table next to the picture of her with that German fella. Her *friend*. His throat tightened. He shook a cigarette out and lit it. "They looked like pretty damn good friends!" he muttered, taking a deep drag. He wondered how the hell to reconcile seeing that picture of Stetti and another guy one minute with her telling him the next that *Friendship takes time—More than we've had*. Huffing, he thought, it was plenty of time for me. Jeeze, I was sweet on her from the moment we met. He snuffed out his Chesterfield and climbed the stairs to his room.

Drake fell into bed, fully clothed. He slept on and off until almost noon. Then he checked out and walked to the train station, where at 1700 hours he'd catch a ride on the First Army HQ shuttle back to the battalion. He glanced at his watch—three and a half hours to kill.

Drake sat outside on the station steps, leaning on a stone column pockmarked by small arms fire during the March fighting in the city. He thought some more about the picture of Stetti with...her friend. Why did it eat on him so? Everybody's got romances in their past. And who knows, maybe they were just friends, though the way his hand perched on her thigh discounted that. Besides, no matter what they *had* been, there was a good chance the guy was permanently out of the picture now...so many German boys had been chewed up in the West, the East, Italy, Africa. Drake felt lousy for thinking that, maybe even hoping for it. What had the fellow done but fall for a girl—just like he had?

He had a vague sense that what really tore at him was more than jealousy, something stronger. But he couldn't quite put his finger on it. Then it came to him: Had Stetti stage-managed the whole picture-with-the-boyfriend deal? Drake repeated the scene in his mind. Knowing he was watching her, she had held her cigarette just so over the ashtray she'd set right in front of the photo. And she made sure to leave his Chesterfields next to the picture, then pointed to them and said, "Don't forget your ciggies." Was she warning him off, making sure he knew she wasn't his girl? Or worse, was she torturing him, perhaps even enjoying it? Tears welled up at the thought that someone he loved so dearly cared so little for him in return. He looked to both sides, embarrassed that someone might be watching, and drew his jacket sleeve across his eyes. When tears kept streaming, he pulled out his handkerchief. But it did nothing to stem the sobs now shaking him by the shoulders. Look at me, he thought, bawling my fool head off in front of a bunch of damn foreigners. I'm pathetic.

Then a bigger notion flashed into Drake's head. Hit him like a right hook to the jaw. This relationship he had with Stetti was his whole life in miniature—frustration in whatever he tried to do. Everything from doing his part in the war to having a girlfriend. Did fate have it in for him? But, to his surprise, that calmed him. As if the right hook had cleared his head. Given him hope. He realized everything was about to change. The day after tomorrow he'd start a new chapter—something completely different. Something that might break the spell.

He took a deep breath. Tracing his upper lip with the nail of his thumb, Drake told himself, you're free to put Stetti out of your mind. You've done right by her—all you could do. Who knows, maybe someday you'll be back and things'll be different. But no matter what, starting Monday, *you're* in the clear.

Drake went inside the station feeling upbeat. He spotted a stern, old woman with a penny-sized mole on her cheek and a table of stuff to sell. He strolled up and scanned her wares. She didn't have much—a few hand-rolled cigarettes, match sticks, five cans of warm beer, some smudged slips of paper, two stubby pencils, a hunk of dark bread, and two dozen tubes of red lipstick. "What happened?" Drake said, pointing to the cosmetics. "Betty Grable drop her makeup case trying to catch a train?"

The woman missed his joke. "*Bier, ja?*" she snorted.

Drake leaned over the table and tapped a can of beer and pointed to the cigarettes. He held up two fingers. The lady opened the can and wrapped it in a scrap of newspaper. When she handed it to him, he caught a whiff the sleeve of her coat—sour as a mildewed dishrag. She pushed the pair of smokes across the table along with a couple of matches. "*Danke,*" he said, counting out four one mark coins and tossed in a handful of pfennigs for good measure. The woman seemed pleased.

Drake shuffled over to the counter in front of a long-closed bar in the station. He lit one of the woman's cigarettes—it tasted like alfalfa. And *wet* was the best thing you could call the beer. When he had finished the smoke and the drink, he walked to the old woman's sales table and tossed down his half-empty pack of Chesterfields. "There you go, granny, upgrade your merchandise."

The old gal smiled for the first time, showing several missing front teeth. She shoved the Chesterfields into her dress pocket and said, "*Amerika gut!*"

Drake hiked to the river and strolled along the walkway he'd taken with Stetti the day they met. He was back to the *Hauptbahnhof* fifteen minutes before the prescribed 1700 meet-up time for returning to post.

On Sunday, 29 April, Drake packed some of his things. He tried to be excited about what lay in store, but his spirits were back in the dumps. Maybe what Stetti was trying to do with her picture had him buffaloed again. And all day a sound echoed in his head: That piercing click her door made when she pushed it closed, cutting him out of her life.

Monday Drake completed paperwork all morning. Rutledge told him to take the afternoon off. He went running, for almost three hours, farther than he'd ever gone. Outside the post, loping easily along roads through lush countryside, he felt unburdened, alive. Like he could have gone on running forever. But that evening, in the dark of the barracks, the emptiness returned.

First thing after morning mess on Tuesday, May First, Drake said goodbye to Pete Pietromonaco and a few other friends. He went outside his barracks to wait for his ride. Looking back at the building, it seemed strange that he'd never see it again. Strange but good—he was ready for a change. Five minutes later, Rutledge showed up in a spanking new jeep. Drake tossed his duffle bag onto the rear seat and climbed in next to the sergeant. "*Avanti!*" said Rutledge as he floored the gas pedal.

When they were halfway to Bonn, Rutledge said, "Next time you're in Cincy, hope you'll look me up." He slowed down and pushed a slip of paper into Drake's hand. It read, *Dick and Jeanette Rutledge. 340 Heartley Street, Cincinnati, Ohio. (Millvale area of town).*

"Like to, sarge." Drake stuffed the paper into his jacket pocket.

"Just so I'll know you made it home OK. Been through a lot together since last summer, you and me. Not like the fireworks in store for you, but plenty for a pair of pencil-pushers." Rutledge brushed the corner of his eye with his thumb. "Damn proud of you."

Drake looked off to the side. "Sure, I'll be fine." He shrugged. "Heck, Berlin's teetering on the brink. The war here's about over. Maybe Japan will quit too." He said it with a hopeful tone for Rutledge's sake. Inside he didn't want that to happen before he'd done his part.

"Ever heard of Okinawa?" Rutledge snorted. "Some pile of sand who knows where in the Pacific? Read about it in *Stars and Stripes*. We've been battering our heads on that brick wall for over a month now. Damn Japanese are hanging in there like it's downtown Tokyo. On their home islands, when it comes down to *their* families and *their* cities and *their* emperor, think they'll just throw in the towel?" He shook his head. "In a pig's eye. Yep, kid, you'll get your fool chance to be a hero."

127

Drake eyed the sergeant. "Hope so. Foolish or not, sarge, I've set my mind to it."

"Sure."

Nothing else was said until they pulled up in front of the *Hauptbahnhof.* Rutledge jumped out of the jeep and grabbed Drake's duffle.

"I can get it," Drake said.

"I know you can, but this once you're getting mollycoddled. Probably be one helluva long time before you get another NCO to play porter for you."

Inside the station there was a table set up under a sign that read, *In-Transit GIs Report Here.* "I'll take it from here, sarge," Drake said.

Rutledge set the bag down. He shook Drake's hand. "God speed, son," he said, his voice breaking.

"I'll be fine, sarge. I'll try to get to Cincinnati." Drake tapped the pocket with Rutledge's address in it. Hee picked up his bag and strode to the check-in desk without looking back.

As he waited in line behind two other GIs, Drake scanned the room. He spied the old lady with the mole selling whatever she had today. Three young children sat on a tattered blanket under her table. A couple of soldiers looked over her dingy wares.

When Drake stepped up to the desk, he handed the corporal a copy of his travel orders.

The NCO scanned his list and ticked Drake's name off. He checked his watch and scribbled the time and his initials on the orders, then he clipped them to his board. "Report to track number seven. That's *Geleise* seven. You're in car number niner zero six. Looking at a ten forty-five departure." He craned his neck to see around Drake. "Next!"

Drake walked by the old lady's table. She took out the pack of Chesterfields he had given her to show she still had them, again saying, "*Amerika gut!*"

He gave her a ten-Mark note and turned to go. Before he could leave, she insisted he take a pencil.

Drake went down the stairs labeled *Nach das Geleise 7*. There were dozens of GIs already waiting on the platform. An MP bellowed, "Wait in the area designated for your carriage, fellas. You'll find the car number written in chalk at your assigned spot."

Drake found 906 chalked on the platform floor. He set down his duffle bag and scanned the faces of the other GIs waiting there. No one looked familiar. He sat on his duffle and took out a new package of Chesterfields.

A tall, gangly private, who'd been doodling on a pad, sidled next to him. "Hey sport," he said, "can I bum a snipe?"

Drake opened the pack and shook out a cigarette for the guy and one for himself. He thumbed the striker of his Zippo and lit the man's smoke then his own.

"Thanks." The private stuck out his hand. "Name's Malarkey. Marv Malarkey. Out of Winslow, Arizona."

Drake shook the man's hand. "Pleased to meet you. I'm Winston Drake. Fellas call me Omaha...or just Drake."

"You're 906 too? Think that means we'll be in the same squad. Hey, come on over and meet the guys."

They sauntered to where three GIs sat. "Gents," Malarkey said, "meet our new squad mate. Calls himself Omaha."

"Or Drake. That's my last name."

A pipsqueak with curly red hair and freckles sat on the platform floor, hunched over a book. He looked up from the tattered tome, *The Cascades, Rocky Backbone of the Great Northwest*. Pushing his black, horn-rimmed glasses up, he gawked at Drake for a moment before scrambling to his feet and extending a hand. "'Lo, Omaha, I'm Arventnor Titus," he said in a rich baritone that seemed at odds with his spare frame. "Guys call me Arvee."

"Good to meet you," said Drake, shaking hands with Titus.

"Titus's gonna be our squad historian," Malarkey said, chuckling, "right, Arvee?"

"History's kind of my hobby," Arvee said. "And languages."

Malarkey pointed to another soldier, a beefy guy sitting on a green metal bench and reading a comic book. "That's Ralph

Davis." The man glanced up, scowling at the interruption. A toothpick dangled from his mouth, and the left side of his face jerked every few seconds with a nervous tic. "Goes by Blackie. He's from Hollywood, California." Malarkey cupped a hand next to his mouth and whispered to Drake loud enough for all to hear, "Word is, he's Bette Davis's kid brother. I'm working on him to have his sis line me up with Ginger Rogers. Plan to take her out dancing…teach the gal a step or two."

Davis glared. He took his toothpick out and pointed it at Malarkey. "Listen, Marvin, you don't quit jerking me around, I'll line you up all right…with my fist." The voice, formed deep in his barrel-like chest, rumbled like thunder. "Besides, I never even seen no movie stars," he snorted, "except in picture shows, like everyone else. So watch your step."

"Down boy," said Malarkey. "No need to go all Hindenburg on me, big fella. I was only kidding."

"Best not kid with me. It ain't healthy."

"OK, Blackie, OK," Malarkey muttered, stepping back. "Save it for the Japs." When Davis looked back at his comic, Marv stuck out his tongue then smirked. He nodded at the fellow dozing next to Davis on the bench. His arms crossed, he'd pulled his garrison cap down over his eyes. "On the left there, we got sleeping beauty, Will Tolliver. Claims to be from Mars."

Titus looked up. "Think it's *Le Mars*…Le Mars, Iowa. You know, the tall corn state?"

Malarkey shrugged. "That so? Guess I naturally figured the planet, green as Will's looking around the gills." He leaned toward Drake and whispered, "Think Private Tolliver might've had himself just little bit too much partying last night."

Drake sat on his duffle bag and finished his cigarette.

Five minutes later another GI sauntered up. "This the meet-up point for 906?" he asked.

Drake looked up. "Think so."

The face of the new GI's lit up. "Omaha! Well, I'll be damned." He took off his hat and moved closer to Drake. "'Member me? Dickie Henderson? From the poker game?"

Drake stared for a second. "Oh, sure. Motor pool mechanic, right? Ohio boy?"

"Yep," Henderson said. "Been trying to forget that card game. I lost a bundle."

Drake nodded. "Think Dutch pretty well cleaned all of us out."

Henderson made the rounds, introducing himself to the others as "Dickie Henderson, automotive mechanic *extraordinaire*." Just as he finished two more soldiers showed up.

The corporal of the new pair glanced at a clipboard of papers he carried. "906, right?"

"You got it, sport," Malarkey said.

The corporal scowled. He scanned the GIs. "Name's Barezzi, Franco Barezzi, your new assistant squad leader." Franco was a slight, olive-skinned guy with the curly black hair and a five o'clock shadow. "Fellas called me Breezy in my old outfit." He glared at Malarkey. "No one ever called me *sport*." Barezzi put a hand on his partner's shoulder. "This *hombre* here's Sandy Berger. From Miami…right, Sandy?" Berger nodded.

"Welcome, Breezy," Marv said. "Where you from?" He flashed Drake a peek at his pad, where he'd scrawled in pencil, *Lookee that kisser. Bet he's right off the boat from Sicily.*

"South Philly born and bred," said the corporal. "Got drafted out of barber college…but don't none of you go counting on free haircuts—" He scanned the group of GIs. "—though a couple of you could sure use one." He asked the men to introduce themselves, which they did. "Anyway, here's the story, fellas. We're due to spend tonight in Paris. Sandy here tells me he was stationed there for three months last autumn. Says he developed quite a taste for those French *mademoiselles*." He slapped Berger's back. "You're going to get us all fixed up with Parisian gals tonight, right Sandy?"

Berger grinned. "Sure…if I can round up that many blind ones on such short notice."

"I'll have you know," said Henderson, "After my weekend pass in France this spring, many a Frog dame were seen putting up

131

most-wanted posters with my kisser on 'em. They dubbed me *Monsieur Le Grand Dickie*." He arched his eyebrows.

"Yeah, right," Barezzi scoffed. "Enough bullshitting. I'm running the show till we get to Paris. We'll meet our squad leader there." He took a paper from his pocket and glanced at it. "That's Sergeant Holt." He eyed the men. "Hercules T. Holt, for what it's worth. Anyway, while I'm in charge, I don't want no trouble. Got it?"

Malarkey put his hands on his cheeks, tilted his head, and batted his eyes at the corporal. "You can count on us, Corporal Breezy, sir."

"Malarkey, I'm getting it loud and clear—if I ever want to start a circus, I'll know where to find a clown." Barezzi's face lit up. "Speaking of clowns, did you fellas hear the news? *Stars and Stripes* ran an extra today." He pulled a copy of the newspaper from his pack and displayed the front page. Black headlines roared, *HITLER DEAD*. "German radio's confirmed it, the article says. Shot himself in Berlin with the Russians beating down his door."

"Suicide?" Henderson hissed, shaking his head. "Lousy chicken shit!"

"One less blowhard in the world," Davis said.

"So, is the war here over?" Drake asked.

"Guess not," Barezzi said. "Least the Krauts are blustering that it ain't, but for how long?"

"Days...maybe weeks," Henderson said, shrugging. "They're screwed."

The men muttered and nodded in agreement.

"Maybe Japan'll follow suit," Titus wondered aloud. "Could be they'll cancel our transfers and send us home, huh?"

"Don't count on it," Drake said. "They're hanging tough on Okinawa. Least that's what I hear."

Breezy glared at Arvee. "Omaha's right—don't count on it, Titus. Or anything else. If the Army wants you wondering about stuff, they'll issue you a brain."

"So Corporal Barezzi," Drake asked, "what about the other guys in our squad?"

"We'll hook up with three others plus Holt in Paris," Barezzi said. "That'll give us our full complement of twelve. From then on, we train, eat, and sleep together. The idea's we become some kind of perfectly meshed fighting machine."

A shabby street urchin, six years old or so, came up to the group. He took a wrinkled apple from his grimy canvas bag. "Sir GI, have you hunger? You can buy with me this pretty apple. For being healthful."

Ralph Davis looked up from his comic book. "Scram!" he growled.

The boy looked bewildered.

"Thought I told you to beat it," Davis stood up.

"Go easy on the squirt, Blackie," Henderson said. "He's just trying to earn a few pfennigs."

Davis glared at Henderson. "Mind your own business." He looked back at the urchin and grinned. "Anyhow, me and the little shit are just having some fun." He took the *Stars and Stripes* newspaper from on top of Breezy's rucksack. He held the front page for the child to see. "I'll buy your apple if you can just answer a couple of questions, Fritzy. Whose picture is this?" he said, pointing to the photo of Hitler.

The child cowered before the six foot, five inch GI.

"Come on, kiddo," Davis said, jabbing the picture with his finger, "who's this, eh? *Who?*"

The urchin, fighting back tears, said, *"Der Führer."*

"Very good," said Davis, nodding. *"Sehr gut."* The child relaxed. Davis pointed to the screaming headline, *HITLER DEAD.* "Can you read this?"

"Hitler," the child said, then he shrugged. *"Ich weiß nicht."*

"Dead? You don't know what dead means?" He looked around at the other GIs, shaking his head. "Stupid little turd can't even read."

"Aw, get off his back, Davis," Drake said. "Can't you see he's scared?"

"Bastards liked kicking ass in Poland," Davis sneered. "And France. Not so crazy about somebody pushing back."

Will Tolliver lifted the cap that had covered his eyes while he dozed. "That's right, Drake, butt out. Can't believe you'd go taking some Kraut's side over your buddy's."

Drake ignored Tolliver. He scrambled to his feet and took a step toward Davis, his fists clenched. "He's just a kid. *Leave him alone.*" Drake was dwarfed by the two hundred forty pound giant, but he kept his glare trained on Davis as he stepped in front of the child.

Davis froze, the twitch on his face going into overdrive.

Barezzi jumped up. He pushed Drake back and stood eyeball-to-chin with Davis. "Goddammit, I warned you guys about giving me trouble. Davis, sit your fat ass down and don't let me hear another peep out of you." He turned to Drake. "You too, Private." He looked at the wide-eyed urchin. "Take a hike, sonny."

The child stood there, looking confused. Drake put a hand on his shoulder. He reached into his pocket and pulled out a handful of coins and bills, all the German money he had left. He pushed the cash into the boy's hands. "For you," he said. "*Gut gluck!* Or however it is you wish a fella well."

The boy eyed the money for a moment then stuffed it into his pocket. He presented the apple to Drake. Standing ramrod straight, he held out his hand and shook Drake's with the formality of a banker sealing a financial transaction. Then he dashed away, a child again.

Drake watched him go then sat on his sack. The air was still thick with tension.

Five minutes later a gray steam locomotive rounded the bend and pulled slowly into the station. The clanging of its bell echoed through the building and pulled the eyes of every GI to it. A pair of American flags decorated the cow catcher. Sooty black smoke and sparks boiled out of the stack and blasts of white steam shot from the driver cylinders. The screech of brakes and the smell of hot metal filled the air as the train crawled by.

The engineer and fireman in the passing locomotive were GIs in uniform and there was a white-helmeted MP riding shotgun on the engine steps. Behind the coal car were a dozen passenger carriages each with a *Deutsche Bahn* plaque centered on the side. Some cars were empty and some were packed with GIs. In the widows were brown paper sheets with three digit numbers brushed on in black paint.

The train shook to a stop. In one of the rear windows of the car that halted in front of Drake and his fellows was a sign reading *906*. A muscular MP stepped off the train and hollered, "Group 906, board up here. Grab your gear and have a copy of your travel orders out. Step lively now." He checked names off of a list on a clipboard he held. "Rear four rows of seats in this car, gentlemen." Barezzi was last in line. The MP eyed him sternly. "Corporal, according to the roster, you're in charge. I want these men in their seats unless they gotta go to the can. Understood?" Barezzi nodded. "Then mount up and we'll get this show on the road." The MP stepped onto the platform and signaled that his charges were aboard with a roundhouse wave of his clipboard. He jumped onto the railcar steps as the train eased from its stop.

When the train had cleared the station yard, the MP called Barezzi to the front of the car to finish up paperwork. With the corporal out of earshot, Davis turned around and glared at Drake, sitting in the back row. "Don't think it's over, four-eyes," he snarled.

Arvee Titus sat next to Drake. "They used to call me four-eyes, too," he said softly, then sighed. "Wish I had the guts to face up to guys like Davis the way you did, Omaha. Ever read Shakespeare's play about King Henry V?"

Drake shrugged.

Arvee hoisted an imaginary sword into the air. "*Once more unto the breach, dear friends, once more.*" He sheepishly lowered his arm. "That Henry, now there's a real hero." He pushed his glasses up and leaned toward Drake. "Scared Blackie will jump you when he gets the chance?"

"Davis? Naw." Drake sniffed. "Standing there, I saw that twitch of his. 'Bout jumped right off his face. Probably not used to having his bluff called."

"They say that about bullies. All the same, I thought it was swell, what you did."

Drake nodded. He closed his eyes, crossed his arms, and slipped down in his seat. Rocked by the swaying of the train, he was asleep in two minutes.

Camp Clay Door

The troop train slow as it approached Paris. With their first glimpse of the capital's eastern suburbs, the GIs aboard, most of whom had dozed through the rest of the trip, suddenly got rowdy. They whistled and hooted at every mademoiselle who happened to be out walking. That stopped when an MP swaggered down the aisle, slapping his night stick on his palm. It resumed when he went on to the next car.

Once inside the city, Cpl. Barezzi stood and hollered, "Quiet down, you knuckleheads!" He shuffled through papers on a clipboard. "About tonight, gentlemen…here's the story. We'll be billeted at some hotel called *Le Cle d'Ore*. Sounds swanky, eh? It's a mile or so from the Gar de l'Est, where we arrive. We'll go together to the hotel, get squared away as far as bunking, and have chow." Barezzi glanced at his watch. "It's now one nine four zero hours. By the time we get all that done, I expect it'll be after twenty-one hundred hours. Says here curfew is twenty-two hundred hours. I s'pose you'll want to go out for a drink or something, so you can brag to the folks back home about painting Gay Paree red. If so, make it snappy. Don't want to piss-off our new squad leader."

As they slowed for Gar de l'Est station, Drake stared out the window, transfixed—the setting sun had painted the buildings of the 10th arrondissement and the city stretching beyond in magical, golden light. Moments later the train snorted to a stop in the gargantuan arrival hall. Drake and the other GIs poured out of the cars onto the platform under the glowing, arched glass ceiling. The mob scattered flocks of the pigeons that had been pecking crumbs from the bricked platform floor.

Barezzi grouped the men of the squad, checked names, and marched them to the end of the platform where a burly MP waited, his shoulders back and arms crossed like he was the king of France. Barezzi walked up to him and said, "My squad's billeted tonight in the Hotel—" He glanced at his paperwork. "—*Le Cle d'Ore*. Know where it is?"

Without breaking his pose, the MP snorted, "Out the main exit and right on Boulevard Magenta. Straight through Place

République to Boulevard Voltaire for a half a kilometer. It'll be on the right."

Ten minutes later, Drake and the other men arrived at the foot of the stone steps under the hotel's marquee. A staff sergeant sat at a desk that had been set up outside for GI check-in. Barezzi presented the group's paperwork.

The NCO glanced at the documents then scanned the GIs with a scowl. He looked over his shoulder and called, "Sgt. Holt!"

A man stepped from the shadows at the side of the hotel door. He was built like a fire plug. His shaved head shined under the lights of marquee. A pair of bushy eyebrows completed the circus strongman image. He stopped at the top step, above the men, and slipped on his garrison cap. He eyed his squad for a moment. "Gentlemen," he drawled, "welcome to Sixth Army." He thrust his hands on his hips. "My name's Holt. H, O, L, T. On Guadalcanal, one of my privates had the balls to call me—right to my face—the meanest son of a bitch in the United States Army. And the ugliest." Holt grinned broadly. "I said, 'Can't take any credit for ugliest cuz that's God-given, but meanest I've worked hard at. So thanks for the compliment, Private. And consider yourself lucky.' Well, I let him stand there with his mouth open like a carp, then I explained, 'You're still alive, aren't you? Unlike those Japanese corpses piled outside our perimeter. That's my doing." Holt spat on the hotel steps. "Don't doubt it boys—when we hit that beach, it'll be this mean, ugly son of a bitch keeping you alive." He plucked a partially-smoked cigar from his breast pocket, struck a large wooden match with a flick of his thumbnail, and lit the stogie. "But enough war stories. Let's get you men settled and fed."

Holt snapped his fingers and the French doorman opened the brass door to the hotel lobby. "Avanti!" he barked and led the men inside. Drake smiled. He wondered if the Army made every sergeant take *Intro to Italian*.

The squad streamed by the reception desk, eyed by the snooty clerk smoking his cigarette through an ivory holder and the bored-looking, blue-uniformed bellboy sitting on a stool. They passed the door to the dining room and the icy glare of the tuxedoed maitre-d'. Went down a long hallway, past the kitchen and finally out the door into the hotel garden. Holt opened a black wrought-iron gate, and they walked across an alleyway to a grassy lot with twenty large tents. Someone had nailed a broken board to a tree and painted on it in sloppy black letters *Welcome to Camp Clay Door*.

"We're bunking in tent number seven, over there." Holt pointed down a row of tents to the right. "Park your gear and grab yourself some ham and lima beans at tent eleven down there—" He waved to the left. "—where all the smoke's coming from." He glanced at his watch. "You got fifteen minutes to be done eating and back to our quarters for a squad meeting."

Drake and the men took off running to stash their duffles and have a quick bite.

A quarter hour later they came back from chow, picking stringy ham from their teeth. Barezzi was waiting in front of their tent. "Line up, men, on the double now. Come on, dress down. Snap to it." As the last GI moved into position, he barked, "Atten-**hut**!" Each man froze. "The squad is dressed and ready, Sergeant Holt."

Holt strode out of the tent and stood in front of the rank. He clasped his hands behind his back and surveyed the men. "At ease, gentlemen. Now that you're squared away, I was thinking—" He thrust his ample nose skyward and inhaled like the air was laced with perfume and possibilities. "—we got us this little stop in Paris. Be a shame not to have a night on the town. Who's up for joining me?"

Drake noticed a devilish twinkle in the corner of Holt's eye. He squinted, trying to read more from the sergeant's face.

The other men glanced at each other, surprise and glee on their faces. "Sure thing!" "Count me in." "You bet." They chorused.

"All right then," Holt said, "hope you didn't eat too many mess hall limas." His hands curled into fists. "'Ten-**HUT**." He fired the order like a cannon blast. "Rrright **FACE**." Holt moved next to Drake, the first man in the file. "Hawk the back of the file,

Barezzi," he hollered. "Nobody lollygags in my outfit." He glanced back to make sure the men looked sharp. "Forward **MARCH**." After ten steps, he boomed, "Double time…**MARCH**." The squad broke into a trot.

"Mind your step," Holt boomed as he turned the unit right at the dim alleyway then left onto Boulevard Voltaire, heading back toward Gar de l'Est. The street was inky dark except for puddles of yellow light cast down from street lamps. "Pick up the cadence," he hollered, "left, left, left-right-left." He eyed Drake. "What's your name, Private."

"Winston Drake, Sergeant."

Holt nodded. "Looking OK there, Drake. Just keep up the pace. No stopping. Except at intersections. Then you march in place till I give the word to move out. Got it?"

"Yes, Sergeant."

"Good." Holt peeled back and ran effortlessly alongside the file. "You men look like crap." He pointed at Tolliver. "What's your name, GI?"

"Tolliver, Sergeant."

Holt scowled. "Well, get your lard ass moving, Tolliver. Is this the first time in your life you've ever run? Pick up the goddamn cadence! Left, left, left-right-left." He eyed the file of men, most of whom were already gasping for breath. "Holy shit, this is the infantry, ladies, not some country club."

As they approached a busy intersection, Holt halted his troop with, "Mark time…**March**!" and raced ahead to flag the cross traffic. When he had the automobiles stopped, he hollered, "Double time…**MARCH**." Jogging in place, watching his squad trot by, he muttered, "Criminetly! If Hitler looked up from hell and saw you clowns, he'd say, 'I got beat by this freak show?' and shoot himself again."

A half block farther, Davis staggered out of the file, dropped to his knees and threw up in the gutter. Holt stopped the squad and stood over Davis, shouting, "Taking a little rest are we, Private?" Holt grabbed the big man's collar and jerked him to his feet. "If I want you barfing out your guts, I'll goddamn tell you. Now get your ass back in formation."

Watching his troop lurch along, Holt got more exasperated by the minute. "Maybe some jody will shape you knuckleheads up. I'll give the call, you echo the response. Remember, first beat's on the strike of the left foot. And make it **loud**!"

"Sergeant tells me here in France"

          "Sergeant tells me here in France"

"Girls don't wear no underpants"

          "Girls don't wear no underpants"

"I don't know but I've been told"

          "I don't know but I've been told"

"What they got is good as gold"

          "What they got is good as gold"

"Sound off"

          "1, 2"

"Sound again"

          "3, 4"

"Break it on down now"

          "1, 2, 3, 4, 1, 2...3, 4"

The squad trotted along the walkways through Place de la République for another half hour. Four more of the men threw up. At last Holt headed the squad back to Camp Clay Door. He halted them in front of tent seven at 2229 hours and checked his watch. "You're twenty-nine goddamn minutes past curfew." He shook his head. "What the hell did I do to get stuck with this ragtag bunch? Well, kindergarten's over, that's for sure. I'm rolling you out at zero five hundred hours, and we'll go out on the town again. Till then, pleasant dreams, ladies. **Dismissed!**"

The men were in their sleeping bags two minutes later. In the dark of the tent, Marv Malarkey uttered the last words spoken that night. "That private of Holt's on Guadalcanal, the one who called him the meanest son of a bitch in the United States Army—he sure had that right." After that, the only sounds were deep, slow breathing and snores.

Do Your Duty, Then Pick Apples

2 May, 1945

When the men stumbled into ranks at 0500, they were joined by three new squad members who had arrived after midnight. The morning run was about the same length and pace as the previous one, but it seemed considerably easier without a bellyful of lima beans and ham.

The squad was back at Camp Clay Door about 0600. Holt gave them twenty minutes to shave and pack up their gear. Then came breakfast—fried Spam, cream of wheat, canned peaches, and coffee. Pretty damned good. At 0730 they were ready for bus transport to the port city of Le Havre. They sprawled on the grass in front of tent seven, most of them snoozing, until 1020 when three buses arrived to take them and nine other squads to Normandy.

Drake's seat on the bus was next to one of the new arrivals, a lanky corporal. "Name's Drake," he said. "I go by that or my nickname, Omaha—it's where I'm from."

"I'm Zimmerman." The corporal shook Drake's hand. "Grew up on an apple farm in eastern Washington. Folks call me Zip."

"Zip Zimmerman, eh? Sounds like the star of some Republic Pictures serial you'd see in a Saturday matinee. Like Crash Corrigan."

"Dad called me Zip cuz I could shinny up an apple tree faster than any other kid in the county." He shrugged. "Since the war started, I've been glad for the nickname. My given name's Adolf."

"They named you Adolf? Ouch." Drake got out his pack of Chesterfields. He shook one out and offered it to Zimmerman. "How about a nail?"

Zip waved off the cigarette. "When I was born, Hitler wasn't a household word yet."

"Guess not." Drake lit himself a smoke. "Could've been worse...like Tojo." He exhaled a stream of smoke. "Anyhow, folks shouldn't hold a fella's name against him."

"*Shouldn't*...like my old lady says, that and a dime'll get you coffee and a sinker." Zip loosened his tie. "So Omaha, how'd you let 'em Shanghai you into this Japanese business when you'd already done your part over here?"

Drake sighed. "That's just it, I never did my part. Up till now I just sat behind a desk. So I volunteered for infantry duty in the Pacific. Guys called it crazy, but I just wanted to do something important…make a difference. You know?"

"Not really. Might've been better off listening to your pals."

"I take it you didn't volunteer, huh?"

Zip crossed his arms and looked out the window. "Yeah, I volunteered. Dunno why. Buddies said I'd already done my part. Landing on Omaha Beach on D-Day. Slugging it out all the way to Germany." He faced Drake, pointed his index finger at his temple, and moved it in circles. "Guess I'm fucking loony. When the fighting died down in March, I'd be in the dumps one minute and giddy as a schoolgirl the next. Then just numb a bit later." Zip shivered. "Talk about nuts, I hate combat, but I can't stand being away from it. It's like if I ain't on the line, I ain't alive." He peered blankly into Drake's eyes.

A minute later the men were quiet and remained so as the bus barreled down a highway tracking the northeastern edge of the Seine valley. When they skirted the city of Rouen, Drake pulled out a map he'd brought. "We should be well over halfway to Le Havre now." He glanced at his watch. "Puts us in there about fifteen hundred hours."

Zip silently kept his gaze trained outside, at the river and the countryside beyond.

Drake cleared his throat. "Down there's where all the June fighting was, right? Can't believe it was less than a year ago." Zimmerman said nothing. Drake looked close and saw, reflected in the glass, tears welling in the man's eyes. "Must be hard, seeing it again, huh?"

Zimmerman nodded without turning away from the window.

After a while, Drake said, "I came in on D plus eighteen. Things were quiet on the beachhead by then."

Zip inhaled deeply. He brushed away the tears with the back of his hand, then faced ahead. 'My outfit was F Company, 116th

Regiment, 29th Infantry Division. We came in at dawn. Hit Dog Red on Omaha Beach. Hell's Beach, we called it. So many buddies…"

Drake gazed at Zip like he was his favorite ballplayer, Pee Wee Reese. "You guys were heroes."

Zip chuckled. "Where I grew up, a hero's a fucking sandwich. That's about it."

"Now we're playing word games, eh?" Drake sighed. "Seriously, being a hero's something no one can take away from you. Long as I can remember, all I've wanted is to be what you already are. I envy you, man."

Zimmerman squinted back, like Drake had spoken in Chinese. "You don't know what…" He bit his lip and turned back to the window. "A hero ain't what I feel like. More like a bastard who lived while buddies like Henson and Withers died back on the beach. Spent weeks after the landing stewing on what I could've done different."

"Look, you did more than anyone could ask. All you brave fellas did."

Zimmerman smiled bitterly. "Yeah, sure."

Drake took out a pack of Juicy Fruit gum. He gave Zip a stick and took one for himself. "Don't make sense, The brass sending you to the Far East."

Zip's face was red. "Didn't you hear me? I fucking demanded it!" Through clenched teeth he growled, "Doncha see?" His eyes were wide, darting. "How goddamn batty I am." He shook his head. "I go through hell. Somehow come out in one piece…well, everything but my brain. And what do I do? Push to the head of the line and stick my fucking hand up when they ask who wants to go again." He laughed so loud men sitting ahead turned back to gawk.

In the ensuing silence, Drake closed his eyes. Was he a chump to be so fixated on doing something big, being a hero? And if he ever did succeed, would he discover like Zip had that it's never enough? That every glass is half empty? Drake inhaled deeply. It won't be that way for me, he thought. He was born a glass-half-full guy. Heck, a glass brimming full guy!

Zip was still peering out the window. At a vast, leafy, green orchard. Drake took his slouch as a reflection of a soul still lying wounded on some spiritual beach.

Drake couldn't leave the man bleeding there. But how to help? "Listen, Zip…" He didn't know what to say next but charged ahead anyway, "You lost some brothers on Omaha Beach. Could be why you volunteered—to get another chance to save a buddy. Nothing crazy about that. Maybe you'll get that chance, maybe you won't. But as a soldier, what you'll sure get is a chance to do your duty. Do your duty, Zip, and you'll go home, a soul at peace. Then spend the rest of your days picking apples." Drake glanced at the sea of fruit trees outside. "Maybe that's all any of us can hope for—to go home and pick our goddamn apples knowing we did our duty."

Zimmerman's jaw clenched and his hands curled into fists so tight his shoulders shook.

Drake's stomach sank. He was preparing to jump to the safety of the aisle, when Zip calmed, took a deep breath, and snorted, "What a crock of shit!" Then he broke out laughing.

After a moment, Drake was laughing too.

The three buses from Camp Clay Door pulled into the military compound of Le Havre's waterfront at 1440 hours. Through the window, Drake could see a couple dozen busloads of GIs already lined up outside six huge olive-drab tents.

After the bus parked at the end of a long row of vehicles, a sergeant and a corporal came aboard. "Welcome to your disembarkation facility, men," the sergeant said. "The staff are here to get you safely and efficiently aboard your vessel, but we need your cooperation to do that." He previewed each of the processing stations the men would pass through. "As you exit the bus, pick up a copy of form DA-254 and a pencil from Corporal Johnson here. Fill it out while you're waiting in line. All right, gentlemen, move out!"

Drake and the others stepped off the bus into the stream of men heading for the line outside of the tent marked *Station A*. Inside, they showed their Form 64-5 Identity Cards, turned in copies of their orders, and picked up more paperwork to complete.

They left the tent, following signs to the medical station, and caught their first glimpse of the only big ship in the harbor. It had two black smokestacks and its hull was painted in maritime camouflage to look like the surface of a white-capped ocean. There was a sailor in blue dungarees and a chambray shirt mowing grass nearby. "Hey sport, is that our boat?" Malarkey asked him.

The Navy man stopped and leaned on his mower. He pulled out a handkerchief, took off his white sailor hat, and wiped his buzz-cut head. "Yep. She's USS *Queen Beatrix*." He put his cap back on. "And she don't like being called a boat, Private. She's a ship."

"Oh yeah? There's a difference?"

"A ship can carry a boat, but a boat can't carry a ship. Better get that straight because our captain, the Dutchman, will be pissed if he hears you call his vessel a boat. Probably make you walk the plank." The sailor stuffed his handkerchief back in his pocket and resumed his mowing.

Inside the medical tent, a stout sergeant who'd lost one arm at the elbow told Drake and the others, "Strip down to your undershorts, men. Grab one of those cartons—" He pointed to stacks of cardboard boxes. "—for your duds, then get in any of the exam lines."

When Drake got to the front of the line, an Army nurse in a starched white dress looked over his paperwork asked a dozen questions from a checklist. She sent him ahead to an Army doctor in a white smock who listened to his heart, checked him for hernia and hemorrhoids, and examined his spine, knees and feet. Next there was a vision test given by a pretty, brunette nurse. Finally a burley nurse named Lt. Armburster gave him a shot in the right arm, two in the left and two in the rump. She also gave him a brown bottle of anti-malarial pills to "take daily on the boat." When he corrected her, "technically, it's a ship," she frowned and hollered, "Next." Drake was glad she'd already given him his injections.

Drake dressed, dropped off his documents at Station C, and got his hand stamped red. He ate in the mess tent—corned beef, boiled potatoes, boiled cabbage, with a bottle of Belgian Jupiler beer. Carrot cake for dessert. Best Army food he'd had since Thanksgiving.

In the tent marked *Station E*, Drake was issued new boots, a helmet, and a duffle bag with wool socks, tee-shirts, tropical weight infantry fatigues, a field jacket, a pulp novel, and a blanket. It was 1710 when he exited and found Sgt. Holt and most of the rest of the squad.

Good Old Trixie

When Drake arrived at the squad meeting point, all the men but Blackie Davis were already there. Titus's nose was stuck in a book and Holt was showing a couple of the GIs how to sharpen a bayonet.

Drake sat at the edge of the group with the two privates he hadn't already met. "Howdy, gents. I'm Winston Drake. I go by Drake. Or my nickname, Omaha." The GIs shook hands.

Beauregard Forgette was a tall, Tums-popping chain-smoker from Texas. He had a small, flat nose, turned up at the tip. Bo announced in a honeyed, nasal drawl, almost a purr, "I grew up punching cattle on my daddy's ranch outside Abilene." He lit a Camel cigarette. "Till last week, I been a driver with Third Army. Stationed in itty-bitty Luxembourg. Whole country's about half the size of our place back home."

Ralston Van Fleet had blacksmith's hands and thick lips that smacked when he spoke. "Call me Rollie. Taught high school shop class and coached hockey in Buffalo. Transferred from Seventh Army, stationed outside Mannheim."

Forgette quickly steered the conversation to the subject of women. "Hey, how about that eye-test lieutenant? Man, what I'd give to get me some of that."

Holt burst out laughing. "Yeah, Forgette, like that's going to happen."

Malarkey pointed at Bo and snickered. "With that puss, you'd be lucky to get a second look from any dame, even that shot nurse…Armburster. Wasn't she something? Arms like Popeye and a face that's probably sunk a sight more ships than it's launched."

Forgette shook his head. "Jeeze man, we're about to set sail and you're making jokes about ships sinking? What's the matter with you?" He flicked ashes from his Camel. "As for me and women, I'll have you know ol' Bo Forgette don't do too bad. Till last week, I been seeing this little yella-haired Luxembourg lady called Arlette. Hated to dump her—she's a horny little filly. And plain beautiful." He took deep drag and spat out a shred of tobacco.

Arvee looked up from his book. "Couldn't help overhearing, Bo. Plain beautiful's an oxymoron." The comment drew blank stares from the men around him. "A contradiction in terms." He shrugged. "Just saying."

Forgette glared at Titus. "You're an oxymoron, fella." He blew a smoke ring at Arvee. "Anyhow, back to Arlette…gal turned all sappy on me, talking about getting hitched and stuff. Reckon this ol' Texas boy ain't ready to settle down. Not yet, at least— shit, I just made twenty-one in April." He peered at *Beatrix* in the harbor. "Hope that bucket's watertight." He shivered and slapped his rear end. "This ass of mine don't cotton to water deeper than a bathtub." When the men around him chuckled, Bo said sternly, "I'm fucking serious, boys."

Van Fleet unwrapped a stick of Beechnut Spearmint gum and pushed it into his mouth. "Dames," he said, crossing his arms. "The ones over here don't interest me."

Glaring, Forgette leaned away. "Ain't a pansy are you?"

"Hell no." Van Fleet jumped to his feet. "Got a wife, my gal June, back in Buffalo. For crying out loud, we got a kid and everything. 'Course I ain't no pansy!"

"Just asking." Forgette snuffed his cigarette in the dirt. "Said you didn't like dames."

"Go sit on a tack, Beauregard. I said I wasn't interested in the dames *over here*." He pulled out a snapshot of his wife and showed it to Drake and Bo. "Who would be when he's got *this* waiting for him back home?"

"June looks swell, Rollie," Drake said. "So what's the story with you? Did ya volunteer for this Sixth Army gig?"

"Volunteer? Kind of. I trained as a vehicle mechanic, but I hated the job. That goddamn grease!" Van Fleet studied his fingernails and scowled. "After a while you taste the stuff in your chow." He shuddered. "Anyway, I still got eighteen months on my enlistment, and they told me the only way to get out of the motor pool was to sign up for infantry. Sixth Army was looking for infantrymen, so…."

Drake lit a Chesterfield. "I was pushing paper in First Army headquarters battalion. With the fighting in Europe winding down,

I volunteered for Pacific Theater infantry duty. Just wanted to do something in the real war before it goes up in smoke."

"You don't look the type," Forgette drawled. He took two Tums from his pack and tossed them into his mouth, then pointed at Drake. "Them glasses." He snickered. "Look like you'd work in a library, alphabetizing books or something. No offense, it's just the specs. And your face."

Drake shrugged. "Not every guy's got a kisser like Bogey. Anyway, how *does* a hero look? Take General Bradley. Nobody's done more to win the war, so he's a hero. But that face of his! He's the one looks like he ought to be shelving library books."

Forgette guffawed "A general working in a library, that'd be a sight. Being fresh outta Third Army, I'm picturing our old man, Blood and Guts Patton, pushing a cart of books. He'd be all spitting and hollering and cussing at those books till they jumped themselves back in place on the shelf."

"So we got a confirmed bachelor—" Rollie pointed to Bo. "—here, and me, happy as a clam being married to my little June Bug. You're the umpire, Omaha. Who's got it right?"

Drake laughed. "I'm probably not the best one to ask." He sighed. "Back in Bonn, I was sweet on a *Fräulein*. That girl was lightning in a bottle! Beautiful, smart...played the cello. Guess I fell pretty hard for her. But she was what you'd call an enigma."

"Enigma?" Forgette said. "I'm not for sure, but that means she's a mite frosty, don't it? Back home we called that kind an ice princess."

"No, enigma means you can't figure them out." Drake inhaled deeply like the air held Stetti's essence. "Believe me, this girl could turn ice to steam. But, doggone it, I never knew if she cared for me or was just using me."

"Are you plumb loco?" Forgette popped another Tums. "Lemme get this straight—you're all worried that a hotsy-totsy gal might be *using you* for a good time in the bunk?" He shook his head and chewed the antacid. "Must be a million GIs around here that'd love to have that problem."

"Good gravy, Bo, give him a break," Van Fleet said. "Omaha's a square guy. Not everybody's got a one track mind."

"It's OK, Rollie," Drake said, "Think I gave Bo the wrong idea. Yeah, she was exciting all right and I loved that…but the next minute she'd treat me like a cigarette butt smoked down to the stub. I would have been OK just helping her out—poor kid and her family had nothing—but she made even that hard." He nodded. "Yep, my Stetti was an enigma with a capital E."

"That's some contradiction," said Titus, eavesdropping again, "an enigma named Steady."

"No, Arvee, it's Stetti. S, T, E, double T, I. That's her name."

"Weird-ass name for a weird-ass woman." Forgette shook his head as he took the last cigarette from his pack of Camels. He crumpled the wrapper and tossed it away, then he lit the smoke with a green-painted Zippo. "Here's what I say, pardner: That broad's bad medicine. Thank the Lord you're free of her. I was you, I'd never give 'er another thought."

Drake shrugged. "Easy for you to say…you're not the one crazy about her."

"I'll butt out then." Forgette leaned back on his gear and took a deep drag on his Camel. "As my daddy used to say, 'A dog do what a dog's gotta do.'"

When Davis walked up, Holt jumped to his feet. "That's everybody. Raise your mitts, men, so I can see your stamps." The GIs did. "Everybody got your new gear and copies of your orders?"

Arvee waved his hand. "Excuse me, Sergeant. What about the stuff we brought with us on the bus?"

"Don't you worry your little mind, Titus. It's been picked up and loaded by Navy roustabouts. You'll collect it on board. OK, shall we go meet *Queen Beatrix*? Fall In! Dress right **DRESS**!" Holt eyed the rank. "Rrright **FACE**. Look sharp, ladies. We're gonna show the goddamn Navy what real class looks like. Cover down. Forward **MARCH**."

152

The squad marched to the back of a long line of GIs waiting to board the ship. When they got to the front, each man produced a copy of his orders and tromped up the swinging gangway.

Aboard the vessel Holt conferred with an enlisted sailor, then said, "Men, we're bunking in D Bay. Coxswain Murphy here's going to lead the way down there and get you situated. Before we sail tonight, the ship's captain wants to have a word with you. Give you the rules of the road, so to speak." He turned to Murphy. "Please proceed, coxswain."

Murphy took the squad through a labyrinth of corridors into the bowels of the ship to D Bay. It was a huge compartment filled with canvas hammocks, four to a stack. There were fifty stacks, accommodating two-hundred men. *Queen Beatrix* had six of these troop-sleeping bays, labeled A through F.

Half of Murphy's orientation concerned use of the latrine, or head as he called it. It consisted of a long, sheet metal-lined trench, six inches wide. Sea water was pumped into one end so there was a constant flow through the trench. This flow flushed waste away, into a holding tank when in port and out the side of the ship when at sea. There were sitting boards at the top of the trench, running along its length. According to Murphy, using the latrine when the seas were rough was "an experience you'll tell your grandkids about, after you've had a few highballs."

Murphy demonstrated how to line a sleeping hammock with the muslin, button-on sheet sleeper lying starched and folded atop each man's bunk. He also showed the men how to open the bay's ventilation ports. Since the vent levers were located high on the wall, a six foot wooden pole with a brass hook on one end was used to pull them open. Murphy called the tool "a Goebbels Stick because, like old Joe, it puts out a lot of hot air."

After the orientation, Drake and the others stashed their gear in wooden lockers lined up at the foot of their stacked hammocks. Then they dashed back up to the deck and assembled for the skipper's chinwag.

With his full head of snow-white hair and a jaw like an icebreaker's prow, U. S. Navy Captain Percival Hooft cut a commanding figure on *Queen Beatrix's* deck. He held a large blue megaphone at his side and scanned the assembly, until the last of the one thousand and fifty-seven GIs and one hundred three sailors of the crew was in formation. Then he nodded to his top enlisted man, CPO Burke, who boomed, "**Attention**."

Hooft stepped forward and raised the megaphone to his mouth. "At ease. On behalf of my crew, I wish to welcome you fighting men of Sixth Army aboard USS *Queen Beatrix*. She's a fine ship with a proud history of service in the Dutch merchant fleet." He put his hand on his hip and inhaled deeply. "Take a good whiff of that, men. Nothing in the world like salt air. Within the hour we'll be underway, setting out on our voyage of over twelve thousand nautical miles to the Philippines. Our planned sailing time is 24 days, give or take depending on weather." The captain looked up as three P-51 Mustang fighters roared overhead. "That's the 332nd Fighter Group, the Tuskegee Red Tails, going out to spot Germans." He watched for a moment as they streaked west. "Now where was I? Oh yes, our route. We'll pass from the Mediterranean to the Red Sea through the Suez Canal. In the galley, CPO Burke has posted a map with our course indicated for the geographers among you. You'll find your sea time will go quickly, men, as it'll be full of training and conditioning. Good stuff! Questions?"

Dickie Henderson's hand shot up. "Sir, should we be worried about U-boats?"

"Excellent question, Private. Here's what I know. Hitler is dead. Today, German forces in Berlin and in Italy surrendered. Though there is yet no formal cessation of hostilities, clearly the end of the Nazi Reich is nigh. As of this moment, we don't know the combatant status of the U-boat fleet, so we'll assume it's still hostile. That said, over the last year we've beat the tar out of the German sub fleet." Hooft shifted the bullhorn into his other hand. "When underway, I'll keep the throttle on Full Ahead. Good old speed, a transport's best defense—you can't kill what you can't catch." He puffed out his chest. "Well, *speed's* pretty near my middle name. Around the Fleet, I'm known as The Flying Dutchman. Throw in naval intel, communications discipline, and dogged surveillance, and you've made a sub crew's prospects dim." He crossed his arms. "Yes, I fully expect to get you fine fellows to the Philippines with dry feet. If there are no further questions, you are dismissed."

An hour after sunset, Drake was on deck when he heard the pitch of the ship's engines increase from a rumble to a growl. He felt a tingling in the soles of his feet from the motor's vibration and looked back to watch the pier slip away. A quarter mile out, black smoke and sparks shot from *Beatrix's* smokestacks, and the grumble of her engines was deafening. Leaning on a railing near the bow, a cool evening breeze caressing his cheek, Drake counted the buoys marking the channel. He lit a cigarette and let his thoughts drift, aimless as a bottle bobbing on the waves.

Arvee Titus walked up. He sucked pensively on a briar pipe packed with Prince Albert tobacco. The sweet aroma sent Drake's thoughts to his father, another Prince Albert man. He closed his eyes and smiled.

"Good old Trixie," Titus said, "that's what Holt calls the ship." He stomped his foot on the hardwood deck boards. "She seems solid to me. Don't you think?"

"Sure. But that won't stop Bo worrying." Drake took a deep last drag and flicked his cigarette butt overboard. "I'm surprised how loud she is."

With black smoke still billowing from her stacks, Trixie cleared the harbor and surged forward in the westerly heading that would take her past Cherbourg then out of the English Channel into the Atlantic.

Holt roused the squad at 0500 hours. He formed them up on the main deck. Seas were rough and spray came over the bow, coating Drake's eyeglass lenses.

"Gentlemen," Holt boomed, "Cox Murphy tells me Good Old Trixie's bow-to-stern length is 422 feet. I'm figuring seven trips around her perimeter is a mile. If we want to get in a four mile run before breakfast, we better get a move on. 'Ten-**HUT**." He eyed the rank and scowled. "Rrright **FACE**."

Holt moved to the center of the file. "Fair warning: I push stragglers overboard. Got it? Look sharp now....Forward **MARCH**." After ten steps, he barked, "Double time...**MARCH**." The men broke into a trot.

By the time the squad had done the first half of their 28 laps, all the men were gasping except Drake and Holt. The sergeant ran alongside Drake. "When I first saw you, Omaha, I thought, there's a damn sissy. But I was wrong. You an athlete or something?"

"Always try to stay in shape. Used to swim—I lifeguarded all through high school. In Germany I took up running on my own. Good for blowing off steam."

"Peel off to the back of the file. Anyone starts lagging, kick 'em in the ass, hear?"

"Will do, Sergeant." Drake circled back to the rear of the formation.

The squad finished their four mile run at 0625. No one was cast overboard.

After breakfast and inspection of their bunking area, Holt took the squad to the stern of the ship for weapons training. Waiting for them was a sailor, a rack of rifles, and three olive-drab wooden ammo boxes. Targets—six human silhouettes with helmets and rifles, drawn on cardboard—had been set-up along the aft railing. There were six shooting stations denoted with sandbags about ten meters from the targets.

Holt spoke briefly with the sailor, then he grabbed a rifle and turned to his men. "Listen up, gentlemen," he shouted into the wind sweeping over the deck, "this is the M-1 Garand rifle. It will shortly become your second best friend in the world. Right behind Sgt. Hercules Torvald Holt. Why? Because your M-1 and me are what keeps you alive." Holt eyed the men to confirm he had their full attention. "Has anyone *not* fired the M-1?" No one replied. "Good. Now get this straight—on the firing range, Gunnery Mate Kearney here is God. Fail to follow his every instruction in even the smallest way, and I reserve the right to substitute your lame ass

Saving Euridice

for one of those cardboard targets. Understand?" He returned his
rifle to the rack.

Kearney gave a talk about range safety and other protocol.
He took a rifle, demonstrated proper loading technique, and
casually put three rounds through the torso of one of the
silhouettes. Then he ejected the clip and the chambered round,
double checked to be sure the weapon was cleared, and returned it
to the rack.

Holt thanked the sailor. He took a rifle from the rack and a
clip of ammunition and stood at a sandbag firing station. Without
saying a word, he loaded the M-1, took aim, and fired off the
whole clip in two bursts of four rapid shots. Every round hit the
target in the center of the head.

When it was his turn, Drake confidently took his place at one
of the firing positions. He'd always had a steady eye, and he
squeezed off two clips, sixteen rounds, putting most of his shots in
a tight pack in the middle of the silhouette's head, like Holt had
done. Everyone else was able to at least hit the cardboard with
their 16 shots—it was only ten meters away, after all—though
Arvee Titus and Marv Malarkey both put most of their strikes
outside the silhouette.

"Lord have mercy, I've seen better shooting at Girl Scout
jamborees," Holt scoffed, "but on the other hand, the only
casualties were cardboard, so I'll call the session a success."

Skirmish at Sea, I

The first afternoon at sea, 3 May, Holt was occupied in a long meeting with the other squad leaders. Drake and the rest of the GIs used the time to polish boots, read, play cards, and nap.

At 1500 hours the sergeant showed up and ordered his men to be on deck in ten minutes for their afternoon run. As they trotted along their 28 lap course, a cool breeze off the water, laced with sea spray, tempered the heat of the blazing sun. The squad finished the run in under an hour, eight minutes faster than they had two days before.

Holt had his GIs sit in a semi circle in front of him. "Before chow, I want to tell you about the enemy you're going to face. The Japanese soldier." He rubbed his hands together and grinned broadly—a bit theatrical, Drake thought. "Japs! *Everybody* knows they're weak little shits. Shuffling around town in bathrobes and sandals. Slanty eyes behind big old coke-bottle glasses." He made circles with his thumbs and index fingers and held them up to his face like goggles, then he laughed. The men laughed too. "Bastards can't hit the broad side of a barn. They're tricky, but stupid. Chattering away in that gibberish of theirs. Am I right?"

Ralph Davis guffawed and muttered something to his buddy Tolliver, sitting next to him.

"Something pretty damn funny, huh, Private?" Holt said to Davis. "Lemme hear it too."

Davis scratched his ear and chuckled some more. "I was just telling Will how I'm going to skewer one of the little turds on my bayonet and hold him up in the air, squirming like a damn worm on a hook." Grinning, he looked around at the other GIs. "That'd be hilarious."

There were nods and chuckles from some of the men.

Holt let them go on for a moment, then he hollered, "'Ten-**HUT**." When each GI had jumped up, frozen at attention, he stormed at Davis, standing inches from his face. "Everything I just said is bullshit, men," he yelled, "same as what came out of Davis here's mouth. Difference is, I know it's bullshit. And you clowns don't." The sergeant glared at his men. "None of you have a clue, do ya? Well listen up, because here's the straight poop: The Japanese fighting man is small, but he's tough as rawhide. While you creampuffs need your Hershey bars and your bacon, he lives on a little bowl of maggoty rice. He's ready to go into battle on an hour's sleep, day or night. If his squad leader says, 'engage that tank barehanded,' he bows and does it. He fights hand-to-hand with skill and tenacity, and he'll tie you up in knots and slit your throat before you can say 'Merry Christmas.' And the biggest difference between the Japanese soldier and you?" Holt's jaws tightened. "He's not afraid to die."

"But sarge," said Breezy, "we've beat 'em time and again. Every island we hit, we take. Bang, bang, bang. Ain't that right?"

Holt peered at his assistant squad leader. "Yeah, we've had success, island-hopping. Because of the heavy firepower we bring to bear. Because we control the skies. Because we come in greater numbers. Not because the Japanese fighting man is inferior." His eyes were dark as storm clouds. "The Brits and us both thought that in the first days of the war, and we got our asses handed to us. Look, I faced the bastards on Guadalcanal. Saw them charge fearlessly, wave after wave, into withering machine gun fire. The Japanese I faced there were the toughest, bravest men I've ever seen, and I respect the hell out of 'em."

Drake raised his hand. "Sarge." When Holt nodded to him, he said, "Something else about the enemy we'll be facing. My sergeant back in First Army pointed out that up till now they've been defending a bunch of islands in the Pacific. Sand piles with names no one knew before the war. When we face 'em, it'll be on the Japanese mainland. They will be defending their divine Emperor. Their homes. Their wives and mothers. With nowhere to fall back to. They'll be playing for keeps."

Blackie Davis put his fist in front of his mouth and, camouflaging it as a cough, grunted, "Fucking kiss ass."

Holt turned slowly and glared at Davis. "Still popping off, Private?"

Davis shook his head innocently. "I just said, 'Fucking kick ass!'" He pumped his fist in the air. "You know, agreeing with my little pal Omaha. That's all." He turned to Drake and grinned.

Holt pointed at Davis and glared. "Got my eye on you, Private." After a moment, he scanned his GIs. "You ask me, Omaha's got it right. You damn well better figure on a fight to the death."

Every man in the squad was silent.

"Which brings me to something every combat GI's gotta face." Holt squinted at the squad, studying them. "You aren't saying so, but I know it's got you worried. *How the hell am I going to handle killing someone?*...I'm gonna let you in on the secret. At ease. Sit down, men." He put his hands behind his back and paced side to side in front of the GIs like a professor. "From the moment I set foot on Guadalcanal, that question clawed at me. Got my answer from something my old man said when I was a kid in Oregon. Place we lived was primeval forest—see, my dad *loved* big trees. Firs, cedar, hemlock. Giants, over two hundred feet high and six feet in diameter. Him and me spent many a morning tromping through the woods. He'd give names to his favorite trees, and he talked to them as we walked by." Holt looked up as if he could picture a Western Red Cedar towering from Old Trixie's deck. "He loved his trees, but the old man was a lumberjack. I could never figure it out—how does a fella who cares so much about trees make his living cutting 'em down? On one of our tromps, I asked him that.

"Dad was quiet for a while, staring at a titanic Douglas fir six feet away. Then he looked at me and said, 'Son, a family man's gotta make a living. It's his duty. A long time ago I learned to see my job not as felling trees, but as processing lumber, turning out logs. It's the only way I can get by.' I applied my old man's logic on Guadalcanal. I drummed it into this thick skull of mine, that my job there was also processing, plain and simple—turning live Japanese soldiers into dead ones. It was my duty. Now you gotta make that same leap. Once you're there, combat won't chew on you so bad. Oh, it'll still scare the living shit out of ya, but that's just the way it goes."

Holt checked his watch. "One thing more. Know it or not, the Army tacked another pair of jobs on my chest when they made me squad leader. These two duties are subordinate to mission number one, helping Japanese make their goal of dying for the Emperor. But I take 'em real serious. My first extra duty is getting you jugheads home safe and sound. Then there's my last priority: Making it back home myself in one piece." Holt stiffened. "I expect to accomplish all three assignments." He cleared his throat. "But be advised, on the way there I'll be the toughest, orneriest SOB sergeant in the Army—you're gonna hate my guts most of the time." He shrugged. "That's the only way I know to succeed." Holt scanned his men. "Just wanted you to know the score. Any questions?" The GIs were silent. "OK, let's get cleaned up and go have us some chow."

The fourth day at sea, mid-afternoon, the skipper announced on the ship's PA system, "We're sailing through the Strait of Gibraltar. If you want to see one helluva rock, hustle up on deck."

GIs who had been below, cleaning and polishing their sleep area, the head, and their personal gear, ran up to view and photograph the landmark. A sailor painting doorframes stopped his work to tell a group of Army men, "These waters used to be crawling with U-boats. They knew surface ships had to sail through this constriction to get into the Mediterranean, so they'd lurk here for the easy pickings. Different now. Like the skipper said, our anti-sub air patrols have chewed 'em up damn good in the last two years. Strait's pretty clear these days. "

When Drake and the others went back down to resume cleaning their quarters area, Blackie Davis and Will Tolliver were waiting there with big smirks on their faces.

Bo Forgette whistled and said, "Take a gander at them two! Look like a pair of hounds that found them a big old meatloaf left unguarded on the kitchen table."

"Just saw the darnedest thing." Davis looked down and started cleaning his fingernails with the point of his pocketknife blade. "A seagull flew by and took a big dump right in Drake's bunk."

Tolliver glared at Drake. "Damn bird squawked that sleeping in shit's what a Kraut-loving brownnoser deserves."

The GIs all went silent as Drake stormed to his hammock. Right in the middle of the bunk were three fat brown turds. Stinking, grotesque, taunting. When he turned back to Davis and Tolliver, the pair burst out laughing.

Drake seemed calm as he removed his eyeglasses and set them on his foot locker. He put his right hand into his pocket to feel for the talisman coin Stetti had given him. It was there— warm, smooth, like it was alive. Rubbing its magic into his fingers, he took a moment to peer without expression at his tormentors.

"Don't think I'll need this," Davis said, handing his knife to Tolliver. He snorted like a bull and stepped forward. "Got a new nickname for you, twerp. Try Winnie the Poop on for size." Snickering, he curled his fleshy hands into fists and thumbed his nose. "Golly, Will, think the little tyke's gonna start bawling right here and now?"

Drake hollered, "Bastard," and charged forward. He buried his shoulder deep into Davis's corpulent gut. Blackie grunted loudly as the two careened back and crashed into a cardboard trashcan, sending its contents skittering across the floor. Drake jabbed a long volley of rabbit punches into his hulking opponent's midsection.

The GIs, cheering and cursing, formed a circle around the combatants.

Gasping for breath, Davis joined his hands over his head and brought them down like a sledge hammer onto Drake's back, breaking off his attack. Davis staggered to his feet and grabbed the Goebbels Stick from its hanger on the wall. He swung the pole in a swooshing arc aimed at his foe's skull. Drake deflected the stroke with his forearm, but it caught the side of his head in a glancing blow, sending him reeling to his knees.

Drake got up, the cut above the ear streaming blood. He ran his hand over the wound and looked at his bloody fingers. He glared at Davis, who cocked the pole behind his back like a baseball batter and panted, "Want some more, you little rat?"

Arvee Titus, all 153 pounds of him, leapt from the side for Davis's weapon, jerking it from his hands.

Drake charged again, planting his shoulder once more into big man's breadbasket. The pair tumbled to the floor. Drake, his expression savage and the side of his head bloody, sat atop his fat foe. He pinned Davis's arms with his knees. Resuming his barrage of rabbit punches, Drake pummeled the helpless giant's face.

Suddenly the circle of GIs around the fight broke open, and a hand grabbed Drake's collar and yanked him off Davis. "What in God's name…?" said Sgt. Holt.

Drake, panting like a wild beast, his eyes still fiery, pulled out his handkerchief and pressed it to the slash on his head. He glared down at Davis.

"Get your ass up," Holt snapped at Blackie.

Shaking his head to clear his brain, Davis rose unsteadily to one knee and stayed there. His face was a bloody pulp, with his nose smashed, his lip cut, and a gash along his eyebrow.

"Help Davis up," Holt said to Breezy and Van Fleet. Take him to the head and scrub that ugly mug of his. "Zimmerman and Titus, get Drake's butt in there too and clean him up. Then you guys escort them both to the medical corpsman's clinic. Down the corridor and to the left. You'll see a big red cross on the door. And you two—" He pointed at Drake and Davis. "—if anyone asks, you cut yourself shaving…understand? Soon as you're done with the corpsman, I want to see you both in the NCO offices. **Now get moving!**"

When Drake and Davis and the men escorting them were gone, Holt said to the remaining GIs, "Any of you who aren't mine, make tracks." When the others were gone, he leaned toward his men. "All right now, what the hell happened here?" Holt's look was dark as a tornado sky.

163

Tolliver scratched his head. "Aw, sarge, Davis was just giving that cry baby a hard time on account of the way he took a German's side over ours back in the Bonn train station. Then Wee Winnie the Poop plain went crazy. Fucking attacked Blackie. 'Course he had to defend himself."

"That's a goddamn lie," Malarkey said. "Look at this, sarge." He led Holt to Drake's bunk. "Blackie took a damn dump in Drake's bed. He's had it out for Drake from the start." He pointed at Tolliver. "And that weasel's been in cahoots with Davis all along."

Holt grabbed Tolliver's shirt front and dragged him next to Drake's fouled bunk. "You fucking piss on my shoe and tell me it's raining?"

Tolliver looked to the side. He swallowed hard. "Guess it's pretty much like Marv said, Sergeant Holt."

"You guess?" Holt shoved him away in disgust. "Listen, eight ball, pick up that fucking mess and take it into the head where it belongs. Haul the sheet to the ship's laundry. Then get a clean sleeper and make up Drake's bunk. After chow tonight, you'll clean our latrine, spic and span. I'll inspect it at 2130 hours and it damn well better sparkle."

Two hours later Drake and Davis hobbled back from the corpsman and reported to Sgt. Holt in the NCO room. Drake had six stitches in the cut over his ear. His jaw was bruised. The knuckles of his right hand were bandaged. Davis had three stitches in the gash over his right eye, which was now purple and puffy. Each nostril was plugged with a cotton wad, and his lower lip was stitched and swollen.

Holt crossed his arms. "Davis, if you *ever* pull a fool stunt like this again, I swear to God I'll have you court marshaled. As it is, you're on report to me for the next seven evenings. Starting tomorrow. Your buddy Tolliver is cleaning up your shit and polishing the head tonight, and you'll be on that duty for a week." Holt stood so his face was inches from Davis's. "Listen, you got two strikes, mister. One more and you're out." He punched his fist

164

into his palm. "And I do mean out. Got it?" Blackie Davis nodded. "OK....You going to be all right?"

"Yes, Sergeant."

"Good. Now shake hands with Drake and go get some shuteye. Zero five zero zero will come around mighty early tomorrow morning."

Without saying a word, Davis shook Drake's hand and shuffled away.

Holt watched him go out the door then turned to Drake. "Gonna live?"

"'Fraid so. Corpsman gave me four aspirin and a snort of medicinal brandy, so I'm pretty good. Said I got a pretty darn hard noggin."

Holt nodded. "The men told me about Davis's little stunt. That lousy four-flusher." He put his hands on his hips. "Should be dressing you down for being a hothead, but, shit, a man's gotta take a stand sometimes. Guess I would've done the same. Or more."

"Thanks, sarge." Drake rubbed the knuckles of his right hand. "I dunno...just can't figure out why Blackie'd want to go and do something like that."

"Known a few like him," Holt said, "fellas that don't think. It's just the way they are." He eyed Drake. "Gotta hand it to you, Omaha...you surprised me again, giving that big lunk a first-class ass-whooping like you did."

"Kinda surprised myself."

Holt chuckled. "Think you just might turn out to be a real infantryman." He put a hand on Drake's shoulder. "I had Tolliver make up your bunk. Go get yourself some sleep. And if Davis says *Boo* to you, I want to hear about it. That's an order."

"Right, sarge."

Drake walked back to D Bay, to his bunk and was asleep ten minutes later.

Skirmish at Sea, II

May 8, 1945

After evening chow on the sixth day at sea, the skipper came on the ship's PA. "Attention all officers and sailors of USS *Queen Beatrix* and US Army personnel aboard, I've got news. President Truman released the following statement to the American people: 'This is a solemn but glorious hour. General Eisenhower informs me that the forces of Germany have surrendered to the United Nations. The flags of freedom fly all over Europe.'"

After a momentary silence, whoops and whistles erupted. There were hugs and handshakes, dancing and prayer, from bow to stern, from below decks to the bridge.

Captain Hooft gave the men a full minute to celebrate. "Attention, men. I want to add that the President emphasized that the war with Japan will continue to absolute victory.'" Hooft cleared his throat. "GIs, be assured my crew and I will do our utmost to get you to the Far East, then victory will be up to you." The skipper let the roar build among the GIs and crew, then he boomed, "Go get 'em, Army!"

Drake and Arvee Titus were on deck the next morning. "Think you must've scrambled something in Davis's brain when you thumped him like you did." Titus pushed his eyeglasses up on his nose. "Last night as we filed out of chow he gave me a stick of Wrigley's."

Drake shook his head. "Life's full of twists, ain't it?" He squinted at the sun. "Think maybe our helmsman's been hitting the hooch this morning?"

"Huh?"

"Seems like we're on a merry-go-round, sailing in circles."

Two sailors walked by.

"Say there, fellas," Drake called to them. "Are we just circling around this morning?"

"Sure are," said the squat sailor with the dagger-pierced heart tattoo on his forearm. "See that speck on the horizon." He pointed into the distance a bit port of the stern. "We're marking time so that ship can rendezvous with us. It's another transport brimming with you Army types. And there's a third on the way too. Scuttlebutt is, we'll convoy for a while."

"Any idea where we are?" Titus asked.

The other sailor smoked a corn cob pipe. He glanced at his watch then squinted at the sun. Shielding his eyes with one hand, he peered to the horizon on the starboard side. "Off Egypt." He pointed. "Should be Alexandria about there, I reckon." The sailors ambled off.

"Alexandria," Arvee said. "Its lighthouse was one of the seven wonders of the ancient world."

"Huh!" Drake took out a Chesterfield and lit it. "If we spend the day sailing loop de loops, maybe we'll be here tonight to see its beam," he said, exhaling the first drag.

"Doubt that. It was destroyed centuries ago. Earthquakes."

The next morning when Holt's squad came on deck for their morning run, there was one large ship a half mile ahead of Good Old Trixie and another the same distance behind. After the run, Drake spotted the sailor with the cob pipe, oiling door hinges. He walked over with Bo Forgette and asked the man, "Guess we're convoying just like you said. How come?"

The sailor put his oil can down and puffed on his pipe for a moment, like he was considering how best to answer such a naïve question. "Watch many of them western moving pictures, do ya?" He took another puff. "Wagon trains going west? They convoyed up for protection from Injuns, right?" He tapped his teeth on the pipe mouthpiece. "That's what ships do in dangerous waters. Reckon the skip's got him some intelligence about submarines lurking on the other end of the canal." He glanced into the bowl of his pipe then took a series of short puffs to get it going. Then he picked up his oil can and resumed his work.

As they walked away, Bo muttered, "Subs! I knew setting foot on this canoe was a mistake."

By the time lunch was over, the convoy was in the canal. Holt's squad had an hour's free time, so Drake and some of the others spent it on the foredeck. As soon as they'd left Mediterranean waters, the air turned blistering hot and arid, so the GIs stripped off their shirts and soaked in the brilliant sunshine on the teak boards of Old Trixie's deck.

Henderson had a pair of binoculars and was peering into the distance. Breezy poked him and asked, "Whatcha seeing out there, bathing beauties?"

"Nah," said Dickie. "Sand mostly. Hoping to get a glimpse of the pyramids."

"Good luck with that," said Arvee. "Unless I'm wrong, the tombs of the Pharaohs are better 'an fifty miles away, and off the starboard side—not the port, where you're looking."

As the men laughed, Henderson swept his glasses forward and trained them on the stern of *Pottawattamie*, the transport steaming ahead of them. "Well hell's bells, can you believe that?" he muttered, handing the binos to Drake. "Take a gander, there on the back railing." He pointed to the ship's stern, chuckling.

Drake stood and lifted the binoculars to his eyes. He saw five bare asses and a GI holding a hand-lettered sign that read *Bite it, Navy*. *Beatrix's* crew must've seen the display too, and radioed ahead, as seconds later a troop of sea police descended on the exhibitors and broke things up.

A few minutes later Drake announced, "I'm cooked." He pulled on his shirt and went inside with Titus, Henderson and Zimmerman. Breezy stayed on deck for more baking.

The convoy cleared the canal before dawn the following night. By noon it had sailed through the Gulf of Suez and into the Red Sea. Soon it connected with its US Navy destroyer escort, USS *Triquot*. As it did, Holt called his squad together. "Gentlemen, Captain Hooft just briefed the on-board Army command that there are reports of Japanese submarines operating in the Red Sea and the Gulf of Aden. Naturally, they'd like nothing better than to ambush us before we get to the high seas of the Indian Ocean. The skipper made the point that any Jap subs in these waters face much tougher odds than we do. Here's why. The USS *Triquot*, which you see on our flank—" He pointed to the destroyer off the port side. "—and her crew are highly experienced and effective sub hunters. The Navy's got antisubmarine air patrols in the vicinity. Plus our ship is well armed and outfitted with sub-detecting sonar. And gentlemen, we're going to be part of show. You hawkeyed GIs will be partnering with experienced Navy crewmen for a surveillance regimen. I'll have your assignments shortly." He scanned the line of GIs before him. "I expect you to keep your morale up and your eyes open. When in doubt, point it out."

As he walked down to D Bay for the afternoon Spit & Polish Fest with Bo Forgette, Drake said, "You look like you just saw a ghost."

Bo said nothing for a moment. Then he rubbed his lips and exhaled deeply. "Fucking subs gimme the yips. Had a cousin in the Merchant Marine. U-boat torpedoed him in the Atlantic. The stories he told..." He shook his head. "Cold, black water. Fire. Real bad medicine."

"Water's not so cold here," Drake said, smiling.

Forgette scowled at him. "Easy for a fucking lifeguard to say. Me, I can't swim a stroke." He shivered.

"Like Holt said, we're taking lots of anti-sub measures. I read in *Stars and Stripes* about the new gizmos they got on sub-hunting aircraft—lets them see u-boats even under water. And depth charges! Imagine being down there with a destroyer lobbing those suckers at you." Drake put a hand on Bo's shoulder. "We'll be fine."

Thirty minutes later Holt met again with the squad. "All right men, no training, no running until we're out in open ocean. For now you'll be pulling watch duty, working with Navy fellas on six hour shifts. Four of you with a sailor. I got a list covering the next twenty-four hours."

"What about inspections, sarge?" said Malarkey. "We get out of them too?"

Holt glared at Marvin. "You're only on watch twelve hours a day. By my count, that leaves you with twelve hours to kill. Of course I'm still doing inspections, Private." He read the first day's postings. "One last thing, anybody falls asleep on watch, I'll personally toss your sorry ass overboard." He grinned. "Hear the water around here's thick with sharks."

Drake glanced at Bo Forgette. The look on his face said that now he'd added sharks to his worry sheet.

Drake's first watch ran from midnight until 0600 on 12 May. With him were Marv Malarkey, Dickie Henderson, and Will Tolliver. At 2330 hours they met with Machinist's Mate Butch Bratgeust of upstate New York, the Navy man in charge of the observer team. He was tall with a melodious baritone that would sound perfect on the radio. "Fellas," the sailor said, "as you can see, the moon is almost full, and the sky's clear...so we'll have excellent visibility. On watch, you want to be looking for a periscope's little white wake. Or maybe a glint of reflected moonlight. Sing out if *anything* catches your eye. Questions?"

"If we spot one," said Drake, "What'll happen?"

"We'll sic *Triquot*, our destroyer, on 'em. If the sub's on the surface, we'll engage with guns. If she dives, there's *Triquot's* depth charges, a submariner's worst nightmare." Bratgeust checked his watch. "You got ten minutes to hit the head and grab your Mae West and a cup of joe. Meet me at twenty-three fifty-five hours at point S-9, that's starboard nine, abaft on the main deck."

"Abaft?" Malarkey asked. "How about you translate that into English, Butch?"

"Toward the stern, on the starboard side." He pointed astern. "You'll see the S-9 sign."

When the men reassembled, Bratgeust distributed binoculars and posted his GIs.

Drake leaned on the railing and peered into the darkness of the ocean. The full moon was behind him so he didn't have to deal with a swath of moonlight dancing on the water.

Marv Malarkey was in a playful mood. When Bratgeust stepped away to report, Marv teased Henderson. "Psst, Dickie...see any pyramids? Or mummies dancing?" He snickered.

"Shut up, Marvin," Henderson hissed.

"Hey, sport," Marv said, "what about moons? Any fat GI asses out tonight?"

"Dammit Malarkey—" Butch Bratgeust had heard the banter. "—cut the clowning. Just keep your fucking eyes peeled for subs fixing to serve us an order of fish."

Drake was glad Bratgeust was cracking the whip. He rubbed his eyes and peered again. He shivered at the night's chill— amazing given how stinking hot the day had been. He slipped his hand into the pocket of his pants and felt Stetti's talisman coin. Instantly he felt warmer. Safer.

At 0130 hours Drake was panning his glasses across the thirty degree arc he was responsible for, when he saw a tiny flash. A spark. There for an instant then gone. Probably nothing, he figured. A stray beam of moonlight dancing on a wave crest. He stared into the darkness. Nothing. But he remembered Holt's words. *When in doubt, point it out.* Drake lowered his binos and called softly, "Hey Butch, come'ere for a second." When Bratgeust was next to him, Drake said, "Out there—" He pointed. "—way out there. Thought I saw...wait, there it is again. Did you see it? There!" He pointed again.

Bratgeust peered through his binos. He said nothing for a moment, then, "Yep!"

"Damn right, I saw it too," Drake whispered.

Bratgeust sprinted to a telephone twenty yards away. He cranked the phone and reported his team's observation and the angular position off starboard. He ran back to Drake's side.

"Any idea how far off it is?" Drake said.

"Hard to say," Bratgeust muttered. "At least a couple kilometers."

Suddenly the starboard pod of quad twenty mm antiaircraft machine guns opened fire, sending a stream of tracer rounds skimming over the water's surface in the direction of the flashes

Drake had seen. A klaxon horn went off and over the PA came the order, "Battle stations. All personnel to battle stations."

"Bet they picked up 'em up on sonar too," shouted Bratgeust over the clatter of the machine guns. "Gives 'em a range to target."

There was a mechanical whir and the twin two inch guns swung into alignment with the target. As soon as they halted, there was a flash of light and a deafening blast, followed by paired rings of smoke moving from the weapons' muzzles.

Drake squeezed his lucky coin in his fist and looked astern just as the destroyer *Triquot* dashed through Trixie's wake toward the target. *Triquot's* forward five inch guns exploded with a blast that Drake felt on his cheek. In the moonlight, he watched the big black rounds streak ahead in a low arc then send tiny white geysers into the air far off starboard.

Drake felt in his knees a subtle shift in Trixie's course. Her engines strained and smoke and fire shot from her stacks.

"Evasive action!" Bratgeust bellowed. "May be a torpedo. Get your Army asses amidships"

"Fish in the water!" the PA boomed. "All personnel brace for torpedo impact."

Drake raised his binoculars. As he panned across the water's surface he saw a white line drawn straight as an arrow and heading for *Beatrix*. He let the binos drop to his chest and, shaking, grabbed a fixture to brace himself. Holding his breath, he watched the white trail of bubbles swoosh just in front of Trixie's bow and head off to port. Drake put the binos back to his eyes. In the distance, he could see *Triquot* racing in a jagged pattern. Huge explosions of water—depth charges, he figured—followed in her wake.

USS *Beatrix* and her convoy mates fell into line, *Pottawattamie* leading and *Jagger* trailing, and steamed full ahead. Thirty seconds later, Drake was knocked forward by a concussive shove to his back and instantly struck by a thunderous blast that left his ears ringing. Without rising from his crouch, he spun around just as an eruption of fire shot skyward from *Jagger's* bow.

For a moment, all he could do was stare, wide-eyed, mouth agape, frozen at the horror of the sight.

Let Go

The explosion that enveloped USS *Jagger's* bow stunned Drake. His ears were ringing as he lurched toward the stern of his ship, with only moonlight to guide him over the cluttered deck. He had no idea what he could do when he got there. He only knew he had to help.

Just as he arrived at the stern, *Beatrix's* floodlights came on, illuminating *Jagger*, dead in the water. She was slumped forward so her stern rode high and her bow low, but for the moment anyway, she seemed stable. Steam and smoke, luminous against the black background of the nighttime sea, poured from her prow. Crewmen with fire hoses were fighting down the last of the flames. Men bobbed in lifeboats on the inky water between the vessels. Others splashed in the drink, thrashing for the white and red life rings tossed to them. Drake saw their open mouths but heard no sound but the hissing in his ears.

Seeing men in the water, Drake's mind flashed back to his lifeguard days, specifically to the Labor Day afternoon he'd failed to rescue Hilda Crabbe at Perritt's Beach. He was pulling off his shirt, about to dive in, when Bratgeust grabbed his arm. Drake turned and saw the sailor's lips move and his head shake, but he couldn't catch the words. Bratgeust hustled him over the chaotic deck toward the midship GI meet-up point. When Drake's ears began to clear, he was able to make out Bratgeust saying, "The oldest trick in the book...."

"Trick?" Drake yelled back.

"One sub draws your attention," Bratgeust said, "and her pal stabs you in the back."

Drake stared blankly.

"There was *another sub*, over there somewhere." Bratgeust pointed to port-side. "She was the bitch that fired the tin pickle that took out *Jagger*." A PA announcement, too garbled for Drake to understand, interrupted the explanation. "Just stay put," Bratgeust yelled as he ran off.

Drake scanned the tumult. A second destroyer, USS *Dresher*, had been rushing to join the attack on the starboard-side submarine when *Jagger* was walloped. Now she was slashing to the other side of the convoy, her bow tossing foamy water to each side, bent on blowing the second shooter to kingdom come. A minute later Drake watched *Dresher* lay out her depth charges—an explosive game of cat and mouse between herself and the Japanese sub.

Bratgeust ran back and enlisted Drake and a dozen more GIs to help in the rescue efforts for *Jagger's* survivors. Near Trixie's port-side railing was a huge, rolled rope climbing web. Lowering the roll, eight feet in diameter and a dozen feet wide, enabled men to climb from the water to the deck. The GIs uncranked the web down to the water's surface. Lifeboats immediately moved to it and oil-splotched men began climbing up. Nearby, medics and sailors were operating a pulley system to raise stretchers with the injured from lifeboats to Trixie's deck. By this time, *Pottawattamie* had made it back and began picking up sailors and GIs, injured and not.

Drake and the GIs were assigned to wait at the webbing roll and grab wet, exhausted survivors as they made it to the top. They pulled the men over the railing and got them resting on the deck with a blanket and a cup of hot coffee.

Ninety minutes later, all the men in lifeboats were safe aboard either *Beatrix* or *Pottawattamie*. A few sailors remained aboard *Jagger*, hosing down hot spots and shuttling equipment and paperwork in baskets by pulley-fixed laundry lines rigged between the vessels.

When a sailor came around pulling a wagon with a large urn of coffee, Bratgeust gathered his team for a rest. "For a bunch of land lubbers, you guys performed damn good tonight."

"Any word about casualties?" Drake asked, taking out a fresh pack of Chesterfields, which he passed around the group.

"Preliminary's all I heard," Bratgeust said, lighting his smoke and Drake's, "but they're saying only nine confirmed dead. A couple of dozen guys with burns or considerable injuries. That's out of ninety-six crew and pretty near nine hundred GIs. So it could have been worse. Like if that fish had struck directly amidships."

"What about the boat?" Henderson said.

"You mean the *Jagger*? She's a ship," Bratgeust said. "Well, she's non-op, but they got the damaged fore compartments sealed off so she won't sink. I figure they'll tow her somewhere and get her fixed up good as new."

"The fucking subs," Tolliver asked, "did we get 'em?"

Bratgeust shrugged. "Reckon only the Jap submariners know whether or not we did…and either way, they ain't talking. All we know is there's no sign of 'em now."

By sun-up, Trixie's crew and GIs had rigged space to park the additional 467 men who'd come aboard. The injured went to an expanded sick bay. Some of the rest were bunked in spare hammocks in F-Bay, but the majority of them had to camp out on deck, sleeping on cots, jerry-rigged hammocks, or the hardwood deck. Holt scoffed that with all the bedding and the wet clothes draped around, Trixie's deck looked "like a damned harem." An hour later, when a patrol boat arrived to babysit the stricken *Jagger* and its skeleton crew, the convoy—now four ships, *Beatrix*, *Pottawattamie*, *Triquot* and *Dresher*—resumed its voyage for the Philippines.

The morning of 14 May, the ships steamed into the Indian Ocean. Holt's boys had already returned to their regimen of exercise and training. On the 14th, after a morning run and breakfast, they had their first session of hand-to-hand fighting techniques. A US Marine sergeant named Cassidy conducted the training. He'd been scheduled to come over from *Jagger* and arrived a day early due to the submarine action. Cassidy was hard, both in musculature and attitude. He was short, five foot six or so, and must have weighed two hundred pounds. His nose had been pounded flat and a notch, quite visible given his close crew cut, was missing from the top of his right ear. He called every one of his students an "Army foozle."

"As Sergeant Holt told you Army foozles," Cassidy growled, "the Japanese marine or infantryman you'll face is one tough son of a bitch. On Tarawa, the little buggers would charge, screaming like banshees, into the teeth of our machine guns and the few who made it through would fight you like you never seen before—

flurries of quick jabs, crazy grunts. They leverage your size and strength against you. I've seen 'em flip Marines twice their weight like flapjacks. We weren't ready for them on Tarawa. My job is make sure you are."

Cassidy's unarmed combat sessions were savage. There was one in the morning and one in the evening. Everybody going full time, with two lines of men facing each other. Both lines would count down and the number 1s fought each other. Same for the 2s, the 3s, and so on. The starboard line was Americans for the first half of the session. Port was Japanese. After thirty minutes the roles switched. Cassidy would holler, "Let's…**GO!**" and the lines would bang together. The Marine didn't believe in pulling punches, his or his pupils'. Lots of lips were split, and hips were bruised. But the men progressed rapidly. By the fourth session, they'd become more aggressive, tougher, and most important, smarter. Even the men who hated Cassidy, and that was most of them, had to admit his two-a-days made them better soldiers and much more confident they'd survive close combat.

From the afternoon of the submarine action, Drake made daily visits to one of the *Jagger* burn victims in sick bay. Like so many other GIs, Winston Sumter had been assigned to surveillance duty the night of the Japanese sub attack in the Red Sea. But Sumter drew a short straw, being stationed on *Jagger's* portside foredeck right above the enemy torpedo's point of impact.

As Drake said to Zip Zimmerman at chow one evening, "Sumter and me, we're about the same. Privates from the Midwest, desk jockeys up to now. Both of us Winstons. But now he's lying below decks moaning in pain and looking like a grilled hamburger, and all I got to worry about is making it through Cassidy's two-a-day slugfests. Luck, it's always important in life, but don't it seem like in combat it's a kajillion times more so? I mean you and I are here forking pork and beans into our yaps and other guys…"

"Fate," said Zip, setting down his fork, "she's a fickle bitch all right. No telling why one guy lives and another don't."

"I don't know whether sitting by Sumter's bed means anything to him. Or even if he realizes I'm there. They got him pretty well doped up. Oh, he'll moan sometimes. And a couple of times, I've heard him mutter Cassidy's close combat command, 'Let's **Go!**' He's fighter, that's for sure." Drake peered into Zip's eyes. "I'd do anything to save him. I figure if I pray hard enough, if I'm good enough company, maybe I can help pull him through."

"Has the doc said anything about his chances?"

Drake sighed. "Not much. Guess no one knows. But he said being there with him, talking to him, helps a lot. The will to survive's a big part of making it."

Zimmerman eyed Drake for a moment then stood. "How do you know it's not just *you,* wanting so bad for Sumter to make it?" He picked up his food tray. "I used to wonder if it was selfishness made me hate losing those buddies on Omaha Beach. Not being able to stand the guilt of surviving." He took a deep breath and walked away.

"One lousy strip of bacon!" Henderson waved the skimpy, overdone strip of pork in the air to make his point to the other men at breakfast. "And the reconstituted eggs? The cookies used to pile 'em on. Now we get a dab. Are the chickens and pigs on strike or something?"

Barezzi looked over his shoulder to make sure no one other than his table mates could hear him. "Gotta be all those extra guys aboard from the *Jagger.*" He pointed his fork at Henderson for emphasis. "What is it, five hundred more mouths to feed?"

Arvee Titus bit off the corner of his toast. "You know, they didn't exactly plan to get the *Jagger* shot out from under them, Breezy."

"Ain't saying they did. But should *we* have to suffer…for their bad luck? We were here first."

"Damn right," said Bo Forgette. "Ship's so cluttered a fella can't move without stepping on one of those *Jagger* foozles. Latrines are all clogged up. Short rations. It's one big snafu."

Tolliver pushed his dish away with half the eggs uneaten. He lit a Lucky Strike. "I say drop 'em off in India or somewhere and they catch their own boat." He shrugged *why not?*

"I'll finish your eggs if you don't want them, Will," Henderson said, reaching for the plate without waiting for an answer.

"Catch their own boat?" Drake shook his head. "Like they're Howard Hughes or something?" He took a last bite of eggs from his plate and stood. "Can't believe you guys! Bet you won't be gripping when one of them takes out a Japanese machine gun nest that has you pinned down." Drake stormed away.

"Jeeze," Bo muttered, "all we said was the plain facts. It *is* damned crowded aboard these days. And they do skimp on chow. But there goes Drake, making a federal case of it."

After Cassidy's morning two-a-day, Drake stopped by the infirmary to visit Sumter. His breathing was more labored than ever and amber fluids seeped through the dressings on his face and hands.

When the ship's surgeon walked by, Drake grabbed his sleeve. "Sumter here's not doing so great, doc. Can't you do anything else for him?"

The doctor glanced at his watch. "Can't give him another hypo for an hour." He gazed at Sumter and grimaced, then he looked back at Drake. A helpless look. He stepped away.

Drake forced a smile. He leaned down and whispered, "Let's go. We can do it."

After a moment, Sumter grunted. He grunted again.

Drake got the idea the grunts meant the man wanted to tell him something. He bent down so his ear was near Sumter's cracked lips.

Sumter just breathed for a while, like he was building his strength. "Can't" he rasped softly, a rustling like dried leaves. A moment later he whispered "Let go." His eyes, surrounded by bandages, caught Drake's, and he blinked, *please.*

The air froze in Drake's lungs. Sumter had been saying, "Let go," not "Let's go" all along. He swallowed hard and nodded.

The men gazed silently at each other for a moment, then Sumter's lids fluttered closed. His breathing slowed and became shallow. He showed no signs of struggle.

Drake imagined a boat drifting off from shore onto a perfectly calm lake. Drifting away so slowly that it left no wake. "So long, buddy," he whispered.

Sumter's breathing was so soft and peaceful in the end that Drake didn't know when it stopped. At some point he realized Sumter was gone and went to fetch the doctor.

The doc checked for a pulse and shined a light in Sumter's eyes. "It's good," he said, pulling the sheet up to cover the dead man's face.

Drake walked out of the infirmary in a daze. He found Zimmerman polishing his boots. "Sumter passed on, Zip. I was with him at the end."

"How was he?"

Drake's lip quivered. "Seemed peaceful. He was ready to go." He wiped a tear with the back of his hand. "Guess you can't save everyone."

"Yeah." Zimmerman set his boot down and stood. He put a hand on Drake's shoulder. "Especially when they don't want to be saved."

Drake gave Zip an awkward embrace.

BAR Keeper

On the morning of 17 May, 1945, PFC Winston Sumter of Olathe, Kansas was interred at sea with full honors somewhere in the middle of the Indian Ocean. Present were a chaplain, a Navy honor guard, members of Sumpter's squad, and Drake. With tears streaming down his cheeks, Drake wondered, *you live twenty years, have a family, do your duty...then it's over?* He bit his lip. *All you get out of it is twenty minutes of seventeen guys' time.*

There was a second burial service right afterward—another casualty from the sub attack. Drake stayed for that too.

When the ceremonies were over, Drake stopped in to see Sgt. Holt. "This morning they buried a couple of the *Jagger* guys who didn't make it. I got pretty close to one of them these last few days. I don't know, sarge, it's really tough business, saying goodbye like that."

Holt eyed Drake. "Sure is. I've been to my share of memorials." He leaned back in his swivel chair. "Taught me to grow thicker skin. That's what you need to do."

"But sarge—"

"Don't 'But sarge' me. Your pal's gone. Simple as that. You moping gets him nothing. Nor you. So get back to duty. Life goes on." Holt picked up his pencil and peered at his crossword.

Drake stared at the sergeant for a moment, then he turned and left. He was steamed. How could Holt be such a jerk? Then it struck him that Holt, Zip, and even Sumpter had given him the same advice—*Let go!* Maybe there was something to it.

After lunch, in the sultry midday heat and the unrelenting sunblast of the tropical ocean, Sgt. Holt assembled his squad. He signaled two naval ordinance men, who carried over a long wooden box and two ammo cans and set them next to Holt's feet. "Thanks," he barked to the sailors. "Gentlemen, as a U.S. Army Infantryman, who did I say was your best friend?"

Marv Malarkey's hand shot up. "You, sarge." He grinned.

"Yeah," drawled Holt without even looking at Malarkey, "and what else?"

"That'd be our M-1s, right?" said Breezy.

"Give the corporal a cigar. Which reminds me…" Holt pulled out a half-smoked stogie, lit it, and took a series of puffs. "Your M-1 *is* your best pal because it keeps you alive. Today, gentlemen, you'll meet *my* best friend. Remember when I told you, as an infantry squad leader, my number one assignment is killing the enemy. Remember?" He nudged the long box with the toe of his boot. "Well, the big dog in here does that better than about anything else." Holt opened lid and took out an angular rifle. He hefted the weapon and took a moment to admire it. He dropped the bipod down from the weapon's muzzle end and slapped in a rectangular metal ammunition magazine. Then he set it down on the deck in front of the men. "Here she is boys, the slinger of lead. The crusher of dreams. The brute that don't take *no* for an answer." His voice rose. "The heavyweight champion of the infantry battlefield.…The Browning M1918A2 automatic rifle. The BAR. Think of it—eighty rounds per minute of mobile fire power in the hands of a single GI!" Seeing the wide eyes before him, Holt knew the killing machine he held would be an easy sell.

Zimmerman nodded. "Fighting our way off Omaha Beach," he said, "the BAR saved lots of GIs, all right. That suppressing fire did one helluva job, keeping Fritzie's head down."

"And on Guadalcanal," Holt said, "with this little honey we held off relentless assaults by numerically superior Japanese forces."

Zimmerman wiped his nose on the back of his hand. "Only problem is the Germans knew what a bitch the BAR is to deal with. So they tried like hell to put 'em out of action. We used to say a BAR man's lifespan is measured in minutes."

"Japs, too. They ain't stupid." Holt scanned his men. The looks on their faces indicated they were suddenly thinking— *Hmmm, might be best to let somebody else be the big hero toting our BAR.* "That's why we're all going to qualify on the weapon. So if one BAR keeper goes down, someone else can pick it up." That failed to brighten anyone's expression. "And we're modifying our squad structure and tactics to protect our gunners. Notice the plural

182

there? Yep, we're going to have two Brownings in the outfit. They'll work in tandem, hoking up each other. Basically, all twelve of us support them. In the attack, we'll be a scout team of three riflemen, two four-man BAR teams, and me. The Browning teams will alternate cover and assault."

Breezy raised his hand. "How're you going to choose your BAR gunners, sarge?"

"A whole slew of ways," Holt said. "Starting today, firing the weapon. Which we're ready to do." He turned to the Navy ordinance men. "Set the targets, fellas."

The sailors fixed two white cardboards with two-foot diameter bull's eye targets above the ship's fantail, twenty yards away. The sailors showed how to maintain and load the weapon. Finally they demonstrated burst firing of the BAR from various positions.

"Now it's your turn, boys," Holt said. "Remember, fire in six-round bursts. And one more thing...I better not see a BAR muzzle pointed anywhere but off the fantail. You get careless on the firing line and you'll be there—" He pointed to the stern of the ship. "—with only a paper bull's eye between your ass and a stream of .30 caliber rounds."

"Come on, sarge," Malarkey said, "We're your little darlings. You couldn't bear to harm any of us, could you?"

Holt glared. "Always a wisenheimer, huh, Malarkey? Ain't you ever heard of Private Willy Stillwell? General Joe Stillwell's black sheep son? On Guadalcanal, he gave me some trouble, so I loaded him in a one-fifty-five artillery piece and shot him into the Coral Sea. Figure the sharks got 'im." Holt shrugged. "General Stillwell gave me a medal. 'Served him right,' Vinegar Joe said." Holt held his stare on Malarkey for a moment, then said, "Anything else from the peanut gallery?" He put his hands on his hips. "Now back to Mr. Browning's rifle. Form two lines for firing, gentlemen, and remember, mind those muzzles."

The GIs each took a turn firing the BAR. Most were wildly inaccurate.

Drake took the last place in line so he could learn from what the others did. He noticed the weapon's powerful recoil led to overshooting the target. Zimmerman had fired the BAR before, so Drake studied his stance. When his turn came, Drake braced himself like Zip had done and focused on controlling the muzzle's updrift. He put twice as many rounds through the target as most of the others of the others had, as many as Zip.

As Drake walked back to the others after firing, Bo Forgette muttered, "Show off."

After the evening run, Sgt. Holt called Drake aside. "Seems like you survived our little chinwag this morning. About tough skin?"

Drake frowned. "Yeah, maybe."

"Good. Have a seat." Holt gave Drake an Old Gold cigarette and took one himself. He lit them with a Zippo. "Like I told the squad today, all twelve of us earn our pay supporting our BARs." He waited for Drake to nod in agreement. "You're a natural with that automatic rifle, Private. You're also a pretty scrappy infantryman. You do things the right way and the men look up to you for that. Even Davis. I've decided to designate you one of my BAR keepers. Got a problem with that?"

Drake relaxed. "No, sarge." A hint of a smile crossed his face. "Guess I'd be honored."

"It's a heavy hunk of iron to lug when the squad's on the move."

Drake puffed his chest out. "I can handle it."

"And you're OK with every enemy soldier putting you in his sights?"

"Way I see it, I'll have eleven buddies looking after me. Yeah, I'm OK with it."

Holt stubbed out his smoke. He took out a White Owl cigar and fired it up. "Got any thoughts on who to pick for the other automatic rifle?"

"Isn't Zip the obvious choice? He handled the weapon real well today. He's experienced."

Holt stared at his cigar. "True...but Zimmerman's fragile."

184

"He's been better since we shipped out."

"Maybe. But there's still something lurking below the surface. I don't want to have to worry about my BAR keepers."

"Rollie Van Fleet's solid," Drake said. "He trained as a mechanic, so he could take care of the weapon. That's a big deal, I s'pose. And he's responsible."

"Henderson's a mechanic too. You're right about maintenance. Yeah, Van Fleet's serious, all right. Just wonder if he's tough enough. Let me think on it. In the mean time—" Holt stood and put a hand on Drake's shoulder. "—I got you as my number one automatic rifleman."

"Thanks for the confidence, sarge. I won't let you down."

"I know you won't, son."

Drake shrugged. "Been thinking about what you said this morning. About growing a thick skin. Maybe there's something to it." He stood. "Thanks for leveling with me."

Two days later Holt announced to the squad that Drake and Van Fleet would be his BAR keepers on fire teams 1 and 2.

In the pre-dawn hours of Monday, 27 May, USS *Beatrix* sailed into Manila Bay on the west side of the island of Luzon.

Later, when they hit the deck, Drake and his squad mates lined up on the ship railing to gawk at the Philippine capital. "Lookee that!" Malarkey said, pointing to the old walled city along the river. "Like some of them castles they got along the Rhine. Only bigger."

"Think it's called the *Intramuros*," Arvee said. "In colonial days it was the Spanish Fort Santiago. That's where the Japs made their last stand in February. Read about it last night."

Drake peered through binoculars at the ancient walls and the buildings inside. "Holy smoke, the place is three-fourths rubble, and even the stuff still standing's had the tar beat out of it. Must've been one heckuva fight. Take a look," he said, handing the binos to Zip.

Zimmerman scanned the *Intramuros*. "Yep, those Japanese...they're in it for keeps."

"Lemme have the glasses," Bo said, yanking the binos from Zip. He peered up a street leading from the waterfront. "I see saloons. And women! I think I'm in love."

"Women?" Davis said. "Gimme those." He scanned the throngs of people shopping, selling, bicycling, repairing buildings. The streets were teeming. "Must be a million of 'em."

"A million of what, Blackie?" Will Tolliver asked.

"Women, dummy. Tell you what, I'm fixing to get me a couple of 'em."

Sgt. Holt walked up to the group.

"Hey, sarge," Tolliver said, "we're gonna get some time off in Manila, aren't we?"

"Ah, Private Tolliver...I can always count on you for a laugh." Holt chuckled as he punched Will's bicep playfully. Then he scowled. "Think this is a pleasure cruise?" he growled. "No, you're not getting any leave. Now form up for our run. And gentlemen, we're doing an extra mile on account of your buddy here, Pvt. Tolliver"

Late that morning, the GIs from the ill-fated USS *Jagger* disembarked and convoyed south to Camp Yankee, their training base. *Beatrix* and her boys sailed out of the harbor, heading north.

An hour underway, the ship slowed and Captain Hooft came on the PA. "Men, the landmass off to starboard is the Bataan Peninsula. It was there a little over three years ago that the infamous Death March took place. To honor the sacrifices our comrades made, I ask that you remove your headgear and spend a moment reflecting on the power of faith and commitment. In the days ahead, especially the darkest ones, remember those men and be undaunted!" Two minutes later the ship's engines throbbed back to life, and she resumed her maritime trek up the Philippine coast.

In the afternoon, *Beatrix* sailed into recently-liberated Subic Bay, then little more than a PT-Boat base of the US Navy. Drake and the thousand-plus others went ashore via shuttling small craft. They boarded canvas-covered deuce-and-a-half trucks for the trip to Camp Dodger, thirty miles north. On the way there, they passed through the deserted, battle-ruined town of Olongapo. For Drake, it was a sobering sight. Though he was sure his cause was right, though he was confident he'd never sink to the inhumanity seen on Bataan, Olongapo spoke a dark and ancient truth—soldiering was an inherently dirty business.

Attack and Defense

The convoy of trucks carrying Drake and the others emerged from dense jungle and drove into Camp Dodger late in the afternoon. The GIs jumped from the decks of the deuce-and-a-halfs onto a soft carpet of hacked, flattened vegetation and sandy soil.

Drake surveyed the scene. He and the others were standing near a double line of barbed wire fencing. Dodger had been carved out of the jungle and was about the size of two football fields laid side by side. Before him was an array of close-packed, green canvas tents. Each big enough to sleep a dozen men. Taking up a quarter of the camp's area, they were perfectly aligned in ten identical rows, twelve tents deep. Like a well-designed city.

But Drake had seen cities before. What was new to him, what held his attention, was the jungle outside the wire. Primeval: The colors, deep and lush, mostly green but laced with yellows and reds and rich browns. The vitality, as if it were one enormous beast, shimmering with life. The mystery. The jungle, simultaneously tantalizing and terrifying. Beyond, to the west, was the South China Sea—unseen but brought near by the sound of its pounding waves, ominous as native drums. And to the east, rising into mists, was a mountain, a silent, green-shrouded giant dominating the landscape.

Arvee elbowed Drake. "It's called Mount Pinatubo."

Drake glanced at his buddy. "How do you know that?"

"Read about it in *National Geographic*. It's forested all the way up. Inhabited by some savage tribe. Headhunters. Maybe cannibals, I dunno. They kill you with poison darts. Article said the Japanese couldn't subdue them so they just left 'em be."

"Cannibals? Betcha they're out there watching us right now." Bo Forgette slapped a mosquito on his neck. "Speaking of man-eaters, that's one less of the critters." He grimaced at the bloody, dime-sized carcass of the insect squashed on his palm then wiped it on his pants. "Gonna take me an extra malaria pill." He rummaged through his rucksack and found his brown bottle of quinine tablets. He took one with a swig from his canteen.

Saving Euridice

Arvee pulled a pamphlet from his rucksack. "Anybody else read this?" He held it up. The title was *US Army Infantry Training in the Philippines. Getting Ready.* "No?" He opened the booklet. "Says here the jungle's crawling with cobras. There's lots of spiders, some big as a dinner plate. Scorpions, leeches, crocs in the rivers, sharks in the ocean—"

"Hey Titus," Malarkey said, "you're leaving out the most lethal critter in these parts, the notorious Philippine screaming green eagle-gator. Why, they're known to swoop in and gobble a fella down before he can say *boo.*"

"A flying reptile?" Arvee scanned a couple pages. "I dunno. Nothing about it here."

"I think Marv's funning you, Arvee," said Drake.

"Maybe." Malarkey patted Titus's back. "But to be safe, sport, you best keep checking the sky. 'Specially if you hear a high-pitched screech."

Arvee scratched his chin and studied Malarkey's face. "Aw, I knew you were joshing all along, Marvin." He held the booklet up. "According to this, the most dangerous varmint around here is the one Bo just splattered. The mosquito."

"No need to tell me twice, partner," Forgette muttered. "I aim to go real heavy on the quinine and bug juice till I'm outta this God-forsaken place." He poured repellant from an olive drab metal vial into his palm and rubbed it on his neck.

Arvee patted his booklet. "This says some dope called DDT knocks out mosquitoes pretty good. Apparently, they douse camp and our training areas with the stuff."

Holt walked up to the group with a handful of papers. "Gather around, men. On behalf of the U.S. Army, welcome to Camp Dodger. I got our unit assignments, the story on billeting, and so on." He glanced at the paperwork. "We're assigned to the 74th Infantry Division. Major General Hal Hamperville commanding. The 74th's nickname is *Hell-Bent* and word is, the general's determined to live up to that. Camp Dodger here's all 443rd Battalion under Lieutenant Colonel Thatcher. We're in Charlie Company, First Platoon. Captain Nichols runs the

189

company and First Lieutenant Happenchance is our Platoon Leader. Seem like pretty good officers. We're Second Squad." Holt shuffled through his papers. "We're billeted in tent 28. That's two-eight."

Holt studied a hand-drawn map of Camp Dodger's layout. "See the tent over there with the red cross?" He glanced to the far end of camp. "That's the hospital. Next to the southern perimeter fence, is the mess hall." He pointed to a tin-roofed pavilion with no walls and picnic-style tables. "Behind it's the kitchen." Holt motioned toward a smaller structure, also open-air, with a half dozen chimneys poking through its corrugated roof. "Behind you's the motor pool." The sergeant pointed to a big structure, open and tin-roofed like the mess hall and kitchen, where the deuce-and-a-halfs had headed after they'd dropped off their GIs. "Finally men, note the sentry towers at each of the four corners of Dodger." They rose in the ten foot cleared strip between the twin barbed wire fences. Four MPs with dogs patrolled the lane between the towers. "I don't advise sleep-walking out there.

"Now we'll drop off our gear at tent twenty-eight. Then Lieutenant Happenchance wants a word with you. Gotta hustle—chow's in thirty-five minutes at the mess building, and afterward there's a mandatory talk by someone from Battalion Medical. Lights out early tonight—we start training tomorrow, bright and early." He stuck the paperwork under his arm. "Questions?" There were none. "All right then, grab your stuff and follow me to our ritzy new digs."

Lt. Happenchance addressed the platoon with a thick Boston accent. "Keep on your toes, men." He glanced at the perimeter fence. "Though we blew the Japanese army out of Luzon, small pockets of lethal guerilla resistance remain in the jungle." He crossed his arms. "Regarding your training, cinch up those chin straps: The real fireworks are just six months away, so don't expect me to pull any punches." He eyed his men for a moment. "Now, who's ready for chow?"

The dinner was canned ham, beans, rice and some delicious chunked tropical fruit Drake was unfamiliar with. After the meal, a medic captain talked about the anti-mosquito program—sleeping tent netting discipline, spraying, and medication—and camp sanitation.

Lights out was called at 2145 hours. In their tropical tent with the canvas sides rolled up to admit the breeze coming out of the west, the GIs of Second Squad laid on their cots uncovered, in their skivvies. A couple of men smoked, though technically that wasn't allowed. "Damn, it's hot," muttered Henderson.

"Yeah," said Rollie Van Fleet, "but the air's a million times better than in those lousy sleeping bays on Old Trixie."

"Don't know which I hated more," said Will Tolliver, "getting broiled on deck by the fucking sun or choking down below."

"Aw, you survived, didn't you?" Holt said. "Now cut the belly-aching and get some shut eye. Oh five hundred hours is going to come awful early tomorrow morning."

First Platoon, with Lt. Happenchance out front, went running out the wire and down the road through the jungle before breakfast. They went out for twenty minutes then came back. Afterward Happenchance said, "Looks to me like Sgt. Holt's Second Squad showed up in pretty good shape. They'll report first to morning chow. The rest of you will stand fast and give me forty push-ups. Nobody eats until he does his forty." He eyed the platoon then handed them over to Sgt. Young, the platoon first sergeant, who dismissed Holt's squad and started the others doing their exercises.

After breakfast, the men policed their living quarters. Holt inspected the squad's tent and the surrounding area. He found an empty, crumpled Lucky Strikes package behind the tent. Holding the offending trash high above his head, he announced, "I don't give a shit who dropped this trash in our area. What really steams me that not one of you lazy bums picked it up." Holt's jaw tightened. "If I *ever* find garbage in my area again, you'll regret it." He carried the cigarette package like it was toxic to the trash bin in front of the squad's tent and dropped it in.

Holt double-timed the squad to the parade ground. He brought them to at ease for the briefing part of the day's lesson. "Mark 28 May on your calendars, gentlemen. Today you start the most important lesson an infantry unit can learn. It's the heart and soul of offensive battlefield tactics—fire and maneuver." He looked at Zimmerman. "Am I overselling, Zip?"

"Reckon not. In the push from Normandy, we used fire and maneuver on every Fritzie position we encountered."

Holt nodded. He picked up a chalk board he had lying at his feet. At the top, he drew a square and wrote *Bad Guys* inside. Below he drew another square and labeled it *Good Guys*. "This is us," he said, pointing to the lower square. "Now, let's assume the bad guys are dug in. We've been assigned to kick their asses out. If this was 1918 in France, we'd charge into the teeth of their position, and they'd chew us up and spit us out. But it's 1945. We're way smarter now. So *before* we try to blast the enemy out, we *suppress* his ability to defend himself. How? We split into two—a fire unit and a maneuver unit. On my '**Covering Fire!**' command, the fire unit opens up with everything they got. It's called *suppressing or covering fire*—a withering rain of lead that makes the enemy stick his head between his knees. Can't shoot if you're ducking down for dear life, right? Two counts after my '**Covering Fire!**' command, the maneuver unit swings around here and stealthfully advances." Holt drew an arcing arrow that moved up the right side of the board and hit the enemy on his left flank. "Who can tell me why our maneuver unit goes all the way around to the side like this? Why not move straight forward? Be quicker, wouldn't it?"

Zimmerman looked around and sheepishly raised his hand.

"Not you, Zip. 'Course *you* know the answer." Holt scanned his men. "Anybody else?"

"'Cause enemy won't expect it?" Malarkey said.

Holt frowned. "Of course they'll expect it," he barked. "This is SOP for every attacking infantry unit in any man's army." He looked scanned his squad. "Well?"

"Because if the maneuver unit moves straight ahead," Arvee said, "they'll be in the line of fire from their own fire team."

"Exactly!" Holt boomed. "Who wants to get shot in the back by his own buddies?" He threw the chalkboard down and put his hands on his hips. "Fire and maneuver. That's why I'm so partial to the BAR—because in the suppressing role, an automatic rifle's fucking fantastic at persuading the enemy to keep his stinking head down. And in the attacking role, once you're up-close, it'll chop up them bad guys in a hurry....Any questions?"

"I say let's just get out there and try it," Malarkey said.

"One more thing and we will." Holt picked up the chalkboard. "On a real battlefield, when a dozen men execute something as complex and dangerous and exciting as a fire and maneuver tactic, they live and die on control and coordination. That's where Corporal Barezzi and me come in. Our job is to shepherd you men. No matter how excited and scared you are, you need to listen and obey. No thinking, debating, hesitating...got it?"

The GIs nodded.

"OK," Holt said, "First you'll get you rifles and blank ammo at the armory. Then we have a two kilometer march outside the wire to our training area." He checked his watch. "We need to be back for noontime chow, so let's move out."

"Sarge," said Bo Forgette, "we'll be busting through jungle to get to our training, right? Arvee was telling us about all the ornery critters that live out there in the wild. Snakes and such. And all we've got in our rifles is blanks? How are we s'posed to protect ourselves?"

Holt rolled his eyes. "First of all, that out there—" He pointed to outside the fence. "—ain't *the wild*. It's called the boondocks. Second of all, you don't need to worry that little head of yours about critters is because H. T. Holt and his good pal, the M1911 sidearm, are looking out for you." He unholstered his pistol and held it up for the squad to see. ".45 caliber automatic, invented by John Browning, just like the BAR. It'll stop a rhino. I keep it with me permanent. And it *ain't* loaded with blanks." He holstered the weapon and huffed. "Now, if Private Forgette's concerns have been adequately addressed—" He glared at Bo. "—can we get back to soldiering?"

After checking out rifles and blank ammunition and a trek through the boondocks, Second Squad spent the morning working on the fire and maneuver tactic against mock enemy positions. After lunch, Holt's GI's paired off with First Squad, taking turns attacking and defending a position. The next two weeks were spent practicing the tactic in various unit sizes up through company and in various environments: In the jungle. On beaches, coming up from the surf. In urban settings, using the deserted town of Olongapo down near Subic Bay.

Another week was spent working on ambushes, both setting them and defeating them. For the latter, Holt's gospel was simple. "In an ambush, the squad's gotta react as one. The absolute worst thing you can do is to stay put. Any concerted reaction, even the most boneheaded thing possible, is better than sitting there, waiting to get ripped to shreds. So leaders, when your unit gets hit, *Do something bold—anything, goddamnit. Right now!* And if you're following, *Follow*, whether you agree with the leader's decision or not."

Every day for physical training there were long marches, usually in full combat gear. And then one Tuesday there was *The Spider's Web*. The platoon was trucked to a clearing in the jungle. They formed-up before a structure consisting of a twenty-foot high crossbar with cargo netting made of one inch rope hanging from each side. On the ground, below the nets, were three foot thick, water-filled rubber bladders to cushion the falls of GIs who didn't make it up or down.

After instructions, the men lined up for their first go at *The Web*. Arvee Titus, stood in front of Drake, eyeing the scaffold. "Rats, that thing's tall," he whispered. "I'm actually not so great at heights."

"You'll be OK," Drake said. "Just don't look down." Noting Arvee's wide eyes, he grinned. "Hey, I'll go first. You just follow me to the top. Besides, if anything happens, there's those water pillows to catch you." He pointed to Bo Forgette ascending the net.

"And look, we make our first climb without gear. It'll be a piece of cake."

When it was his turn on the ropes, Arvee's foot slipped. "Whoa," he shrieked, falling from six feet up onto the bladders.

Drake heard the cry. He scurried down and said, "How about we give 'er a go...together!" Arvee was shaking. "Look, Titus, I'm not going over the top without you," Drake growled. He extended a hand to Arvee. They climbed side by side and made it all the way to the crossbar. Giddy with a mix of elation and exhaustion, they came down to the cheers of their comrades.

On the first day of climbing, most of the men fell at least once. Within a week, no one did. *The Spider's Web* had been beaten.

Monday, 25 June was spent on shooting drills five miles north of Camp Dodger. After checking out weapons, there was a long, hot march through the dense jungle to get to battalion firing range C. In the morning, the GIs of Second Squad checked out live ammo and shot at stationary bulls-eye targets. After a lunch of sandwiches, bananas, and coffee, they went on a patrol simulation exercise—a walk-through, blank ammunition course. It consisted of a jungle path with pop-up cardboard human silhouette targets appearing from behind foliage, up in trees, and so on.

The men were exhausted after marching back to Camp Dodger. They finished cleaning their rifles and turned them in to the armory just in time for evening chow. After eating, the medical staff gave Company C a class on field-treating common battlefield injuries.

Drake had started a letter to his mother when lights out was called at 2130 hours. He stuffed the pad of lined paper and his pencil in his duffle and happily closed his eyes. Within a minute, he'd drifted off to sleep serenaded by the soft chirps of crickets in the distance.

He dreamed that he was back in Germany. In Bonn. Late one balmy evening, he was walking through ruined streets of the city, looking for Stetti's place. At one house, Malarkey was sitting out on the porch steps, whistling. Seeing Drake, he hollered, "Watcha looking for, sport?"

Drake couldn't remember the name of Stetti's street. He mumbled, "Some girl," and walked on. Eventually he came to a familiar-looking row of houses. He saw Stetti's home down a block or so. There was a jeep parked outside and who but Dutch Scholz was getting into it. Drake ran, calling and waving, but the jeep drove away before he could get there.

At the house, he spotted Katarina out front, and he dashed up to ask her if Stetti was home. But the old woman was sound asleep, and no matter how vigorously he shook her shoulder, she didn't wake.

Drake was ready to give up when he spied Stetti, brushing her hair and watching him though a second floor window. He gasped at her beauty and tried to say, *I came back for you.* His mouth moved, but no sound came out.

Up in the window, Stetti didn't react. She didn't smile, didn't wave, her lips didn't move…she only watched, cold as a marble statue, and kept brushing her hair.

Even the thud of the explosion brought no reaction to Stetti's face. Nor the shouting. A moment later there was second concussive thud, this one louder, closer. And a burst of firing, like the noise on the shooting range.

Suddenly Drake was wide awake. It was dark, but he could faintly see Holt fly up from his cot, reach into the holster hanging from the tent post, and draw his pistol. He heard Holt snap back the bolt to cock it and watched him dash out of the tent.

Drake recalled his training—*under attack, follow your leader*. He grabbed his bayonet and was right behind the sergeant. In the moonlight, he saw Holt, barefoot and wearing just his olive drab skivvies, square into a firing position. Beyond him, Drake watched transfixed as a figure ran awkwardly toward them, shouting wildly, with a rifle-fixed bayonet pointed at Holt's chest.

Boom, boom. Holt calmly squeezed off two quick shots. The charging soldier went down like he'd hit a brick wall.

Drake followed Holt as he shuffled toward the fallen enemy, keeping his pistol trained on the man. The soldier lay sprawled on his back in the space between two tents—his only sign of life, the gurgling sound of his gasped breaths. Standing over the moon-lit figure, Drake peered at his tattered, dust-gray Japanese uniform, a widening, wet, red splotch centered on his chest. The man's glassy eyes were open, and his scraggly beard was matted with sweat and dirt. The cloth cap he'd worn, tan with a golden star on the front, lay on the ground, next to his rifle.

The soldier croaked something and, with a quick sweep of his hand, yanked the pin from a hand grenade that hung from his uniform.

"Grenade," shouted Holt as he shoved Drake back and leapt on top of him, shielding him with his body.

Drake lay frozen with fear. The image of Stetti's lucky schilling flashed through his mind. But it was in his pants pocket back in the tent. If only he had it in the palm of his hand to squeeze now. After a few more seconds—it seemed like forever—he was thinking maybe the grenade was a dud when the deafening explosion slapped his cheek. Instantly, he heard the angry zip and zing of shrapnel shooting through the air and peppering the earth around him. Then, as quickly, everything went still…leaving only the faint chirps of far-off crickets.

Seven of Hearts

"Think I twisted my ankle," murmured Holt, seconds after the grenade's blast. "Shit!" He'd rolled off Drake onto his side, just as men came pouring out of the adjacent tents.

A flashlight beam lit up Holt's face, then it darted to Drake's. "You guys OK?" It was Breezy's voice. "That was one helluva—"

"Medic!" Arvee Titus's piercing holler seemed incongruous with the skinny, white legs sticking out of his baggy undershorts. "We need a goddamn medic here ASAP."

Drake looked at the three GIs with their flashlight beams trained on Sgt. Holt's foot. In the moonlight he could see their faces—Breezy, Titus and Malarkey.

"I'll go," Sandy Berger said, running off.

A few feet farther off, Rollie Van Fleet and Zip Zimmerman were pointing their flashlights at the Japanese soldier. "Sure he's dead?" said Van Fleet.

"Got no chest," hissed Zip, "'course he's dead."

Holt started panting.

"You OK, sarge?" Drake peered at Holt's face, darkened by shadows. He knelt and squeezed the sergeant's hand.

"Don't...worry," Holt whispered.

Drake peeled off his undershirt and covered the sergeant's lower leg. "Where's the goddamn medic?" he hollered over his shoulder. When he looked back, his shirt was already red with blood. He raised the covering to examine Holt's foot. "Come here, Zip. Take a look." He held the shirt up so Zimmerman could see the wound. "Think we ought to make a tourniquet?"

Zip grimaced. "I ain't a medic, but..."

"Somebody get me a belt," Drake yelled. "Hurry up, dammit."

By the time Blackie Davis held out a belt, the medic ran up. He uncovered Holt's foot and shined a flashlight on it. "Son of a bitch," he muttered.

"Needs a tourniquet, don't he?" Drake said.

"Yeah. Give me a hand. In my bag—" The medic nodded to the satchel he'd brought. "—you'll see an elastic band and a peg. Gimme it."

"Train the light on his foot," the medic said to Drake, handing his flashlight. He twisted the tourniquet, and the bleeding slowed immediately. "What's the sergeant's name?"

"Holt," said Drake, "our squad leader. He stopped the Jap. You're going to be able to save him, aren't you?"

"Trying." The medic ripped open an envelope and dusted the wound with its white powder contents. "Need a runner," he said, grabbing Tolliver's sleeve. "Go find Captain Burgess. Think he's over by the motor pool with other casualties. Tell him we're bringing a tourniquet job to the dispensary. Possible limb excision. Tell *Captain Burgess*. Got it?"

Tolliver nodded and ran off.

"We're going to improvise a stretcher," the medic said. "Get me a cot." When Malarkey and Henderson brought one from the tent, he ordered, "Flaten the legs. We're going to move the sergeant on it. I want six of you. A man hefting each corner, one out front with a lantern and one along side with a flashlight trained on the sarge's foot. I'll be working the tourniquet. Got it?"

Drake, Malarkey, Henderson, Davis, Zimmerman, and Van Fleet went with the medic and Holt. When they got to the dispensary tent, medical staff took over. Drake and the GIs were left standing outside. It started drizzling.

After five minutes, Drake said, "Better go back. Holt's with the pros. Come on, guys."

The six GIs walked back in a downpour. The rain was warm. Heavenly. It washed off the mud, sweat, leaves, and blood so that when they got back to Tent 28 they were soaked clean.

Inside, they toweled off and put on dry underwear. Drake told the squad how the whole engagement had come off—how brave Holt had been. He broke down when he talked about Holt shielding him from the blast with his own body. It wasn't until 0330 that Breezy ordered, "Lights out, fellas. Try to get some sleep."

Drake lay in the dark wondering why he'd never been the one doing the saving. Maybe some guys were cut out to be heroes and some weren't. And he kept seeing the gash in Holt's foot. All the blood. Drake fell asleep praying there'd be good news from the medics the next day.

Corporal Barrezi's hands were shaking when he spoke to the squad in the morning. "I talked to Lt. Happenchance just now. He asked me to take over squad leader duties. For the time being." He took a gulp of water from his canteen. "Said I could get a promotion out of it...if I get the job permanent." He hunched his shoulder. "Not that I'm bucking for it. I want Sgt. Holt back just as much as the next guy."

"Any word on how he's doing, Breezy?" Drake asked.

"The lieutenant hadn't heard. He said the medics were swamped. On account of the multiple casualties." Barezzi leaned toward the men like he was about to pass along *Top Secret* intelligence. "There were two raiders. Jap soldiers who probably got stranded and were out in the boondocks on their own. Left to fight the war solo, I guess. Coming through the fences, they shot one sentry dead, wounded another. One of the sappers hit the motor pool with gasoline bombs and grenades. Started fires. A dozen vehicles torched. One mechanic burned pretty bad. MPs had a bigtime shoot-out with the guy outside the motor pool. Killed him. The other guy was the one Holt shot. He'd been running around the camp crazy-like. Firing into tents. Set one tent on fire with a gas bomb. Burned a half dozen GIs from Fourth Platoon, Bravo. Couple of 'em died—"

"Wasn't Deschamps was it?" Tolliver said. "Ernie Deschamps? Buddy of mine. He was assigned to Bravo Company. Fourth Platoon, I think."

"The lieutenant didn't give me any names." Breezy rubbed his eyes. He looked like he hadn't slept much. "He suggested somebody from the squad spend the morning with Holt. Let him know we're pulling for him." He took off his helmet and tossed some playing cards in it. "I thought we'd draw to see who goes. Obviously I won't draw since I'm squad leader."

"Acting squad leader," said Drake.

Breezy shrugged, like it was a technicality. "Yeah, acting squad leader. I put nine spades and one heart in here." He shook the helmet. "The guy who draws the heart visits Holt."

Breezy held the helmet high and everyone reached in and took a card. Davis drew the seven of hearts. "Guess it's you going, Blackie."

Davis shrugged and kicked at the sandy dirt. "I dunno…seems like it outta be Drake. He was there with Holt last night." He offered the winning card to Drake. "Here, you go."

Drake looked at his feet. "But you drew the heart, Blackie."

"Davis is right," said Zip to Drake, "you go, kid. And why don't you take some of his stuff over to him. Might make him feel more comfortable. "

Drake scanned the men around him. He suddenly felt very close to them. "Sure, I'll go." He took the seven of hearts from Davis and shook his hand. "Thanks." He stuffed the card in his fatigue shirt pocket, picked up Holt's duffle, and trotted off toward the dispensary.

Three minutes later Drake was at the medical tent. As he opened the flap, a groggy-looking private carrying a tray of shiny surgical tools and a stack of white bandages scurried by. Drake grabbed his sleeve. "Can I see Sergeant Holt? How is he?"

The private seemed confused for a moment, then he said, "Oh yeah, Holt. The foot job."

"Well, how's he doing? Where is he?"

"He made it. He's…" The medic looked around the tent. He set the tray on a table and rubbed his eyes with a towel. "Back over there…I think." He pointed toward a dark corner. "Sorry, it's been a long night. What time is it anyway?"

Drake glanced at his wristwatch. "Zero eight fifteen." He hurried toward the bed in the far corner.

Holt was sleeping. Peaceful. He looked good. Except for the IV drip, you'd think he was napping. Drake was elated to see him like that. He set the duffle down and looked for a chair.

A captain with a stethoscope draped around his neck came up. "What are you doing here? Did you sign in?"

"No, sir. Sgt. Holt here is our squad leader. The guys sent me over to see how he's doing."

"Well, go John Hancock the book. Back by the door." The doctor glanced at Holt's chart. "The sergeant's pretty well doped up but you can grab a chair and sit with him. Just don't get him worked up. If anyone asks, tell them Captain Burgess said it was OK."

Drake signed in, then he pulled up a stool and sat next to Holt's bed.

Fifteen minutes later Holt stirred and mumbled, "Water."

Drake hustled off and got a cup of water and a straw from the bleary-eyed private. He put the straw to Holt's lips.

Holt took a tiny sip and his eyes opened. "Omaha? Is that you? Are you OK?"

"Thanks to you I am."

Holt closed his eyes. "Good."

"The guys all send their best, sarge. Can't wait till you're back in the saddle with us." Drake grinned. "Guess we're a bunch of saps for abuse."

Holt's eye lids fluttered opened. He peered at Drake. A tear tracked down his cheek.

Captain Burgess returned. He looked over Holt's chart. "Time to take a look at those dressings, Sergeant. Just be a minute." He lifted the sheet covering Holt's legs. Next to Holt's bare left ankle was a bundle of bandages where the right foot should have been. Seeping blood saturated the bottom of the dressing.

Drake jolted to his feet. Then his knees went weak. His head spun and a spasm in the gut shot bile into his mouth. He collapsed back onto the stool.

202

The doc glanced at Drake. "Get some air, partner. I'm going to rebandage the stump. This kind of bleeding in the first twenty four hours after an amputation's completely normal. Come on back in ten minutes."

Drake eyes met Holt's. Both men were fighting back tears. Drake rose and stumbled out of the dispensary. Outside it was sunny and bright. A cool breeze blowing in from the ocean nestled his cheek. It was beautiful. It was heartbreaking. Drake wiped his eyes on his sleeve. He took out a cigarette and lit it. He sucked the smoke deep into his lungs. It calmed him.

When Drake went back in, Holt was alone.

The sergeant's eyes were dry. Except for the stubble of beard, he looked his old self. "Damn, what I'd give for a cigar about now." He shook his head and grinned at Drake. "And a couple fingers of rye whiskey."

Drake's lip trembled. "I...I didn't know about..."

"No? Aw, how could you have? Just found out myself." Holt forced a laugh.

"You protected me with your body." Drake swallowed hard. "I always wanted to be a hero, but in that split second, it was you."

"Wasn't nothing heroic about it. More like pure reaction. There was a hot grenade and I jumped as far from it as I could. You just happened to be in the way." Holt winked. "Just bad luck to catch a hunk of shrapnel from the fucking thing." He rubbed his eyes. "My ex-wife always said I had two left feet. She can't say that no more."

Drake thought about how little he knew about the man laying there crippled—his life outside the army. About how much he looked up to the guy. The army was that way. It brought men together as brothers...but distant ones. "So how'd you become a professional soldier, sarge?"

"Grew up in Oregon and got hitched to a local gal. Took the family to California during the dust years. Wife left me flat busted, so I joined the Army. That was nineteen and thirty-seven. Been all over with the service, including hell and back." Holt's eyes closed. "Now, who knows?"

203

"It's just not right, a hero like you that's the heart of the Army." Drake shook his head. "Now maybe you're…." He bit his lip. "And me, some measly private who's never done jack in the military's supposed to pick up the slack? Fat chance."

"Pull your chair close, Omaha." Holt waited for Drake to sit. "Ya know, you got it all wrong. The army doesn't need heroes. Not many of 'em anyway. Mostly it needs GIs who do their damn jobs. Whatever they're asked to do. Guys who aren't squawking all the time. Aren't always playing some angle. Trying to weasel out of stuff." He shrugged. "The army needs men like you, son." He eyed Drake and shook his head. "You don't look like much, but hell, it's leading young troops like you that rolls this old sergeant outta bed every morning."

Drake laughed. "What do you mean, *don't look like much?*"

Holt scowled. "Well, to be blunt, you don't exactly look like a fella that hunts rattlesnakes barehanded. Skinny, four-eyed like you are. But I tell you what, you tear through a damn job like crap through a goose."

Drake shook his head. "I try…it's just that I'm so damn average at everything."

"Average? You? Naw, you're one in a thousand. A regular pistol! Fact is, you make every other member of the unit better by your attitude and *espirit*. It's called leadership. Shit, I'll take a leader over a hero any day. As my drill sergeant in NCO school told us, 'Leadership is heroism multiplied.'" Holt winced as he shifted in his bunk. "I saw it that first night in Paris, when I took the squad out for a run. Look, I know how it is, training an outfit. When you're assigned a bunch of green GIs, it's like getting a handful of nickels. Your job's to turn 'em into quarters. With you, I got a shiny silver dollar."

"Mighty nice of you to say."

"Had a clue even before I set eyes on you. See, I get evaluations on each of my new men, ones your previous sergeants wrote. Don't recall the name of the guy who did yours."

"Rutledge?"

"Yeah, that was it…anyway, Rutledge called you a buzz saw. Said you always do your best. That other GIs look up to you. He felt lucky to have had you in his organization."

"Rutledge wrote that?"

"Damn straight." He grabbed Drake's sleeve. "Don't you let it go to your head, hear?"

"I won't, sarge. Hey—" Drake pointed to the bag on the floor. "—I brought some of your stuff along."

"You did? Good, cuz I'm in big time need of my shaving kit. And you know, there's something I want to give you. Open my duffle. See a silver flask in there? Grab it for me."

Drake examined the flask as he handed it to Holt. It had a Japanese symbol engraved on it.

Holt took off the cap and sniffed the contents. "Mmmm. Genuine Jap sake. Found it in one of their bunkers on the Canal. I was going to drink it, but something told me to hold off. Our division translator said this—" He tapped the symbol. "—is their word for *Victory*. I decided to carry it all the way to Japan and drink it soon as I set foot on their home soil. A slap in their face, I guess." He glanced at his bandaged stump. "Looks like I won't be making that landing now. Kind of hope you'll complete the job for me when you get there. What do you say? You'd play delivery boy for your old sarge, wouldn't you?" He pushed the sake into his private's hand.

"Sure I would." Drake clutched the flask. "You can count on it."

Holt took Drake's wrist and squeezed it. "I know I can. Hope it tastes good as it smells."

Dr. Burgess came back. "Truck's here, Sergeant."

Holt looked at Drake. "They're evacuating me to a regular hospital in Manila. Me and a couple of others banged up in the fireworks last night." He turned his face to the side. "Don't give your new squad leader too hard a time, huh?" he said, still looking away.

"It's Breezy. Our new squad leader's Breezy."

"Breezy?" Holt glanced back and shook his head.

Drake looked at the doctor than back at Holt. "You're leaving...now?"

The doc held Holt's wrist while looking at his watch. "Sixth Army's facility in Manila is equipped and staffed to handle serious injuries like the sergeant's. We're not." He picked up Holt's chart and jotted down his pulse rate. "Need you to vamoose now," he said to Drake.

Drake took Holt's hand. He leaned over, pulling himself into an embrace. "You take care, sarge." He was crying. "Thanks for what you made of me and all the other guys, too."

"It's my job." Holt sniffed. "*Was* my job." He turned away again and ran the sleeve of his pajama shirt over his eye. "Now get the hell back on duty. There *is* a war going on, you know."

Preparing for War, Preparing for Play

Right off the bat, filling Holt's shoes was tough for Corporal Barezzi. Without much experience, his decisions were more like guesses. Guesses set in quicksand. And unlike Holt, he didn't understand the basic precept of military leadership: Your men's unquestioning compliance is essential not only to accomplish the mission but also to keep them alive. Giving the impression you know what you're doing is as important as actually knowing it.

Two days after Holt's injury, Breezy's Second Squad was assigned to take a jungle forest hilltop from dug-in defenders of First Squad. Breezy assembled the squad and briefed them using a relief map. "This is our objective, men." He circled the high ground with a pencil. "We're here, along this line. How about if team Alpha under Private Malarkey pours suppression fire on the objective? Then Corporal Zimmerman can maneuver team Bravo off to the east here and engage the objective on its flank. Any questions?"

Marv raised his index finger. "Just a suggestion, sport, but how about if Zip takes Bravo up the west side? See, on the east there's a cliff to get over. Here." He drew an arrow indicating the location of the steep terrain.

"In the immortal words of General Patton," Zimmerman said, "I say *nuts* to that."

Arvee Titus cleared his throat. "I believe that was General McAuliffe."

Zip looked confused. "Huh?"

Titus sighed. "The one who said, 'Nuts!' It was McAuliffe....101st Airborne's commander. At Bastogne." He looked from man to man. "Well, it was McAuliffe."

No one spoke for a moment, until Zip blinked and continued where he'd left off, as if Arvee hadn't interrupted. "Look, Breezy, west's a longer route, and see over there—" He pointed to an exposed face of the hillside. "—I got no cover to mask my advance."

"But it does lead to higher ground," Tolliver said, tapping the map to the west of the objective. "Better for pounding their exposed flank."

"Everybody hold your horses," Barezzi huffed. He turned to Zimmerman. "You're the one leading the flanking maneuver, Zip. Whatever way you want is OK with me. You call it."

Zimmerman shrugged. "East it is, then…I guess."

Drake rolled his eyes, glad the defenders were First Squad firing blanks and not Japanese marines desperately defending their homeland.

That evening just before chow, Barezzi was accompanied by a young buck sergeant when he came back from briefing Lt. Happenchance about the exercise. "Men, this is Sergeant Ames. He's our new squad leader." Breezy looked relieved to have been relieved.

Forrest Ames had a long, thin face. His dark hair was buzzed close on the sides with a frizzy, stand-up top. He'd grown up in Tupelo, Mississippi and had been assigned to the quartermaster section of battalion headquarters. "Hope y'all can see your way to cutting me some slack. Just made sergeant in April, fellas, and this is my first leadership gig, so figure on some OJT for a spell. Point is, I feel real lucky to lead y'all. Lieutenant says Second Squad is one of his best." Ames chuckled. "'Don't screw it up,' was the last thing he told me."

Friday morning Drake and Zimmerman were called to see the lieutenant just after breakfast.

"Think we're in trouble?" Drake asked.

"No fucking idea," said Zip. "Probably sending us home. Hardy har har."

In the platoon leader's tent, they saluted and reported in.

"At ease, gentlemen," Happenchance said. He offered them cigarettes. "I had a chat with Sergeant Holt before…well, before he was wounded." He peered into both men's eyes. "He recommended you two for promotion. Your records support the recommendation, so I put it in to battalion. Col. Thatcher approved the promotions and gave me the signed paperwork this morning." The lieutenant stood. "Sgt. Young," he called to his first sergeant.

Young barreled in carrying two sets of chevrons and some papers. He handed them to Happenchance and picked up an ashtray. "Snuff the smokes." Then he boomed, "'Ten-**HUT**.'"

The lieutenant glanced at the paperwork and returned it to Young. He pinned on Zimmerman's new sergeant stripes and shook his hand. He stepped in front of Drake and pinned corporal stripes on his sleeve and shook his hand. "Proud of you two. You both earned this promotion. And you'll see Uncle Sam's appreciation reflected in your next pay envelope. So, sign the papers Sgt. Young has, then get back on duty. Dismissed."

Zip and Drake saluted and left with the first sergeant. They signed the documents of promotion. As they hustled back to the squad, Drake felt a little extra spring in his step.

That evening the troops got a Camp Dodger first—Zip called it *canned morale*—a movie was shown. It was the new Warner Brothers adventure film, *To Have and Have Not*, starring Humphrey Bogart and introducing Lauren Bacall, a young American starlet making her A-picture debut. As usual, Bogey played an antihero—a tough ex-pat American fishing boat captain working in Vichy-controlled Martinique. He agrees to smuggle French Resistance fighters out of the Gestapo's clutches. With many close scrapes and lots of bravado, the anti-hero Bogey pulls off the caper. What most viewers, including the Camp Dodger GIs, liked best were his on-screen fireworks with co-star Bacall, whom he dubs 'Slim.'

Drake was thoroughly smitten with the character of Slim because for him she was a theatrical portrait of Stetti. Sure, Hollywood got the hair color wrong—Bacall's honeyed blond was more girlish than Stetti's jet black. But they got the girl's hard, exotic beauty right. And the purr in her sultry voice. From the moment they met, Bacall had Bogey twirled around her finger. Later, as he watched a flat-broke Slim pick a rich sucker's pocket, Drake smiled, remembering the day he first saw Stetti working the outdoor tables of *Die Marionette* tavern in Bonn. But his favorite part was the film's ending, when Bogey, the American, gets his girl. Drake hoped it foreshadowed what was in store for Stetti and him.

The heat and the bugs and the constant thirst…they were murder. Bayonet drills were the most exhausting thing Drake had ever done. But some training was fun and exciting too. Drake felt like an actor in an adventure movie. Like acting, it was relatively safe—certainly compared to the actual combat it was supposed to approximate. "Everybody's firing blanks, for christsakes!" as Holt used to say when his men were tentative.

Drake especially liked the simulated amphibious landings. His company did lots of these. They took place on the volcanic sand beaches of Anawangin and Nagsasa Coves, southwest of Camp Dodger. At first they involved Second Squad wading out into the surf, then turning around and storming ashore, using fire and maneuver tactics to work their way off the sand and up the rocky hills surrounding the cove. As things progressed, the drills involved larger assault units and personnel playing Japanese defenders in fortified positions on the hillsides.

In mid-July armor was thrown into the exercise mix. Coming ashore with the infantry were "Donald Duck" swimming Sherman tanks—with normal treads for moving on land and propellers for driving in water. Fitted with steel pontoons to keep them afloat, the tanks made a powerful impression, firing their main guns from the water before hitting the beach.

In all the beach assault exercises, there was a common element, at least as far as Drake was concerned. With his first tread on sand, he'd say, "Here's to you, Sarge," and take a swig from his canteen, practicing for the ceremonial drink of sake he'd consume on Japanese soil. It became a good luck ritual.

Sgt. Ames called the squad together after chow one evening. "Gentlemen, I just got word that the battalion's fixing to bump up the training up a notch. Turn us into pros at the fine art of the amphibious combat landing. Lieutenant says they'll haul us way out to sea, and we'll board landing craft for actual run ins and beach landings. Just like hitting a real hostile objective. Some of the exercises will even be live-fire. Y'all better cinch down those chin straps!"

The GIs of Second Squad whooped and hollered. But the men's eyes, darting from one comrade to the next, reflected fear. They'd all heard what a bloodbath the invasion of Japan was expected to be. *Live Fire* reminded them Operation Olympic was only months away.

On Tuesday, 24 July Captain Nichols, Commander of Company C, assembled his men after breakfast. "I've been pleased with the effort and the results of our training, gentlemen. In less than two months here at Camp Dodger, Charlie Company has melded into an impressive fighting unit that I'd be proud to lead through the gates of hell. Now we still have a lot of work to do before we really earn our pay in November, when we punch the Emperor right in the mouth. But we're getting there. To show my appreciation of your fine work, I'm issuing the entire company a weekend pass commencing at noon this Friday and running through sunset on Sunday. More on that later." Nichols checked his watch. "OK, in forty minutes, First and Third Platoons are due on the bazooka range, and Second and Fourth are scheduled to practice pitching grenades at the foxhole field. After lunch we'll switch. All right, men, let's go out there and make some noise!"

Nichols spoke to the company again after the flag raising ceremony on Thursday morning. "Tomorrow after noontime mess your weekend pass begins. I want you to have a good time. However, there's rules you need to follow. First Sergeant Tubbs will review those with you now, so listen up! Top..."

Tubbs was a tanned, crew-cut man who wore dark glasses night and day. His uniform, with creases sharp as his bayonet, was always impeccable. He strode to a position in front of the battalion flagpole and thrust his hands on his hips. "Men, Captain Nichols has generously granted us the weekend off. Here are the rules I'll hold you to. Number one, do not be late to sign in Sunday evening." He scowled menacingly. "The CO said you need to be back by sundown Sunday. My almanac says the sun'll set at nineteen forty-eight hours. I want you in, safe and sound, signed, sealed, and delivered by nineteen thirty. Don't chisel me on the time. It's real simple—return to duty late and I'll courts marshal your AWOL ass. Number two, once you sign out noon tomorrow, you're on your own. You can sleep here at Camp Dodger or on the beach. Maybe you can find a place to bunk in San Narcisco. Up to you. There'll be trucks shuttling back and forth. Just don't sleep in the jungle. Like fishing? For a few bucks a dozen guys can hire a boat to go out. Number three, don't overdo it. The locals will sell you beer on the beach. Be sober when you report Sunday. Don't get too much sun. And don't you dare drown or get eaten by sharks! I expect 100% turnout Monday morning. Number four, and most important, men: Don't say a word about why you're here to any civilian—the guy selling you a beer, the gal who finds you so handsome she wants to lose her virginity to you, the old lady making you rice and gravy, the five year old offering you a stick of gum for a penny. Say nothing about Operation Olympic or November. Nothing about the number of GIs in Dodger. Not even the brand of cigarettes your squad leader smokes. Got it? Remember, loose lips sink ships."

Later that morning, marching into the jungle for mortar practice, the squad took a cigarette break. Marv Malarkey called the men together. "Hey fellas, I sat at breakfast yesterday with a guy delivering ammunition. Fella named Appleby. His battalion's based up north of here—place called Camp Redleg. Told me his company got their weekend leave a while back, and his squad hired some fisherman to sail them to Manila for a night. Cost 'em a few bucks apiece. In Manila, they ate good, drank good and got fucked good. Time of their goddamn lives. He told me the guy with the boat's name is Tomas. Has a crate docked in San Narcisco harbor. White with pink trim. Can't miss it. What do you say we do it? Together, like brothers. Something to remember forever."

"We could all get tattoos!" Tolliver said. "My uncle was in the Navy in the Twenties. Got him one on leave in the Philippines. 'Didn't hurt much,' he said."

"I'm getting one that says *June Bug* in a big red heart," said Rollie Van Fleet. "The old lady'll be tickled pink!"

"Whoa!" Arvee Titus held his hand up. "Top didn't say we could go as far as Manila."

"Didn't say we couldn't, *tight-ass*," Tolliver replied.

"Well, we ought to ask, fellas," Arvee said, "just to be sure."

"Fucking out of your mind, sport?" Malarkey said, laughing. "No, we're not going to ask."

"My brother's a Marine," said Ames. "Said the gals in Filipino whorehouses are covered, head to toe, with tattoos."

"Even down there?" Van Fleet pointed to his crotch.

Ames nodded. "Yessiree, Bob. They'll give you a guided tour for an extra buck."

"I saw that same story somewhere." Tolliver said.

"They got crap like that in comic books?" Davis snickered.

"Hey, I read other stuff too."

"Yeah, girlie magazines. And I betcha it's more gawking than reading."

Malarkey waved his arms. "Gentlemen, please!...So, we're all in, right? We'll go to San Narcisco together Saturday morning and find this Tomas guy. And come Saturday night, it'll be *Hello Manila!* We'll be drinking the beers and bedding the babes."

"And showing off new tattoos," said Tolliver.

"You got it, sport." Malarkey looked around at his squad mates. He made hard eye contact with each man, sealing their pledge to go.

Drake had remained silent through the discussion. Though Tolliver was technically right that going to Manila for the night hadn't been forbidden, Drake thought it was a bad idea. He pictured Sgt. Tubbs blowing his stack if he found out. But he'd go along with his squad mates. Like Holt always preached, *Units need to act with unity.* Whether it was an ambush in the jungle or a hare-brained scheme, Drake believed a team member's best choice was acting in concert with his fellows. Besides, there was something he wanted to do in the big city.

Breaking Eggs

Like most of Charlie Company's complement, Drake and the boys of Second Squad spent Friday afternoon 27 July on the beach. They swam, drank warm beer, and played ball. That night they slept on the sand.

Early Saturday morning, with Marv Malarkey in the lead, they slipped away from the others and hurried to the tiny marina just south of San Narcisco. There were only two boats docked there and one had pink trim. The GIs walked out the pier to inspect the craft, which up close was in sorry shape. The paint was peeling. Part of the deck rail was missing. The crate stunk of dead fish. "Not too bad," pronounced Malarkey. He pointed to the side of the boat where *La Sirena* was written next to a whimsical drawing of a mermaid. "Think that's what Appleby called her."

At the end of the pier, two men were sitting on stools, mending fishing nets. Marv approached them. "Hey sport, where do I find a guy named Tomas? Fisherman. Runs that *La Sirena* tub." He pointed to the pink-trimmed boat.

One of the men squinted at the American. "*La Sirena?* Tomas?"

"Yeah, that's it."

"*Policía?*"

"Huh? No, I'm not a cop. My buddies and me, we're GIs. We want to go by boat to Manila. You know…" He pantomimed ocean waves.

The Filipino stood up. "With paying, mister?"

Malarkey pulled out a wad of US dollar bills, twenty of them.

"I am Tomas." He took the wad from Malarkey and counted out eight dollars. He gave the rest back. "Eight American dollars are now. Eight to coming back. OK, mister?"

"Deal."

Tomas pointed to Marv's watch. "To Manila is five hours. Want beer, mister?"

"Beer? Sure thing!"

"Two dollars." Tomas held out his hand.

Malarkey paid him. "Is the beer cold?"

"Cold?" Tomas laughed. "Yes, cold as the air. We leave now ten minutes, mister." He held his hands out with all his fingers extended. "Ten minutes? OK?"

"Sure."

It took half of the ten minutes for Tomas to get the diesel engine of *La Sirena* started. A boy wearing only a pair of shorts came out on the pier pulling a wagon with two dozen clanking brown bottles of beer in it.

Bo Forgette had been standing apart from the rest of the GIs. As the beer was carried aboard, he came up to Malarkey and said, "If it's all the same, think I'll pass on this little excursion." He glanced at *La Sirena* and shivered. "That boat...it's a goddamn wreck."

"Bullshit!" Marv said. "We all agreed, Forgette. You can't back out now."

"I'm scared, man." Bo pulled out cash and handed him a fold of greenbacks. "Here's five clams. That'll cover my part."

"Forget it, cowboy," Ames said, "you're going." He huffed. "Somebody sees you around here, they'll wonder where the rest of us are. Start asking questions. Then we're all screwed."

Tears welled in Forgette's eyes. "I can't do it, Sarge."

"Yes, you can." Drake put an arm around Bo's shoulder. "Sit next to me. I'll be your own private lifeguard. And, hey, lookee that—" He pointed to an old, paint-splattered life vest on the deck of the boat. "—a Mae West. You can wear it."

Forgette wasn't sold, but he let Drake guide him on board. He put on the life vest and sat stiffly next to Drake near the stern. The rest of Second Squad climbed aboard.

The boy untied the idling boat, pushed it from the pier with a long pole, and it was off.

Drake watched Tomas at the wheel. He was a wiry little guy, tough looking. His face and hands were tanned a deep brown and crusted with salt. He had a stiff moustache and thick hair, jet black. Drake leaned toward Bo and hollered over the racket of the engine, "Tomas don't look like Bogart, but he handles *La Sirena* with the same flair that Bogey did in *To Have and Have Not,* doncha think?"

With sea spray wetting his face, Forgette clutched his life vest. He nodded in reply without looking at Drake.

La Sirena sliced through the ocean at a pretty good clip, but the run to Manila still took the five hours Tomas had indicated.

As soon as the vessel tied up, Forgette was the first man off. On the dock, he grinned and quickly was his old self, joking with the others and drinking a beer.

Malarkey stood on the edge of the pier and hollered to Tomas, "Tomorrow. Sunday. Twelve thirty hours." He squinted at the sun. "Just after midday. We come here." He stomped his foot on the dock's wooden planks. "We go back then. San Narcisco. Got it?" He pointed out to sea.

Tomas nodded. "Yes, just here on half past twelve. With eight dollars, mister. I come."

La Sirena sped off and the GI's did the same. Van Fleet, Tolliver, Forgette, Henderson, and Breezy went looking for a tattoo parlor. Ames, Malarkey, Zimmerman, and Berger ran off to find the red light district.

Drake, Titus, and Davis went into a waterfront bar just down the rubble-strewn street to have a beer. The place was called *El Naufragio.* There were only a couple of other customers when the GIs entered. An ancient jukebox played earnest-sounding ballads sung in a strange language. Though it was hot in the bar and the stench of stale beer and sweat was strong, the darkness inside and the chill of the drinks made the place dang pleasant for a trio of GIs on weekend leave from infantry training.

Drake checked his watch. "Eighteen hundred hours. What do you say we go out, fellas, and rustle up something to eat?"

Their noses led them to an open-air café. They feasted on fish, sausages, tomatoes, and sweet potatoes—all skewered on bamboo and roasted over charcoal. For dessert they had fried bananas.

As they finished eating, Davis said, "Don't know about you, but I'm about ready for a little female companionship." He belched. "You with me, fellas?"

"I'm up for giving it a shot." Arvee looked at his buddies expectantly. "Get it? *Up* for giving it *a shot?*"

Davis laughed, but Drake just shook his head.

On the street, the sun was low over the bay. An occasional breeze cut the heat. "Think I might just try to find the Army hospital," Drake said. "See how Holt's doing."

Davis glanced at his watch. "Gee, ain't it kinda late for that? You can go tomorrow. I'd say you'd best come on along with us and get laid. Do you a world of good. Besides, if you don't, you'll never hear the end of it from the guys."

"That's for sure." Arvee lit his pipe and drew a puff. "How much you guess it'll cost?"

"A lay you mean?" Davis shrugged. "Beats me." Four sailors were approaching on the sidewalk. "Let's ask those swabbies." When the sailors were close he said, "Hey, fellas, any good cathouses around here? Something you'd recommend?"

"Down the next street to the right," one sailor said. "A block or so. There's a few of 'em."

"So, how much will it set us back?" Arvee asked.

"Well, they pay us," the same sailor said. He and his mates laughed. "For you…eh, depends on what you want. The works is about eight bucks." The seamen moved on.

"Seems kind of steep," sniffed Arvee when the sailors were out of earshot.

Drake chuckled. "Is that so, Private Skinflint?"

Titus crossed his arms. "Hey, where I come from, eight bucks is a lot of dough."

The GIs followed the sailor's directions to a block-long stretch of battered buildings. The sounds of wild partying throbbed from every open window. Sandy Berger and Marv Malarkey sat outside one of them, smoking cigarettes. Waving, Davis called, "Yo, fellas!"

"Where you been?" Berger said without getting up.

"Had a beer," Drake replied, "and ate. Up by the waterfront. What are you two doing?"

"Just taking a break, aren't we Marv? Sarge and Zip are inside."

"How is it?" Arvee asked.

"Fantastic," Marv said. "If you go in here, be sure to ask for Lin...or is it Lon? I dunno. Pretty girl. Young. Knows all the tricks in the book. Tell her Marvelous Marv sent you."

Davis and Titus went inside. Drake sat with Berger and Malarkey and had a smoke.

"Not going in, sport?" Malarkey said.

"In a minute."

Berger took a last drag and stubbed out his cigarette. "Saw Tolliver and Van Fleet. With their new tattoos. Jeeze, did they ever look sore! Think I may pass on getting one."

After five minutes Drake sighed and stood up. Looking like he wished he was somewhere else, he glanced at his watch. "Guess I'll go check things out," he announced.

"Remember, ask for...." Malarkey scratched his head. "Um, they'll know who you mean."

Drake went inside. A portly, middle aged woman wearing a floral-print dress sat on a sofa near the door, smoking a black cigarette in a pink wooden holder. A skinny white cat lounged on her lap. Without getting up, she said, "Hello, GI. You come the right place. Best place...for a girl. You see?" She pointed into a parlor. Three women were inside. A plump one ate pieces of fruit with her fingers, another sat at a piano, distractedly striking random keys, and the third, a kid really, paged through a magazine. None of them had tattoos.

The girl with the magazine was pretty, slender, sixteen or so, and her hair was black as Stetti's. Her skin was exotic, the color of Hershey's chocolate. She wore a faded, pink satin dress and no shoes. Drake pointed to her. "OK?"

"Betty!" The madam winked. "She best one."

Drake looked into the girl's eyes. He knew Betty wasn't her real name. "How much?"

"Best girl in Manila. Ten dollars everything."

Drake shrugged. He reached into his pocket and pulled out his bankroll. He counted out ten one-dollar bills.

Betty took Drake's hand and led him down the hall to a door with a brass 6 on it. One nail was missing so the number might have been 9 hanging upside down. Inside, Betty sat Drake on the bed. She stood before him and began to unbutton the top of her dress.

Drake gazed at her face—cute, girlish, too young to be pleasing men for money. He moved her hand from the buttons. "Hold on," he said. "Speak English?"

Betty didn't seem to understand. She peered into Drake's eyes like she hoped they might translate for her.

Drake pointed to her mouth. He shook his head, saying, "You don't have to talk." He patted the bed next to him. "Sit." He patted the bed again, and taking Betty's wrist, he eased her next to him. "You just listen," he said squeezing her hand. "It's all you have to do." He took out his Chesterfields and offered her one.

Betty took the cigarette and placed it on the nightstand next to the bed.

"I've got a girlfriend in Germany. Haven't seen her in almost three months." Drake touched Betty's hair. "Her hair's like yours." He talked for another quarter of an hour, barely looking at the girl. Then he stood, gave her three dollars more plus the rest of the pack of Chesterfields, and left.

Drake was glad he saw none of his mates outside. He walked back to the waterfront and got a shabby room for the night. $1.50.

Early Sunday morning Drake asked a pair of MPs where the US Army hospital was located. They gave him a ride there. On the way, he worried that Holt might already be gone.

Drake signed in with an orderly just inside the hospital door. Holt was listed as being in ward room 2-F.

The instant he opened the door, Drake spotted Holt in the fourth bed on the right. As he hustled toward the sergeant's bedside, Holt looked up from his *Life Magazine* and broke into a big grin. "Well, dog my cats! Drake! I can't believe it."

Drake pumped Holt's hand. "How are you doing, sarge?"

"Good as can be for a one-footed foot soldier."

"So when do you ship home?"

Holt shrugged like he didn't care. "Who knows? The sawbones told me all the hospital boat beds are going to Okinawa casualties." He grabbed Drake's wrist. "Say, what's that on your sleeve? You made corporal! Congratulations."

"Thanks, sarge. Lt. Happenchance said you put in a good word for me. 'Preciate it."

"Shit, Drake, you *earned* that promotion." Holt took a white enameled water cup from the table next to his bed and sipped. "So, what else is new back in camp?"

"Well, Zip made sergeant. Same time I got promoted. Think I told you they made Breezy acting squad leader when you...got hurt. But they gave somebody else the job after a few days."

"Hmm. Not surprised. Barezzi is all right, but he's too *by the book*. Needs to rely on himself a little more. That comes with experience. So, who'd they make squad leader?"

"Sergeant named Ames. Forrest Ames. From company HQ."

Holt winced. "Face like a horse? Hair like he stuck his dick in a light socket?" He shook his head.

Drake shrugged. "He seems OK."

Holt closed his eyes. A moment later they flashed open. "Say, what the hell are you doing here in Manila?"

"Company Commander gave us a weekend pass. The whole squad came."

"They let you come all the way here?"

"They didn't exactly *let* us come. Didn't say we couldn't either. Some of the guys wanted to chase women. Some figured to get tattoos. Cold beer's in there somewhere too."

Holt's jaw tightened. Then it relaxed. "So you didn't disobey an order...exactly. And you had reasons for bending the rules." He nodded. "You know, that's good. You can't make an omelet without breaking eggs. Soldiers need to do that sometimes. It's something Americans got in their blood. Hell, it's how we beat the Nazis and it's why we'll chew up the Japs and spit 'em right out. So, yeah, break some eggs...when there's a good reason. And wine, women, and tattoos? Well, there's worse reasons." Holt rubbed his chin and eyed Drake. "But I don't see no tattoos on you. And you don't seem hungover. *And* you're here with a broke-down old sergeant rather than going at it with some saucy tomato. So what's *your* excuse for bending the rules?"

Drake shrugged. "Guess I wanted to make sure you're keeping out of trouble." He winked.

Holt glared at Drake. "Don't try to razzmatazz me, dammit! You bent the rules out of sentimentality." He grabbed Drake's shirt. "That ain't a good reason. In fact, it's a damn lousy one." He jerked Drake closer. "You better listen and listen good, kid. Sentimentality bores into you like a leech. In combat it'll get you killed. Sure, when the bullets fly, your buddies are what you're fighting for. You'd die for them. That's sentiment...and it's good. But once somebody's out—transferred, or wounded, or dead— they're history. You write 'em off. Cuz if you don't, you get soft as a rotten apple...and you're worthless to your buddies and to yourself. Sentimentality's a bunch of crap. I warned you, Corporal! Told you how it about strangled Zimmerman. And now you're letting that leech dig its sucker into you."

"But I..." Drake's gaze went to the floor.

Holt sat up in bed. "But what? Just get the hell out. I had high hopes for you, and you let me down. Big time." When Drake just stood there, the fire in Holt's eyes flared. "Listen, damn you. Never visit me again. Don't send a Christmas card. Cross me off any list you got. Far as you're concerned, I'm dead. Worry about that jackass Ames and the rest of Second Squad. They're what matters now." He crossed his arms and turned his face to the wall. "Go on, get lost."

"But sarge—"

Holt looked back and glared at him. "You're a fool, Drake." When tears welled in his eyes, he turned away again. "Just get the fuck out and don't come back. *Ever.*"

Drake swallowed hard. After a moment, he turned and left. At the door, he glanced back. Holt was still facing away. Drake walked down the hall and out the building with tears streaming down his cheeks. He took a pedicab ride to the waterfront and waited for the rest of the squad, wishing he'd kept a couple of cigarettes.

When the others returned to the pier, they asked what he'd done in Manila. "Drank some beer, rented a girl named Betty…and learned a lesson," was Drake's sullen reply.

Tomas returned at half past noon. On *La Sirena's* deck were six baskets filled with large fish with iridescent scales and bulging eyes. The captain bought six chunks of ice from a girl on the dock, one for each basket.

La Sirena made good time getting back to San Narcisco, and Second Squad's GIs shuttled back to Camp Dodger, arriving just as the sun started to ripen red, low in the west.

The squad members lined up to sign in at a table outside the company HQ tent. Like a hawk on a telephone pole, First Sgt. Tubbs silently oversaw each man enter his signature and report time.

As they walked back to tent 28, Malarkey burst out laughing. "Told you we'd pull it off."

"Gotta hand it to you, Marvin." Van Fleet slapped him on the back.

Berger snickered. "Did you see Tubby when we signed in? He had *no* clue."

"Gotta say, I was kind of worried," Arvee Titus told Drake, "when I saw the name of the boat. *La Sirena.* Know what it means? The Sirens were mythological Greek women. They sang these Orphic songs—entrancing, magical—to lure sailors to their doom on the rocks. That's how come *siren song* means something that sounds good but ultimately leads to disaster. The Germans have a version of the same myth—beautiful girls living along the Rhine River, the Lorelei. They sing men to their ruin too. *Naht euch dem Strande!*" he said theatrically, looking into the distance.

Drake grabbed Titus's elbow. "What's it mean, Arvee…that German saying?"

"Something like 'Draw near the shore!' That's why you call a dangerously seductive woman a Lorelei."

Tolliver shook his head. "Leave it to Professor Titus to tell you stuff that don't matter."

But it did matter to Drake. Questions rattled through his head: A seductive woman living along the Rhine? Dangerous? Maybe playing the cello rather than singing? Was he just a sucker blindly drawn onto the rocks?

"My only point, Will," Arvee said, "was *La Sirena* seemed like a hard luck name for a boat that could end up getting us in hot water."

"You worry too much, sport," Malarkey said.

Tattoo Blues

Tuesday, 31 July, Charlie Company conducted their first landing craft exercises.

Early that morning, each of the four platoons tromped from the beach up the steel ramp of a waiting landing craft, commonly called a Higgins Boat. When the whole platoon was stuffed in like cigarettes in a pack, the ramp was cranked up. The boat's diesel engine growled to life and backed the craft off the beach. Out it charged toward open waters.

When the Higgins Boat with Second Squad was out a half mile or so, it stopped. Breathing Diesel exhaust and tossed by the swells, half the men lost their breakfasts. Drake gripped the plywood side wall worrying the boat might be swamped or fall apart. He leaned toward Bo, sitting next to him and grinned. "Gotta hand it to Mr. Higgins, he knows how to build a rugged boat." Bo, staring at his boots, didn't reply.

Lieutenant Happenchance stood unsteadily next to the boat driver. "We're stopping here where it's not so rough as farther out." He pointed to the white caps to the west. "Don't worry, fellas, your bellies will adjust to this pretty quick. A few days at most. Today will be simple. We'll just go full blast to the beach, drop the ramp, and storm imaginary enemy positions."

By day's end, the platoon had made five round trips out and in.

Pvt. Rollie Van Fleet missed the landing exercises. He had reported to sick call that morning. The tattoo he'd gotten—a red heart captioned *June-Bug 4-Ever* on his bicep—was swollen and oozing yellow fluid. It hurt like the dickens. As he applied ointment, the medic said, "Probably an infection or an ink allergy. I got open beds, so you can spend the day."

Ames and the squad had just gotten their dinners and were seated in the mess hall when Sgt. Tubbs stormed in. "Second Squad, leave that chow and double time it to the flag pole at the parade ground. Be there in ninety seconds."

The men ran to the meeting spot with worried looks on their faces. The looks became even darker when they saw Van Fleet, his arm in a sling, already waiting under the flag. They fell into line and snapped to attention as the company first sergeant stood in front of them.

"What in the name of hell fire and damnation did you jackasses think? That your dumb old sarge was born yesterday? That you'd bamboozle him no sweat? That he wouldn't wonder how Van Fleet got a botched tattoo job?" Tubbs glared at the men. "Well, did you?" he roared.

"No, Sgt. Tubbs," the squad replied in unison.

"You didn't?" Tubbs hollered. "Then you're the stupidest sacks of shit in the United States Army, risking my wrath for one night of whoring!"

Sgt. Forrest Ames gingerly raised his hand. "'Scuse me, First Sergeant, we didn't think we could outsmart you. We just thought you wouldn't find out." He smiled weakly.

Tubbs walked to Ames' side and, grinning broadly, put his arm around him. "Well, bless your heart, sergeant. You don't think I'm dumb...just incompetent." The grin disappeared. Tubbs cocked his fist and shot it into Ames' stomach, sending him to the ground. "Did I say you could take a snooze, Ames? Get back on your feet."

With a wild look in his eyes, Tubbs marched back to his spot, facing the line. "Anyone else want to try to tell me why I shouldn't string you jackasses up like Christmas lights on the perimeter barbed wire?"

Drake swallowed hard and stepped forward. "First Sergeant...look, nobody's saying we didn't bend the rules, but fact is, we didn't disobey any direct orders by going to Manila Saturday. No one flat out told us not to go." Drake saw Tubbs' eyes get wide with rage, and he knew his ship was taking on water in a stormy sea. He held a finger up. "Our old squad leader, Sgt. Holt, used to say good soldiers break an egg sometimes. What I think he meant was unless something's against a direct order, you can't be scared to do it, to break that egg, *if* there's a good reason."

"That's right, First Sergeant," Zip said, stepping forward. "Ike himself said he wanted GIs making quick decisions on their own—improvising, he called it—rather than waiting for instructions from above." He stepped back.

Drake figured he had only seconds to pull the pan out of the fire. "You see, Sergeant Tubbs, Holt believed improvising is the biggest edge a GI's got. He told me that flat out." The fire in Tubbs' eyes died down. "Well, after two months at Camp Dodger, Manila sounded pretty darn good. Listen sarge, we're about to wade into whatever Japan throws at us. We weren't trying to pull one over on you. We just saw a chance to live big. Maybe the last one we'll get." He shrugged. "We took it and now we're ready to face the music."

Tubbs glared at Drake for a moment more, then his look softened. "Hercules T. Holt is my friend." He chuckled. "We made an omelet or two in our day. What's your name, Corporal?"

"It's Drake, Sergeant."

"Drake. Hmm, maybe Holt mentioned you once or twice." Tubbs scratched behind his ear. "Men, Drake here is right—I didn't say you couldn't go to Manila. But that's not why I'm going to let Saturday night's indiscretion pass, *this one time*." He sighed. "A soldier *shouldn't* go by the book all the time. You do have to take a risk once in a while. Just be willing to stand behind your call afterwards. Manila on Saturday was a jackass stunt, but I'm not going to bust your balls for it. On account of how Drake squared it up." He looked at Van Fleet. "Get back to sick bay for the night and I'll expect you in formation with your squad at morning assembly. The rest of you are dismissed. Go get your chow."

Every day, the amphibious assault exercises increased in scope. After the treacherous single-platoon landing practices on 31 July, Drake made sure he had Stetti's lucky schilling in his front right pocket every day. He filled his canteen with the ginger tea recommended by the battalion medics, saving the last sip, 'Holt's swig' he called it, for the beach when he was safely ashore.

Thursday, Higgins Boats, four abreast, brought in four platoons. Friday there was a platoon of defenders ensconced in bunkers in the jungle above the beach waiting for the landing.

Blanks were issued. Every GI strapped on full assault gear, about seventy-five pounds.

When the boats' steel ramps hit the wet sand at surf's edge, the defenders opened fire. Though he knew it was all play-acting, the short space between him and the muzzle flashes and crackle of gunfire turned Drake's legs numb with fear.

Coming in next to him, Zip Zimmerman was scared too—but worse than that, the rush of memories of Normandy hit him like a club. He sank to one knee and bowed his head.

Seeing Zip, Drake's fear evaporated. "Let's go, buddy. Come on, you're all right." He grabbed Zip's arm and pulled him to his feet. "Keep your head down and move those boots." They ran forward together, then hit the sand and fired while their comrades advanced.

An exercise moderator hollered, "Incoming artillery," and tossed an explosion stimulant ten feet ahead of Drake. "Cover," he yelled at Zip as he pitched himself onto the ground. The simulator hissed then exploded, showering the pair with sand and leaving their ears ringing. "Gotta move again," Drake shouted as he pulled Zip into a crouch and hustled forward with him. The pair continued their stop and start course up the beach, in the face of the defenders' fusillade and the flash, bang, and smoke of artillery simulators. When they reached the line between open sand and jungle, the end point of the exercise, Drake and Zip collapsed.

After a ten minute break, First Platoon returned to their Higgins Boat. The craft hauled its exhausted GIs out two hundred yards, turned around, and the exercise repeated.

In the third run of the exercise, Drake and his First Platoon mates moved into the jungle to play defender. It sounded great, since it was out of the sun and didn't involve running with full assault gear. But training is never easy—in addition to the simulated assault, they had to fend off a real and relentless one: Wave after wave of mosquitoes.

At Camp Dodger after evening chow, Charlie Company assembled for an exercise debriefing by the CO, Captain Nichols. He ended his comments with a preview of the next phase of training. "Monday, gentlemen, the shit gets real." He explained that a transport ship which had just delivered a battalion of green troops was anchored two miles off their exercise beach. They'd motor out there in Higgins Boats, climb the cargo nets, then form up on deck and simulate an amphibious assault, start to finish. "Believe me, fellas, you've never had fun till you've shinnied down a slippery, wind-flapping net into a Higgins Boat jitterbugging on storm-swept seas." Nichols glanced at his clipboard. "Before we turn you loose, Sgt. Tubbs has a word about maintenance. First Sergeant…"

Tubbs strode forward. "Boys, your gear took a beating this week. Especially your weapons. This is going to be a maintenance weekend, and I want everything put spic and span. On Sunday afternoon I will personally inspect every damn soldier and every damn stick of gear. It better be perfect because next week is going to be a test for man and machine alike. Speaking of tests, I just got a weather update. It's looking real nasty for Monday. That'll make a tough day tougher. But we like that, don't we?" Tubbs paused for a response. It didn't meet his expectations. "I can't hear you," he roared. "We like that, don't we?"

"Yes, First Sergeant!" came the booming response.

"Better….Now grab some rest tonight. And tomorrow get to work on your gear. I'll see every one of you Sunday!" Tubbs scanned the ranks in front of him. "Dismissed!"

Second Squad prepared all weekend for Sgt. Tubbs' inspection. By sixteen hundred hours Sunday, 5 August, each man had arrayed his pristine gear as prescribed on his shelter half. When Tubbs, with another NCO, approached their tent, Sgt. Ames called the squad to attention. The GIs lined up exactly two feet behind the line of their equipment. Each man snapped into a stiff *Parade Rest* position with his weapon tucked at his side. It began to rain.

"Gentlemen," Tubbs said, "in case you don't know him, this is Battalion Command Sergeant Major Castro. He'll be inspecting you today…Sgt. Major" Tubbs stepped aside.

"Good afternoon, men. I'm working my way through the battalion to get me a firsthand take of the command. Today Charlie Company's up. Let's see what you got." With Ames providing each man's name, he worked his way down the rank, checking gear and weapons.

When it was his turn, Drake raised his BAR to the position of *Inspection Arms.*

Castro took the weapon and checked it for cleanliness and proper lubrication. "What's the maximum effective range for your weapon, Cpl. Drake?"

"326 meters, Sgt. Major."

"How's your personal accuracy at that distance?"

"I expect to cut down any exposed enemy with my first burst, Sgt. Major."

"And what if your enemy's a little girl in a kimono running at you with a sharpened bamboo stick? Or maybe she's got just a pair of chopsticks. Are you confident you'd cut her down too?"

Rain mixed with sweat trickled down Drake's face, burning his eyes. He tried to blink it out. "To be honest, Sgt. Major, if she was a ways off, I'd probably look for uniformed enemy soldiers to take out first."

"And if she's the last attacker still on her feet? Just five meters away?"

"Then I think I'd probably knock the stick away and subdue the kid. She's a civilian after all." Drake wiped his eyes with the back of his hand. "And someone's daughter."

Castro eyed Drake for a moment then thrust the BAR back into his hands. He moved on to the next man without saying a word. Maybe he had a daughter of his own.

Sea of Fury, Sea of Repose

All night on 6 August rain pummeled Drake's tent. Gusts of wind set it flapping like it wanted to fly away. The downpour slowed at dawn and stopped completely during morning chow. But by the time Second Squad mounted their truck for the trip to the beaches, the storm was raging again.

When Drake and the others jumped out of their deuce-and-a-halfs, the rain was relentless. Men stuffed their rifles into the plastic gun bags they'd been issued. The sea beyond the sand boiled with whitecaps. At the water's edge, surging surf tossed the Higgins Boats around like corks. The platoons formed up next to their trucks. Uniforms, packs, and equipment that had weighed 60 pounds dry were quickly sodden and felt more like a hundred.

In his position in the formation, Drake was close enough to the company commander, Cpt. Nichols, to hear him over the din of the storm, speaking on his radio with 74th Division HQ. "No sir, a little rain doesn't bother us. It's the seas. The whitecaping waves." There was urgency in his voice. "But General, I've never seen anything like it. The Higgins Boats—"

Nichols rolled his eyes as he listened to the officer on the other end of the line. "Yes General Hamperville, I *am* familiar with the training schedule." He continued to listen, trying to get a word in. "Yes, sir, I know the Navy's transport ship is spoken for after tomorrow. If we could just—" He bit his lip. "Yes, I've seen the forecasts too, General....No, sir, I'm not suggesting that tomorrow will be any better. But this *is* a typhoon, sir." He pulled the receiver from his ear and glared at it then listened again. "General, no one is saying we won't have rough weather when we go in for real. Look, sir, I'm not sure you appreciate how bad—" His shoulders sagged. "Yes, General, I understand....Yes, we can give it a go....Of course I'll keep you posted, sir....Thank you, sir. Out." He hung up the receiver.

Nichols met with his four platoon leaders. They huddled in the driving rain, the wind snapping their ponchos. After two minutes the platoon leaders ran back to their units.

Lt. Happenchance stood in front of First Platoon. "Division won't scrub the exercise," he shouted over the wind, "typhoon or not. Swimming Sherman tanks were s'posed to be going in with us, but that part of the exercise got scrapped. Guess those tanker boys are scared of a little weather." He glanced at his watch. "In three minutes we mount the Higgins Boats. Questions?"

"I have to piss, sir," hollered a man in the middle of the formation.

"Go in place" barked Happenchance. "Let's be careful out there, men. Keep your weapon in a gun bag. Everyone have a lifebelt? Squad leaders, make sure your men are wearing one."

As Sgt. Ames checked out the men, Bo Forgette leaned over to Drake. "Shit," he hollered over the racket, "this's like the rain we get back home." He wiped his eyes with the back of his hand. "Reminds me of the time my daddy and me were moving a herd of cattle when a bad storm blew in. Thunder and lightning like you never seen. Spooked a dogie, and I rode into a canyon to fetch 'er. I must've been fourteen or so. Anyhow, out of nowhere, this flash flood comes a-crashing down the gulch. In no time flat, I got water over my saddle. Reckoned I was done for, but I latched onto a scrubby tree and hung on till the storm passed." Bo peered out at the crashing whitecaps and shuddered. "Still get fucking nightmares of water sucking me down."

Drake squeezed Bo's arm. "I won't let that happen."

The lieutenant blew his whistle. "Mount the boat!"

The steel front deck of the Higgins Boat clanked down. The vessel bucked under the assault of the waves trying to toss it onto the sand. With the slippery deck and the pitching, GIs stutter-stepped to the stern and threw themselves into their assigned places.

When the boat was loaded with GIs, the ramp came up. The driver revved the engine, furiously fighting the waves to pull away from the beach. At last he got the boat turned around and started the long churn out to the troop ship.

Drake made sure he sat next to Forgette. He saw terror in Bo's eyes each time a wave broke over the bow, sending a briny shower on the men huddled inside. "Gonna be OK, buddy," Drake yelled, "remember you got that life belt on. It'll keep you everything but dry, even if we do go for a dip....Which we won't."

Bo pounded the boat's plywood sidewall with the heel of his fist. "Got a real bad feeling about this crate." He tossed a couple of soggy Tums into his mouth.

"Just stick by me," Drake shouted over the storm and the growl of the Diesel. "Like I said, I'm looking out for you." He peered into Bo's rain-spattered face and winked. "Hey, I'm a lifeguard, right?" Then he recalled Hilda, the girl who'd drowned on Labor Day at Perritt's Beach. On his watch. He pictured sand-flecked hair matted to her face and shut up.

It took an hour, but finally First Platoon's Higgins Boat pulled alongside the cargo net of the huge troop transport ship and tied up. Bobbing and tossing back and forth as the boat was, the transfer of men to the rope net was treacherous. One GI from Third Squad got his hand crushed between the Higgins Boat's railing and the side of the ship. Unable to climb, he was hoisted to the deck in a cargo sling. Everyone else made it to the top somehow. Comrades and the ship's crew grabbed exhausted GIs when they reached the top of the net and hauled them over the railing.

On the ship's deck, GIs lay bushed and battered by the wind and rain. The crew of the transport brought out hot coffee, candy bars, and cigarettes. Most of the men had something but a few of them were so worn out all they did was grab a wet snooze.

After twenty minutes aboard, First Sergeant Tubbs blew his whistle and hollered into a megaphone, "Fifteen minutes till we go back over the side, men. One five minutes to debark."

Drake looked at the beaten men around him. He approached Tubbs. "First Sergeant, some of the boys can't make the climb down to the Higgins. Not yet."

Tubbs scowled at him. "Lieutenant asked HQ for a delay and they said no dice. Look, the climb down should be easier than coming up was. Then all we got to do is sit back and enjoy the ride to the beach." He squinted into the streaming rain. "Besides, maybe the storm's letting up a little." He didn't sound convinced.

Drake glanced back at the men. "Here's an idea. How about we down the net without our packs? That's sixty pounds of dead weight we won't have to haul. You can lower the gear down to us using cargo slings." He pointed to the riggings the Navy had used to raise the soldier from Third Squad who injured his hand. "The men, sarge…lots of 'em got nothing left in the tank."

Tubbs sighed. "I agree, Corporal, but this exercise is supposed to simulate the real thing. On the big day, bushed or not they're going to have to go down the nets with all their gear."

"For the real thing we won't be coming from land to the ship and having to climb up the net in the first place. We'll already be aboard. Well rested. This isn't realistic." Drake took off his helmet and eyed the sergeant, rain pelting his face. "Just saying, don't get anyone banged up—you're going to need every one of us when we hit those beaches for real."

Tubbs put a hand on Drake's shoulder. "I'll run it by the lieutenant. Take a breather while you can." He spotted Lt. Happenchance smoking a cigarette under cover and ran over to him.

Five minutes later Tubbs spoke to the GIs through his megaphone. "Listen up, men. We're about to head in for the assault. Grab another Hershey Bar if you want. And some good news…I went to the lieutenant and recommended lowering your equipment down to you after you get in the boats. Why risk getting anyone hurt? Lt. Happenchance green-lighted my plan. Now, the weather's still damn nasty. When you go over the side onto the net, take it slow and easy. Keep your weight on your legs. Watch your grip—those ropes are slippery." Tubbs glanced at his watch. "Two minutes until we put men on the net. Two minutes."

All of First Platoon's GIs made it safely into the Higgins Boat. They waited, their craft clipped to the cargo netting, while the other boats loaded.

Packed into his spot in the landing craft, Drake wiped rain from his glasses and looked up when Davis, sitting next to him, pointed to Second Platoon descending to their boat. They were coming down the wind-whipped cargo netting without their gear, which was being lowered alongside them. "Hey, fellas," Blackie said, "lookee that! They're copying us."

"My mother says," Titus chirped, "imitation's the sincerest form of flattery."

Davis looked at Arvee and shook his head.

"All I can say is," Forgette hollered from the other side of Drake, "you gotta hand it to sarge and the lieutenant! All this wind and rain and such, I'da been scared shitless tackling that rope ladder with a Studebaker strapped on my back."

A big wave broke over the side of the Higgins Boat, soaking the cluster of Second Squad men on the starboard side. "Shit!" yelled Bo as his pack of Tums flew from his hand into the water in the bottom of the boat, which by now was up to the men's ankles.

"If they had our backs," Tolliver griped, "we wouldn't be out here in this fucking tornado."

"You mean, *this fucking typhoon*," mumbled Titus.

"When we head in—" Drake lifted his boot out of the water and watched it drip. "—it'll suck most of this water out the back of the boat." He leaned toward Forgette and grinned. "Back at camp tonight, you can read the new *Superman* comic I got from my mom yesterday. It's a good one. Some professor blasts Superman with an atom smasher."

"Why'd anyone wanna kill Superman?" Arvee put his arm through the sling strap of his M1 and adjusted its position on his shoulder. "Except Lex Luther, of course."

"Shut up, Titus," shouted Bo, "I don't wanna know what happens."

"Well," sniffed Tolliver, "for sure Superman's going to be OK. He *always* is."

The last men of Second Platoon and their gear were secure in their Higgins Boat. From the other side of the ship, the boats of Third and Fourth Platoons came around and tied in.

Aboard one of the other boats, Cpt. Nichols addressed the company through a megaphone. "Nice job, boys, debarking the ship. OK, this is it. Just a few final instructions. First make sure your life belt is snug. It's rough out there. Anything can happen.

Boat drivers, keep a tight rank going into the beach. I want all four boats hitting sand at the same time." He glanced up at the driving rain. "Good luck, men. I'll see you on the beach." Nichols nodded and the company bugler rose unsteadily. He blared out the notes of the cavalry charge.

The engines of the Higgins Boats revved, and four abreast they began their dash to the beach, about two miles away. The boats churned up the backs of waves and careened off the crests, crashing back into the sea with huge sprays of white water. The wind was blowing at an angle to the course of the boats, so the drivers had a continuous battle to maintain their heading.

As they were trained to do, the assault troops in the Higgins Boats kept their heads down to avoid catching a round fired from the beach. Since everyone was using blanks, that wasn't necessary, but given the pouring rain, the men were happy to comply.

About half way in, the wind picked up, swirling in every direction. The drivers were unable to hold their craft on a straight course. The seas were so rough that in troughs they couldn't see anything but the walls of water surrounding their boats. Rain and spray whipped from the ocean surface pelted them. They were driving blind.

From his place near the back of the boat, Drake watched First Platoon's driver. It looked like a fire hose was trained on him, and he struggled mightily with the steering wheel. More worrisome to Drake, his face was gray with terror. Drake reached into his pocket and fingered his lucky shilling—Stetti's talisman had its work cut out for it today.

A moment later, out of nowhere, Drake glimpsed a dark blur of motion off to his side. He turned to see one of the other boats crashing down from a wave crest and yawing right for him. It looked enormous. Five feet off his side, it punched into the churning brine, sending a wall of white water surging over the whole platoon.

The next thing Drake knew, the bow of the other boat was under his craft, lifting its starboard side, with him and his buddies, out of the water. Then a wave reinforced the other boat's shove and sent Drake and the GIs next to him even higher. The momentum tossed Drake and the half dozen others sitting around him into the air. Two of the soldiers crashed down on their comrades in the boat, but five men including Drake were hurled into the foamy sea.

In the churning water, the weight of his sodden gear dragged Drake down. He struggled to kick to the surface but couldn't. He undid his chin strap and pushed his helmet off. He let the sling of his BAR slide off his shoulder and slipped out of his pack. Now his kicks sent him shooting upward.

Gulping in air at the surface, he found himself right next to a heaving Higgins Boat. A hand reached out to him. He looked up and saw Breezy's face. As he reached up, he thought of Bo Forgette and jerked his arm back in the water.

Drake took a lungful of air and plunged into the sea to find his buddy. He kicked himself down and spied a figure struggling underwater. Drake darted to him and grabbed the man, who was still now, from behind. Drake pulled off the fellow's pack and helmet and let them sink away, then he hauled him to the surface. He towed the feeble, sputtering GI to the edge of the pitching Higgins Boat. Clutching the side railing, Drake looked at the guy's face—it was Blackie Davis.

"Pull him aboard," Drake hollered at Berger and Zimmerman. When they'd grabbed Davis, he gulped another deep breath and plunged back to find Forgette.

The crashing waves filled the sea with tiny, sparkling bubbles. Unlike the surface where water raged and surged, the ocean below swirled and swept more slowly, beautifully…but with incredible power. Drake was pushed ahead one moment and held back the next. He spotted a dark figure in the radiant water. The person seemed to move only in reaction to the whims of the sea around him. Drake swam to the GI and pulled off his helmet and pack. Holding his collar, he tugged the man to the surface. Bobbing there, Drake located the Higgins Boat about fifteen feet away and swam to it, towing the limp soldier. As soon as he got there, hands reached down and hauled both men aboard.

Drake knelt gasping, peering at the body sprawled there on the deck. He didn't recognize the face, with its wide-open, bulging eyes and the big purplish bruise across one side. Someone said, "Jesus Christ, it's Titus." The words hit Drake like a club. The nicest, smartest guy in the unit. His friend. He glanced at the churning sea, thinking Arvee's glasses were somewhere out there.

Then Drake remembered Bo, thought how panicked he must be, and moved for the water.

"Hold it, Drake," Ames shouted over the storm's roar, "you're staying right where you are." He and Zip grabbed Drake's arms.

Drake jerked himself free. "Forgette's still out there," he screamed. "I promised..." As he stepped to the railing, ready to dive back in, someone from the front of the boat hollered, "Got a survivor in the water up here."

Everyone watched as an exhausted GI was pulled from the sea. A moment later someone exclaimed, "It's Tolliver. Will Tolliver. He's alive!"

Drake yelled, "Bo!" and turned to the water again.

But before Drake could spring, Zip tackled him and two other GIs held him down. "Easy, buddy," Zip whispered in his ear, "it's been too long. You did all you could."

Physically spent, pinned to the deck by his buddies, Drake shook with sobs and surrendered.

Hold on to Your Hats

When the engine of First Platoon's Higgins Boat revved to resume its trek back to shore, Zip took Drake's hand and pulled him from the deck. "Shit happens, man. We gotta move on."

On one knee, Drake peered into Zip's eyes. Though he knew it was true, he felt too guilty to move on. He stood, bracing himself on Zimmerman's shoulder, and scanned the churning gray sea off the stern. He owed that one last look to Bo Forgette. As the site of the disaster slipped into the distance, Drake sank to his seat.

No one spoke as the boat plowed through the thrashing waves. Swept by wind-driven spray, all the GIs aboard could think of was making it back to shore in one piece. But for the men in the back of the boat, there was more. They had to look at Arvee Titus's body, which the lieutenant had covered with his poncho, lying in the couple of inches of water sloshing around on the deck.

On the way in, Drake wanted to be sitting near his friend's corpse. Watching over him. His memories of Arvee were strong enough to momentarily push aside regret at not saving Bo. He recalled his brawl with Blackie Davis, when Titus jerked the club out of Blackie's hands to make the fight fair. He smiled, thinking of the bookish kid who knew as much as an encyclopedia about subjects ranging from the ancient city of Alexandria to jungle spiders. Yeah, he already missed Arvee.

When First Platoon hit the beach, the other landing craft were already in. Even the GIs in the Third Platoon boat, the one that had collided with them, didn't know men had been lost in the incident. That's how rough the seas were—almost immediately they had lost contact with the boat they hit. As Titus's poncho-draped body was carried on the medics' stretcher to an ambulance, the other men of Charlie Company watched in stunned silence.

Back at Camp Dodger, at evening chow, Lt. Col. Thatcher spoke to the men, informing them of the loss of Titus and Forgette. He called for a moment of silence, then said, "There will be a memorial ceremony tomorrow at zero nine hundred hours for our fallen comrades. Weather permitting. I know it's tough, losing members of the battalion...for some of you, buddies. But it's part of this business, and you need to step up and march on. By the way—" Thatcher glanced up at the ceiling of the mess tent, rippling in the wind. "—word is, the storm's officially been designated a typhoon…as if we need a weatherman to tell us that. Anyhow, I'm scrubbing tomorrow's scheduled training. Use the time to get your gear and yourselves squared away." Thatcher checked his watch. "One last thing. Armed Forces Radio announced that earlier today the air force dropped some newfangled blockbuster bomb on a target in Japan. Biggest one yet. I tell you this as a warning—lest you hear and get your hopes up. Bombing's never won a war. Not when the Krauts bombed the Brits or when we bombed Germany." Thatcher crossed his arms. "And it ain't going to happen now, stubborn as the Japs are." He leaned toward the men "Infantry wins wars. We do it with bayonets jabbed into our enemy's cold, dead heart. That's the way it's always been. Just saying, boys, don't any of you go making plans for Thanksgiving at Mom's."

Drake walked back with Zimmerman to the squad's tent in wind-driven rain so strong that the GIs had to lean into it to keep from being blown back. "Look," Zip shouted over the roar of the storm, "it's rough, losing a buddy. I know you were close to Titus." He shook his head. "Shit, after 6 June of '44, I quit making friends."

For a long time Drake didn't reply. Finally he said, "Sure, it's hell about Arvee. He was swell, when you got to know him. But it's even tougher with Forgette. See, Bo was so damn scared of the water—" His lip quivered. "—and I promised to look after him out there." Drake took off his glasses and wiped his eyes with his wet sleeve.

They walked on. Drake was glad for the *tat-tat-tat* of rain splattering on his helmet. Anything was better than trying to explain his feelings.

"Listen to me, Drake. Don't beat yourself up about Bo. His number was up. Simple as that. Hell, you tried to watch out for him. If you need to kick yourself, do it for making a promise you couldn't keep." He shrugged. "On the other hand, I reckon it gave

Forgette considerable comfort out there, knowing you were watching over him. That counts for something."

When they made it back to their tent, the first things the squad mates saw were Bo's and Arvee's belongings neatly set out on their cots, ready to be sent home. Drake turned away and climbed into his bunk, fully dressed. He laid there silent for the rest of the evening.

All night long the typhoon raged, shaking the tent with wind-hurled rain and feeding the impromptu rivers flowing through Camp Dodger. Drake lay awake on his cot, listening—the weather was a perfect mirror for what he was feeling.

Tuesday morning about dawn, the storm suddenly let up. By 0900 hours, when Drake and most of the rest of the men the 443rd Battalion assembled for the memorial ceremony, patches of blue sky had broken through the clouds. That'd please Arvee and Bo, Drake thought.

The 74th Infantry Division chaplain, Cpt. Myhre, came in a jeep from the HQ at Camp Giant to preside over the ceremony. He stood behind a podium on the open rear deck of a deuce-and-a-half truck. A pair of steel pot helmets and three stacked M-1 rifles had been placed at the front of the improvised dais. The men of Second Squad, the home unit of the deceased GIs, stood in front of the battalion formation.

The chaplain read some passages from the Bible. He talked about the importance of service and the mystery of the Divine's plans. It didn't make much sense to Drake. If Bo and Arvee were serving God, doing something good and important, something He wanted done, what sense did it make to kill them off? The *mysterious plans* stuff that people like the chaplain always fell back to seemed weak as used dishwater to Drake. But, he told himself, can't be too hard on the padre—if you're in the mystery business, what else can you say?

The chaplain did catch Drake's ear with one idea. He urged the men of the 443rd to look forward—not to dwell on setbacks but rather to throw themselves into their training, preparing for the

241

noble work that was to come in November. The accident had left Drake washed out. Drained of all enthusiasm. For the first time since he joined the army, he'd wondered, *What's the point?* Now, with the padre's pitch, the fire in his belly was rekindled.

At morning formation, two days later, 9 August, a private reported in to fill one of Second Squad's vacant slots. Oskar Silverthorn of Pine Ridge, South Dakota was pure-blood Ogallala Lakota Sioux, tall and athletic but shy. He and Drake hit it off from the start. With Stetti's admiration for Indians, Drake fantasized about telling her someday that one of his best army buddies was a Sioux warrior.

Silverthorn blended in fairly well. In excellent shape, he pulled his weight from the start. The only trouble came from Tolliver. At breakfast one morning, he muttered to Drake and a couple of others, "It's bullshit. We lose Bo, and the Army says 'take a redskin in his place.' Trading a cowboy for a fucking Indian—what kind of a deal is that?" When he called Silverthorn *Chief* to his face, a line was crossed. Drake pulled Tolliver aside and told him, corporal to private, to straighten up. But the abuse continued, so Drake enlisted Davis to confront Will. From then on, Silverthorn was Oskar, and Tolliver, pissed as he might have been, kept his trap shut.

On the afternoon of 9 August, Second Squad and their Charlie Company comrades were back conducting combat exercises in the ruined town of Olongapo. A squad from Bravo Company, playing Japanese defenders, set up ambushes in bombed-out buildings and improvised bunkers. Charlie Company, spearheaded by Second Squad and three clanking Sherman tanks, fought their way in and secured the simulated Japanese village.

That night at chow, the word spread that a second *big* bomb had been dropped on Japan. Sgt. Ames told the men at his table what he'd heard from another battalion NCO: "Colonel Thatcher was talking on the radio with a buddy in the Sixth Army G2 section who told him, 'You know those two blockbusters we dropped in the last few days? Well, they weren't just high explosive suckers, but something entirely new. Reports call them *atom* bombs. Supposed to be way more powerful than anything else.' Thatcher's G2 pal said there's hope among the Air Corps types that these bombshells are so fucking destructive that they might *persuade* the Japanese to surrender." Ames shrugged. "Mind you, I'm not getting my hopes up, fellas."

"Atom bombs," said Drake, rubbing his chin. "Think *Popular Mechanics* ran an article about that one time. Said it works on the same principle as the sun's power."

"Doesn't make sense," said Rollie Van Fleet. "Everything's got atoms—you, me, everybody...everything. We don't go blowing up, do we?"

"Don't know about that, Rollie," said Marv Malarkey. "When they served bean soup for noontime mess—yesterday, wasn't it?—well, it had you farting so much in the tent last night, sport, I was thinking we could drop *you* on Japan and wipe out the whole lousy country. Want blockbuster atoms? Your fat ass's loaded with 'em, big time."

On the morning of 14 August, at Charlie Company's weekly administrative assembly, Drake was called to the front of the formation.

With Drake standing at attention before him, Cpt. Nichols took a paper from a manila folder and read the following citation: "For distinguishing himself by heroism in saving a drowning comrade during training exercises on 6 August, 1945, Corporal Winston Charles Drake, United States Army, is awarded The Soldier's Medal. Following a collision at sea during a training mission, Corporal Drake, without regard for his personal safety and despite the fact that typhoon conditions prevailed, dove into the ocean off the Philippine island of Luzon and saved a member of his rifle squad then recovered the body of a deceased soldier. His bravery is in keeping with the best traditions of the United States Army and reflects great credit on himself, his unit, and the military service."

First Sergeant Tubbs handed Nichols a box. The captain took out a bronze medal with a red, white and blue ribbon and pinned it on Drake's uniform. He shook Drake's hand.

After Tubbs dismissed the company, Blackie Davis was first to approach Drake. "Tell you what," Davis said, "I'm real fucking glad I didn't rip your head off when we had our little tussle back on Good Old Trixie." He shook Drake's hand. "And glad you aren't the grudge-carrying type neither, or I might still be out there—" He pointed west. "—sleeping with the fishes."

"I'm just happy I spotted you there in the drink, Blackie. Course, big a lug as you are, how could I miss you?" Drake's eyes filled with tears.

Davis bear-hugged him.

"Just wish I could have found Bo, too," Drake whispered, "and gotten to Arvee sooner."

After a moment, the men broke their embrace. They glanced with embarrassment at their comrades looking on. Davis shook Drake's hand again and hurried away.

Wednesday, 15 August, training in landmine clearing was on the schedule. After a morning session on the mechanics of the various types of anti-personnel and anti-vehicle devices, Charlie Company was trucked into the jungle to an area planted with dummy mines that the men would practice detecting and disarming.

Just after fifteen hundred hours, Cpt. Nichols' jeep roared up to the simulated minefield and screeched to a dusty halt. The company commander terminated the training and called his men together. "Gentlemen, hold on to your hats....The war's over!" Nichols paused to give the news time to sink in.

At first no one said anything. The befuddled GIs looked at each other, wondering if they'd misunderstood. Then, slowly at first and building to a roar, they broke into whoops and whistles.

Nichols held his hands up, which had little effect. He hollered, "Listen up, men." When some order was restored, he said, "Word came down from Sixth Army. It's been authenticated. The Japanese emperor has announced the surrender to his people.

Now, we don't have a ceasefire order in place, but Allied Command has directed that we don't initiate any offensive operations. We're to remain on high alert and defend ourselves in case of attack. Since we don't have orders to stand down, for now we'll continue training. I'll keep you posted as I learn more." Nichols turned to leave but stopped. Looking back at his men, he said, "It's been going on a long time, this goddamn war. Sometimes I thought it'd never end. But I guess it has. And I say credit for that doesn't go to the emperors or presidents. Nor to the generals or the admirals…Or even to the captains." The men laughed. "It goes to the fighting men like you." He saluted then turned to Sgt. Tubbs. "First Sergeant, how about you lead the men in a cheer? For themselves! They've damned-well earned it."

Tubbs hollered, "Three cheers for the United States, for the good old US Army, and for you, the best fighting men in the world. Hip, hip…."

"Hurrah." The response boomed like a cannon.

"Hip, hip…."

"Hurrah."

"Hip, hip…."

"Hurrah."

Nothing much happened for the next couple of weeks. Training ceased. The men were confined to the grounds of Camp Dodger. They polished their boots and maintained their gear. They played cards, baseball, horse shoes. They put on skits. They wrote home.

Drake started keeping a journal to help him deal with his ups and downs. He described the elation he and his comrades felt, knowing they wouldn't have to invade Japan. No killing or being killed. He mused about going back to civilian life and how the service had changed him. He wrote about the friends he'd lost: Jimmy La Roux, the truck driver killed during the Battle of the Bulge. Hercules Holt. Winston Sumter who died of burns in Trixie's sick bay. Bo Forgette and Arvee Titus. He wrote about them hoping they'd somehow know they hadn't been forgotten. That maybe it could even bring them back, in a way. It didn't work, especially for the last two. He just couldn't get around the fact that about the same time Bo and Arvee were drowning in a freak accident, the atom bomb's detonation was starting a chain reaction that would end the war and make their deaths meaningless. If the bomb had come just a few days earlier, Bo could have gone back to Texas to punch cows—far, far away from water. And Arvee could have written books or worked in a library or taught *MacBeth* to tenth graders. Death at the twilight of a war is as cruel as it gets.

Drake likewise hoped his journal might help crystallize his thoughts about Stetti. He never had much success—it was tough to pin down an enigma or write objectively about a Lorelei.

He couldn't shake his frustration at feeling he hadn't accomplished much...not much that mattered anyway. Sure, he'd been promoted and awarded a medal, but that seemed like peanuts next to his hopes. Every time he'd stepped up to the plate trying to hit a homer, fate had thwarted him. In the end, he decided the journal idea was a dead end, and he burned the book in the mess hall incinerator one morning while on KP.

That evening he dug to the bottom of his duffle bag and found the silver flask of sake Holt had given him to drink after he stormed ashore onto the Japanese mainland. Now he'd never do that. He gulped a slug. It was so sour, he spit it out. He looked at the Japanese symbol etched on the flask. Holt had said it meant *Victory*. Sour—that's about what this victory tasted like to him. Rollie Van Fleet wanted the flask as a souvenir and offered to buy it for a buck. "It's yours," Drake said, "for nothing. Cuz that's what it's worth to me."

The official surrender was signed 2 September on the Battleship Missouri. A day later, word came down that GIs who wished to apply to continue on active duty could do so, though nothing was guaranteed. Everyone else would shortly be shipping back Stateside for discharge.

Cpl. Winston C. Drake had no interest in staying in the army. On 4 October, 1945, he boarded a troop transport ship sailing for the USA.

Part III   Suite's Finale

Lorelei Song

Omaha, Nebraska. February 24, 1946

For Drake, things back home moved in slow motion. Everything was easy. Every day was the same. The quiet was an itch he couldn't scratch.

Drake couldn't turn to the guys he'd known before the war. His best friend Rob Drabik had joined the Marines right out of high school. He died on Tarawa. Drake couldn't relate to his other pre-war friends. Most had served. It changed them. Some returned thinking their war days had been the best of their lives. They hung out together, telling the same stories over and over, finding them endlessly fresh and exhilarating. Others came back broken, physically or mentally. Some both. Like Buddy Perritt, who lost the sight in one eye and both legs at the knee from a bouncing betty mine in Germany. Buddy spent his days looking out his bedroom window, smoking Lucky Strikes, drinking cheap whiskey and listening to Sinatra records.

Other old friends hadn't served for various reasons. They acted like the war was a toxic subject. Probably embarrassed, Drake figured. Just being around them made him jumpy.

Drake knew everyone who'd served was profoundly affected by the experience. Vets felt loss or fulfillment or gratitude or pride. But no one else's reactions matched his—frustration and disappointment. It made for a chasm between him and his fellow veterans.

From the time he left the Philippines, Drake had the same dream almost nightly. It recurred for months, even when he was separated from the service and home. It always started with him on a ship. He would be standing along the railing when he'd hear Bo Forgette, calling his name from the water. Drake knew from the voice—the sweet, almost musical drawl—that it was Bo. He'd scan the sea, but he could never spot his buddy. Invariably, Bo's call would fade slowly away. As it did, Stetti's voice replaced it.

He'd peer into the distance and see her, standing on boulders along the shore. She played a violin rather than her cello and sang an enchanting song. The only words Drake could understand were, "Draw near the shore." Somehow he knew she was singing to him. He'd dash to the ship's bridge to ask the captain to put him ashore, but never managed to find him. And when he returned to the railing, Stetti and her song were gone.

The dream was persistent, coming every night as it did. In that it was like the recurring nightmare he'd had in high school after the Labor Day drowning of Hilda Crabbe—how he would swim out to save her and she'd grab his foot, pulling him down. Drake never understood why while dreaming the same thing again he never thought, *Oh, this again.* It was always new and fresh. But the strangest part was the way he hated and loved it. Every night, he went to bed both unsettled by what was in store yet looking forward to it. Not finding Bo at the beginning was always gnawing frustration, as was Stetti's disappearance at the end. But in between there was the intoxicating pleasure of her beckoning call. When he woke, Drake never was able to recall the melody of Stetti's song. In his dream it seemed so natural and perfect—so unforgettable—but somehow, in the morning, the tune was always gone.

Drake's mother, Alice, worried about what she saw after his return from Asia. At breakfast one Saturday morning she said, "Not sleeping so well these days, are you, honey?"

Drake shrugged. "I dunno." He didn't look up from his oatmeal. "All right, I guess."

"I hear you tossing and turning. You make sounds, sometimes shouts. When I look in, you're asleep. But fitfully. Is something wrong, Win?"

"Sometimes I dream about stuff from overseas, Mom. A GI I knew who drowned during training. This German girl I met. No big deal…I guess."

"A girl?" Alice said.

Drake watched his mother's plump face light up. He knew she'd worried about his love life since he'd written to tell her Janie Stabler had *Dear Johned* him.

Alice leaned in. "Tell me about her."

Drake looked out the kitchen window. "Name's Stetti....Tall. Beautiful." He turned back, worried his description might have offended his short, stout mother. She gave no indication it had. "Plays the cello. What I can't figure out is that in this dream I keep having, she's got a violin. Doesn't make sense."

Alice sipped her coffee and shrugged. "A violin's a baby cello, I suppose."

"Dreams..." Drake shook his head. "I dunno."

Alice got up and put an arm around her son's shoulder. "When your father returned from the war, he had trouble sleeping for a while. Lots of men do."

Drake glanced at the picture of his father, Alexander, on the wall. He recalled the mild, reliable man he'd admired so growing up. The man who always dressed neatly and never used language stronger than *goldarn* and *dangnab*. The man who never complained about his war-related breathing difficulties. Ever since his dad's lung cancer took him young in 1935, Drake had felt a vague obligation to carry on his legacy.

Alice's eyes got a far-off look. "I remember it so well—your dad would wake up gasping and choking, muttering about gas in the trenches. That went on for months, but eventually the bad dreams ended. I'm sure it'll be the same for you."

Drake didn't look at his mother. "Yeah, I s'pose."

Alice rubbed her son's back. She kissed the top of his head, then got the coffee pot and refilled their cups. She turned on the Philco and dialed in a popular music station. Doris Day's *Sentimental Journey* was playing. Smiling, she sat at her place and, watching Drake, ate her cereal. Alice was a short, stocky woman with a kind, round face. As a widow, she'd quit teaching and took a better-paying job in the Omaha city treasurer's division. By the war's end, she'd risen in the municipal government to head the payroll office. Alice was as deft with people as she was with figures, and when he returned from overseas, she used her connections in city hall to get her son a position in the county assessor's office.

When *Sentimental Journey* ended, Alice sighed. "I love that song." Next on was Al Jolson's hit from the 1920s, *Red, Red Robin*. She swayed to the music and whistled the tune. When the song ended, a sonorous ad for Sanka came on. "Dreams," she murmured. "Folks say they usually mean something." She put more sugar in her coffee and stirred it. The spoon and the cup made tinkling music. "Don't you agree, Win?"

Drake didn't look up from his oats. "I guess. If folks say so…"

"'Specially if the same dream comes knock, knock, knocking every night. Maybe if you figured out what yours meant, it'd leave you alone. Then you could forget this faraway foreigner and concentrate on what's next door…all those lonely American girls who dream of meeting a fella like you."

Drake glared at his mother. "Not sure I want it leaving me alone, Mom." He picked up his cereal bowl and coffee cup and carried them to the sink. "Guess I'll take Rylee for a walk."

Drake headed for Benson Park with his mother's dog, a little canine firecracker with curly white fur. Leaning into the stinging north wind, he thought about how much he hated his job with the county. The people he worked with had been there forever. They all seemed to be just marking time—and now he was doing the same. It was bad as his desk job at First Army Headquarters. And here there was no Stetti to spice-up his weekends.

As they stepped into the park, Rylee tugged at the leash and yapped at a squirrel sitting on a low limb of an oak tree. The critter chirred back at her. A noisy face-off between my pooch and a tree rodent, Drake thought—that's about as exciting as it gets around here. He wondered if a squirrel was actually a rodent or not. Arvee would have known.

At the end of the walk Drake stopped at the postbox and picked up the mail. As he put the bundle of letters and periodicals on the kitchen table, the cover of the *Life Magazine* there caught his eye. Under a headline screaming, "Europe's New Dark Age," the cover picture was heartbreaking—grim-faced people in ragged clothing lined up in an unnamed city for a bowl of soup and a chunk of bread. But what grabbed Drake's attention was a figure walking next to the line. Facing away from the camera, it was a woman with long black hair, wearing a dark coat. And she was pushing a starkly white baby carriage. She stood straight and tall, in contrast to the dark-eyed, huddled people in line. A shiver shot down Drake's spine. Though he couldn't see the woman's face, he was overcome with the belief that it was Stetti.

Drake sat at the table, staring at the cover. Pondering the implications: Stetti had a baby! Considering the timing, it could be his. Maybe the woman he loved and his child needed him to save them from a real life nightmare of social and economic collapse. A nightmare…his nightmare! He remembered what his mother had said about it: that a violin is a *baby* cello and that dreams bring messages. Maybe, he thought, his subconscious somehow already knew he'd fathered a child, and his recurrent dream was trying to deliver the news.

A question swirled in his mind: Had Stetti finally come to appreciate how crucial he was to her future and her baby's? If he truly loved her, he should assume she had.

That evening at dinner, a stew of pork, potatoes, carrots and turnips, he asked with all the casualness he could muster, "Mom, how did having me change things for you?"

Alice arched her eyebrows and smiled. "I learned a lot, like how to translate a baby's various cries into English. And I got pretty good at operating on very little sleep."

"But did it change *you*? How you see the world and stuff?"

"Like night and day, Win. I was still teaching before you came into our lives. I loved touching young minds. It seemed so important. And it was. But when you came along, the rest of the world shrank into the background. All I could think of was opening life up *for you*. Sharing it with you. With you and your father. Our family became enough for me. More than enough….Everything."

"Me being born…" Drake gazed up at the ceiling and sighed. "Guess I didn't know I made such a difference." Looking back at his mother, he reached out and took her hand. "I wonder, do you think it's the same for other moms too?"

"The birth of a child? I expect that every mother would say it changes everything. Forever."

In that moment, sitting at the dinner table holding his mother's hand, Drake knew what he had to do. Wanted to do. *Would* do. He'd rescue Stetti and his child. Bring them out of their nightmare to the security of America. Take care of them. Make a family.

Later, as they cleared dishes from the table, Drake announced, "I've decided on something." He took a deep breath. "I'm going back to Europe. To Germany. I owe it to Stetti, that girl I met there. She needs me."

Alice's brow furrowed. "But honey, things are in such turmoil there. I was just reading—"

"I know. That's why I need to go."

Alice put an arm around her son's shoulder. "You're a good man, son. Loyal, responsible. But people are on the move. Refugees they're called. Finding someone?" She shook her head. "Might be impossible. Why don't you write? Make a connection that way. Maybe the best thing you can do is send money. If things are bad as it sounds."

Drake pushed his mother's arm away. "Dammit, I can't write," he barked. "I don't have an address." He lied— *Chorsängerstraße 25* was etched into his heart. "I need to show up in person."

"And if she's gone somewhere…?"

"OK, so I don't know for sure where she'll be." He thought of crazy old Katarina, sitting on the steps, singing. "But there's people in Bonn who'll know how to reach her if she's moved on." Drake looked at his shoes. "Probably. Besides, I've got to go. There's a baby involved." He shrugged. "Might be, anyway."

"A baby?" Alice put her fingertips to her lips. "I don't get it, Win. You've known this all along and suddenly you have to make a beeline back there?"

Drake glared at his mother. "Look, I don't *know* anything. Except that everybody back there's got it rough. The baby…well, I just figured that out."

Alice stared at her son, bewildered.

"You're the one who explained it," Drake huffed. "This dream I told you about. You said dreams are trying to tell us something. And that a violin is a *baby* cello." He crossed his arms, a figurative Q.E.D.

Alice looked even more confused for a moment, then she smiled fondly. "Aw, Win honey, who knows what dreams mean? Surely they can't tell us things we have no way of knowing.

"Look, I just know what I know…and I'm going!"

"But your job…"

"It's crap."

"Such language! This isn't some army barracks, young man."

"Sorry, but that's what my job is. And it'll be here when I get back. Or something else will. There's a million jobs."

Alice threw her hands up. "But…but you'll need a passport. That'll take awhile to get. Thank goodness. Give you time to come to your senses."

"Don't need one, Mom." He smirked. "When they demobilized us, the War Department put a clause in everybody's orders that allows them to be overseas for an additional year. Those orders and my army I.D. are as good as a passport." Drake pulled out a tan tri-fold card. "Got it right here, my Form 65-4." He held the I.D. out for his mother to see. "Photo, physical descriptors, fingerprints. It's all here."

Alice took the I.D. and inspected it like she was hoping to find an error that invalidated it. She handed it back without a word.

Drake folded the card and stashed it in his shirt pocket. He noted the resigned look on his mother's face and put his arm around her shoulder. "Mom, I'm going. I have to." He grinned. "I'll be fine."

"But honey, what if you can't find her? Such a long way...perhaps for nothing."

"You worry too much."

On Monday morning, Drake quit his job. He went to the bank and closed the account he'd built up with savings from his military pay. He packed a suitcase. The next morning he was standing in snow flurries outside Omaha on the eastbound highway hitchhiking. Six rides and three days later he was in New York. A day after that he landed himself a job as a deck steward on the *SS Île de France* ocean liner, sailing March seventh for Southampton, England.

After the Atlantic passage, Drake hitchhiked to Ramsgate on the southeast English coast and caught a ferry to Ostend, Belgium. From there he traveled by train through Belgium to the border crossing outside Aachen in the British Occupation zone, arriving March 19, 1946.

Paper Roses

When he got to the front of the line at the British Army border control station, Drake nodded to the corporal standing behind the tall desk and produced his War Department discharge papers and identification.

Sporting a moustache broad as a brush-swipe of black paint dashed cheek to cheek above his mouth, the Tommy looked the part of a grizzled vet. The block of ribbons on his chest suggested that he'd done his part, defeating Hitler. But with the war over, his eyes were dull, like he wanted to be in his neighborhood pub, nursing a pint of warm bitter. "Yank, eh?" he snapped, squinting at Drake's paperwork. After a moment, he snorted and shuffled back to a bank of filing cabinets and ledgers. He lit a cigarette, pulled a thick book with *US, De-Du* painted on the spine down from the shelf and paged through it. Then he nodded at the book, closed and returned it to the shelf. He took a form from a pad and brought it to the desk where Drake waited. "Purpose of proposed travel within the British Occupation Zone?" he grunted without looking up.

"I'm going to Bonn to find my fiancée. German national. Met her when I was there with First US Army."

"Name?" the corporal barked.

"Winston C. Drake."

"I can see that," growled the clerk, holding up Drake's ID. "What's your fiancée's bleeding name?"

Drake rolled his eyes. "Her name's Euridice Bloomstedt."

"Spelling?"

"B, L, O, O, M, S, T, E, D, T."

"The given name, if you please...*sir.*"

"E, U, R, I, D, I, C, E."

The Brit snorted, "Sounds more like a bloody disease than a *Fräulein's* name." Perhaps Drake's scowl chastened the clerk, as his demeanor abruptly turned polite. "If you'll excuse me, sir, I'll get the Lieutenant's approval of your forms straight away." He carried the paperwork with Drake's ID to the desk of the officer in charge.

The ruddy-faced lieutenant scanned the papers casually, stamped each of the three copies *Approved*, and handed them back without a word.

The corporal clipped a copy of the document to Drake's identification papers and handed them to him. "Approved for twenty days travel inside the British sector. Renewable if required at any military control office. Good luck finding—" He glanced at his copy of the form. "—*Fräulein* Bloomstedt. Should you require assistance in that endeavor, sir, we're happy to help an old ally." He reached over the desk and shook Drake's hand.

Drake thanked him and walked through the exit of the control station. The passenger rail office was a block away, and he went there to get his ticket for Bonn.

Three hours later Drake was in a second class coach car heading east. He arrived in the Bonn's train station in the early evening. He stepped from his car and looked up at the high ceiling. Being back in Bonn gave him chills. Part of that was looking across the platforms to track number seven, where he'd met Arvee Titus the previous May. Tears welled in Drake's eyes. "I'll never forget you, buddy," he whispered. "Promise." He shook his head at what he'd been through in the last year. All of it had begun right here.

As he walked through the cavernous building, his thoughts turned to Stetti—how she was somewhere nearby, probably in dire straits. Maybe she'd given up hope he would return, even though he'd promised. "In time you'll learn to trust me, sweetheart," he whispered. "I'll always be there for you." He stepped outside into the frosty evening air. There was a skiff of snow on the ground. He glanced at his wristwatch. Given the hour, he decided to wait until the next day to see Stetti. For old time's sake, he took a room at his old digs, *Hotel Heinrich der Heilige*. He requested and got #220, the room he'd shared with her the first night they spent together. A nod to the Fates never hurts, Drake figured.

Drake woke early the next morning. After breakfast, he got himself a snazzy bow tie at a haberdashery next door to the hotel. He put it on, then found a toy shop and purchased a rattle for the baby. He crossed the street to the makeshift stand of a shivering old *Frau* selling dusty paper flowers. It could have been the same woman he'd seen in the Bonn train station almost a year earlier. Drake bought all six of the pink roses she had. After rounding the corner from the woman's stand, he shook the dust off them and set out for *Chorsängerstraße*.

Drake found Stetti's street. In the cold morning wind, even with the sun breaking at times through the clouds, it was dark and desolate. Some of the houses were still abandoned. Then from a block away, he spotted Stetti's place. His step quickened.

He stopped for a moment and stared at the house. The sight of it took him back to the night she played the cello piece she written for him. The night she'd given him the talisman. The night she'd secreted him up to her room and made love to him. Remembering the scene, it came to Drake that the piece Stetti had written for him had the same tune as the intoxicating song she sang in his recurring dream.

He inhaled deeply. The lungful of sharp air snapped him back to the present. His legs charged with energy, Drake bounded up the stairs to the front door. He knocked. No answer. He used his ring to rap on the glass. That brought a shuffling of feet inside.

The door creaked slowly open. Katarina's face appeared. When her eyes focused on Drake, they began to sparkle. *"Ein Gast!"* she squeeled.

Drake took her expression to mean she remembered him. "Katarina," he chirped, "how's tricks?" She didn't react. "Stetti? Is Stetti at home? You know—" He pointed inside and thought for a moment. "—*im Hause?*"

She smiled. *"Stetti,"* she murmured, like the sound of the name was soothing, *"Schöne Stetti…"* Her eyes went wide as if she thought everyone must know she was gone. *"Stetti weg."* Katarina started to close the door. *"Auf wiedersehen!"* she sang.

Drake held the door open with his foot, but before he could say anything, a man's voice boomed, *"Stetti?"* from inside the house. That was followed by urgent sounds of thumping and shuffling on the floor. *"Die Hure! Kommunistische Hure!"*

A red-faced young man hobbled to the space next to Katarina and leaned on his single crutch. He was missing his left leg below the knee and his left sleeve was empty, pinned go his shirt front. *"Die verräterische Stetti is tod für meine Familie,"* he screamed, elbowing Katarina to the side. *"Für alle guten Deutschen Volkes."* He wiped his eyes. *"Früher habe Ich sie als meine liebste fickende Schwester genannt für Gottes wegen!"* He huffed, then leaned on his crutch and pointed with his hand like a pistol. *"Engländer?"*

Drake swallowed. "American. I'm an American."

The man eyed Drake, then lowered his hand. His twitching eyes were still dark with rage. *"Macht nichts. Raus, Amerikaner!"* He shoved the door, but Drake's foot held it open.

Drake heard a woman's voice behind him, on the steps from the street. *"Entschuldigen sie? Kann ich Ihnen helfen?"*

Turning about, he faced a middle-aged woman, fine despite her tattered black coat and the darned gray scarf over her blond hair. "Sorry," he said, "I don't speak German."

"It isn't a problem, young man," the woman said, "I speak some English." She looked around Drake and said soothingly, lovingly to the agitated man inside, *"Kurt, warum gehst du nicht in dein Zimmer. Alles ist in ordnung."* When the scowling man hobbled away, the woman turned formal again. "Good morning, sir. Please excuse my son, Kurt. His crude language. He comes not long now from a Soviet war prisoner's camp. I am Doctor Keller. Birgitta," She thrust out her hand and shook with Drake. "May I help you?"

"The name's Drake. Winston Drake. From America. You know, the US?"

Birgitta half-smiled. "Certainly I've heard of America."

"Sorry. 'Course you have. I was…I am the friend of a woman who lived here. Stetti. Actually Euridice Bloomstedt's her name. It was just after the war. I'm hoping to see her."

"Mr. Drake, you said? The GI she knew? The one who arranged food for us in the last year?" Tears filled her eyes. Not waiting for an answer, she rushed forward and threw her arms around him. "It was you kept us alive when there was nothing else last summer. Before the Red Cross came to the city. We owe you everything." She took a step back and held Drake's hands.

"Wasn't a big deal." Drake fidgeted. "I only sent a little dough to Dutch. He did all the leg work." He squeezed her hands. "Glad it helped."

"For us it was the difference..." She released his hands and squared her shoulders. "You came to see Stetti? It grieves me to tell you she left my home, in the last autumn time...in October."

She's not here. The thought put Drake into a tailspin. Then he considered the timing—it jibed with her going off to have her baby. Maybe to her family. His eyes lit up. "I think Stetti was pregnant. Is that why she left? Maybe to Dresden where her folks are?"

"I have no thought that Stetti was with a child. As her physician, I would have known such a thing, except in the first days. Even if she were, she would not go to Dresden. Her family *was* there, but they are gone...dead. From the Allied bombing. All Dresden is dead."

"Like you say, even her doc might not know, at first." He considered what that would imply—that she became pregnant after he'd left Germany, but he forced himself to push that thought aside.

"A pregnancy—" Birgitta shook her head. "No, I don't think so. Stetti is not one for motherhood."

Drake's fists clenched. "Maybe she *wasn't*, but people change! Especially when they're expecting."

"Some women. But not Stetti. Rather I suppose she goes to the East for playing her *precious* cello...with some orchestra. I don't want to know where." Birgitta sniffed. "I am very sorry I cannot help the man who gave life to my family."

"East? What do you mean by east?"

"I expect she goes to a city in the zone of Soviet occupation. Stetti..." Birgitta shook her head. "Certainly not Dresden—not there, tasting the ashes of her family. Perhaps Berlin...or Leipzig."

She glanced off in the distance. "Stetti kept an infatuation for communistic ideals. In my son Kurt, that belief seeded great anger on her. You see, he fought against Russian reds. He saw their barbarity." Her jaw tightened. "Stetti was a sister to him. To have her *choose* to go east to live with them...the ones who maimed him? Raped his country? It is too much for Kurt."

"For you too, I guess?

Birgitta's eyes darted to Drake, then she looked away. "For many of us."

"I'd say lots of Stetti's goals are pretty darn noble." He sniffed. "And the Russians? Sure they were brutal to Germans, but from what I hear, it went pretty much both ways."

"Is it so? Ask my aunt in Berlin, made to watch her young son clubbed to death and her daughter raped and murdered. Their sin? Being German." Birgitta glared at Drake as she slipped past him to the door. "I regret that your long travel here must come to nothing. Good day, sir." She stepped inside and pulled the door closed.

Drake stared at the rearing unicorn figures etched on the glass plates on each side the door. The cracked one on the right was still crudely mended with amber glue, same as when he used to call on Stetti almost a year earlier. He gazed at the fake roses in his hand. Feeling as shabby as they looked, he tossed the flowers onto the stoop next to the door.

The cracked glass, the faded paper roses...and Stetti gone. All part of the same story.

Help?

After leaving the house on *Chorsängerstraße*, the next thing Drake knew he was standing in his hotel room, his head spinning. The walk back was a blur. Maybe both his mother and Birgitta were right—he'd come all this way for nothing.

Without thinking about it, Drake's hand went into his pocket and found his talisman. He brought the lucky schilling out and rubbed it. "Don't know how you'll do it," he whispered, "but somehow you gotta come through for me." He kissed the schilling good luck and put it back in his pocket.

Drake fell onto the bed, exhausted but unable to sleep. Was he stupid for coming? Or stupid for waiting so long to come—had he blown his one chance for a special life? Before Stetti, everything about him was totally ordinary. Gray. Then she walked into his world and changed all that. Now she was gone and his future had faded from her Technicolor back to his black and white.

After a dark hour, Drake decided to get out of the hotel room. Maybe have a drink. It might clear his head. Or deaden it. Either would be OK. He'd noticed a small beer place around the corner. It would do.

Drake walked out of the hotel to the bar. The sign on the building read *Ratskeller Der Schwan* under a dreary, yellowed painting of a fat, graceless fowl, more goose in its bearing than swan. Drake opened the door and peeked inside…tiny, dingy. It stank of stale beer and smoke. *Ratskeller* has the right ring to it, he thought, like some rodent's tunnel. Though this place had no appeal, the word, *Ratskeller*, triggered a memory—of Stetti's favorite bar, one named for the underground lair of a nobler creature, a dragon: *Fafner's Höhle*. The hope that she might be there lit a spark in his soul—it seemed unlikely from what Birgitta told him, but a long shot is better than none. He pulled the door closed and stepped back on the street.

It took Drake a moment to recall how to get to *Fafner's Höhle*. He couldn't remember the address, but he knew the direction. He took out his talisman schilling and rubbed it hard as he set off, walking briskly. Ten minutes later he came to a street named *Moselweg*. He knew right away it was the one he wanted. Two blocks down, he came to the tavern's door. Drake's heart pounded as he pushed it open and felt his way down the rickety staircase into the place. He strained to acclimate to the darkness, hoping to spot Stetti before she saw him—it would be great to surprise her.

Drake's heart sank when it was clear Stetti wasn't there. At first he didn't recognize any of the eight people inside. Then the woman behind the bar caught his eye. She pointed to an empty table in the corner and nodded for him to take a chair there. As he looked harder at her broad, factory-girl's face, he thought maybe he had seen her before. When she came around the bar and he saw her thick legs and pendulous breasts, it hit him...this was Stetti's friend, the barmaid-prostitute to whom she'd given the *Immer* perfume he brought her. *What was her name? Gretchen? That seems right.* He sat at the table she'd indicated.

The waitress brought a rag and wiped a puddle of spilled beer off of Drake's table. She looked at him and giggled—tinkling bells followed by the snort of a sow. *"Guten Tag, mein Herr."* She bent over the table, displaying her barely-contained cleavage, and placed her hand on his. *"Was trinkst du, meine Liebe?"*

Considering the view, Drake thought of asking if milk was the daily special. Instead he said, "You're Gretchen, aren't you?"

She bolted straight up.

"Sorry," Drake said. "'Fraid I don't know German. Do you speak English, Gretchen?"

"A little English." She held her thumb and index finger a half inch apart. "For Tommies. Like you. Always pushing on me with questions. I can say only what I always do: I am only a drinks server in this place." She eyed Drake. "You are *Englisher* police?"

Drake shook his head. "Nope, I'm American. Not police. Just traveling here to find my girl. Name's *Stetti*." Her eyes widened. "You know her, don't you? We used to come here last year when I was a GI. I'm Drake. Winston Drake. Remember?" When the girl kept silent, he took her wrist and pulled her close. "You *are* a friend of Stetti's, aren't you...Gretchen?"

262

The waitress trembled.

Drake softened his grip and peered into her eyes. "Don't you remember me?"

She stood rigid. "Maybe I do...maybe not."

Drake patted her hand softly. "Don't worry. All I'm asking for is a little help, finding Stetti. So I can take her away—" He looked around the room. "—from all of this. Bring her back to America with me. Give her a new life."

She scowled. "Make of her a good capitalist, eh?"

Drake chuckled. "Give her a life without all the hardships. You'd want that for your friend, wouldn't you?"

"You *aren't* a policeman, are you?"

Drake grinned. "Nope."

The girl crossed her arms. "So, what if I am called Gretchen?"

"Nothing...just trying to sound friendly. Since I'm asking a favor." Drake raised his hands. "Look, it's this simple, do you know where Stetti is?"

"You would take her away?" Gretchen glared, then her look softened and she shrugged. "Perhaps....Stetti and I speak with the telephone sometimes. But I must have her permission to say more."

"Sure," Drake said. "Can't go telling telling every Tom, Dick, and Harry where she is."

"I don't know these men you say." Gretchen leaned forward and whispered, "I will ask Stetti if she wishes for your visit. Come back tomorrow evening. After the dinner hour."

"Here's a buck says she will, Gretchen." Drake slapped a silver dollar on the table. "Remember, my name's Drake. And hey, tell her I know her *little* secret." He winked. "Just say, a little birdie told me."

"Knowing secrets can make danger." She studied Drake's face and shook her head.

"I'm not scared to lay my cards on the table. Guess I like living dangerously." He rose from his chair and headed for the door. Over his shoulder he called, "Till tomorrow night."

263

Help?

The next evening Drake was back at *Fafner's Höhle* at 7:00 p.m. He waited near the door, watching Gretchen serve glasses of amber beer and sausages from a large tray to four stout old-timers. When she was done, he walked with her to the bar. "Did you reach her?"

"I spoke with Stetti, yes. She is surprised you've come."

"Surprised good, I hope." Drake grinned. "What did she do when you said I knew her little secret?"

"Stetti wonders, what is the secret you know? She wants you to say it to her."

"Just let me know where she is, and I'll tell her anything she wants to hear. Say, how's she doing?"

"She is well. She tells to me she is never happier than now."

"You mean, with me coming, right?" Drake smiled broadly. "So, when can I see her?"

"Stetti must first have the instructions of her officers. For your visit."

"Instructions?"

Gretchen bit her lip. "Perhaps I misspeak. The English…it is not easy, you know. Stetti must get the official permissions. From her authorities. A formality. I talk with her tomorrow. Return here next evening on this hour. For now, please sit. Drink a liter of good beer."

Drake came back a day later.

Gretchen was watching for him and came over as soon as he appeared. Looking to the side, she said, "Tomorrow you will see your Stetti. In her home in Leipzig, four hundred kilometers to the east. All is in order for your travel."

"Hold it." Drake grabbed her elbow. "Leipzig…that's Ruskie territory, isn't it?"

Gretchen looked angry. "I said Leipzig, did I not? Of course it is on the Soviet sector."

"Well, is that a problem?"

"A problem? Not if Stetti invites your visit. She arranges everything. Do you change your mind, mister?"

"No, 'course not. I just thought—"

"Don't think. Only do." She took a paper from her apron pocket and scanned it. "You must take train 457, leaving Bonn station at 06:52 hours. Change to train 1124 at Marburg and travel to the border crossing station in Bebra. A visa awaits you in the Soviet documents control office. Train R5 takes you direct to Leipzig." She glanced at a paper in her hand. "Your arrival is 17:13 hours at main station Leipzig. I have written everything for you. Stetti's address is here." She pointed. "*Goerdelerstraße 137. Flat 207.*" Gretchen thrust the paper into Drake's hand. "Now go. You make an early departure in tomorrow's morning."

"Thank you, Gretchen. I—" Drake reached to take her hand.

She pulled away from him. "You mustn't thank me," she said, stalking away.

Being Led...On

Saturday, 23 March, Drake was on the Bonn railway platform, ticket in hand, forty minutes before the scheduled departure of train 457. At 06:46 a gray locomotive pulled into the station. As it passed, hissing a cloud of white steam, he could see in a space under the engineer's cab, darker than the rest, the faintly visible image of a swastika, painted-over. He boarded a second class car, and the train departed right on time.

Thirty minutes later the train passed into the American sector, marked only by a one minute stop for US Army MPs in white helmets, belts, and spats to replace the British escorts aboard. An hour later at Marburg, Drake changed trains. Before he knew it, his train was pulling into the terminal stop of its run, the border town of Bebra, at 11:50.

When Drake entered the US Army border crossing control office, a tinkling bell, the kind they have on the doors of pawn shops, announced his arrival. A boney, old NCO, hunched over a book and puffing on a briar pipe, sat at a desk marked *SSG C. Boyle, Empfangsoffizier*. At the sound, he looked up and said, *"Kann itch Ihnen behilflich sein?"*

"Howdy, Sergeant," Drake said. "Can you run that by me again, in good old English? I'm American."

Boyle stood. "Why hullo, partner. Figured you were German, like most of the folks we get through here. I'm Staff Sergeant Clancy Boyle." He shook Drake's hand.

"Winston Drake. Pleased to meet you."

"That German lingo was me asking if I could help you."

"Sorry to interrupt your reading. Looks like you are into a good part there."

Boyle held the book up for Drake to see. "I do like my westerns. I'm a Wyoming boy, after all. This one's *Rescue at Rattler Ridge*, one of those Sheriff Duke Orpheus adventures Tim Kenny writes. His Medicine Bow series. Darn things all have the same plot—the sheriff's gal, Lola Delovely, gets herself in a fix, and Duke rides in on his shiny Palomino and rescues her—but I love 'em." He set the book down. "So what can I do you for?"

"Some advice, Clancy. I need to visit the Soviet sector to pick up my girl...um, my fiancée, and bring her out of there. We're gonna get married. She's got a visa lined up for my trip. Guess I pick that up on across the border. Anything special I need to do?"

Boyle shrugged. "Get your head examined, maybe."

"You think it's crazy to go into Soviet territory, eh?" Drake sniffed.

The sergeant laughed. "That too. But I meant getting married. It's like a turkey accepting an invite to Thanksgiving dinner." He laughed again. "Just funning you, partner."

Drake nodded. "Is there a problem going into the Soviets' territory?"

"Nope. 'Course getting out...now that's another matter." Boyle chuckled. "Seriously, we don't advise Americans to go over the border. That's the official policy, at least. There's a fair amount of tension right now between us and them. A couple weeks ago we picked up one of their agents down toward Frankfurt. Apparently they're mad as hornets about it. So going there right about now...well, could be ticklish." He shrugged. "But we can't stop you." He leaned toward Drake and whispered, "And unofficially, I'd say you'd most likely be OK. Last week we had an old-timer come all the way from California to go to Leipzig. Wanted to stand in the same church Johann Bach did. Know who that is?"

"If you mean Johann Sebastian Bach, sure. I'm not some dumb yokel, you know."

"No offence meant, partner. Just that *I'd* never heard of this Bach fella before that Californian came in, beating the drum for him. Told me he was one helluva song writer...the Hoagy Carmichael of his day. Anyhow, Mr. California went to Leipzig and came back fine two days later. Trip went slick as a whistle, he told me." Boyle relit his pipe. "Way I see it, you and that Californian have something in common. You're both in love. And what do they say? Love conquers all. Right?"

"What about getting back into the American sector? That gonna be any problem?"

"Let's see your papers."

Drake handed the sergeant his ID and discharge orders.

Boyle reviewed the documents and handed them back to Drake. "Should be no sweat for you. Now this gal of yours, a German national is she?"

Drake nodded.

"Well...there's three factors that decide admission: Linkage, merit, and compassion. Wives and children of Americans—they have linkage. So do fiancées. People who've done something for us, either during the war or since—they have merit. Then there's need—folks can be admitted on compassionate grounds, at the discretion of our CO, Major Parsifal. Think of the three factors as legs of a stool." Boyle inspected his pipe. He scraped out the bowl with a penknife, then took out a tin of Prince Albert tobacco and refilled. After tamping with the tool, he fired the briar with an olive drab Zippo and took a contented puff.

Drake smiled at the ritual. His father used to go through the same song and dance, and the smoke's aroma was as sweet as his dad's. When Boyle was settled, Drake asked, "So let's say we show up in a couple of days and apply. We got your linkage covered. Merit? Maybe. Regarding need, how would you peg the odds we'll find your CO in a generous mood?"

"Umm, not bad." Boyle knocked on the top of his wooden desk. "Guess you could say Parsifal's learned compassion pretty good in this assignment. What with all the displaced persons we deal with."

"Well then, I s'pose it's worth risking a trip to hell and back to save my little lady."

"Like Sheriff Orpheus, huh?"

"Yeah." Drake paused, then took the toy rattle from his pocket. "Clancy, there might be one other thing." He shook the rattle. "A kid."

"How old?"

"A baby."

"Yours?"

Drake's brow furrowed. "Course it's mine!" he huffed.

"Then it's no problem, partner."

Drake closed his eyes and smiled. "Swell."

Boyle opened a wide ledger book. "Let's see your papers, lad." He took the documents and wrote down Drake's name and other identifiers. "Destination?"

"Leipzig, Germany."

Boyle wrote that. "In your own words, what's the purpose of your travel, partner?"

"To pick up my fiancée, like I said. And our kid."

Boyle wrote some more, then he had Drake sign in the last column. "You're all set. Pass through the gate and report into the Soviet office on the other side. They'll make you cash in a certain amount of money into Soviet German script. And you'll have to spend it all before you leave." He stamped the papers. "Good luck finding that gal of yours."

"Got her address right here, Clancy." Drake waved the papers Gretchen had given him and grinned. "Shouldn't need any luck." But just to be sure, he found Stetti's one schilling talisman in his pocket and gave it a squeeze.

Drake walked through a gate in a chain-link fence and across ten meters of land laid bare to the dirt. On the other side was a guard post—a Soviet soldier sat in a small shack.

The man jumped up as Drake approached. "*Halten Sie!*" He raised his rifle. "*Für das Durchfahren?*"

Drake held up his hands. "English, *bitte?*"

The soldier looked puzzled for a moment, then he picked up the telephone, cranked it and conversed in Russian. After he hung up, he held out his index finger. "*Moment.*"

Drake lowered his arms.

Two minutes later a Soviet lieutenant with a red star on the front of his brown peak cap hustled out of the building behind the guard post, holding some papers. "You are Mr. Drake? Yes? Mr. Winiston Drake, please?"

"It's *Winston*. Like Churchill. Yes, sir, I'm Drake."

"I am Lt. Nakitov, here for helping your travels. Come with myself." The officer led Drake past the guard house into the office.

269

He stepped behind a desk and stood stiffly. "Your documents, please." After getting them, he reviewed the I.D. using a finger to guide his eye and compared it in detail to the papers he already had. Finally he nodded sharply. "Sit, please," he said, indicating the chair next to the desk.

Drake sat and took out a package of Chesterfields. He shook out a cigarette and offered it to the lieutenant. "Smoke?"

Nakitov nodded and took one, then he sat.

Drake lit the officer's cigarette and his.

The Soviet leaned back and scanned Drake's papers. "To the eye, all is fully in order."

Drake exhaled. "Glad to hear it. I'm hoping to head on and catch a train leaving about 16:00 hours today."

"Head on? This means consider?"

"No, Lieutenant, I meant *leave*. You know, say *Auf Wiedersehen*. Am I cleared to go?"

"*Moment*. I must record the particulars of your travelings. I am informed your destination is Leipzig."

"Right, Leipzig. It's east of here." Drake fidgeted and checked the time. "They told me to take the R5."

The lieutenant glared at Drake. "We know of Leipzig's location, thank you. And of Route R5's schedule." He cleared his throat. "The purpose of your proposed travels, please?"

"To visit a friend."

"And the name of this lady friend, please."

Drake furrowed his brow and peered at Nakitov. "How do you know my friend's a lady? I never said that."

The Soviet looked flustered. "Of course Comrade Bloomstedt is a lady! Please to state me the name of your lady friend for completing my document."

Drake shrugged. "OK. It's Euridice...Bloomstedt. Stetti's what I call her."

The lieutenant glanced up. "Thank you for telling that," he said with exasperation.

The tone made Drake uneasy. But it was more than that. What's up with this game of asking what you already know? Drake stubbed out his cigarette. He cocked his head and stared at the lieutenant. Studying him.

The Soviet's eye twitched. He smiled like a kid caught shoplifting an apple. He took a deep drag on the Chesterfield and patted his forehead with a handkerchief. "If you please to tell me, what is the time length of your proposed traveling to engage Comrade Bloomstedt?"

"To *engage* her?" Drake smiled and stroked his chin. "Dunno. Maybe four days." He had the officer backpedaling, and he liked it. "That OK with you, comrade?"

Nakitov took a last puff and put out his smoke in the ashtray. "Sir, is not a problem…for me." He wrote a long entry then handed Drake a sheet of paper crammed with numbered paragraphs, in German with print so small a watchmaker would have trouble reading it. "For your informing, please accept the regulations on your very welcomed travels, sir. Relax for a moment while Comrade Kuznetsov prepares a camera for the capture of your image." He nodded to a burley soldier sitting at a nearby desk with his fingers hovering over a typewriter's keys, but not typing. "By the way, we have what's called the *Zwangsumtausch*. It is a compulsory exchange of western currency into local script. You must purchase one hundred Marks per day of your travels. So four hundred, please. Or the equivalent in another western currency. I can transact."

While Drake and the officer did the money exchange, the big soldier silently went to the other side of the office. He took the black cloth cover off a large, tripod-supported camera with a big silver flash. He fiddled with the device for a minute, then stood stiffly next to it.

The lieutenant rose and said to Drake, "Please for stepping to the floor's white line."

Drake glanced at his watch. His train was scheduled to depart in twenty nine minutes. "It's getting late. Sure I'll be OK, making the R5?"

Nakitov smiled placidly. "Sir, this train does not leave without you."

Drake shrugged. "Mighty accommodating," he said, stepping toward the camera.

When Drake's toes were on the white line, the photographer took two shots, each made dramatic by a blinding flash that momentarily filled the office with cold, white light. The first was front on and the second in profile, just like police mug shots.

Nakitov casually checked his pocket watch. "Ah, thirteen forty hours. It makes eleven minutes until your route's published departure for Leipzig. The station is nearby, but for certainty I will inform the train master you make your way there now."

"Appreciate that," Drake said. "I'll be able to find the station no problem?"

"My comrade escorts you." Nakitov nodded to the photographer and picked up the receiver of a candlestick telephone. As he dialed the railway, Kuznetsov hoisted Drake's satchel and led him out the door.

Sitting on the gently swaying train, Drake had a strange feeling of discomfort. Like what he felt, talking to the Soviet lieutenant at the border crossing. It sure seemed like he was being led. Maybe led on. Every step of the way. First by Gretchen, who'd engineered every part of his journey. Then by Nakitov, who already knew the script of Drake's travelogue by heart, asking questions just for show. Holding the train's departure for him. Playing a role.

After a while the train's rocking motion soothed his concerns. These nice people were just trying to help him find his love. Making it possible. And he returned their kindness by suspecting something sinister? Don't be so dadgummed suspicious, he told himself.

Sitting there, his mind drifted back to the day he met Stetti, 27 March, 1945, and he realized that it was just about a year ago. He pulled out his ticket to check the date. To think, he told himself, you're just four days short of knowing Stetti a year!

Ninety minutes later, Drake stepped onto the platform in Leipzig's main train station. His eyes went wide at the sight of the huge arching canopy of steel and glass overhead. Swept along in the rush of early evening commuters, he passed through the cavernous main hall of the station and into the rose twilight of the square outside. His pulse racing, Drake took out the paper with Stetti's address on it. He smiled, thinking she must know it was his train's arrival hour. Perhaps right now she was standing at her window watching for him on the street below her apartment. Perhaps cooking a celebratory dinner for them—he pictured champagne on a candlelit table. Perhaps she was sitting on the sofa nursing their sleepy baby. The image made him feel in his pocket for the rattle he'd bought in Bonn.

Drake found a city map on a kiosk in the square. Looking back and forth from his paper to the map, he searched in vain for *Goerdelerstraße*. He was almost in a panic when he felt a tap on his shoulder. His heart skipped a beat as he spun around.

But it wasn't Stetti he faced. It was a slender, rather plain girl with mousy brown hair spilling out from her bright red, wool headscarf. She wore a thin, burnt-umber cloth coat, too big for her birdlike frame. She leaned on a worn wooden crutch. Drake felt instant comfort in her earnest expression.

"Good evening, sir. Are you lost?" The girl's eyes said *I want to help*. "May I assist you finding an address?"

"English?" Drake exclaimed. "How did you know I'm a foreigner?"

"You look American." The girl swallowed hard. "Perhaps." She shrugged. "And I study the English language. I hoped to help you and practice at once."

"Guess I'm lucky you came along. *Goerdelerstraße* is the street I'm looking for. " He pointed to the address on his paper.

"Certainly I know where this street is. *Goerdelerstraße*. Number 137. It is there—" She pointed to the south. "—perhaps two kilometers. I am going that way. I can accompany you. Tell me your name, sir."

Drake held out his hand "Winston Drake." As they shook hands he eyed her closely. She looked familiar. Then he realized—it was the scarf. So bright red. He'd seen her in the mob on the train station platform. She'd been standing off to the side, watching people. He remembered thinking when he saw her there that she was watching him.

"Winston, like the Englisher Churchill, eh?" The girl beamed. "I am Hilde Krebs." She pulled her scarf off of her head so it hung loosely around her neck and glanced back at the train station entrance. "Shall we go?"

Drake glanced at her crutch then down to her right foot. Her high-topped shoe was odd—thick and clunky, to accommodate what he figured must be a misshapen foot. He'd known a classmate, Randy Mortensen, with a deformity called clubfoot. Randy's foot was twisted so that the arch curled inward, leaving him to walk on the side of his foot and ankle. This girl seemed to have the same handicap.

"Oh, it isn't a problem. I hobble along rather well, you'll see." She indicated south with a wave of her hand. "We will walk there, across *Richard-Wagner-Straße*."

"Sure this isn't out of your way?"

The girl suddenly looked sad. "No, helping you is what I am here to do." She glanced again in the direction of the train station. "My purpose," she said softly.

It struck Drake as an odd way to put it. "Your purpose?"

Hilde bit her lip. "My English is clumsy. Please see over it." She looked away. "I meant only that...it is good to be useful to a stranger" When she turned back to him and smiled, it looked forced.

Just then, a bus's headlights illuminated Hilde's face. Drake saw tears welling in the corner of her eye. "Are you OK?"

"It's only the wind," Hilde said, wiping her eye then jabbing her hands in her coat pockets. "Brisk, isn't it?"

They walked down *Katharinenstraße*. Hilde had been right—though her gait was herky-jerky, she moved right along. She seemed happy again, pointing out a grand building on the left, glowing in the faint moonlight. "It is what we *Leipzigers* call *Das Alte Rathaus*. The old city hall, you would say in America. It dates from the Sixteenth Century. Before Johann Sebastian Bach was born. Whenever I pass it, I think, imagine, my eyes now see the same building his so often did!"

She explained that their destination was recently renamed for Carl Friederich Goerdeler. "He is my hero. Only a year ago, he gave his life opposing the Fascist Reich. He loved Germany enough to try and kill Hitler. With Bach, I count him as the greatest Leipziger."

Drake told Hilde about the reason for his trip. About Stetti. About how wonderful, how beautiful, how perfect she was. She seemed uninterested. As if she'd already heard that screed. Gotta be the story of her life, Drake thought. The story of every plain girl: Meet a guy, and sure enough, he's got his eye trained elsewhere. On someone beautiful.

Twenty minutes later they turned onto *Goerdelerstraße*. Hilde turned pensive again.

Drake spotted a number on a house. "We must be getting close. There's four sixty-two. We're looking for—" He glanced at his paper. "—one thirty-seven."

"Yes, I know well the place of one three seven. It is just nearby." She gazed ahead like she could see the apartment building in the distance.

When they stood in front of 137, Drake was surprised by its dullness. As if Stetti's living there should give it pizzazz. It was hulking. Gray stone. The white marble frontispiece over the door had once given it a name, some character. Now that name was unreadable, chipped and cracked as the stone was—probably war damage. The only elements of interest were dramatic shadows cast by the moonlight. A few of the windows were lit but most were dark. He wondered which one was Stetti's. Had she turned off the lights so she could watch for him better? Would one of the windows spring open and her beautiful face appear, calling down to him, proclaiming to the whole world, "Drake darling, you've come!" With sobs of joy, "You've come!"

Instead, all was silent, dark, electric, like a cat sleeping...or a panther ready to pounce.

"Now that I have done what I must," Hilde said, "I'll take my leave, Mr. Drake." Her eyes got big. She touched his arm, took a deep breath as if she wanted to say something important...then shrank back and without another word, turned and limped away.

Candle in the Window

Drake hardly noticed Hilde step away. All his thoughts were on Stetti, on being reunited with her in mere seconds. He stood in the street entranced, his body tingling.

An approaching automobile brought him back to the moment. He stepped to the sidewalk and the car passed. As he watched its taillights move off, a swath of space in front of the vehicle was illuminated by its headlights. The quiet street was deserted…except for a pair of shadowy men in brimmed hats and long overcoats, on the other side fifty yards down. They froze in the glare until the car passed. Then they stepped into the dark doorway of an apartment building. Drake figured they'd gone inside until he saw the flare of a match struck and then a pair tiny glowing points. He shivered. Nothing's biting as a damp winter night in Germany, he thought, remembering the time he'd spent stationed there a year earlier. "Nice, ain't it," he whispered in the direction of the pair across the street, "ducking the cold for a while with a smoke in the shelter of that door stoop."

Squeezing his lucky schilling into the palm of his hand, Drake took a deep breath and dashed up the steps to the door. Inside, he went down a long hallway to the stairs at the side of the building. Up two flights he bounded then walked down a dark corridor till he came to number 207. He stood for a moment, peering at the door, finished in glossy black enamel. The white number was painted on, in an ornate style like the writing on a Coca Cola bottle.

Seized by panic, Drake could barely draw in a breath. No sound came from the apartment. No light slipped under the door. There was no sign that Stetti was inside. He put his talisman back in his pocket and raised his hand to knock, then lowered it. Because as long as he hadn't done so, there was possibility. Once he did, things would go inexorably either right or wrong…and if wrong, he knew he'd never have a happy moment again. After a moment, Drake set his jaw, closed his eyes and rapped softly.

He was about to knock again when the apartment door sprang open. Drake's knees went weak. Stetti stood before him in the doorway, the light of the single bare bulb hanging behind her in the center the room, creating a glow around her tall, slender figure. Everything about her was severe: The woolen, charcoal-colored tunic with buttons to the throat. The high-collared corbeau linen blouse underneath. The mid-calf length skirt, straight and crisp. But it was the darkness of her face, framed by her straight, black hair, that held Drake's gaze. Because it said everything. There was no smile, no warmth, no emotion. He had dreamt for a year of her smoldering lips. Now her mouth was a harsh, frozen scissure. Her eyes, no more the liquid, sparkling, green portals of a fiery soul, were cold and dangerous. When she said, "Come in," her icy tone sounded as ominous as a shouted *Get out!*

Drake stepped inside, and she gave the door a push with her foot, swinging it shut with a reverberant clack.

They stood facing each other in the small, austere room. Like prize fighters sizing each other up before the opening bell. As if trying to divine what was to come from the way the other shifted their weight or clenched their fist or twitched their eye.

Then Drake's gaze fell on Stetti's cello, resting on a stand in the corner of the room. Its soft, curved, feminine lines. Its rich cherrywood, polished to a gleaming luster. Its strings and bow, in which the magic of music lived. He saw it and thought of the *folie* she'd written for him and played almost a year ago. Through his mind swept a snatch of that melody which was at the center of the dream that had drawn him back to find her. For a moment, the cello and the music pushed aside his shock and his fear. "I had to come back to find you. To see you." He held his hand out. "To save you."

Stetti stared at him. As if she needed time to comprehend what he'd said. Then she shook her head and the look of her eyes changed from cold disinterest to rage. "To save me?" she sneered. "Imperil me is more like it. You and your clumsy meddling forced me to act. I *had* to save myself...prove my loyalty. And Gretchen, you left her defenseless with your threat to expose *our little secret.* Tell me, what is she to do now?"

"Look honey, you've got it all wrong. I only..." Drake wanted to explain what he meant by *little secret*—*their* baby. But seeing his dream smashed, he couldn't go on.

Stetti seemed to have no interest in explanations. Her fingers coiled into clenched fists. "I didn't want to have to do—" She glanced out the window. "—this." Glaring at him, she snapped, "You left me no choice, damn you." Then her eyes changed again, as if they'd suddenly filled with profound sadness. "Why *did* you have to come?" Her shoulders sagged. "There was never anything here for you."

Drake stood dead-still, staring at the floor. Stunned. When he looked up, tears filled his eyes. "There's no baby, is there?"

Like a coiled cobra, Stetti locked him in her gaze. "You're a fool, Winston Drake."

The words stung, and the pain only grew when Drake recalled Holt saying the same thing to him in Manila. He lowered his gaze, admitting to himself it was true.

Stetti lit a candle, carried it to the window and slowly raised the tattered tan shade. She held the flame near the glass and moved it back and forth. Then she stood for a moment, staring down to the street. Without looking back, she said, "Get out."

His body numb, Drake's brain seized by a memory—Stetti explaining her name the day they met. She'd related the myth of Orpheus and Euridice, declaring that Orpheus hadn't ventured to Hades to save his wife...he'd gone out of his own need. Had he done the same? Crushed by this doubt, he rushed to her side and held her waist. She wouldn't look at him. His eyes followed the track of her stare. To the moonlit street below. To the pair of men in the brimmed hats and overcoats looking up at him. He watched one of them raise a Luger pistol and pull the bolt back, cocking it. The men dashed for the apartment's front steps.

After a frozen instant, the instinct to survive surged through Drake, sweeping everything else aside. He pushed Stetti away and dashed for the door. Damn her, he thought, for being so cold, so cruel. Damn me for being so stupid, so blind. And damn Fate for being out to get me.

279

Oblivious to the physical world around him, he crashed into the wooden kitchen chair, sending it careening across the floor and clattering into the stove. He stumbled but somehow kept moving. A second later he was at her doorway. In a blur, he fumbled with the knob and hurled the door open. Without a glance back, he careened blindly into the dark corridor.

Ditching the Goons

When Drake stumbled into the dark corridor outside Stetti's apartment, he instantly sensed the presence of someone standing inches away. Waiting for him. His heart sank. He peered, expecting a brimmed hat. Instead he made out something red, a scarf. It's that girl who brought me from the train station, he thought.

Hilde took Drake's hand. "Come." The clatter of men dashing up the staircase grew louder by the second. "You have to trust on me."

The image of the man down on the street cocking his Luger flashed through Drake's mind. When the girl jerked his arm again, he followed.

Hilde led him down the corridor, the rapid-fire thumps of her crutch reverberating on the floor. Drake could barely keep up.

They passed two doors and stopped in front of the third. "It has a vacancy," she said, pulling him in and easing the door closed. She turned the deadbolt and guided Drake through the empty apartment to the kitchen window in back. There was no shade, and gray moonlight streaming in provided faint illumination. When bootsteps clunked in the hallway, Hilde put a finger to her lips and murmured, "Shhh." She waited for shouts in the corridor to mask the sound she made opening the window. Pulling Drake close, she whispered, "We can escape on the fire ladder. Say nothing."

Hilde climbed onto the iron catwalk. Drake paused to take the baby's rattle from his pocket, gaze at it for a moment, then set it gently next to the sink. He followed Hilde out. The pair shuffled along the catwalk to a ladder that led to the alley below. Slinging her crutch over her shoulder, Hilde stepped nimbly down the rungs to the paving bricks. Drake came right behind. Sticking to the shadows, they hurried to the corner and rounded it, moving away from the apartment building. "Take my arm," Hilde whispered, out of breath. "A couple draws less attention."

Sirens sounded behind them. There were muffled shouts and distant police whistles.

Drake looked over his shoulder. "I want to thank you…but I forgot your name."

She glared. "You're not the first."

After a few steps, Drake said, "Don't be sore. Tell me again. I'll remember. Promise."

"It is Hilde. H, I, L, D, E, should you want to mention me in your memoirs."

"Thanks, Hilde." He squeezed her wrist. "It's a pretty name."

She looked at Drake and half-smiled. "You're welcomed."

With every step down the dark residential street, the commotion on *Goerdelerstraße* grew fainter. Drake's optimism rose. "So, where are we going?"

"My brother's flat. Not far."

A block later he stopped her. "Why are you doing this...Hilde?"

She didn't look back. "Keep moving."

Shortly she steered Drake into a stairwell leading down into a basement apartment. She rapped on the glass of the door with a spoon hanging from the jamb by a string. *Tap, tap.* Pause. *Tap, tap.* Pause. *Tap, tap.* After a moment, a light came on inside. An unshaven young man peered out. The door opened.

Hilde and the man spoke softly but quickly back and forth in German. The words *Winston* and *Drake* were the only ones Drake recognized. Then she turned to him. "Mr. Drake, I present my brother—" She nodded at the man. "—called Johannes."

The men shook hands. Johannes's features were mild, with pale blue eyes behind round, wire-rimmed glasses. His ears caught Drake's attention. They were disfigured, rough around the outsides, as if mice had nibbled off the edges.

Seeing Drake's stare, Johannes touched his ear and said, "*Rußland.*"

"He explains his ears were frozen in Russia," Hilde said. "He hears well but can't speak English. His French is good, if that is possible for you."

Drake scrunched his nose. "'Bout the only French I know is *Hinky Dinky Parlez Vous.*"

"It makes nothing. You should require no conversing." Hilde glanced at her watch. "Now I must appear to the captain of my

282

agency. You can stay hidden here, with Johannes." Hilde shrugged. "Early tomorrow I return."

"But won't you be in hot water?" Drake asked. "For helping me?"

Hilde blew on her hands. "Hot water…mmm. But I've no time for a bath." She flashed a shy smile. "Don't worry. All they know is that I performed my assignment—bringing you to Stetti's flat. No one saw me creep quietly back. Through the alley. Or enter in the rear with the fire escape and the vacant flat to wait for you." She knocked on a wooden cabinet door. "Now my captain thinks only of missing prey." She glanced at her misshapen foot. "Like everyone, he overlooks me." She turned to leave then looked back. "Tonight, I glad for it."

Hilde returned early the next morning. Soon after, Johannes left.

Behind drawn shades, Drake and Hilde sat at the small kitchen table. "Johannes goes to his job with the railroad," she said. "We both have wished to leave the Soviet zone for some time. Now we think we can do that and help you, too. But you must trust us."

"Not sure I have much choice." Drake cocked his head. "But you and Johannes do. Why *are* you helping me? Seeing that rough-looking pair outside Stetti's place, guns drawn and all, it seems mighty risky."

"It is. Those who would stop us are ruthless. In our offices only last week I heard two Soviet agents laughing and talking over lunch. One said a young couple from Jena had let slip that they planned to defect. A good citizen reported their treason. The agent tracked this husband and wife to a place near the border and stopped them. He offered to let them go in exchange for their money, then shot them like dogs before they took ten steps. The pleasure for him was that in addition to the bribe, he also collected an official reward for stopping two enemies of the state."

Drake shook his head. "I can't let you do it. Risk your neck to save me."

"Johannes and I aren't saints. Crossing the border without you, we are just two Germans pleading for refuge in the West. Our case for asylum is stronger if we've helped you. We have long dreamed of a life of freedom. With you, we have our best chance." She smiled at Drake. "Besides, you are in peril. We won't abandon you."

"Abandon me to what? Look, all I did was come to see my girl. Least I thought she was. And I'm an American citizen, goldangit. Just a year ago, I was fighting Hitler along with the Soviets. Once all that gets straightened out, surely they'd let me go."

Hilde peered at Drake. "Naïve one, our agency views any effort to lure citizens to the west as espionage. Spying cannot be *straightened out.*"

"So your agency knew all about my plans?" Drake folded his hands. "Guess I got one question." Tears welled in his eyes. "How deep was Stetti involved in this dirty deal?"

Hilde looked away and took a deep breath. Then she faced Drake. "I am just a lowly foot soldier in the Soviet security agency in Leipzig. I take orders. Though they tell me little, my ears are sharp. What I heard is that when you sought out Stetti, she reported it, out of loyalty to the Party. Our captain called your mission an espionage. Clearly you had found out that Stetti and her contact in Bonn are involved in intelligence gathering, and you threatened to expose their mission. Later the agency came to see your travels here as an opportunity. A chance to catch a source of information on an enemy's projects *and* a potential...we say *Verhandlungmasse*, something to use for trading."

"A bargaining chip," Drake muttered, "that's what it's called in English."

"A chip for bargaining? Yes. And that would be your best outcome. Otherwise, perhaps it is a long holiday in Siberia for you."

Drake scowled and shook his head. "It's all plain crazy—I'm no spook!"

Hilde cocked her head. "What is the spook that you are not?"

"It's slang for spy. But it's nothing to do with me. Like I said, I'm just a guy who came to see his girl. To try and help her. I was in love with Stetti, for Christsakes!"

Hilde shrugged. "Perhaps. But our agency believed otherwise. They made your travels easy. Arranged your visa and itinerary. Many actors played their parts. Because of my English skills, I was selected to meet you at the station. Besides, who suspects a cripple? My job was to verify your identity and convey the confirmation by slipping off my scarf. Then to deliver you into the jaws of the trap. Stetti was the bait. In her apartment, she captured your offer to take her to the west on a concealed voice recorder then signaled *proceed* to the agents on the street by moving a candle in her window. So yes, Stetti was involved. But was it vile disregard for you? She would insist it was virtuous loyalty to the Party."

Drake's shoulders sagged. Stabbing pain ripped his gut. "I'd hoped she wasn't in on it." He shook his head. "What a chump I was!"

"You trusted. Here, no one trusts…is that better? It's why I want so desperately to flee."

Drake nodded. "You got a plan, I hope."

"As I told you, Johannes works in the rail authority. He has sympathetic friends there. Some smuggling goes on. We plan to make a smuggling, not of schnapps or tinned meat, but of people— you and me. The details are many. Leave them to Johannes. Be content to know he has a great reason to succeed. Love. He dreams of seeing again a girl living in the west. "

"The thugs after us, they're from this agency of yours, huh?"

"They are," Hilde said. "It is the local office of Soviet NKVD, a Russian gestapo."

Drake shook his head. "What chance do we have, up against a gang like that?"

Hilde put her hand on Drake's. "The NKVD is everywhere, relentless and brutal. But we have our cunning." She smirked.

Drake looked into her eyes—there was no fear. He recalled her calm getting him safely out of Stetti's building right under the goons' noses. He winked at her. "Tell you what, cool as you are under fire, my money's on us."

When Johannes came home that evening, he looked worried. Smoking a cigarette Drake gave him, he spoke to his sister in rapid-fire, clipped sentences.

Hilde listened calmly. She poured beer from a large brown bottle into three glasses and let Johannes's nervousness burn itself out. When he'd finished talking, she turned to Drake. "Did you know you are a big celebrity?" She raised her beer glass to him. "Johannes days your picture is distributed to ticket sellers and trainmen working every line running to the west. It is the same for autobus transit and local police. He sees agents lurking throughout the train station and on many street corners."

Drake winced. "That don't sound good."

Hilde shrugged. "An inconvenience, certainly. But don't forget the ace in our sleeve, our cunning." She smiled and sipped her beer. "And our advantage in having a spy in their midst." She nodded to Johannes. "Naturally the goons expect you to make your escape west, where safety is." Her grin was big as a harvest moon. "So, we will go east."

"The old switcheroo...that could work, I guess." Drake's brow furrowed. "But at some point we'll need to double back, as they say in Hollywood westerns."

"I have seen American western films. Before the war. But then I hadn't English, so I understood no speaking. Yes, we will turn back later, but from someplace other than Leipzig. A place unexpecting. It is one of the cunning aces in our sleeves."

"Clever. Glad we're on the same team." Drake rubbed his palms together. "OK, let's hear the whole scheme."

"Johannes can travel openly. You cannot, being a famous American spook." She grinned. "Nor me, once I fail to report for my next duty. The plan? Tomorrow Johannes will smuggle us, concealed in one of the cars of a train he works on." She shrugged. "That is it."

"A little short on details, aren't you?"

"Johannes has the whole plan written here." Hilde tapped her temple with her index finger. "We must trust him. We have no other choice."

"And crossing the border? It's Soviets, not your brother's pals, who control that."

"We depart the train before there and cross to safety on feet. At some unofficial point. You are right that the danger there is large, travelling open grounds, with guards nearby."

Drake glanced at the crutch, leaning on Hilde's chair. "Dashing across the border on foot? I've seen the Russian soldiers stationed there. They got rifles big as cannons. We'll have to step lively. Sure you'll be OK?"

She clenched her teeth and stood. "Worry about your own stepping, sir." She took her crutch and hobbled out of the kitchen.

A Rolling Coffin

March 25, 1946

The apartment was pitch dark when Hilde woke Drake. *"Guten Morgen, mein schlafmützig Herr.* The time makes nearly 4:00." She switched on the light. "We must leave in the next minutes so we can walk before the day is lighted. Few people will be up, and in the dark we can see police headlamps before they see us."

Drake sat up and rubbed his eyes. "What did you call me? *Schlaf-something*? It means dreamy…as in handsome, right?" He faked a yawn. "The ladies are always calling me that."

Hilde giggled. "Hmm, American girls must be easily pleased," she said with a smirk. "As for *schlafmützig*…it means sleep-capped. In English you say sleep-headed, don't you?" She eyed Drake, head tilted, studying him. "Handsome? Hmm…a little."

Drake was surprised by the flirtatious tone. Up to now Hilde had been as serious as her face was plain. He respected her, even liked her, but she was more comrade than female. Was that changing? "Sleepy-headed. That's what we say in English."

They left the flat at 04:10, an hour before Johannes was to depart for his railroad job.

Walking in the cool darkness felt swell to Drake, though he guessed some of it was the excitement of their stealthy, dangerous journey. "Johannes said pictures of me were plastered all over the train station and the place was crawling with goons. Shouldn't I have a fake moustache or a hat I can pull down over my eyes?"

"Don't worry. We don't go in the station."

Drake waited a moment for her to go on. When she didn't, he said, "So…are we jumping aboard the moving train like a couple of hobos?"

"That sounds dangerous. No, after it leaves the station, the train stops near the outside of Leipzig for water. We wait there and Johannes will bring us aboard then."

"Slick!"

It had just started to drizzle when the pair arrived at the railroad water tank at 05:50. The location, along the tracks in an area of abandoned, bombed-out factories and warehouses, was overgrown with tall weeds. They huddled under the elevated tank to keep dry.

An hour later, a faint light appeared far down the tracks in the direction of Leipzig's center. "Johannes said to wait thirty meters from the tank, so other crew members won't see us board."

They walked up the line and stood under a small, leafless tree. Three minutes later the engine eased slowly by them and stopped at the water filling station. Johannes opened the door of a passenger car nearby. He peered up and down the line to be sure it was safe, then waved for his sister and Drake to hurry aboard.

Inside the train, Johannes, wearing a dark blue trainman's uniform, whisked them to a compartment whose doors had been tied closed with gray cotton cord. A sign on the glass read, *In Reparatur. Gesperrt!*, and there were tools spread on the floor. When he'd opened the door and they were inside, Johannes stood on the seat and removed a panel from the ceiling. Extending his hand to Hilde, he said, "*Kommst du! Schnell!*" He helped her onto the seat then easily lifted her lithe body to the space above then handed her crutch up. "*Und Herr Drake,*" Johannes said.

With a boost from Johannes and a pull from Hilde, Drake scrambled into the hiding hole.

Johannes whispered something to Hilde then raised a finger to his lips. "Shhh." He slid the cover panel back into place, making it completely dark for the pair inside.

A moment later the train jerked ahead and slowly picked up speed. "Now we can speak, but it cannot be noisy," Hilde murmured.

"Cozy in here, ain't it?" Drake said.

"The closeness…does it make disquiet in you?"

"You mean, does being cooped-up like this gimme the willies? No. How about you?"

"For me it makes more comfort than the rain and cold outside. Our travel to Dresden is a little more than two hours. You may sleep if you wish, *mein schlafmützig Herr*. Perhaps you'll dream of easily-pleased American girls."

"Or persnickety German ones."

"Persnickety? This word I don't know. It sounds vulgar."

Drake snickered so loud Hilde had to quiet him with a firm *Shhh!* "Persnickety means fussy," he whispered, "you know, the opposite of American gals." He closed his eyes, intending to catch forty winks.

Instead he thought about Stetti. Fussy wasn't the right word for her, but everything she did was on her own terms. With her, it always seemed like she was driving...and he was supposed to feel lucky to be along for the ride. Those times with Stetti—in hindsight, how wonderful they were mattered less than his feeling vaguely unworthy of them. Like Stetti wanted him taking it that way. It was a heckuva lot different from the last couple of days with Hilde. They hadn't been what he'd call magical, but he was at ease with her, like he belonged there. He looked in her direction, and though he could see nothing in the darkness, the sound of her soft breathing was comforting.

After many short stops along the route, the train made a longer halt. Drake could hear conversations, shuffling feet and station announcements—must be in Dresden he figured. Shortly, the compartment door opened and Johannes spoke to Hilde through the false ceiling.

She touched Drake's arm. "We are in Dresden. After some time for the passengers to disperse, my brother will lead us to a train going west. For now, we must remain quiet."

Johannes returned to the compartment ten minutes later and removed the cover panel. While he was helping Hilde and Drake down, he briefed her on the arrangements he'd made.

"Johannes has purchased a hat for you to wear as we walk to the next train. His friend in that crew will put us in a compartment like this one, made for smuggling. Johannes will ride below us. Have you Soviet script we can give for Johannes's friend?"

Drake pulled out the wad of money he'd purchased at the border. He offered it to Hilde who took a few bills. "Keep the rest," she said, "for bribing at the border." She handed the money to Johannes and took the brown fedora he was holding. She placed it, nice and low, on Drake's head. "Now, say nothing more until we are safely hidden in the next train."

They walked silently through the crowded station to the platform for western departures. A train was stopped there. Waiting next to a car in the middle was a heavy man in a blue railway uniform. He looked up and down the track and said in a pipsqueak voice, "*Kommen sie mit.*" He led them into the car, to a compartment labeled *Reserviert.* Johannes passed him the money, and he ambled away looking satisfied as a bear who'd just eaten a bushful of berries.

"The train will leave in twenty minutes," Hilde told Drake. "We must hide ourselves quickly before crewmembers and passengers arrive." The pair scrambled into the smuggling space, a much tighter fit than the one in the last train, and Johannes sat below, reading a newspaper.

Soon there was a swell of voices and shuffling as passengers climbed aboard, lugging clunky suitcases. A woman in a frilly, old fashioned dress, leading two young children, slid open the compartment door. "*Frei?*" she asked hopefully.

"*Nein,*" said Johannes, pointing to the *Reserviert* sign on the door. He shrugged. "*Verzeihung. Es tut mir leid.*" Reopening his paper with finality, he leaned back in the seat.

The woman huffed, slammed the door, and stalked off, her children in tow.

Three minutes later, with hisses and clanks, the train eased out of the station.

In the smuggling box over the false ceiling, Drake started to panic. The close quarters seemed to push in on him, more with each passing mile. Lying on his back, the box's top an inch from his nose, his chest tightened. He tried to focus on the rhythmic swaying of the train as it chugged west. Rocking that might ordinarily have been soothing became claustrophobic with the closeness pressing in on him. The air seemed heavy, and he started to pant, trying to push the spent breath from his lungs. Hilde took his hand and squeezed it. Her touch said *You're not alone,* and the panic in him began to ebb.

Drake thought about the escape from Stetti's place, when he couldn't recall Hilde's name. That was lousy. Now it was worse— even after being together a couple of days, here in the dark he couldn't picture her face. All he could remember was her short, mousy-brown hair and crippled foot. He bit his lip. She *was* plain, forgettable, but that didn't make it OK.

As he clung to her fingers, his breathing slowed. And suddenly he saw her in his mind. It was her eyes. They weren't magic, hypnotic like Stetti's. Hilde's eyes were dark brown, quiet, but early that morning, when she'd said he might be handsome, they'd come alive. It was that image he pictured, when she playfully shed her cocoon.

Ten minutes later, Drake heard the compartment door below swish open. "*Papiere, bitte,*" a man's baritone voice demanded of Johannes.

When Drake cocked his head, Hilde's fingertips flashed to his lips. The breath froze in his lungs.

The men below conversed for a minute, cordially calling each other *Kamerad.* There was the sound of shuffling papers and clunking—perhaps the stamping of documents. Then the compartment door slid closed and the only noise was the train's wheels.

After a minute, Hilde whispered, "That was the *Zugführer,* the boss of the train. He checks Johannes's documents. My brother tells him he travels from Bautzen to Gerstungen to visit a sick sister. I believe we remain safe, for now."

Eighty minutes later, the train slowed as it entered a noisy station. It stopped. Outside were the sounds of a crowd on the platform. "It must be Leipzig," Hilde whispered. "Quiet!"

The compartment door slid open. Someone came in and spoke with Johannes. A deep voice—it was the *Zugführer.* After a moment he left.

Fifteen minutes later the train departed the station, and ten minutes after that Johannes let Hilde know what had happened.

Afterward, she whispered an update to Drake. "The stop was Leipzig as I guessed. Johannes saw many policemen on the platform, mingling in the crowds waiting to board. The *Zugführer* gave him a copy of your picture. He asked if Johannes had seen you. Of course, he hadn't." She squeezed his hand. "The man instructed Johannes to sound an alarm if he observes you. For security, the Leipzig passengers were boarded onto a separate carriage." She sighed. "It seems we are still obscured."

Drake wanted to kiss her…he told himself it must be because things were going so well. "*Wunderbar!*" he breathed.

The train chugged on, and after a while Drake closed his eyes. He was exhausted but couldn't sleep. His thoughts were back on Stetti. He'd thought of her little since the blow-up in Leipzig. But now his mind was in a rut—he couldn't let go of the moment when she snarled, "Get out." The icy hatred in her voice when she'd called him a fool and scorched him with, "There was never anything here for you." That from one who had meant everything to him! Tears welled in his eyes, and he shuddered with a sob.

Hilde didn't speak, but she placed a hand on his shoulder.

Drake pictured her leading him from Stetti's to safety, a happier thought. Her thin, pale cheeks. Plain mouth. And most clearly, her darting, dark eyes, expressing fear, courage and urgency, all at once. She cut quite a figure—small and strong. Incongruent as a mouse in battle armor. The image was what he needed, one powerful enough to dislodge a nightmare.

Too *Gut* to Be *Treu*

Drake slept in the smuggling box until Johannes's tapping on the panel woke him.

"*Ja?*" Hilde said.

Johannes stood on the seat and whispered to her.

When he had finished, Hilde said urgently to Drake, "Johannes says we are near to Gerstungen. Soon it will be the time to leave from the train. Before its station stop."

"Jumping off? Sounds tricky."

"Johannes was told the train will slow outside the village when it passes on some temporary tracks. We must jump then. At a ruined building. We can hide there if we must."

Two minutes later the panel to the hideout slipped away. "*Komm schnell!*" Johannes barked.

Hilde and Drake scrambled down. Johannes peeked out of the compartment to be sure the aisle was clear. "*Gut!*" he said. "*Wir gehen.*" He took Hilde's hand and led her out.

Hilde looked back at Drake. "May luck join us!"

The train slowed to a crawl. On the left side were a few cottages, ahead on the right, a large dilapidated building. The three hurried to the front of the car, and Johannes opened the right-side exit door. When they were even with the building, he looked at Hilde and nodded. She stepped to the bottom stair and jumped. As soon as she had landed awkwardly and tumbled to a halt by the door to the wrecked structure, Drake whispered, "Geronimo!" and leapt. He came down like a bundle of laundry then watched Johannes step gracefully off the train and halt, standing up, twenty feet down the line. Drake sprinted to Hilde's side and said, "You OK?" When she nodded, he pulled her to her feet as Johannes ran up.

They stood before the entryway to the bombed-out hulk of a building. The door lay knocked down under a pile of charred rubble just inside. A sign under the eaves read *T. Eigen, Fabrik der feinen Konserven.* Johannes pushed his companions into the building, and they hid inside the doorway. As the end of the train passed, Hilde gasped, "We are alive!"and embraced her brother and Drake.

Drake peeked out as the train moved off down the track. "Hope nobody saw us."

Johannes led the way over the debris-strewn floor to the back of the former canned goods factory. The roof of the rear half of the building had collapsed and parts of the walls were missing. He pointed to a line of trees fifty yards off. *"Rasch, zu den Bäumen!"* He took his sister's hand and they traversed the open space, with Drake close behind.

They hid among the trees, catching their breath. Johannes surveyed the area around them, then spoke to Hilde and pointed.

"Johannes believes that way—" She pointed with a nod of the head. "—is correct. But he can't say how far the border is."

They hurried along the line of trees, using them for cover. Their advance was parallel with the train tracks, so the direction seemed right. But then the trees ended, and the tracks curved, and more houses made the trio go farther off their intended bearing. After an hour, Johannes stopped and shook his head. *"Ich weiß nicht,"* he groaned, *"wo wir sind. Wir müssen um Hilfe bitten."*

Hilde leaned toward Drake and whispered, "Johannes thinks we must ask for help." She saw a flash of fear in Drake's eyes. "Don't worry. Local people cross to the west frequently. It is too much trouble and expense to pass through the official transit points. We heard it is easy to pay a little to someone for help getting across."

Drake bit his lip. "You know best."

They walked on and soon saw an old woman forty meters off. She sat in the sunshine on the trunk of a downed tree, smoking a cigarette. At her feet slept a small gray dog.

Johannes pointed. *"Das aussieht wie Marco."* he said quietly. Studying the woman, he nodded and murmured a comment.

"He says the dog looks like our mother's pet, Marco. And the woman looks nice, he thinks. He believes we should ask her for help. Do you agree?"

"What else can we do?" Drake glanced at the woman. "Probably someone's grandma." He shrugged. "If you can't trust a grandma…"

"We'll approach her. Give me your script so I can offer something for her help." As Drake handed her the cash he had, she looked sternly at him. "We mustn't say English around her. If she speaks to you, let me reply."

They approached the woman. Hilde greeted her, then introduced Johannes and Drake.

The woman nodded *hello* and yacked for a while, with ample pointing and gesturing. She had a whiskey voice.

Hilde said, "*Sehr gut*," and handed the woman four bills which seemed to please her greatly. Turning to Drake, Hilde winked and said loudly, "*Gehen wir, Liebe.*"

The four set off. Johannes walked ahead with the woman, chatting with her and carrying her pet. He made a big deal of the dog, stroking its ears and speaking to it in what sounded like baby talk.

Behind them, Hilde let a dozen meters of distance build, then she whispered to Drake, "Her name is *Frau Guttreue*. She knows the countryside well and goes often across the border illegally. To avoid the crossing tax. I told her Johannes is my brother and you are my husband." Hilde glanced at Drake to see his reaction. "I explained your silence by saying you are dumb." She shrugged. "I said we travel to visit our sick mother in Bebra, and we haven't time to apply for a *Sichtvermerk*—you can call it a traveling permission."

"So, we'll just tag along with Granny Gut-whatever and keep our fingers crossed?" Drake's brow furrowed. Then he noticed Hilde was nervous too. Leaning close, he said softly, "Your dumb husband, huh, little wifey? I promise to be silent as Charlie Chaplin."

Hilde smiled. "Imagine," she murmured, "a simple *Fräulein* married to a famous American film star!"

When Drake broke into a Chaplin-esque waddle for a few steps, Hilde grabbed his arm and gave him a fierce look. "Don't make me laugh and betray our secret!"

"OK, OK."

"We must be serious, Drake. *Frau Guttreue* said the patrols today are many, all looking for a dangerous spy." Her look brightened. "Perhaps it makes good for us. They may be too busy to care about three good citizens only wanting to visit a poor, sick mother."

They entered a thickly wooded area. A dozen meters into it, Johannes, who was still ahead, walking with *Frau Guttreue* and her dog, turned and spoke to Hilde. She replied, *"Sehr gut."*

When Johannes had reengaged the old woman, Drake whispered, "What's good?"

"She told my brother that the border isn't far. After the woods, we can see a nearby road, then a little farther, a small river. The water marks the border to the American sector."

"Is there a bridge or something so we can cross?"

Hilde shrugged. "Johannes can ask." She called to her brother, who slowed for her. While they were speaking, *Frau Guttreue* approached Drake. When she said something to him in her raspy German, he shook his head and pointed to his mouth. She leaned toward him, cocked her head, and squinted, like she was studying his face. After a moment, she sniffed and smiled, the grin spreading from her eyes to her mouth.

Hilde turned and saw the encounter. She hurried over, exclaimed, *"Frau Guttreue, blick, ein Distelfink!"* and pointed to a goldfinch in a tree. Before she could react, Johannes took the old woman's elbow and urged her onward. He asked about a bridge. She chattered a long answer, with lots of pointing and gesturing. When she finished, he turned to his sister and passed along the information.

After a moment, Hilde leaned toward Drake and whispered, "There is no bridge, but she knows a place where the river is short. We can cross it with wet feet."

"Wet feet for safety, pretty good trade." Drake touched her hand, and when she looked at him, he whispered, "Done a lot of walking, Hilde. On top of that tumble from the train. You doing OK?"

Hilde's eyes sparkled. "Yes, OK. I'm used to walking. I only hope not to slow us."

"Not a bit," Drake said. "Fact is, it's all *I* can do to keep up." He stopped to behold the withy end of a low branch of one of the slender trees lining the path. The tip was just budding out. He glanced ahead to be sure *Frau Guttreue* wasn't looking back. "It's springtime. Everything's new." He turned to Hilde. "Ain't it beautiful!" Like before, he had a powerful, crazy urge to kiss her, but he held back.

Seeing the buds seemed to please Hilde too. She looked into Drake's eyes. Maybe she even saw craziness in them, as she took his hand and squeezed it. "Spring is my favorite time too. And this spring, with some good luck in the next minutes, perhaps my life can become completely good and new. For the first time since I was a child."

Drake reached into his pocket and pulled out his lucky schilling. "I got a piece of good luck right here." He rubbed the coin between his thumb and index finger. "Want to rub off some for yourself?" He offered the coin to her.

"No, thank you." She looked down. "I feel lucky enough just being here with...."

They walked along in silence. Soon, the woods began to thin, then they stepped into a clearing. Immediately, the old woman held her hand up and breathed, "*Stillstehen!*" She pointed to a small military vehicle parked on the road below them. Two gray-uniformed men leaned on the fender, smoking. "*Die Soviet Polizei,*" she whispered, motioning for everyone to move back into the woods.

The two women conferred in soft German for a moment. Hilde turned to Drake. "Geld, bitte," she said, rubbing her thumb and fingers together. When Drake didn't seem to understand, she glared at him and mimed the word *money.*

Drake's face lit up, and he pulled the roll of script from his pocket. Hilde took half and handed it to *Frau Guttreue,* who put the cash in her coat pocket. When she moved to take her dog from Johannes's arms, the animal cowered and turned its head from her.

She gave it a swat on the rump and jerked it away. Clipping a leash on its collar, she led the dog off, walking out of the woods and down the hill toward the policemen. All the way, the animal kept looking back for Johannes.

"She will pay the Russians to finish their cigarettes down the road," Hilde said to Drake, "so we can make our way to the river and cross."

Drake glanced down the hill at the old *Frau*. "Bribing the cops to look the other way, a trick right outta Al Capone's book." He chuckled.

"In Germany we don't have the book you mention, but *Frau Guttreue* says looking away for money is quite ordinary on the borderland."

From the cover of the woods, the three watched the woman approach the Soviets.

When she was fifteen meters from them, her dog started barking. The cops spun around then smiled when they saw who was approaching. One of them called out in crude German, "*Ach, Frau Guttreue, sind sie so schnell wieder zurück?*"

The woman and the Soviets spoke for a moment, then she reached into her pocket and pulled out not money but a piece of paper. She unfolded it and showed it to them, pointing adamantly to something printed there. Then she directed their attention up the hill, pointing to the place in the woods where Drake, Hilde, and Johannes were hiding.

The policemen turned to look where she indicated. One of them raised binoculars and scanned the woods. The other reached into their vehicle, pulled out a microphone on a coiled cord, and spoke briefly into it. Then the men charged up the hill, pistols drawn.

"Holy shit," Drake said. "Did we just get sold out?"

"*Ausreißen!*" Johannes yelled, taking off on the path back into the woods.

Hilde and Drake, hand in hand, followed close behind.

Frying Pan, then Fire

In his first steps running from the Soviet cops, Drake remembered what Sgt. Holt said about reacting to an enemy attack: *When the other side hits you, clobber him back. Pronto! Clobber* was the word Drake fixed on. A minute later, the three came to a bend in the path. Drake pulled up and hollered, "Johannes!" Hilde and Johannes stopped and looked back. "Hilde, keep going," Drake yelled, pointing ahead. "*Schnell!*" After she lurched off down the path, he growled, "Johannes—" and slammed his fist into his open palm. He picked up a broken tree limb big as a baseball bat and pointed to a cantaloupe-sized stone on the ground near Johannes's feet. "Grab that!"

Johannes lifted the rock and held it chest high with both hands. Drake raised his timber up like a club and made a throaty, snarling noise. He gestured for Johannes to hide behind a tree on the left side of the path. He stepped behind one on the right.

Waiting for the Soviets, Drake seethed at having been betrayed all down the line, from Stetti, to Gretchen, to Nakitov, to the NKVD operation in Leipzig, and to *Frau Guttreue*. A lethal betrayal—he recalled Hilde's story of the agent laughing as he bragged about gunning down the young couple from Jena and collecting a bounty. Drake gritted his teeth. "Somebody's going down the crapper," he hissed at Johannes, "and it ain't gonna be us."

When the first policeman came around the bend, Drake jumped out, screaming like a panther. Strength surged through him, as if a wild beast within had awakened and taken over. He swung and struck the cop smack dab in the throat. The man's feet went forward, his head backward. He hit the ground stone still, face up, eyes wide open.

The second Soviet bellowed and leveled his revolver at Drake's chest, ready to fire. The same instant, *Frau Guttreue's* little dog, its leash trailing through the air, leapt from behind, sinking its teeth into the back of the policeman's calf. Screeching, the man spun around. He kicked the dog in the face, sending it tumbling into brush along the trail. As he turned back, he was struck on the shoulder by the rock Johannes heaved. Before he

Saving Euridice

could recover, an arcing swing of Drake's bat sent his pistol sailing far into the brambles. Disarmed and battered, the policeman sank to his knees, cowering.

Spiritual fire still engulfed Drake as he swept his club back, ready to deliver the *coup de grace*. But Johannes grabbed weapon before he could swing and shook his head gravely at Drake. Turning to the Soviet, he pointed down the path away from the border and shouted, "*Hier raus!*"

The terrified policemen scrambled to his feet and hobbled away, passing Hilde who had heard the commotion and returned.

Johannes picked up the dead man's pistol and flung it far off the trail. He stepped over the body, walked to where the stunned dog lay in the brush, and lifted it up. When he cradled it in his arms and gently stroked its bleeding jaw, the dog licked his face.

"We must go," Hilde said, tugging Drake's arm.

He nodded vaguely but didn't pull his gaze from the Russian's face. The man's pale blue eyes were fixed skyward. A stream of blood trickled from the corner of his mouth. It tracked down his cheek to his ear. Thick, bright red, the color of life, its languid flow confirmed Drake's fears—the man was dead...by his hand.

"You did what you had to do," Hilde snapped. "It saved us."

Drake's mouth was open, his stare blank, entranced by the line of red.

Hilde huffed. "Pull yourself together!" She pinched his elbow. "We cannot stand still."

He didn't seem to hear. His gaze drifting aimlessly over the body, he drew his arm free.

"Come with me *now!*" Hilde growled. When Drake still didn't move, she slapped his face with all her might and turned to go.

The sting of the stroke jerked Drake from his fog. Tears filling his eyes, he ripped his gaze from the man he'd killed and watched Hilde step around the body on the trail. After a choking breath, he dropped his bat and followed her.

They hurried down the path in silence, Drake in the rear. At first his legs were rubbery, but gradually the numbness ebbed. Watching his two friends running, it struck him—they're alive, by God! As is the Soviet who staggered away, battered but still breathing. Maybe he had a family in Moscow. Now he'd see them again. By the time they came to the edge of the woods, the fog in his soul was clearing.

When the three stepped into the open, *Frau Guttreue* was waiting by the Soviet vehicle. Seeing them without the police, she shrieked, tossed away the cigarette she was smoking, and scurried off down the road.

"Think you got yourself a dog, Johannes," Drake said. "Treat him nice, that mutt saved our hides."

Hilde translated for her brother as they hustled to the Soviet vehicle.

When they were there, Drake yanked out the radio microphone. He flung it with the ignition keys into the weeds.

Hilde picked up a paper from the ground. She held it for Drake to see. "This is what *Frau Guttreue* showed the policemen. It says that you are an American spy. And offers a reward for information helping your capture."

Drake took the flyer and stared at it for a moment. The pair of stark mug shots printed in the center were the ones taken at the Soviet border control office. "Ain't that swell," he growled, refolding it and stuffing it in his shirt pocket. "When I make it back, maybe I'll frame it to hang over my mantelpiece."

"Now we must go," Hilde said, looking around, "or you won't have a chance to display your souvenir."

The three hurried across the forty meter strip of shrubs and weeds to the stream that marked the border to the American zone. The sun was low in the sky. Drake figured they had maybe two hours of daylight left to cross the river and get to a US border outpost, or at least to a good place to spend the night.

The stream didn't look deep, but the water was flowing fast. Hilde bit her lip. "It might be dangerous. I don't swim." Her eyes darted from the water to Drake. "I'm afraid."

Drake thought of Bo Forgette. He squeezed Hilde's hand. "Let me go first," he said, "to see how tricky it is."

He splashed across the twenty feet of surging water. "Not too bad," he called. "Barely above your ankles." His pants were wet to the knees. "Johannes should come next, since he's got the pup. Then I'll help you."

Hilde translated Drake's suggestion and Johannes gingerly stepped into the water. The dog squirmed, but soon they were most of the way across.

The sizzle of bullets slicing through the air and the little geysers of water they made hitting the river's surface momentarily froze Drake. He spied two Soviets, standing fifty meters from the eastern bank, firing pistol shots at them. The spray of blood from Johannes's shoulder and the sight of him dropping to a knee in the stream unlocked Drake. He rushed into the water, put an arm around the wounded man's waist, and hauled him and the frantic dog toward the western bank of the river. Almost there, he shouted over his shoulder, "Hilde! Come on, girl, you gotta cross now. Those goons mean business!"

After he'd helped Johannes to safety behind a small tree, Drake turned back just as Hilde, about halfway across and engulfed in a hail of spattering revolver shots, lost her footing and splashed into the water. The current swept her along to a point where the river narrowed. And deepened. An instant later, her head slipped below the churning surface.

Drake dashed along the bank, rounds snapping by his nose, then charged into the river where Hilde went down. He found her under about a foot of eddying water and pulled her to the surface. With Drake hauling her through the surging water and singeing gunfire, they made it to the western bank and collapsed, exhausted. He threw himself over her, a human shield. Sure he was scared, but more so elated—he heard sputtering breaths coming from the girl in his arms.

Suddenly there was a thundering sound nearby. A familiar *thud, thud, thud, thud.* Drake looked up to see five US military police in sparkling white helmets, belts and spats. One of them was making all the noise, firing a BAR into the air. The other four had M-1 carbines trained on the pair of Soviet guards across the river. The fire from the other side abruptly ceased. Drake glanced back and saw the Red Army men backing off.

One of MPs ran up to Drake. "*Sie sind beide unverletzt, mein Herr?*"

Drake wiped water from his eyes with his sleeve. "Run that by me in English, fella. I'm one of you guys."

The MP yelled over his shoulder, "Sarge, got an American over here." He turned back to Drake. "I was asking if you two were OK."

Drake looked at Hilde. She was shivering and coughing, but she seemed unhurt. "Got a blanket? She's chilled to the bone. And my buddy over there took a round to the shoulder. Better check him out pronto."

The MP glanced back to the tree where Johannes was. "Nelson and Fetterman are there with your pal. Nelson's a trained medic, so he's in good hands." He hollered to the pair of soldiers still eying the Soviet side, "Couple of blankets over here, Burkhart, on the double."

Hilde looked up at Drake, her teeth chattering so hard she could barely speak. "I think Johannes was injured. See to him first. I'll be fine."

"A medic's minding him already. We'll check on him soon as I get you warmed up."

An MP brought two olive drab wool blankets. Drake put one over her shoulders and head like a hood. He wrapped the other around her torso and legs. When she'd stopped shaking, he picked her up and carried her toward Johannes.

On the way, Hilde burst into tears. "I was so afraid. When I slipped on the river stones. And I went under the water." She nestled her head to his chest. "You saved me, Drake."

Drake halted. "Saved you?" The idea seemed new to him and he smiled. "Guess maybe I did." He brushed the matted brown hair from her face and wiped her eye with a corner of the blanket. "You don't have to be afraid. Neither of us do. Not ever again." He kissed the top of her head.

"But I lost my crutch. In the river."

"I'll get you a new one. Heck, I'll do better than that, if you come to America. There's lots of good doctors there. We'll get the best foot doc to fix you up, good as new. You won't need crutches or special shoes anymore."

When Hilde silently looked away, Drake scowled. "Aw, never mind," he muttered, resuming his walk to the others.

They stopped in front of Johannes, who was leaning on the tree and being tended to by Corporal Nelson. Hilde asked the GI, "Can my brother become well?"

Nelson looked up and grinned. "Not sure how the Ruskies ever beat Hitler, lousy shots as they are. So, this is your brother, ma'am?" Hilde nodded. "It's just a nick. He'll be OK. To be honest, the fella you should be worrying about is me...when I tried to pull your brother's mutt out of his clutches, damn thing near bit my hand off." He looked back at Johannes. "What's its name?" he said, pointing at the dog. *"Was ist Ihr Hund genannt?"*

Johannes thought for a moment. *"Caspar. Sein Name ist Caspar."*

Dusky twilight was falling when two MPs brought a stretcher and carried Johannes to their deuce-and-a-half truck, Caspar nestling in the crook of his arm. They loaded him onto the floor of the canvas-tented truck bed, and Hilde, Drake, Nelson, and two other MPs climbed onto the benches along the side. The vehicle rumbled off.

Drake eyed the GI resting the BAR between his knees. "I toted one of those babies when I was in a rifle squad last year. It sounded darn familiar and awful sweet when I heard it thumping away back there. What's your name?"

"Fetterman, sir. And yours?"

"Drake, Win Drake. This is Hilde and her brother Johannes." He turned to Hilde. "It's Krebs, right?" Hilde nodded. "Mighty obliging of you fellas, showing up when you did."

"Pleased to be of service. Kinda fun getting into a shooting match with those Ruskies, 'specially when we got 'em outgunned like that."

"So...what happens now?" Drake said.

"We got a call in to the post dispensary. We'll drop off this fellow—" Fetterman pointed to Johannes. "—plus Rin-Tin-Tin there, so a *real* medic can see him." He elbowed Nelson in the ribs and chuckled. "You two, we'll get you signed in for an interview and get your paperwork started. Same as anyone who sneaks across the border."

Thirty minutes later, Drake and Hilde were sitting in a small, brightly lit office, sipping mugs of hot coffee and nibbling on slabs of apple cake. In walked a beaming SSG Clancy Boyle, the fellow who had processed Drake through the border crossing a few days earlier. "Well, Mr. Winston Drake, aren't you a sight for sore eyes!" He shook Drake's hand then sat behind the desk. "When we caught wind of all the *escaped American spy* radio traffic and saw copies of the wanted posters...well, I didn't like it one bit."

"You and me both, brother."

Boyle turned to Hilde and smiled. "And this would be the fiancée you told me about, I reckon? *"Sprechen Sie English, Fräulein?"*

"You bet she does," chimed in Drake. "Matter of fact, darn good English."

"Oh not so good," said Hilde softly.

Boyle rose and stood next to her. He gently took her hand. "What's your name, hon?"

"I'm called Hilde Krebs, sir."

"Welcome to the American sector of divided Germany, *Fräulein* Krebs. I understand there were some fireworks at the river. And you got yourself soaked. You doing OK? Anything I can get you?"

Hilde looked at the floor. "My friend Drake saved me from the water, and your men defeated the shooting guards. Now I am safe and warm and fed. I want for nothing."

306

Boyle headed back to his chair. Halfway there he stopped. "Say," he said to Drake, "didn't you mention a kid you'd be bringing out too?"

Drake squirmed. "You must've misunderstood," he mumbled. "Never was a baby....Maybe you're thinking of Hilde's brother."

"Huh?" Boyle shrugged. "Could've sworn...Oh well." He plopped down in his chair. "Say, it's been a helluva day. How about we get you two some shuteye now? We'll start the official interviews tomorrow."

Drake lay in his bunk staring up at the ceiling. He couldn't lose the picture of the dead Soviet border guard, that trickle of blood. "How do you justify killing a man?" he whispered. Out of nowhere, Sgt. Holt came to mind again. Drake recalled the night the sarge got his foot blown off. Good old Holt, Drake thought, after he'd protected our squad by killing the Japanese infiltrator, he'd thrown himself on me to shield my ass from the grenade blast. How different was it from what I did today? I killed a man who threatened my friends in the woods and covered Hilde with myself on the river bank? I s'pose if Holt was a hero, then...

He also thought about the ferocity that had surged through him, attacking the Russian guards. For the first time in his life he'd felt dangerous. Imagine, he thought, what I can do any time I wake that beast inside me again! He pictured himself storming up Omaha Beach on 6 June and singlehandedly wiping out a whole bunker of defenders on the cliffs above. He heard his wide-eyed comrades saying, "Holy cow, Drake, how the hell did you do that?"

Cradled in those thoughts, Drake slipped gently into deep, silky sleep.

Commitments

The next morning, Drake was in the chow tent, surrounded by a dozen MPs, eating scrambled eggs, fried Spam, and toast. Hilde came in. Without a crutch, her awkward gait was painful to watch. Drake jumped up and helped her to the chair next to his. He got her a tray of food and a mug of coffee. "Like your joe black?" he said, pointing to the drink.

"Have they milk?" Hilde asked.

"Think I saw an armored cow up there. I'll get you some." A moment later, he was back with a can of milk and a white hand towel draped over his forearm. He tipped a splat of milk into her coffee and said, "For madam," in a bad French accent.

A sergeant poked his head through the mess tent door. "Time to mount your patrols, boys. Move it...on the double." The MPs filed out of the tent, leaving Drake and Hilde alone.

"I haven't had a breakfast like this since before the war. People say America is a land of endless bounty. Now I see it must be so."

"Yeah?" Drake said without looking up from his plate. "Why would you care?"

"Because it seems impossible, next to what I know."

"But yesterday, when I mentioned going there, you didn't seem interested."

Hilde stared at him. "Girls I knew used to dream of going to America. I'm rather plain-faced. And crippled." She looked away. "I can't have such dreams."

Drake peered at her, his eyes sparkling. "Maybe you can...now. Maybe I can make some dreams happen."

"But you hardly know me...how can I matter to you?"

"Last couple of days, it kept hitting me—I like being with you. It seems natural. Then yesterday, when I thought those Russian cops might get their grubby mitts on you, or worse, well, I just lost it. I killed a man, for Christsakes! And when you went swimming in that stream, I knew that nothing in my life mattered as much as fishing you out safe and sound. Sure, I did those things to save you. But maybe doing 'em saves me too." He took her hand and squeezed it.

They looked at each other for a moment, then Hilde pulled her hand away. "What is the point of dreaming when a bureaucrat can send me back in an eye's blink?"

Drake ate his last bite of Spam. He put his knife and fork on the tray and pushed it out of the way. "That's just it. These American officials like Boyle and his boss, a captain named Parsifal, don't decide on whims. They use three specific factors: One of them's merit—like have you done anything good for the American cause? I guess no one can claim better than what you did, saving me from the frying pan in Leipzig. Second, there's compassion. You and Johannes would sure be in the soup if they toss you back there, 'specially after what happened in those woods. Linkage is the third. They believe you're my fiancée. That's one mighty strong chainlink."

"But I can't ask you to lie for me."

Drake smiled. "You aren't asking. And far as I'm concerned, I'm not lying." He took her hand again. "Look, I don't want to put you over a barrel, but, doggone it, if you can see a future with me, I say let's give it a shot."

"You can imagine spending your life…with a cripple?"

"Not crazy about that word, Hilde," Drake huffed. "But, if it's you, yeah, I can. Besides, like I told you, we're going to get that foot of yours fixed up when we get stateside."

Hilde's eyes filled with tears.

Drake reached out and wiped the wet tracks on her cheeks with the towel he'd played waiter with. "Can I take the waterworks for a *yes*?"

"One thing still reserves me. Just days ago you admitted you loved someone else. I have spent seven months in Stetti's shadow, little more than a servant to her. In the West, I might step out of her shadow, but not with a man still under it." She took his hand. "*Yes* isn't for me to say. Not until you know, you've left Stetti behind. Being sure takes time."

Drake was quiet for a moment. Then he swallowed hard and said, "Guess you're right. I owe that to you. To us." He took out a pack of Lucky Strikes he'd gotten from an MP and offered one to

Hilde. She shook her head. He lit it for himself and took a deep drag. "Look, we interview with Sergeant Boyle this afternoon, me at thirteen hundred hours, you at fourteen hundred. We need to settle this by then. Let me spend a few hours doing some soul searching. I promise to be straight with you. If I can't say 'yes' with confidence, I won't do it at all." He stood. "I'll find you at twelve thirty or so." He ran out of the room.

Drake went back to the Quonset hut building that served as the enlisted men's barracks. With the MPs all on duty, it was deserted. He sat on the bed he'd been assigned and lit another Lucky. Stetti...how *did* he feel about her? He remembered her playing cello outside her house in Bonn a year earlier. Just for him. Pictured her naked beauty in her room later that night. Then he recalled the next morning, when she told him to get lost. And just days ago in Leipzig, after he'd come so far, she'd said, 'there's nothing here for you'...after selling him out. He hated the roller coaster ride. "God, I *want* to be out of that damn woman's shadow," he whispered, stubbing the cigarette into an ashtray.

Drake reclined on the bed. The image of Sgt. Holt, lying in his hospital bed in Manila, came to him. And he recalled the last advice Holt had given him—that ties to the past can ruin you *and* others who depend on you. 'Cut those ties!' he'd said. 'Focus on the present and the future.' Like that was something you decided to do, then did. Well, maybe it was!

Drake jumped up. He felt suddenly free. Free of Stetti. Free of the roller coaster. Free to commit to Hilde. He knew that for now it was only a feeling. But he believed he could turn it into fact. He ran out of the barracks.

He found Hilde sitting on a bench outside the post dispensary. "I was visiting Johannes," she said. "It was time to clean his wound, so I left. It can't be twelve-thirty already, can it?"

"Nope." Drake glanced at his watch. "Eleven-fifteen. But I don't need any more time. I figured out that it was the idea of Stetti that I loved, not the person. I didn't realize it, but in a lot of ways I hated Stetti the person. Look, I don't want to spend my future loving an idea." He took Hilde's hands in his. "I want to love a flesh and blood person. Somebody who makes me happy." His face glowed. "You."

"You said *want* many times. But how do you know you *can?*"

"I believe I can. That's enough for me. How about for you?"

Tears tracked down Hilde's cheeks. "It is enough," she said, her voice cracking.

Drake threw his arms around her neck and kissed her. "Whew!" he whistled.

Hilde eyes were wide, joyful. "On the train, I wondered if our lips would ever touch."

"Strange," Drake said. "A couple of times these last few days I thought about kissing you too, but I figured it was just being happy—like at a ballgame you might smooch the girl next to you when DiMaggio jolts a homer in the last of the ninth."

"I don't know about ballgames….just that I'm excited and happy now."

"I only meant maybe the real reason I wanted us to kiss was I was falling for you. Only I didn't know it yet." He shrugged and kissed her again. "How about we walk a little?"

They strolled, hand-in-hand, for a couple of minutes. When they came to the post flagpole, Drake looked up at Old Glory and said, "One thing could still gum up the works. What did you and Johannes do during the war?"

"Johannes was conscripted in…perhaps 1941. He served in Belgium and in Russia. He was wounded and nearly froze in 1943—the cold took the outer parts of his ears and some toes. But it probably saved him as he was evacuated to Germany. Many others never came back. He spent the rest of the war convalescing and working as a civilian in the rail yards."

"His service…was he SS?"

Hilde giggled. "Johannes an SS storm trooper? I can more easily imagine him as a ballerina. No, he was a low-level enlisted man in the regular army, the *Wehrmacht.*"

"OK. How about you?"

"I helped in a school in Garmisch, my village, until 1944. Then I went to Munich to the Messerschmitt factory there. I worked on the jet production line for the number 263. It was called *Die Schwalbe*. In English, The Swallow. The Fuhrer believed it could save Germany."

Drake's eyebrows arched. "Thank goodness he was wrong."

"Thank goodness. In 1945, they moved me to Leipzig to translate English language documents at a *Luftwaffe* base. When the war ended, I was stranded there. Johannes took a job with the rail authority in Leipzig to be near me."

"You were *ordered* to work at the Messerschmitt plant and the airbase? Be sure to emphasize that in your interview." Drake inhaled deeply and gazed into the distance. "So tell me, what was it like, living under Hitler, then Stalin?"

"Dreary, frightening, suffocating. My soul has been sick for as long as I can remember. When the Soviets came in and the war ended, I thought things would be different. Probably worse, since Russians and Germans have bad blood. I was surprised. Aside from the flags and the uniforms, nothing changed." Hilde sighed. "How can systems with ideals so opposite make the same result? I suppose once men taste power they prefer it to their ideals."

"You say nothing changed. I guess that's not true for Jews...or for Reds, huh?"

"Yes, Jews were no longer hunted. But the Soviets put them in the huge, second-class basket with everyone but themselves. We non-Russians were tolerated as long as we made no trouble. Those that did—" She snapped her fingers. "—they disappeared."

Drake embraced Hilde. "I guess the last few days we were big-time troublemakers, so I'm tickled pink to be this side of the border. Got no interest in disappearing."

Drake met with SSG Boyle that afternoon. Being a U. S. citizen, the interview was mostly formality. The probing questions involved Hilde and Johannes.

"Regarding Miss Krebs," Boyle said, "let me be sure I have this straight—you're not married, but you are engaged to be, correct?"

"Right." Drake looked at his hands. "To be honest, I haven't given her a ring yet. But we've exchanged promises, and in our hearts and minds, we're engaged."

"Good, Mr. Drake. Now, how about you give me an example of something Miss Krebs has done that serves the interests of the United States of America?"

"Sure, if you'd call saving my butt serving America's interests....When the Soviet gestapo in Leipzig had me in their cross hairs, Hilde Krebs sprung me from their trap and hid me." Drake paused to let Boyle catch up, writing the story into his notes. "Then she and her brother risked prison time and probably even their lives sneaking me out of the Soviet sector. I tell you, Sergeant, there's no way I'd be sitting here now, but for those two heroes."

"Anything more you can add?"

"Guess there is one more thing, Sarge. You said your Captain Parsifal was a pretty compassionate fellow, right? Well, he should know that sending those two kids back to the Soviets, is like signing their death warrants. Hilde says, defectors are branded enemies of the state. I'd be pleased to tell the captain myself, if you think it'd help."

"If there is any question on their status, Drake, I'll make sure you get the chance to do that. Trust me." Boyle looked over his notes. "Oh yeah, there is one more thing to I need to clear up here. Any idea of what it was made the NKVD want to come after you, anyway? All you were doing was visiting your girl, right?"

Drake paused. He didn't want to muddy things by bringing up Stetti and he wasn't about to lie. Blatantly, at least. "Yeah, all I was doing was visiting my girl." He shook his head and shrugged. "Who knows what's in the screwball brains of a bunch of Soviet goons?"

"Yep, who knows?" Boyle put his pencil down. "Unless you want to ask me anything, that about does it for our interview."

313

Drake shifted in his seat. "Just one thing, Sarge. Right before the border, a couple of Soviet guards were chasing us. Guns drawn and all. Anyway, we got into a fight. A hand-to-hand deal. I had a piece of tree limb, against his revolver. I hit him pretty good, maybe—" He closed his eyes and shook his head slowly. "—well maybe I killed the guy. Whatever I did, guess it was self-defense…but you know the Russians won't see it that way. So, what do you think? Will they try to get me sent back for trial? Or maybe even come after me?"

Boyle leaned back in his chair. "Before you escaped, we heard a lot of radio chatter about 'the American spy.' It stopped soon as you crossed the river. Typical of the Soviets—they're practical SOBs. Admit a mistake? Nah. Might get you shot." He winked. "With screw-ups, the SOP is bury 'em deep. Like nothing ever happened." He closed the folder labeled *Winston Drake*. "Nope, don't think we'll ever hear a fucking peep about your incident."

Drake closed his eyes and exhaled. "Thanks."

"I'll interview your friends today," Boyle said, "unless Mr. Krebs isn't up to it. Hope to resolve their cases by the close of business tomorrow." He rose and shook Drake's hand.

Drake left the interview room. Hilde was sitting outside the door. She looked like a kid with a toothache waiting to see the dentist. As he walked by, Drake gave her a *thumbs-up* and grinned encouragement. Then he stopped, went back and kissed her. "You'll be fine, sweetheart." That brought a smile to Hilde's face.

The next afternoon, Drake and Hilde were summoned to Boyle's office. When they got there, Johannes was already waiting outside, his wounded arm in a white sling. His dog Caspar slept in his lap.

A minute later, Boyle appeared and solemnly said, "Follow me, folks. Better leave your dog here, sir." Hilde translated.

Johannes tied the leash to a chair. He bent down and roughed-up the fur behind the dog's ears. "*Aushalten sie, Caspar!*" he murmured. The dog dutifully lay down, chin resting on its forepaws.

Boyle led the way down a corridor to the end office. The sign on the door read *Parsifal, R., Cpt. U.S. Army.* Boyle knocked, opened the door and shepherded the three in.

Parsifal, a tall, knightly man with sandy-blond hair, stood. "Welcome! I won't keep you in suspense." He picked up papers from his desk. "Mr. Drake, we're pleased to have you safely back. You're free to go as you wish." He handed Drake his travel documents. "Miss Krebs, as Mr. Drake's fiancée and an otherwise worthy applicant, I'm glad to authorize your travel within the American sector of Germany and on to the United States in the company of Mr. Drake. In the U.S., you'll have status as a documented alien with the right to apply for citizenship as prescribed by law." Parsifal handed her a folder of authorizations, signed and stamped and impressively official looking. "And you, Mr. Krebs, as a worthy applicant for asylum, here is authority for you to reside within the American sector of Germany in a place of your choosing." He handed Johannes a folder of documents. "Congratulations, and once again, welcome."

The three thanked Cpt. Parsifal and left his office smiling broadly. Outside, Drake said, "Well, we made it! What do you say we go into Bebra tonight and have a beer to celebrate? I'm buying. Then tomorrow we hit the road." He took Hilde's arm. "You and me, babe, we got an ocean to cross!"

"Johannes told me that if we gained admission," Hilde said, "he will travel to Belgium to find his sweetheart. It was near Liège, during the war, that he last saw her. The place is on the way of our travel. May he go with us?"

Drake shrugged. "Beer tonight, Belgium tomorrow? Don't see why not. Tell Johannes that I got a gal out of our little caper, and I'd be glad if he does too."

315

A Mother's Grave

The next morning, after a night drinking beer, Drake, Hilde, and Johannes, with Caspar too, were on a train heading west into Belgium. Since he'd served there during the war, Johannes, chattering nonstop, played tour guide for his sister. Hilde passed the stories on to Drake. "Johannes says this eastern slice of Belgium is German-speaking. This I didn't know. Soon we'll be in Wallonia, where the language is French, which Johannes speaks quite well."

When the train stopped in Liège, the travelers got off to have lunch and change lines. An hour later they we heading southwest, and forty minutes after that they got off in the crossroads village of Lefebvre on the banks of the Meuse River.

Johannes left the others on the platform. As he walked away, Caspar padded along at his side. Hilde told Drake, "He goes to find a driver who can take us to a certain convent outside the village. The nuns run a boarding school where his friend lives."

Drake opened his last pack of Lucky Strikes. He took out two and lit them together. He gave Hilde one then took a deep drag on his. "So, what's the story on this girl of his?"

"Johannes was assigned to the small garrison here when the *Wehrmacht* occupied Belgium. As he tells the story, one winter day he rescued a pretty young student who had injured herself on the ice. His heart was melted from the first sight. He returned the stricken girl to her school and brought a doctor for treatment. Later he began meeting the girl—secretly since it was against orders. They fell in love. It ended when Johannes was sent to the eastern front, but before he left, he vowed to return. Her name was Eva."

"Ah, loyalty! Your brother's a real prince."

"For strangers, anyway. For a sister he can be monstrous."

"Like a lot of brothers."

"He used to write me, mooing over his Eva like a lovesick cow. I said, 'Find yourself a nice German girl.' 'No one,' he said, 'can compare to my Eva, the most lovely thing on God's earth."

"Oh I don't know," Drake said. "German gals can be darn lovely too—look at Stetti." As soon as the name left his lips, he regretted saying it. "And you too, Sweetie, of course!"

She looked like she'd been kicked. "You needn't...."

"Don't know why I mentioned her," he said, shaking his head. "I can be so stupid!"

"What you said about Stetti wasn't stupid. It was true. Feeling you must include me...yes, that is stupid. Drake, I know what I am. We have mirrors in Germany, you know."

Drake took her hand. She pulled it away. "Listen here!" he said. "You wanna talk about looks? Hey, I shave every day, and I know this kisser of mine ain't much to write home about. Big deal. What matters is you're my girl, and I like everything about you—your heart, soul, moxie, *and* looks. I wouldn't change a thing. That's the darn truth."

"Wonderful...but is there another truth? One hiding in the shadows? Drake, it must come out! Despite your pledge of yesterday, I believe you can't get Stetti out of your mind. She's there, behind every moment, every thought. That's the truth that haunts me."

"Not so! I mentioned her, talking about German beauty. It's just a fact, the girl's a looker. And she's one German woman we both know. I was just making a point. I could've mentioned Marlene Dietrich instead. Wish I had. Look, I understand Stetti's a loaded name for us. That's why I feel stupid for putting it out there just now. I am sorry." He peered into her eyes and took her hand again. Now she didn't pull away. "Hilde, I love you, for crying out loud. I don't want to hurt you. Ever. I know I need to be way more considerate."

"As I said, honesty about my face, about my foot, doesn't bother me. I know beauty is only skin deep. I also know I'm clever, interesting, faithful. And I know you're lucky to have me, sir! What I don't know is if you've completely left Stetti behind."

Drake pulled her close. "Well I know it. I don't love her. I don't want her anymore. You *are* clever, interesting, faithful...plus brave and considerate and a ton of other good things. Yes, I do know I'm lucky to have you." He kissed her. "And I know I love only you. I just need to be better about showing all that."

317

"Every lover must work to show those things." Hilde sighed. "As for Stetti, she is an enigma, outwardly perfect, but flawed inside. She lacks the gift of empathy. I was her faithful..." She looked up. "In German we say *Dienerin*, it means a female servant."

Drake shook his head in disgust.

"I knew my place—I was there to serve, to reliever her of the small so she could accomplish the grand." Hilde gazed down the tracks, into the distance. "You know, she never called me by my name. It was always *Krüppel*." She glanced at her crippled foot. "I suppose she did that to remind me of my status. And hers."

Drake nodded. He could see Stetti doing that.

"I don't envy her. It can't be a good way to live." Hilde looked at Drake. "She's not really an evil person. Perhaps she was given too much—beauty, intelligence, strength, artistry. *Everything*. It blinds her. Yes, her gifts allow mighty accomplishments. Her music. Her work for The People. But what matters to her is *The People* collectively, not *people* individually. She can't see the inconsistency. I suppose the world is better for her genius—" Hilde shook her head. "—but not those who must live next to her."

"None of that matters now." Drake took her hand again. "She's out of your life."

"And out of ours?"

"Yeah!" He hated the question. "Ours too. Look, I know I need to quit saying dumb things that make you wonder. I can do it, just give me a chance."

She squeezed his hand.

A minute later Johannes returned to the station, riding with Caspar in the back seat of a pre-war Renault clunker. The driver was a grizzled, old, pipe-smoker named Hervé.

Drake whispered to Hilde, "Guy's got a nose big as a Buick!"

"What is a Buick?"

"A car. A *large* American car."

Hilde eyes went wide and she elbowed him. "Shhh!" Then the sternness she wanted to show was scotched by a giggle.

318

They got into the car, Drake and Hilde sitting in back, Johannes with Caspar on his knee up front. As they pulled away from the station, Johannes turned and gleefully spoke to his sister. She translated for Drake. "Johannes thinks it makes luck to have Caspar along. He says his girl Eva has a little dog looking just the same. He thinks they can be friends."

"How long ago did he know this girl?"

Hilde shrugged. "It must be, perhaps 1942."

"And he hasn't heard from her since?"

"I don't think so."

"1942's a long time ago. Johannes should be careful, getting his hopes up like this." He thought of adding that he knew that from experience, but caught himself.

Fifteen minutes later the Renault turned into a drive, barely visible for all the weeds, and stopped at a closed wooden gate. Its green paint was peeling and the hinges were thick with rust. A faded sign over the gate read *Ste. Sébastien*. Johannes got out with Caspar and walked around the gate. Drake and Hilde followed. They approached the stone building of the convent school through an overgrown field. It was apparent that the school had been abandoned for years. As he reached the slate steps leading up to the decorated metal door, Johannes turned back and looked at his sister, tears streaming down his cheeks. He tried the door. It was locked.

A moment later, they heard the sound of a hammer pounding stone. It came from behind the school. They hurried around the large main building and saw an old man and three old women sprucing up a grave marked by a wooden cross in the small cemetery next to the chapel. The man was chiseling letters into a granite headstone. One of the women weeded the grave top, another arranged white stones on it, and the third sat on a nearby bench praying the rosary.

Johannes walked alone to the people. He tied Caspar's leash to a wrought iron fence then spoke with the woman pulling weeds. After a minute of conversation, Johannes burst into sobs. He fell to his knees, folded his hands, and bowed his head. He stayed there two minutes.

When he came back to his sister and Drake, he was trembling and pale. He put his arms around Hilde, buried his face on her neck and spoke to her, breaking down in tears again.

Hilde guided him to the chapel steps and helped him sit. Then she turned to Drake. "The old woman told Johannes that the school has been closed for years. Since one of the nuns was killed during the Occupation. After that, the students and nuns all left, some to a school in France. As for his Eva, they don't know where she's gone." She glanced at the old people working. "The grave is for the mother superior of the convent, hanged by the SS for harboring Jewish children. Johannes came to know her after he'd saved her student Eva. He said the nun's name was Mother Catherine...that she was unforgettable."

"Didn't know she'd died, huh?" Drake shook his head. "Must've been a big shock."

Hilde's eyes went thundercloud dark. "Not died...she was murdered by Germans. By my people and Johannes's." She swallowed hard. "He didn't know."

A moment later Johannes got up and strode back to the gravesite. He took a scouring brush from a bucket and picked up white stones from a bushel basket. He began scrubbing the stones then laying them out on a canvas to dry.

When he'd done several stones, he returned to Hilde. Now there were no tears. Instead his eyes sparkled and words sprang from his mouth. After a moment he kissed his sister and shook Drake's hand. Then he went back to work, holding the chisel for the old man.

Hilde watched him for a minute then turned to Drake. "We can leave now."

"But...what about Johannes?"

"He will remain. He said the people of Lefebvre are building a memorial to the heroic nun. He wants to stay for a few weeks to help. As a German, he feels obliged. And as one who admired her, he wants to add his mark to her tribute. When he has done his part, he may look for his Eva, but for now working here is enough. He asked me to tell you he wishes us the greatest joy."

"So we're just going to leave him?"

"Of course," Hilde said. "He knows you and I must have a separate life as husband and wife. No one else may share that with us. Parting now, when he has taken on this mission, makes the most sense to Johannes. And to me." She took Drake's hand and they walked slowly back to the Renault, where the old man with the Buick-sized nose puffed on his pipe, waiting to take them back to Lefebvre's train station.

When Drake arrived with Hilde in Southampton, England, he was happy to find the *SS Île de France,* in port. "That's the ship I crewed on, coming over here, honey. Made a pretty decent deck steward, if I do say so myself. If I talk to Mr. Graham, the head steward, I'll bet he'd hire me for the next sailing west." He squeezed Hilde's hand. "Might even take my word and put you to work too. Pay's not much, but we save the fare on top of it."

They went to the ship's on-shore administration offices and waited on chairs outside the one labeled, *Michael Graham, Chef de Personnel des Navires de Croisière.* On his return from luncheon, Graham didn't notice Drake sitting there until he grabbed the knob of his office door. Then he spun around. "Mr. Drake! You made it back. What a pleasant surprise." He looked at Hilde. "So is this the girl you told me about? The cellist?"

Drake jumped to his feet. "No sir, she doesn't play the cello. Think that got mixed up somehow. Probably my fault. This is my fiancée, Hilde, and we'd be pleased to work your next sailing to the States. If it's possible."

Graham opened his door. "Come in please." He held it open and studied them as Drake put his arm around Hilde and helped her hobble into the office. "Have a seat." He walked behind the desk and sat on his sumptuous leather chair.

"Are you looking for crew members, sir?" Drake asked.

"I am always looking for *good* staff."

"Well, you know about me, and I'll tell you this little lady, my fiancée, is hardworking and real good with people. Like I said, her name's Hilde Krebs."

"Mr. Drake, I will always have a place on staff for you." He leaned back in his chair and gazed at Hilde. "Miss Krebs...I observe that you have a handicap. Tell me about it."

"Sir, I was born with a bad foot. *Der Klumpfuß*, we Germans call it. Mr. Drake and I escaped from Leipzig in the Soviet sector, and I lost my crutch in the river at the border. I do much better with—"

Graham raised a hand to stop her. "On the *Île de France*, we take pride in offering our passengers the very highest level of service. We can't make allowances for staff with...limitations. What makes you think you could meet our standard, given—" He eyed her misshapen foot. "—your handicap?"

Hilde held her head high. "If passengers appreciate dedication and hard work, then I can meet your high standard of service. Also consider that my language skills would be useful with German-speaking travelers."

"Yes," said Graham, "if we had any. Given the economic situation, German voyagers sailing to America tend to use, shall we say, less expensive options for passage." He stroked his chin. "However, we do have some Germans in low-level crew positions. Communicating with them can be problematic. Perhaps having a go-between on my staff would help." A hint of a tear welled in Graham's eye. "Additionally, I have a sister with an affliction like yours. She is indisputably one of the most capable individuals I have ever known." He tented his fingers and leaned back in his chair. "Based on your language facilities and your positivity, and on Mr. Drake's endorsement, I am persuaded, Miss Krebs, to offer you a position. Of course, you'll need a crutch. Rough seas and all." He scribbled a note on a pad of paper. He tore off the top sheet and handed it to Hilde. "Take this to the ship's carpentry shop. They will fabricate a crutch for you. I want it painted white." He checked off boxes on each of two forms and handed them to Drake and Hilde. "Present these to the staff outfitter for your uniforms. We sail the day after tomorrow. You'll both be busy preparing."

That evening Drake and Hilde ate dinner on board in the main dining room with other staff and crew. Afterward, they had the night to themselves. It was cool and drizzly, but the couple found a sheltered spot on deck and sat, holding hands and watching the lights of Southampton.

"You know," Drake said, "I read somewhere that a ship's captain has the power to marry people on the high seas. I think we ought to consider diving right in. How many people have the chance to get hitched on the *Île de France*? By a genuine sea captain?" He kissed her. "Not to mention how much I wish we were husband and wife." He put his hand on Hilde's knee. "What do you say?"

"I say it sounds like the most romantic thing in the world."

"OK, we'll talk to Captain Daland tomorrow morning."

The *Île de France* put to sea on the last day of March 1946. It was a sailing made memorable by the fact that Édith Piaf was among the passengers. The Little Sparrow, having dodged accusations that she collaborated with the Nazis, was at the height of her popularity. Loving the spotlight, she agreed to take the ship's stage for several *impromptu* concerts during the voyage.

On the first sailing day, Piaf picked out Hilde as her preferred ship's staff member. As she put it to Captain Daland at dinner that night, "Can it surprise you when one Little Sparrow befriends another?" Each morning at 09:00 promptly, Piaf required a tall glass of freshly-squeezed orange juice and a flute of champagne, served in her stateroom, specifically by 'that sweet little crippled thing, *la piaf allemande*.' The chanteuse may have also had a more practical interest in Hilde. De Gaulle had asked her to do a concert tour of France's German occupation zone in 1947. She would perform on French military posts and, to foster Franco-German reconciliation, in Mons and other German cities. Ever the cagy performer, Piaf understood the power of connecting with her audience. To that end, she got Hilde's help with something she wanted to use on the tour, German lyrics for one verse of a new song she'd written, *La Vie en rose*.

The second day at sea, Captain Daland conducted the ceremony joining Drake and Hilde in matrimony. The wedding was performed on the ship's bridge, with Drake's new pal Walt Winkler as best man and Edith Piaf as maid-of-honor. Photographs were taken of the wedding party and of Drake and Hilde standing at the helm pretending to fight over control of the ship's wheel. Graham had arranged a small reception in the captain's *salle d'attente*. He ordered champagne, cake, and the chef's specialty, *Le trio de Normandie*—raw oysters, broiled lobster, and *Coquilles St. Jacques* sautéed in butter. As they cut the cake, Edith serenaded the newlyweds with a theatrical rendition of the classic love song, *Plaisir d'amour*. That night, on Chief-of-staff Graham's orders, the couple slept in one of the ship's grand stateroom suites.

As they were drifting off to sleep, Drake whispered, "Glad they took pictures. Without evidence, who'd believe that Edith Piaf sang at our wedding."

Hilde nestled to her new husband's chest. "I am glad for everything."

New York to Omaha, with Goebbels Between

The *Île de France* put into port in New York on April 8, 1946. Piaf, the first passenger to debark, walked down the gangway to the *staccato* welcome of a hundred flashes of news photographers' cameras and the *fortissimo* adulation of the mob of fans assembled on the pier to greet her.

Two hours after The Little Sparrow whisked away in a shiny black limousine, Drake and Hilde traipsed the same gangplank and set foot on American soil. Their steps were made lighter by what Hilde carried in her jacket pocket— an envelope with the fifty dollar tip Piaf left for her. After clearing customs, they took the subway, and with several transfers, arrived in Brooklyn. The Drakes checked into in The Hotel Bossert, left their luggage, and went to spend the rest of the day on Coney Island's Steeplechase amusement park. They rode the Parachute Jump—Drake had wanted to do that since following the exploits of the 101st Airborne Division at Bastogne during the Battle of the Bulge. For lunch they ate Coney Dogs.

The next afternoon Drake took Hilde to Ebbets Field for the Dodgers' season opener against the Boston Braves. When the Dodgers took the field, Drake stood and whistled. "See the guy wearing number one?" He pointed to the smallest ballplayer on the field. "That's Pee Wee Reese, about the best shortstop playing the game right now."

Hilde listened intently, believing that every good American wife must know her baseball. When Reese came up to bat in the bottom of the first, she rose from her seat and cheered. She told a stranger sitting next to her, "Mr. Pee Wee is my dearest shortstopper!"

Drake got them both 15¢ hotdogs at the end of the third inning, saying, "You know Humphrey Bogart, right?"

"Only from the Hollywood film we saw on the ship."

Drake rolled his eyes. "Well, yeah. Anyhow, he says, 'A hotdog at the ballpark beats steak at the Ritz.' Guess he should know."

Hilde took a bite and wiped the yellow mustard from her mouth with a paper napkin. "Its taste is very good." She scanned the fans in the seats around them, many of whom were munching dogs of their own. "Who knew America was the land of bread-covered sausages!"

The next morning, just before he and Hilde boarded a Pennsylvania Railroad liner for their trip west, Drake sent a telegram to his mother: *DEAR MOM HEADING OMAHA SAFE AND MARRIED STOP ARR APR 14 ON CHICAGO MILW STOP LOVE WIN END*

The first night on the Pennsy, after making love in their sleeper compartment, Hilde lay smiling in Drake's embrace. "We're getting better, I think," she said. "Don't you?"

Drake kissed her ear. "Practice makes perfect, as they say. And I do like practicing. My only worry is we're getting so good, we won't ever want to do anything else."

"And we will become degenerate?" Hilde slipped her hand down his chest to his belly. "I will risk it if you will. Again." Going lower, she felt his erection growing. "It seems our friend answers for you." She eased herself onto Drake and guided his penis inside her. "Yes, better and better and better," she moaned as electricity surged through her, collecting like static in a thundercloud where their bodies joined. Then, powerful as a lightning bolt and as inexorable, the energy exploded in a few seconds' rumbling.

Lying happily spent in his wife's arms, Drake was struck by the delightful complexity of the person who'd come into his life outside Leipzig's train station just a few weeks earlier. In that short time, his perception of her had gone from flimsy caricature—the crippled waif, the mouse in battle armor—to complete human: a tough, tender, brave, vulnerable, clever, sensual...woman. So powerful was the feeling that he had to whisper the truth in her ear, "Hilde, you're the best thing that ever happened to me. I'm so darn lucky!"

"And me?" she said. "Lying here with the hero who carried me from darkness into the light...I feel lucky too."

"Me, a hero?" Drake let the notion tumble in his brain. "For so long that was all I wanted. As much as I tried, it never clicked. Then, what do you know, when I wasn't looking, it just up and happened! Guess you don't get to choose to go out and be a hero. You just do your best every day, and once in a while fate aligns the stars, then whamo!"

After breakfast in the dining car the next morning, the Drakes lounged in their Pullman compartment. Drake paged through a *Time Magazine*. Hilde gazed out the window at the scenic Chestnut Ridge stretching north near Latrobe, Pennsylvania. Right before her eyes, the land seemed to be coming to life after a long winter.

Drake closed his magazine. "I was just reading about all the crazy stuff in Hitler's brain. The Aryan link to some ancient race of humans. Visits from outer space men. Paranoia. Talk about an inmate running the asylum!" He lit a cigarette. "You told me what you did in Germany during the war. Teaching school. Working in that jet-airplane factory. Translating for the *Luftwaffe*. But you never said what it was like, living in a place with Nazis in charge."

"You speak of *Der Führer's* paranoia as if it were a defect. Don't you see, he needed it. As Stalin and all other dictators also do. Because every human heart they wish to control hungers for the opposite—for freedom. A *Führer* without paranoia is an ex-*Führer*."

"I suppose." Drake scratched his ear. "They say Hitler could cast a spell over his audiences like no one else. Did you ever hear him speak?"

"Only on the wireless. I never saw the man. But I did once meet Joseph Goebbels, the Reich Minister of Propaganda."

"Oh yeah? He was a bad apple, but clever as the devil, right?"

"The devil? Yes. He was one of the most powerful Nazis. He visited my school once. I must have been ten or so. It was soon after his gang came to power, and Herr Goebbels liked to travel around, promoting proper Nazi virtues in youth. Because of a poem I wrote on the bright future of Germany under the *Führer's* leadership, I was one of a dozen children selected to meet the Propaganda Minister. We formed a line, with our parents standing behind us. I was wearing a white peasant-style dress my mother sewed for the occasion. We waited an hour—Herr Goebbels was an important man, too important to be on time." Hilde gazed at the ceiling as if watching a newsreel of the event projected there. "Surrounded by a military escort, he swept into the assembly room. I can still see him in his handsome double-breasted suit with swastika armband, looking radiantly happy, like he loved spending time with young people. Strange, since in the end, the coward murdered his own children."

"Murdered his kids?"

"Yes, to *save* them!" Hilde's jaw clenched, then she sighed and resumed her story. "I stood in the middle of the line of students, and I remember watching as he spoke to each child in turn, asking about their studies, tousling their hair, encouraging them. When he came to me, he shook my hand and, smiling like a kindly uncle on Christmas morning, asked to hear some of my poem. After I'd finished, he pinched my cheek. He was about to step to the next student when my father raised a hand. 'Excuse me, Herr Propaganda Minister, but may I add that you and my daughter have more in common than a love of Germany? You see, Hilde is clubfooted, just like you!'" Rubbing her eyes, Hilde suddenly looked exhausted. "I'll never forget the transformation that swept over Goebbels' face. His beaklike mouth clamped shut and his eyes went storm cloud black. With military precision, he turned on his heel and left the assembly room. The next morning I was sent to another school."

Drake touched his wife's shoulder. "I don't know what to say."

"You needn't say anything. What matters is, that time is over." Hilde forced a smile.

In Chicago a day later, the Drakes transferred to a coach car of the Chicago, Milwaukee, St. Paul and Pacific Railroad for the last leg of their trip to Omaha.

On Sunday, April 14, 1946, they were halfway through Iowa. Drake, anxious to be home and bored with cornfields, slouched in his seat, drowsing. Hilde was too fascinated to sleep. She scanned the seemingly endless farm fields, showered in sunshine. Some were still fallow from the winter, a few with patches of snow remaining. Some were green with newly-sprouted crop—*alfalfa*, Drake had told her. What she didn't see were people. "Strange," she said, "in Germany the fields are so much smaller, and the farmers so much more working in them. My uncle always dreamed of going to America. He told me, 'In America, crops plant themselves, and machines make the harvest. All the farmer must do is count his money.'"

"Don't know about that," Drake muttered without opening his eyes. "Round here, farmers claim it's bankers counting all the money. Guess that was so during the Depression," he mumbled. "Once we went to war, word is the clodhoppers made out like bandits."

"Living on the earth, it seems so pure. Man's natural state." Hilde turned to Drake and touched his elbow to make sure he was listening. "Perhaps we'll have a farm someday. Can that be so, my sweet?" When he didn't answer she shook his shoulder.

"Farming? Sure, we'll see, honey." Shortly, Drake's doze turned audible.

Hilde peered out the window. The sunshine was gone—black clouds filled the sky. A moment later, as splatters of rain slapped the glass, the train began to slow. She glanced at Drake's wristwatch—ten minutes until their scheduled arrival at Omaha's Union Station.

Navigating the Shoals

Marching through the car, the conductor trumpeted, "Omaha, Omaha, this stop is Omaha." He picked up Drake's and Hilde's ticket stubs, telling them, "Your stop, folks."

Drake's eyes fluttered open. "We're here?" As the train entered the station, he leaned over his wife to survey the platform. A moment later he pointed to a short woman wearing the knee-length blue raincoat and holding a red umbrella. "That's Mom," he said over the screech of brakes and the hiss of steam. The Milwaukee Road train shuddered to a halt.

The rain had slowed to a misty drizzle. Alice scanned the windows of the passenger cars for a glimpse of her son. Rapping on the glass, he caught her attention. A huge smile poured over her plump face, and she waved enthusiastically. She folded her umbrella and toddled to the door nearest his window.

Drake descended the steps to the platform and set down his two small suitcases. He helped Hilde off the train, then turned to hug his mother. "It's good to be home, Mom."

"I'm so thrilled to have you back, Win. I did worry, you know!"

"Shouldn't have." Drake put his arm around Hilde and eased her to the fore. "Mom, I want to introduce my wife, Hilde."

Hilde extended her hand. "I am very pleased to meet you, Mrs. Drake."

Alice stared at the frail, plain girl in her son's embrace. Her eyes darted to the crutch she was leaning on and to her foot. "Oh, you've sprained you ankle, my dear."

Hilde's eyes fluttered. "It's my foot, ma'am. Damaged since birth."

"We're going to see if the docs here can fix it." Drake looked at Hilde and winked. "Mom, you won't believe how great Hilde gets around even with..." He shrugged.

"Sure she does, Win." Alice looked at her son, then at Hilde, then at Drake again. "So, you really are—" She blinked then smiled, like even the notion was silly. "—married?"

Drake glanced at Hilde and grinned. "Yep. We got hitched on the ship, by the captain. How's that for ooh-la-la! We figured, why wait?"

"Yes, why wait?" Alice said. "I suppose." She looked around the platform. "Should we find a porter to help with the luggage?"

"This is all we got, Ma." Drake picked up the suitcases then turned to Hilde and winked. "We kinda had to skedaddle on a minute's notice. It's a long story."

"Oh my," said Alice. "But Hilde, dear, what about your cello? Surely you didn't leave that. Drake's told me so much about your wonderful playing."

Hilde looked at Drake, helplessness etched on her face.

His stomach sank. "I, ah…" He set the suitcases down and closed his eyes.

A hint of a smile came to Alice's face.

"The cellist, Mom," Drake said, "that was somebody else. A friend. Like I said, it's all such a long story." He glanced at Hilde. "But what matters is Hilde's my wife, and we're safe here together."

"My gracious, it must be *quite* a story," Alice tittered. "But then, I suppose it's none of my business unless you want to share it. I'm only your old mother after all."

"Sure, later." Drake picked up the suitcases again. "I'm starved. Let's go get a bite to eat, shall we?"

"I was planning to make eggs and corned beef hash," Alice said.

Drake looked at Hilde. "Fried eggs plus potatoes and meat. How does that sound, sweetie?"

"Very good," Hilde said softly.

On the drive home, Drake held Hilde's hand. "We want to get a place of our own, Mom, but I was hoping you wouldn't mind if we stayed with you until we get that worked out. Maybe a couple three weeks. Have to get a job first thing, of course."

Alice looked into the rear view mirror at Hilde, sitting glumly next to Drake. She licked her top lip and her eyes sparkled. "Of course, Win."

The next morning Drake woke early. After tossing all night, Hilde was finally peaceful, so he let her sleep and went downstairs to the kitchen. His mother was there perking coffee. He kissed her and sat at the table.

"So our little German guest is a late sleeper?" Alice said.

"*Our German guest?*" Drake glared at his mother. "Her name's Hilde, Mom. And she happens to be my wife." He got himself a cup of coffee and stood by the table. "If you really wanna know, she had a pretty rocky night. All the traveling, I s'pose. So I'm letting her sleep in."

Alice folded her arms. "I saw Janie Stabler at the grocer's last week. She *was* married, as you know, but it didn't work out...so now she isn't." She shook her head. "Young people!" She eyed Drake. "She asked about you. Said you should call when you got back."

Drake scowled. "Why are you telling me that? 'Course I can't call her. Don't want to either. I'm married, gol dangit."

"Well, did I know that when I talked to Janie? No, I did not! *I* found out after the fact. By a telegram no less! Of course, I'm just *Old Ma.*"

Drake set his cup down and took a step for the door.

"Win, Honey, sit down. Try to understand what a shock it's been. My baby...married!" Alice walked over and stroked his cheek. "Seems so sudden. And to a foreigner. A *German* no less! Same as those people who gassed your father. Have you forgotten how he caughed up blood before he died?" She placed a hand on his shoulder and looked at the floor. "And she's a cripple! I know you feel sorry for—"

Drake pushed her hand away. "Who I feel sorry for is you, thinking that, Mom. Hilde and I'll go out today and find an apartment."

"Oh Win, that didn't come out the way I meant it to. I only want what's best for you, and I think when someone hurries into something, even with the best intentions, they can come to regret it later on."

"Like I said, we'll find a rental and make sure to be out today." Drake left the kitchen.

Three weeks after they'd moved out of Alice's home, Drake and Hilde were finally getting their feet on the ground. Drake got a job with the Union Pacific Railroad. After his first day at work, he told her, "As the greenest switchman in the Omaha District, I'm on the extra board, working if and when the company needs me."

"Will you drive a train or be a conductor like Johannes?"

"Neither, I'll be on a switching crew. With two other guys and an engineer. We run a small locomotive in the switch yard, shuffling rail cars around, making up freights. According to this list called a pickle sheet."

"Pickles?"

Drake could tell from Hilde's look that he'd lost her. "No, not what you eat. A pickle sheet's what we call the list of all the cars and the order the railroad wants 'em in."

"But why call it a pickle?"

Drake thought for a moment then shrugged. "Who knows. Anyway, after we assemble the train the way they want it, a line crew takes it out on the road to its destination. Being low man on the totem pole, I'll work mostly evenings and nights, but the pay's darn good. And the yard boss told me the way business's booming, I'll get lots of hours."

The Drakes' apartment was on the south side of Omaha, near the rail and stock yards. Theirs was one of three rentals on the second floor, in between the apartments of Bobbi Hadley and the Lettermans, Bart and Cézanne.

Hilde and Cézanne hit it off just fine. Cézanne was a war bride from Toulouse, France. She and Hilde bonded over their newcomer status. When Bart was at work as a mechanic in an auto repair shop and Drake was sleeping after a night shift, Hilde would bring over the ironing and the girls would have fun, listening to music on the radio and chattering while pressing the men's shirts, boxer shorts, and handkerchiefs.

Bobbi was another matter. Her husband had been killed in the Battle of the Bulge in December 1944. Only twenty-two, she was alone with a pair of sons, ages two and four. Her mother babysat the boys three days a week while Bobbi worked in a dentist's office, but making ends meet and raising her sons alone was tough. And her future looked bleak.

Hilde could tell from the start that Bobbi disliked her. She tried to win her over by offering to watch the boys or cook dinner for the family any time that might come in handy. Bobbi curtly turned down every overture.

One May night, when he came home after a four to midnight shift, Drake found his wife crying at the kitchen table. He put his arm around her, eased her head to his breast, and whispered, "What's wrong?"

Hilde sighed. "It's Bobbi. She hates me." She paused a moment, studying her folded hands on the table. "No, I think she's just very unhappy. Widowed at twenty. Now she sees a woman next door who is German, like the man who killed her Carl. A woman quite lucky in life—waltzing to America with a husband who survived the war. A husband to nestle her head when she's sad." She kissed Drake's ear. "A woman next door with a future when she has none. No wonder she treats me as she does."

"Look, honey, you've answered her slights with kindness. You were trying to help, but did you?" Drake peered into Hilde's eyes. "You say Bobbi's sour on life, and I think you're right. So what if your kindness only fuels more resentment? It's like you're saying, 'I'm so dang la-dee-da, it doesn't matter how a grubby little zero like you acts.'"

"So what should I do? Sock her nose?"

Drake chuckled. "Probably not right out of the gate. But I'd say, stand up to her. When she puts you down, let her know you're not taking it." He glanced at the ceiling. "There was this big lug in my army outfit. Blackie Davis. From the minute we met, the guy had it in for me. Always pushing, pushing, pushing. Well, one day he pushed a little too far." He decided to leave out the part about finding turds in his bunk in D Bay of Old Trixie. "We went at it—

fists, feet, teeth and about every other part of us—and though Blackie was twice my size, it pretty much came out a draw." Drake laughed and shook his head. "You should have seen the two of us! Looked like we'd gone face first through a meat grinder. But you know…from that day on, I never had a problem with Blackie."

"So you *are* saying I should sock her nose?"

"No, Hilde, but it might straighten things out if you let her know, *verbally*, that you're not taking her guff anymore." Drake leaned in. "Best part is, it's probably the kindest thing you could do for her."

The next morning, Hilde passed Bobbi in the corridor outside their apartments. "Hello. How are you today?"

Bobbi huffed, her only answer.

Hilde spun around. "Wait one minute, Bobbi. I greet you civilly and you don't respond? I know you lost your man in the war. I can only imagine the pain of sleeping every night in a bed with a hole where your Carl should be." Hilde's gaze was fiery. "But you aren't the only one with pain. Every morning I wake with a foot hurting so much I want to chop it off. Every night I go to bed wishing I had two sons to tuck in and kiss goodnight."

The women stared at each other for a frozen instant, then Bobbi broke into sobs. Hilde too. They rushed to each other and embraced there in the corridor, too overcome to say anything. From that moment on they were fast friends.

Treating Lobry de Bruyn Alberda van Ekenstein's Patient

The Drakes had been in Omaha five months. Though many days were still handsome with sunshine, the air had traded a languor born of summer's heat for the urgency of autumn at winter's approach. Maple trees knew it. Birds knew it. And Hilde knew it, because her foot was bothering her.

Drake didn't like that.

"It always aches in the cooler weather, my sweet," she said. "I'm used to it."

"Nope," he said, shaking his head, "we've put it off too long already. We're going in to get that foot looked at."

Drake made an appointment with Dr. Brookings, the family doctor. He examined Hilde's foot. "We like to deal with problems like this in infancy. Other than the accomodative shoe you wear, I'm just not sure what can be done at this point." He scribbled down some information on a slip of paper and handed it to her. "Here's the number of Dr. Vernon Clarkson, an orthopedic specialist—a bone doctor. Let's see what he says."

A week later Dr. Clarkson examined Hilde. "I'm sorry I can't be more encouraging," he said when he'd finished his evaluation, "but at your age, Mrs. Drake, treatment options for your deformity are *extremely* limited. At best, reconstruction tends to afford only limited improvement and often does more harm than good. And treatments are of long duration and quite painful. A most difficult treatment with a very poor prognosis? I can't subscribe to it."

Hilde's face was pale. She stood to leave. "Thank you for your time, Dr. Clarkson."

Drake jumped to his feet. "Hold on a second, hon," he said to his wife. He turned to Clarkson. "Doc, you didn't say treatment *couldn't* work, right? Look, Hilde's suffered with this, er, disability all these years, and it's painful as heck. We know treatment's going to be tough, but we're in this together." He looked at Hilde and nodded for emphasis. "And that's how we think we can get through it. Together."

Clarkson pursed his lips. "That's admirable, sir, but in cases like this…I can't, in good conscience, proceed with anything but—" He grimaced. "—a disarticulation at the ankle."

"Disarticulation?" Drake said, "That means…?"

"It means an amputation of the foot, Mr. Drake."

Drake felt like a guy on an elevator when the cable breaks. He looked at Hilde—she was in the same plummeting car. His thoughts went back to the army hospital in Manila when he saw the bloody bandages on the stump of Holt's leg after his amputation. "Cutting or not cutting—that's the only option you're giving us?"

Clarkson averted his eyes. "I can't in good conscience recommend anything in between. Here's what it boils down to: Hilde, can you live with this handicap or not?"

Drake stuffed his hands in his pockets and looked at the floor. He swept an arm around Hilde's waist and whispered in her ear, "We're not licked yet, sweetheart." He eased her toward the door.

"Just one moment," Clarkson said. "There is one colleague of mine I recall mentioning treating the clubfoot deformity after childhood. I think he was referring more to teenagers than adults, and his patients didn't become Olympic foot racers. But, Mrs. Drake, if you'd take a risk for the chance at *some* improvement, you can see him. He might take your case." He scribbled on a tablet page and tore it off. "Dr. William S. Maugham is his name." He handed the paper to Hilde. "Phone his office."

Two weeks later the Drakes were sitting in the pale green waiting room of Dr. Maugham's orthopedics specialty practice. After they filled out a questionnaire concerning Hilde's medical background and her handicap, they were shown into the examination room. They sat there, looking at the impressive bank of framed certificates covering one wall. After twenty minutes Maugham came in. He was a handsome man with darting eyes, a pencil-line mustache and a leonine mane of gray hair, looking every bit Hollywood's version of a physician in his starched white lab coat. He examined Hilde's foot, reviewed the X-ray films his assistant took, then saw her and Drake into his consulting office. Reclining in his leather chair, he clasped his hands together and sighed, "I wish you had come to see me—" He glanced at Hilde's age on the chart. "—twenty-one years ago, young lady."

"But I grew up overseas—"

"You take me too literally, my dear. I only meant that your disability, *talipes equinovarus*, is relatively easy to treat in infancy, because the tendons, ligaments, muscles and even the bones are pliable then. I liken them to green shoots on a woody plant. In infancy, the foot is readily reshaped because those pliant components can be manipulated by braces, casts, and surgery. So, remedy is straightforward early on, *but* impossible at twenty-one?" Maugham shrugged. "In severe cases, yes. However, I'd rate your deformity as moderate. Four on a scale of one to ten. Perhaps only three and a half. At its heart, the treatment is essentially a physics problem. Structural reengineering. To be fair, many of my colleagues would say the risks trump the potential benefits. I disagree. But you, young lady, are the final arbiter on that point."

Hilde and Drake looked at each other. "What's your plan, Doctor," Drake said.

Sitting behind his large mahogany desk, Maugham lit up a cigarette. "First, tell me, Mrs. Drake, what's been done about your foot."

"I grew up in Germany. My family was poor, and my parents felt they couldn't afford expensive treatments. At least not for a daughter. They had a healthy son, afterall. Besides, they were very religious." Tears welled in Hilde's eyes. "They told me my deformity was part of God's plan, and who were we to tinker with it. When I was seven or eight, a teacher arranged for her cousin, a famous doctor, to see me. He wanted to treat me with a combination of casts and braces and surgery over many months, and the kind man offered to do it at no cost, as a demonstration of treatment options after infancy. But my timing was bad. For this was 1934 and the Nazis had just come to power. They made laws limiting the treatment of cripples and *the nervous*, as they called mentally sick persons. For both economy and racial hygiene. I recall the doctor telling my parents and me he wasn't allowed to proceed. He had tears in his eyes."

Maugham shook his head. "Yes, nasty theories foisted by quacks were embraced especially, but not exclusively I regret to say, in Nazi Germany." He stubbed out his cigarette. "The idea that physical and mental defects correlate to social deviance was used to justify pure evil. In a way though, you were lucky. You shared your handicap with Joseph Goebbels, the German propaganda minister, so clubfoot, in particular, had a less disfavored status."

"I know about Herr Goebbels." Hilde smiled at Drake. "There is also the fact that *der Klumpfuß* didn't restrict one's work with the hands or the mind, so some of us cripples proved useful, especially as fighting casualties mounted."

Drake held Hilde's hand. "They put her to work in their jet airplane factory, doc."

"Ah yes, those nasty Messerschmitts." Maugham stroked his chin. "Your mention of a famous surgeon you saw in Germany leaves me curious. You don't recall his name, do you? Germany had several medical innovators back in the Twenties and Thirties."

Hilde looked at the ceiling. "I do remember he had the largest, most pompous name imaginable. To a child, the lettering on the glass of his office door seemed endless. But I can't recall just what it was. His practice was in Munich, if that helps."

Maugham smiled. He stood and pulled a thick tome from his bookshelf. He held it so Hilde could read the gold lettering on the black leather cover: The title, *Die Anatomie und die Pathologie des Fußes*. The author, *Herr Doktor Professor Siegfried Lobry de Bruyn Alberda van Ekenstein.*

"That's his name!" Hilde exclaimed.

Maugham beamed. "*The Anatomy and the Physiology of the Foot.* A modern classic treatise in orthopedic medicine. And an author with a name like that!" He seemed to shiver with delight. "To think, you were his patient and I could now fulfill his intention."

Drake looked at Hilde and took her hand. "So you'll help us?"

"I'll certainly try."

The following Thursday, Hilde's first surgery was scheduled. The night before, Drake's mother, Alice, came to the hospital with a large bouquet of carnations. Hilde hadn't seen her since they moved out the previous April. Alice had tried to reestablish a relationship on a couple of occasions, but Drake put her off. Now, with the surgery at hand, he relented.

"I'm so happy to see you, dear Hilde," Alice said. She embraced her daughter-in-law in the hospital bed and whispered, "Honey, I feel so bad about the way I behaved when you and Win arrived last spring. The news that you were married was so sudden, and my son being all I had left..." She straightened up and wiped her eyes with a hanky. "There's no excuse for the things I said, and I've regretted them since the day you two moved out. I hope you can find a way to forgive me."

Hilde glanced at Drake, standing to the side with his arms crossed. "Of course we forgive you." She peered at Drake. "Don't we, sweet?"

"If you're good with it, Hilde."

Hilde shot him a stern look.

Drake walked to his mother and gave her a hug. "Love you, Mom."

"I've missed you so much." Alice looked at Hilde. "Both of you." She took Hilde's hand. "And you, little one, you're so brave, facing this."

"Your son is my strength. And now I have you, too. I'm not afraid."

Thursday morning, Drake saw Hilde before she went into surgery. "I'll be thinking of you, wishing us luck, every minute you're in there," he said.

"A little luck can't hurt," she replied.

"That's what I was thinking. I even brought my good luck shilling to rub while your surgery's going on." He took the coin from his pocket, breathed on it, and polished it on his shirt sleeve. "I know it's superstitious, but this little charm's always come through for me before."

Hilde shrugged. "You keep your talisman. I'll put my trust in Dr. Maugham's scalpel, thank you."

A moment later two nurses in surgical gowns rolled a white-sheeted gurney into the room. "It's time, Mrs. Drake," the tall one said.

Hilde scooted onto the rolling bed and with Drake holding her hand, she was wheeled down the hall to the operating room.

Maugham performed a series of seven surgeries on Hilde's foot and ankle over nine months. He built up some bone structure with grafts, removed problematic portions of other bone, and moved tendons and ligaments.

The day after the final surgery, Maugham came to Hilde's room for a post-operative examination. When finished, he spoke to Hilde and Drake. "We'll have to wait until the swelling goes down to know what we've got, Hilde. Functionally, at least." He lit a cigarette. "Physiologically, I've built you one hell of an unnatural skeletal foot and joint. I don't claim to be the anatomical architect the Maker is, but I've got my fingers crossed that I was able to jigger something more serviceable that what you were born with."

"When will we know, doc?" Drake asked.

"First indications in weeks. For a final verdict of efficacy, well, figure months at least. Only this brave little lady—" Maugham took Hilde's hand and squeezed it. "—can ultimately judge my work. Pain and facility will be her criteria." He made a notation on her charts and glanced at his watch. "Gracious! Late for my shattered ankle in room 219. I'll see you tomorrow, Hilde."

When the doctor was gone, Drake sat on the bed next to his wife. "I know we're in for some rough sledding for a while, but I'm optimistic this is going to turn out good." He pulled a silver coin from his pocket. "I've been working my lucky schilling pretty hard every time you were under the knife, and it's never let me down yet."

Hilde smiled. "This is the talisman Stetti gave you in Germany?"

"Yeah. Just before I shipped out for the Pacific." Drake rubbed the coin between his thumb and index finger. "She got it as a music award when she was a kid at school in England. Said it

341

kept her safe during the bombing." He shrugged and offered the schilling to her. "Come on, give it a squeeze. Can't hurt."

Hilde examined the engraved image of King George VI then turned the coin over. She stared at the disk, studying it. "This can't be right," she muttered, biting her lip.

"What do you mean?"

"The date." Hilde held the coin out for Drake to inspect. "See, it's 1940."

"So?" he said. "She gave it to me in '45. Spring of 1945."

"But she can't have gotten it as a student in England. Not if it wasn't minted until 1940. Because her overseas studies must have been well before the war's start in 1939."

Drake took the coin and held it so the light coming through the window made it easy to read. He studied it. Looking for something Hilde had missed, something that reconciled the 1940 date with the story Stetti had told him. But a minute later, he knew—his wife hadn't missed anything. Tears welled in his eyes. The talisman had been the one shred of good he had taken from his time with Stetti. He'd believed in it. "I'll be darned," he hissed, "if that woman didn't play me for a sucker *every* stinking step of the way." He swallowed hard and shoved the coin back into his pocket.

Hilde read the embarrassment, the anguish, in the pallor on her husband's face. "It doesn't matter, my sweet. It *is* only a token. And you do have me to count on. Like I have you. Over this ordeal, you've been my talisman. My strength. Let me be yours."

Drake pressed his lips together to halt their trembling. "Sure." He took Hilde's hand and squeezed it. "Like you say, it really doesn't matter. It was always just a nothing trinket. Only, I didn't realize it until now."

"Put you faith in us. *We're* something that does matter. Something lasting."

Six months later, Hilde was walking better than before her surgery. She still required a special shoe, but it was less clunky and conspicuous than her old one—Hilde loved it. Her foot's appearance was far from normal and it still ached, especially when she was on it a lot, but the pain was definitely less.

Before breakfast on Mother's Day, 1948, she told Drake, "Remember when we crossed the river from Soviet Germany to the West? I lost my crutch, and you told me not to worry. You promised you'd take me to America and find a doctor who could repair my foot. It was barely two years ago! I looked into your eyes when you said it and they seemed so confident, so resolute, that I believed you. I *believed* even though I *knew* it was impossible." She burst into tears and buried her face in his neck. "You promised a miracle and you kept it."

"Guess I just went by the old saying, *Love Conquers All.*"

When Hilde's tears slowed, she looked into Drake's eyes and took his hands. "I've never been out dancing. Never once. Can we go dancing, sweet? To celebrate?"

"I'd *love* to, honey. Yeah, dancing! What a swell way to celebrate your new foot!"

Hilde glanced at the floor. Shy. "Yes, to celebrate my foot." She looked into his eyes. "And Mother's Day!"

Drake caught the glow on her face just as the words *Mother's Day* hit him. "Are you telling me what I think you're telling me?"

"If it means that next Mother's Day you'll have to bring me breakfast in bed *and* take me out dancing, then yes, that's what I'm telling you."

Eight Bucks a Seat

December 8, 1950

D rake had worked the midnight to eight o'clock shift the night before. When he woke at mid-afternoon, he found a note pinned to his shirt hanging on the back of the rocker in the bedroom. *Sweetie—With Arvee and Bo at the playground. Back about 4:30. Making spaghetti and meatballs for din. Love, H.* He checked his watch. Hilde and the kids'll be home in half an hour, he thought, lighting a cigarette and heading downstairs. Just enough time to change the gasket in that dripping kitchen faucet.

They had been in their bungalow for almost a year now. They'd bought the place just two months before Bo was born in March. Between the rickety old house, and the hand-me-down Plymouth coupe from Mom, and the two boys—Bo in diapers and Arvee learning to walk—there was always something pulling at Drake. But he had never been happier.

In the kitchen, Drake got the screwdriver and pliers from the cabinet under the sink. Before he could start on the valve, he noticed the *Time Magazine* left open at his place at the mint-green Formica dining table. Setting his tools down, he took a last drag on his cigarette, turned on the tap to douse the butt, then flicked it into the wastebasket. He stared at the magazine, like there was something ominous about it, sitting there open at his place. Waiting for him. He took a deep breath, walked over to the *Time* and picked it up.

Open to the Arts section, the headline read, *European Cello Sensation Sets US Tour Dates*. There was a monochrome picture of Stetti, in a sleek, long, black gown, with those white pearls of hers. Backlit by a bright spotlight so her image seemed to glow with energy, she embraced her cello like a lover. She looked breathtaking.

Drake set the magazine down and stared out the window. He hadn't thought about her in months. Maybe not in a year. He picked up the *Time* and peered at the picture. His stomach felt like he'd been punched. He didn't want to give a hoot about her and didn't think he did, but his physical reaction was saying otherwise.

He sat at the table and pulled a pack of Chesterfields from his shirt pocket. He shook one loose. As he flicked open his old GI Zippo to light it, he recalled that playful word *ciggy*—what Stetti used to call his smokes when she wanted to bum one off him.

He read the article:

>*What does it take for music over two hundred years old to threaten to displace the likes of Bing Crosby and Patti Page in the front window displays of record shops on Main streets across the country? How about a comely Fräulein who, with a new high fidelity recording, has breathed excitement into what has become one of the revered archetypes of the classical string music repertoire. The lovely lady is West Germany's Miss Euridice Bloomstedt and the music is Johann Sebastian Bach's 'Six Suites for Unaccompanied Cello.'*
>
>*Bloomstedt made news last year when she defected from Red-controlled East Germany, reportedly escaping, raked by a hail of gunfire, across the border in a motorcycle sidecar. She made her flight to freedom in the company of automobile racer and Romanian playboy-prince Adolphus-Rupert of Wallachia. The exiled heir to the vacant Romanian throne was seriously wounded in their dash through a fortified border control station and died in Frankfurt two days later.*
>
>*As for the music, the Suites, championed by Spanish cellist Pablo Casals and popularized by his classic recordings of the 1930s, are admired for their achievement of polyphony from a single musical line. In 1937 Bloomstedt was Casals' young student in England, and until the start of the Second World War he was something of a mentor to her. In 1945, they reconnected. Casals comments in the album notes, "This amazing woman has managed to bring fiery*

passion to the Suites without diminishing their elegance and almost mathematical perfection."

Now American audiences will be able to hear Bloomstedt in the concert hall when she performs Bach's Suites during her upcoming tour of major U.S. cities. In March of next year, she will appear in New York, Philadelphia, Boston, Washington, Cleveland, Chicago, and San Francisco. If the popularity of her recording is any indication, tickets to her concerts will be selling like proverbial hotcakes.

Drake sat smoking at the table, his mind a jumble. When the front door opened, he turned to see Hilde and the boys come in. She let go of Arvee's hand, and he squealed, "Dada!" and careened toward his father with outstretched arms.

Drake grinned and stubbed his smoke into an ashtray. He jumped up, caught his boy, and raised him toward the ceiling, making the nasal hum of a climbing airplane. After bringing Arvee in for a landing on the kitchen floor, Drake walked to Hilde, took baby Bo from her arms and gave her a kiss. "How was the park?"

"Cold," Hilde said. "Feels like it could snow." She took off her coat and Arvee's and draped them over the back of a kitchen chair. "I think Bo needs to be changed."

"I'll do it," Drake said. He grabbed a folded diaper from the pile in the boys' room and changed the baby. "Should I put the little guy down for his nap?" he called from the bedroom.

"I'll feed him first."

She nursed the baby on the living room sofa. Drake sat with Arvee on his lap, reading *Mike Mulligan and His Steam Shovel*. The toddler pushed Cheerios into his mouth as he pointed to pictures in the book—shovel, Mike, dirt, smoke, hole—and named them.

Ten minutes later, as the boys slept in their room, Drake and Hilde sat on the couch. After a minute of silence, Drake stretched and yawned. "So…snow, huh?"

Hilde turned to look at him. "I take it you saw the article."

346

Drake shrugged. "Yeah. So what?"

"Johannes said in a letter last year that Stetti had defected from the DDR. I thought about telling you—" Hilde glanced at Drake and took his hand. "—but didn't. It was a news sensation in West German papers and a propaganda coup for the Federal Republic. You hadn't heard?"

"Nope. And don't give a darn, neither."

"But you must admit, it makes for quite a headline. Stunning artist makes a thrilling escape through hailing bullets with her romantic Romanian Prince Charming."

Drake huffed. "Sounds just like Stetti. She gets the dang headlines and her boyfriend gets a backside full of lead. Besides, as I recall, when you and I crossed from East to West, we braved some fireworks too. 'Course, we didn't get written up in *Time Magazine*."

"We could go to the concert, you know. Chicago's not so far away. Just for curiosity."

Drake jumped to his feet. "Heck no, I'm not going all that way and spending a ton of dough on a ticket to see someone who tried to get me strung up!"

Hilde took Drake's hand and pulled him back down to the sofa. "We have your train privilege so the travel would be free. I'm not saying we should go." She put her arm on his shoulder. "I'm only telling you we *can* go…if you want."

"Well, I don't." Drake crossed his arms dramatically.

"Fine." Hilde caught his attention and made a sour face, mimicking his expression. "Don't look so glum…it might make me wonder why a European cellist's visit to distant American cities upsets you so."

"Do I look upset?" He huffed and gazed out the window. "It's just that things are going so well for us. Like my mother used to say, 'A bad penny always turns up.'" He shook his head. "Why can't she just stay where she belongs—on her side of the Atlantic."

Hilde turned his chin to her. "Bet you a nickel I can chase that frown away. I heard a riddle on Arthur Godfrey's radio program this morning." She waited for his full attention. "What do you call a giant nose without a body?"

Drake shrugged and shook his head. "Dunno."

Hilde giggled, thinking of the punch line. "OK, are you ready?" She cleared her throat. "Nobody knows." She stared at Drake, waiting for him to catch on.

After a moment, his blank expression hadn't changed.

Hilde tilted her head. "No Body Nose," she said excitedly. "Get it? No Body Nose."

Drake looked at the goofy grin on his wife's face. He sensed how much she wanted to cheer him up. How confident she was these days in them and their marriage. He chuckled. "No Body Nose." He shook his head and pulled some coins from his pocket. He pushed a nickel into her hand. "Don't spend it all in one place, girlie." He grinned then peered deep into her eyes. "I love you, Hilde."

Two months later, on page one of the Arts section of the Sunday edition of the *Omaha World Herald* newspaper, a headline in big black letters announced, *German Cello Phenom Adds Omaha Stop to U.S. Tour*.

Drake had worked a night shift, and when he got up that afternoon, Hilde showed him the article. "You can't say it's too far away anymore, Win. Let's go. If you want, we'll wear disguises like a couple of spooks. I'm curious to see her after all these years. Aren't you?"

He eyed the newspaper like it had been used to wrap fish. "Curious? Tickets'll probably be three maybe four bucks...a couple, at least. I'm not that curious. If you need to hear her, I'd say, buy the dang record."

"And a Victrola to play it on? Dear, I said I want to *see* her. What are you afraid of? She won't even know we're there, in the cheap seats back in a dark corner of the hall."

"I'm not scared of anything. Certainly not some *German Cello Phenom!*" he sneered. "I'm just not that interested."

Hilde took his hand. "There was a time when I feared Stetti more than anyone else in the world. Like she could take everything that mattered to me with a snap of her fingers. But I'm not afraid now. I'm sure of you. Of myself. Of us." She kissed his cheek. "Think about going. If you change your mind, whistle." She winked. "You know how to whistle, don't you, sweetie?"

On the afternoon of March 1, a couple of weeks before Stetti's concert, the Drakes' telephone rang. Hilde answered.

"Hello." The man's voice was urbane. "Is this the residence of a Mr. Winston Drake?"

"Yes," Hilde glanced to the bedroom where Drake was sleeping. "Why do you ask?"

"The Winston Drake who served in the army, in Germany? At the end of the war? Knew a German civilian there called Euridice Bloomstedt? In Bonn?"

"Yes. Who is this calling?"

"I'm Louis P. Fischer. I'm promoting a concert tour Miss Bloomstedt is doing this month. You may have read that she has added a March 14 performance in Omaha to the schedule. Anyway, Miss Bloomstedt asked that I send a pair of tickets with her complements to her old friend, Mr. Drake. I obtained this telephone number from the directory and want to confirm the address before I arrange for delivery."

Hilde's mind raced. Would Drake want the tickets? Did she?

"Are you still there, ma'am? Can you give me a correct address for Mr. Drake?"

Hilde bit her lip. What could it hurt to take the tickets, then decide about going? "Yes, it's on Davenport Street." She was so flustered the house number momentarily escaped her. "That's er, 3511...yes 3511 Davenport Street."

"In Omaha, correct?"

"Yes, Omaha. 3511 Davenport Street in Omaha."

"Got it. Miss Bloomstedt will be pleased that I was able to locate Mr. Drake. I'll arrange for delivery this week. Thank you for your assistance, madam."

Hilde was peeling potatoes the next day when the doorbell rang. She dried her hands and opened the door. A boy in messenger's uniform, complete with bow tie, held a large manila envelope and a clipboard.

"Sign for Special Delivery, ma'am," the kid said, handing her the clipboard and a pen.

"Are these concert tickets?" Hilde said.

"Wouldn't know that, ma'am. I'm just the messenger."

Hilde signed and took the envelope. The boy stood on the porch eyeing her expectantly.

"Let me get you something." Hilde went to her handbag on the kitchen table and found her coin purse. She pulled out a shiny dime and gave it to the boy, who tipped his hat and dashed to the stairwell. She went to the window and watched him climb aboard his bicycle and pedal away.

Hilde put the envelope on top of the frig and went back to peeling her spuds. She decided to wait for the weekend to tell Drake about the tickets.

Friday night Drake was off work. On Saturday morning Hilde handed him the envelope, "This came by a hand delivery. Take a look."

Drake opened the envelope and eyed the tickets angrily. "You bought these? Holy cow, eight bucks apiece! Honey, we can't afford that."

"They were free. Complements of Stetti—that's what the man said. And yes, I saw the price. Can you believe it?"

"From Stetti? How can she know about us? Say, are you mixed up in this somehow?"

"Not at all. A man called, asking if you were the Mr. Drake she knew in Germany. When I said you were, he had the tickets sent over. He said Stetti wanted you to have them."

Drake looked at the tickets again. "Eight bucks! That can't be right. Who can afford to throw that kind of dough around? Howard Hughes, I guess. Clark Gable, maybe."

"I think we should go. Don't you wonder what she looks like now?"

Drake was silent for a moment. He took out a pack of Chesterfields. "Want a smoke?"

Hilde looked away. "I don't care for one."

He lit a cigarette and took a deep drag. He glanced at the tickets again and shook his head. "Eight bucks." He stuffed them back into the envelope. "Maybe I'll take along that talisman shilling and give it back to her...she'll need some luck, asking folks to fork over eight-bucks to see her play that oversized fiddle of hers."

Suite Journey

The evening of the concert, the Drakes dressed in their Sunday best. He wore the spiffy, gray gabardine suit Hilde made him purchase for Arvee's baptism. She wore the green, knee-length, wool broadcloth party dress she'd gotten the previous holidays. It had lacey frills at the collar and hem. They drove downtown and parked on Farnam Street across from the Art Deco Paxton Hotel. Walking the four blocks to the Orphuem Theater, they arrived a half hour before the concert's starting time. The display on the brightly-lit theater marquee read, *Tonight Only, Cellist Euridice Bloomstedt   8PM.* A line of taxis and limousines discharged their passengers, many in tuxedos and gowns, lending excitement and elegance to the scene.

Drake noticed a young woman in a frayed, blue cardigan sweater, standing off to the side behind a wooden crate. *15¢* was scrawled on the box in red paint and there were a dozen long-stemmed white carnations in a milk bottle on top. He reached into his pocket and touched the concert tickets as if the fact that they'd been free gave him permission to splurge on flowers for his wife. He walked to the stand and bought four carnations and presented them to Hilde.

She kissed his cheek and broke off one flower for his lapel buttonhole.

Drake lit a cigarette, and they stood outside watching the throng. After five minutes they entered the lobby and handed their tickets to the usherette. She said, "Right this way, please," and led them down the aisle to the third row from the stage. "You're in seats eleven and twelve, there in the middle." She illuminated them her small flashlight. "Enjoy the concert."

They climbed over the people already in their places in row C. After they sat, Drake looked around at the filled theater and said, "Pretty swell seats, huh?"

Hilde giggled. "I feel like a VIP,"

Drake winked at her. "You've always been very important in my book."

At five past eight, a thick man in a too-tight tuxedo waddled onto the stage. He had slicked-back hair and heavy, black-rimmed glasses. He stood behind a microphone at center stage. "Good evening, ladies and gents, I'm Bert Selkirk, proprietor of the Orpheum. I'm happy to welcome you to our first live concert since we converted to moving pictures twelve years ago. We've been closed the last week, restoring the theater to its former glory in honor of tonight's big event. Please take a minute at intermission to look around. Then come back and see a movie." He pulled a slip of paper from his pocket and glanced at it. "Tomorrow we start a five day run of *The African Queen*, starring Humphrey Bogart and Katherine Hepburn." He checked his notes again. "Guess that's it from me. Enjoy the music."

Next came another tuxedo-clad man. He looked like he had been born in formalwear. Tall and debonair, he held the microphone close to his mouth and purred, "Ladies and Gentlemen, I'm Louis P. Fischer, the promoter of Miss Bloomstedt's tour of select American cities. We were pleased to have the opportunity to add Omaha to the schedule, and we're happy to be here—" He took a moment to survey the theater's ornate interior. "—in this wonderful venue. Ah, the Orpheum, home of Orpheus…what better place for a performance by an artist named Euridice? Miss Bloomstedt has created quite a stir in the normally staid world of classical music with her new recording of Bach's cello suites. Of course you already know that. So I'll turn the stage over to her and you can hear for yourself what all the hubbub's about." He extended his right arm. "Please welcome Miss Euridice Bloomstedt, coming all the way from her home in Frankfurt, Germany to perform Johann Sebastian Bach's *Six Suites for Unaccompanied Cello*." The audience applauded as the lights went half down. Fischer exited, carrying the microphone and stand. Then the lights went full off.

The ripple of applause continued as a spotlight illuminated a circle of curtain, stage right. The light was brilliantly cold in the hushed, darkened theater. A moment later, Stetti stepped with her cello into the spotlight's glare and the collective breath of the house froze solid at the sight: The tall woman with straight black hair. Her string of milky pearls sizzling on the ebony background of the long, satin gown clinging to her sleek body. That face, her flashing green eyes and red lips intense against alabaster skin. The way she moved, gliding across the stage in the disk of light. With the applause and cries building, she stepped to a simple wooden chair at center stage. When she stopped there and turned to the crowd, the ovation became a roar. Stetti bowed crisply and let the acclaim wash over her.

Drake's heart raced as he scanned nearby audience members, each heartily sounding a welcome. He guessed they were tingling with the same jolt of electricity he felt. Leaning toward his wife, he said, "Stetti's got no idea what she's doing to these folks."

Hilde glanced at him. "She knows exactly what she's doing."

He looked at Stetti's luminous green eyes surveying the house, the hint of a smile they bore, and he knew Hilde was right. He also knew that no matter their history, he was again falling under her spell. No, he didn't want to cast aside his present life and throw himself at her feet. But at that moment, like the rest of the audience, he found her charms irresistible.

Without a word, Stetti sat and positioned her instrument. When she raised her bow, the crowd fell silent. She launched into the *Prelude* to the *First Suite*. Its optimism and resolve created a natural flow that instantly pulled Drake in, then swept him along with her. Though she had him from the first draw of her bow, it was the second movement, the *Allemande*, that cemented the bond with its brightness. For Drake, falling for the First Suite, as its brightness spun out, was easy as soaking in a hot bath. It made Stetti's power seem benign. He closed his eyes and smiled.

Into the *Second Suite*, the comfort Drake had enjoyed just minutes earlier vanished quick as a bow stroke in the *Courante* movement. He looked at Stetti twenty feet away on the stage—her expression of self-satisfaction was the same one he'd seen when she took money from his pocket in the Bonn hotel room.

As quickly as the *Second* pulled Drake's spirits earthward, the *Third* buoyed them up. Not by jaunty lightness as the *First* had done, but by the precision of its motion. He recalled the night he'd first heard Stetti play in Germany, she'd stressed that Bach's suites were dances. The *Third Suite* was movement, and he was her dance partner. As the *Gigue* drew to a close, Drake hated to see it go.

When the last notes of the *Third Suite* faded, Stetti stood. The hall exploded with raucous applause. She bowed and for the first time looked directly at Drake. It was just for an instant, but it sent a shiver through him. Then her gaze swept away, back to other concert goers. Stetti raised her bow and the clapping ebbed. She cleared her throat. "Thank you for your warm welcome and for your appreciation of Bach's genius. For me, it is a great privilege to perform these suites. I shall now pause for twenty minutes time. *Bis später.*" She nodded to the audience and placed her cello on a stand next to her chair. The applause resumed as she walked off the stage.

Drake and Hilde stood. He looked around at the audience. Seeing so many of them smiling and talking reminded him of the intermission in the little concert hall in Bonn when Stetti had played *The Suites* in 1945—happy people anxious to converse about the experience they had just shared. He gazed at Hilde and took her hand. "Enjoying it?"

"Very much. She looks softer than five years ago. Happier."

Drake shrugged. "I suppose. What do you say we go out to the lobby and stretch?"

People filled the lobby and spilled out into the street. People smoked, sipped soda pop, and chatted in animated tones. "Folks seem to like it, huh?" Drake said.

"They do." Hilde scanned the crowd. "Oh, the woman there—" She nodded toward a tall blonde, wearing a mink stole and a red turban. "—she brings her son to the park. Her name is Froma. Bobbi said her husband's a doctor." She scanned the crowd. "See anyone you know?"

"The man by the cigarette machine is a train dispatcher at Union Pacific."

"The one reading his program so intently?"

"No. The fella smoking a pipe. Name's James Carlos. Usually goes by JC. Best train dispatcher on the whole darn line. The gal he's with must be his wife."

"I should hope so!"

"Heard she's a war bride. Dutch, I think. Or maybe Belgian."

"She's beautiful. I love the red and black velvet dress."

"Let's say hello." Drake took Hilde's hand and led her to the Carloses. "Hi, JC. I wanted to introduce my wife, Hilde."

JC raised his pipe, a kind of salute. "Have you met Andrée, my wife?"

The couples shook hands. They chatted about the concert and about the pair of young children they each had. When Andrée heard where Drake and Hilde met, she said, "I read Leipzig was Miss Bloomstedt's home before she defected to the West. Did you see her perform there, Hilde?"

"I never did." Hilde glanced at Drake. "But knew her. We worked in the same government agency there."

"Small world, eh?" said JC. 'So Drake, maybe you'll talk your wife into taking you backstage after the concert to meet her old friend."

Drake looked at the floor, wondering what to say. Before he had to reply, the man standing alone next to them, the one reading his program so ardently, interrupted. "Excuse me, sir," he said, leaning toward JC and pointing to the short biography of the composer in the pamphlet. "It talks here about some keyboard music Bach wrote. The *Goldberg Variations*. Who was this Goldberg fellow anyway?"

Drake was dumfounded by the inquiry. First, that a stranger would butt uninvited into a conversation like that. Then that he'd ask something so esoteric. And ask it so directly to JC, ignoring the rest of the party. Drake's astonishment only increased with Carlos's reply.

JC took a puff through his pipe. "Ah yes, The *Goldberg Variations*..." He paused for a moment as if hearing a snippet of Bach's masterpiece in his head. Then he told Johann Gottlieb Goldberg's story and how Bach came to compose the well-known aria that begins the set and the thirty variations on its bass line that comprise the work. JC went on to elaborate on the intricacies of the music over the next few minutes in a scholarly discourse rivaling anything you'd get in a composition class at Julliard.

The flabbergasted stranger shook JC's hand and backed away, his eyes wide.

The lights in the lobby flashed, indicating that the intermission was ending. Drake and Hilde said goodbye to the Carloses and headed back to their seats. "What a performance JC gave. I wanted to applaud," Hilde said.

Drake smiled and shook his head. "Yep, that guy...he's sure something, all right!"

When they came to their aisle, an usher was waiting there, holding a small white envelope. "Mr. Drake?" he said.

"That's me," said Drake.

The usher handed him the envelope. "From Miss Bloomstedt."

Drake and Hilde went to their seats and sat. He clutched the unopened note.

"Aren't you going to look at it?" Hilde prodded.

Drake didn't move for a moment, then he sighed and opened the envelope. He took out the card inside and read it. *Drake, I hope you'll say hello after the concert. I would love to see you. And there is something I need to say. Please come backstage to my dressing room. Stetti.* Drake made a sour face and handed the note to Hilde.

She read it. "Will you go?"

Drake huffed. "Don't see why I should. Who knows, she might have a couple of goons waiting to jump me."

Hilde took his hand and squeezed it. "It would be nice to thank her for the tickets."

"It'd be nice if they served ice water in hell too," Drake whispered as the lights dimmed. "Don't mean it's going to happen."

Stetti came out to an ovation. A microphone had been placed at center stage, and she spoke for a moment about the program.

She ended her comments, saying, "For me personally, *The Suites* are reason enough to live. And their composer, Johann Sebastian Bach, is proof of the limitless potential of humanity. In a century of world wars, Bach and his music give us hope." The sentiment brought more applause which Stetti acknowledged with a bow.

An usher removed the mic, then Stetti sat and began *Suite Four*. The movements seemed to Drake to comprise a journey— pulling him so powerfully that his grip tightened on the armrests of his seat. There was the climb to heaven with the lofty eminence of the first three, back to earth with the heartrending humanity of the *Sarabande*, on to the easy commonality of the *Bourees*, and finally to the joyful spontaneity of the *Gigue*. He was glad to let Stetti lead the way, and he loved the fact that Hilde was going along too, right there at his side.

After the flights of the *Fourth's* journey, the steady, brooding power of the *Fifth* seemed resolute, relentless. Drake knew this music wasn't just inviting him to march on with it, it was commanding him.

When Drake realized Stetti had begun the *Prelude* of the sixth and last suite, he felt a pang of regret. He didn't want what he was feeling to end. The buoyancy of the movement only made it harder, as if it were mocking his dread. He looked at Stetti. There was joy, anticipation on her face. And he understood what she'd meant about hope and purpose pouring from Bach's music. For her, it wouldn't end when *The Sixth* did. So, why should it for me, he wondered. The tender, floating airiness of the *Allemande* and the *Courante* bolstered his new optimism. As Stetti played the *Sarabande* with eyes closed, her peaceful expression perfectly matched the sweetness of the music. Finally, the irrepressible jollity of the *Gavotte* and the *Gigue* made for an unexpectedly easy, upbeat ending to *The Suites*.

Applause filled the hall. Stetti rose, holding her cello up, a triumphal salute to the crowd's acclaim. She bowed and started for the curtain at stage right. But half way there she stopped, scanned the audience, then fixed her gaze on Drake.

Auf Wiedersehen

For Drake, when Stetti paused halfway off stage and peered at him, time stopped with her.

She waited a moment then returned to center stage. Applause thundered. Stetti signaled and an usher brought out the microphone.

She raised her hands and the crowd fell silent. "I rarely do encores. Only on special occasions. Of course, performing Bach's Suites is always special. But tonight, more so. For this evening a treasured friend is in the audience. A hero, really. This man kept me and my family from starving in the post-war times of famine in Germany. I've never thanked him properly. In fact, at our last meeting I treated him rather badly, which I deeply regret. I won't embarrass him tonight by asking him to stand. I'll only say his nickname as a GI in those days was Omaha." Her eyes darted to Drake, and she smiled. "I once dedicated a composition of mine to him. This short piece is my improvisation on the well-know tune, *La Folia d'Espagne*. Many, many others have used the melody in their works, including Bach himself…in his so-called *Peasants' Cantata*. In honor of my friend, Omaha, tonight I'll play my improvisation on the *Folia* bass."

Stetti sat motionless for a moment, her eyes closed, paying respect, it seemed, to the music she was about to play. Drake studied her face. Hilde was right—she did look softer than he remembered. And happier.

She drew her bow over the strings in a slow, simple start to the *Folia*. The melody was instantly familiar to Drake. It carried him back to the night she played it for him in front of her house in Bonn. How anxious she seemed to present it then. And how it pleased him. Drake closed his eyes and let himself return to that magical night. Until his memories went to their lovemaking afterward. His eyes popped open, and he shook his head. When the scene was cleared from his thoughts, he glanced at Hilde, embarrassed.

As Stetti's improvisation continued, she elaborated on and decorated the base melody. Watching her immerse herself in the playing, Drake recalled his recurring dream, when she sang "Draw near!" to him from the shore. How he'd longed for her! Another glance at his wife banished the thought. He was awed at the power of Stetti's improvisation to capture him. He knew he should fight it, but leaving himself exposed felt so sweet. It had always been like that with her. All he could do was wait for the piece to end, though deep down he wanted it to go on forever. Tears filled his eyes.

When the piece ended, Stetti stood, holding her cello high as she had after *The Sixth Suite*. Acknowledging the thunderous applause, she bowed and blew a kiss to the audience. *"Auf Wiedersehen!"* she called and walked off the stage with her instrument.

The applause went on, but Stetti didn't return and slowly it died down.

Drake discretely wiped his eyes and looked at Hilde. He exhaled, almost a whistle, but couldn't manage a word.

Hilde put her arm in his and nestled to his shoulder. "So, I'm not the only girl who calls you her hero!" She looked up and smiled at him. "I'm glad she played the encore in your honor. I would have thought such generosity impossible for her, but she made it look easy."

Audience members were standing, starting to file out of the theater.

"Well?" said Hilde.

Drake sniffed. "Well what?" He looked away.

"Will you see her, of course?"

"Aw, let's just go home. She doesn't really want to see me. All that on the stage…it was just part of the show."

"You're afraid."

"Afraid?" Drake huffed. "Heck no!" He knew he was. Maybe most afraid of what he'd been feeling, especially during the encore.

"Were I you, I might be afraid too." Hilde took Drake's hand. "But if you don't go, you'll leave things forever unresolved. I think you'll regret it."

"I won't go without you." Drake looked into her eyes. "Come on." He reached into his pocket and pulled out his shilling talisman. "We're protected by a magic charm after all."

Hilde nodded.

They went to the side of the stage where an usher was standing. He was the same lad who gave Drake the note from Stetti. "Miss Bloomstedt invited my wife and me backstage to see her after the concert. Where do we go?"

"Follow me." The usher led Drake and Hilde up some steps and down a hallway. The door on the end had a handwritten sign, *Miss E. Bloomstedt*. He knocked and said, "A couple to see you, Miss Bloomstedt. The ones you invited."

The door swung open and there stood Stetti. She was wearing a long silk robe, a Japanese floral print in black, gold and red. She bit the side of her lip and said, "Oh Drake, you came!" Then her eyes went to Hilde and she froze. "And you? Impossible! It's…?" Stetti cocked her head and her face took on a look of shy discomfort, like a kid caught by mom sneaking cookies just before dinner.

"It's Hilde." Hilde said.

"Yes, Hilde. Of course."

"In Leipzig, I doubted you even knew my name."

Stetti looked at the floor. "Perhaps you won't believe it, but from the day you left, I regretted how I'd treated you—" She looked up. "—Hilde. I knew you defected with Drake, but I assumed you remained in Germany. Since I came west, whenever I tour the cities of the Federal Republic playing concerts, I find myself searching the faces of people on the streets, in trains, in my audiences, looking for you. Hoping for a chance to apologize for my…shabbiness." She took Hilde's hands and kissed them. "Can you forgive me?"

"It was long ago. In difficult times. And from childhood, I learned resentment brings me nothing but pain, so I avoid it. Yes, from today, we are friends."

When the women embraced, tears welled in Stetti's eyes. "So, you and Drake…?"

"Yes, we're married. We have two wonderful boys."

Stetti nodded like she envied Hilde a bit, then she snickered. "So do I. Or is it three? I sometimes lose count of my boyfriends. Of course mine are grown up. Mostly." She shrugged. "What can I say? I like juggling chaps."

"Since now we're friends," Hilde said, "I can't help but ask, why did you leave the DDR? You'd been such a dedicated Marxist. You were the last one I expected to defect."

Stetti eyed her coolly, as if she didn't like the question, then her look softened. "In the early days of Germany's socialist East, Euridice thought she had found Elysium." She smiled, perhaps recalling that time. "But she came to see that those in charge there, our dear Soviet comrades, were not resolute." Stetti looked away for a moment, then turned back. "It wasn't my ideals that were deficient, you know, it was the Russian leadership." Her gaze turned steely. "I was then, and I remain a dedicated Marxist. Committed to the People."

The tension in the air vanished when Stetti turned to Drake and smiled fondly. "And you, Drake! I owe you an explanation. It's why I came to Omaha, partly at least. In my early days in the Soviet sector, I felt part of something important a grand experiment to elevate humankind. Then you said you were coming to Leipzig, and your visit put my loyalty in doubt. Don't you see, it jeopardized everything I hoped to accomplish. Therefore, I put Party interests before my own and reported your plans to my superiors." She touched his arm. "When word came that you had made it safely across the border, I was secretly thrilled."

Drake smirked. "Well, you needn't have worried." He took the schilling out of his pocket, flipped it into the air with his thumb, and caught it. "After all, I had this little piece of magic right here—the good luck talisman you gave me in forty-five. Remember? The British coin you won as a *student* in England?"

Stetti's eyes lost their sparkle. "I must confess. I really got it from an English soldier not long before I met you. He said it would bring me luck, and it did. When you were about to leave, I had to do something. In return for all you had done for me. I had nothing but the coin. So I invented the tale about winning it as a music prize. I thought if I gave it a story, you would believe more strongly in its power. As with any charm, the power to protect comes from the belief, not the token. If a lie serves a good purpose, is it a bad thing?"

Drake wanted to yell, *Hell yes it is*. But he only said, "That's one way to look at it." In his visions of what he would do if he ever had the chance to confront Stetti about the schilling, he'd always thrown the coin at her feet. But now, unforced, she'd admitted her lie. Besides, she had a point—it had been a source of courage on many occasions since that night in spring of 1945 when she gave it to him. He shoved the shilling back in his pocket.

There was an awkward silence, then Stetti said, "Did you enjoy the concert?"

"It was wonderful," Hilde said. "Such good seats. We never could have afforded them."

"At eight smackers, that's for sure," Drake said. "You once said hearing this music's like going to heaven, and you proved that again tonight." He took out a pack of Chesterfields. "Say, ladies, how about a—" He grinned. "—ciggy?"

"A ciggy!" Stetti cooed. "I'd *love* one."

"Me too," said Hilde.

Drake passed them cigarettes and lit the three smokes. "I've been wondering, how did you know to look for me—for us—here in Omaha?"

"I recalled your nickname, as I said from the stage. You said it came from your home town. You told me Dresden could be my nickname, remember? You said your city was named for the Omaha tribe of Indian people. It was only a guess that you might live here, but a good one. When Louis wanted to add a city to the tour, I asked for Omaha, thinking perhaps...." She put her cigarette in an ashtray and opened a cardboard carton next to her dressing table. "I have something for you. Something authentic this time." She took out her three disk album recording of the *Six Suites*. She used an ivory fountain pen to sign it *March 14, 1951, Orpheum*

Theater, Omaha US. For my dear friends, Drake and Hilde. Love, Stetti. She handed it to Hilde.

"We don't have a record player," Hilde said.

"But we've talked about getting one. Now we'll have to." Drake looked at the album's cover. It has a monochrome line drawing of Stetti and her cello, in white on a black background. It showed her pearls, and in the drawing's only color, her luminous green eyes. The sensuous curves of her cello drew his gaze like a Lorelei's song. How could anyone not fall for her? A glance at his wife standing next to him instantly resolved the difference between falling for someone and being in love. Taking Hilde's hand and kissing her cheek, he thought, Drake, you're one lucky fella. Drake glanced at his watch. "I s'pose we should go, don't you think, hon?"

Her eyes glistening—she knew she was lucky too—Hilde nodded.

Stetti embraced first Hilde then Drake. *"Auf Wiedersehen,"* she said.

"Wiedersehen," said Hilde.

Drake put his arm around his wife and eased her into the hallway. He closed the door, saying, just before it clicked shut, *"Auf Wiedersehen, Stetti."*

Made in the USA
Columbia, SC
21 May 2018